Keverne Barrett lives in the north of England, where she works as a civil servant. *Unsuitable Arrangements* is her first work of fiction.

unsuitable arrangements

keverne barrett

Library of Congress Catalog Card Number: 91–67839

British Library Cataloguing in Publication Data
Barrett, Keverne
  Unsuitable arrangements
  I. Title
  823[F]

  ISBN 1-85242-248-3

First published 1992 by
Serpent's Tail, 4 Blackstock Mews, London N4
and 401 West Broadway #2, New York, NY 10012

Set in 10½/14pt Goudy by Contour Typesetters, Southall, London
Printed in Finland by Werner Söderström Oy

This volume was published with assistance from the Ralph Lewis
Award at the University of Sussex

for Christopher

with special thanks to Joyce and Duncan

....

unsuitable
arrangements

part 1

My mother never spoke of my father's family; when questioned she was vague, indifferent, infuriatingly uninformative about all his relatives. I did not remember my father; he was dead before my third birthday. None the less, I had a clear, if perhaps idiosyncratic, idea of what he was like. My mother was a diffident mediator in our relationship. She spoke often, wistfully, of what my father would have thought of a given topic. Usually his opinions were coupled with a longing that he were there to witness the event (for example, my minor role as an angel in the school nativity, with a halo fashioned of a hanger and cardboard wings covered with kitchen foil, or my first communion, when I wore a white lace dress and veil) or profound relief that he was not (when I had broken something or misbehaved). Never did my mother seem unsure as to what my father's views would have been.

By contrast the photographs seemed curiously insubstantial. I knew by heart the wedding picture on the sideboard and my favourite, a studio portrait of the young lieutenant. He was handsome, of course, but his features seemed elusive, unformed on film. Aside from the wedding album and my baby album there were few pictures, mostly family snapshots of special occasions, my mother shadowy in black, me dominated by my many cousins.

There were two pictures of my uncle. The earlier was on old-fashioned stiff card with a brown vellum cover and bordered oval frame, of the two boys together, the younger cherubic in a sailor suit and brown curls, the elder gawky and sullen in an Eton collar, hair slicked flat to his skull, both with the same intense dark eyes. The other picture was a snapshot of the brothers in uniform, the taller with eyes narrowed against the sun, not sullen this time but inscrutable, my father grinning candidly, eyes crinkled with amusement, both nondescript. In the days of waiting it never occurred to me to unearth the pictures; probably I would not have been allowed to.

But these images had no more bearing on reality than most of the characters that peopled my mind. The cosy families of the Bobbsey twins and Honey Bunch were mixed with the more pungent adventures of frontier settlers and wagon train families, as well as improbable child heroes of wars, against Indians or redcoats, Confederates or bluecoats. My father seemed much more plausible in costume settings. It was easier to imagine him in knee breeches and tricorne hat going off to war than to conjure him arriving in a tree-lined suburban street of rambling clapboard houses and handing his hat and raincoat to the ever-cheerful black housekeeper. Whatever the costume and backdrop, my mother was never part of the fantasy.

Had my reading been more extensive, I would have identified my fate with that of the young Tudor Elizabeth, alone and friendless under the rule of lunatics, no adult trustworthy. As it was, I tended to picture a series of exigencies beginning with my repudiation by my Uncle Pat and Aunt Beth for nebulous and unimaginable reasons and culminating in subsistence with a churlish family of migrant workers, wearing a flour sack dress and picking fruit in the sun, barefoot, until I fainted, in the manner of Lois Lenski.

In my more realistic moments – which were few – these notions were overshadowed by the concrete characters in my life. My daily existence was almost exclusively female; the men were distant and incomprehensible.

Uncle Pat had all the careful dignity of a small man. He bore a strong family resemblance to my mother, but was reddening, fattening, running to seed early under the twin burdens of his prodigious family – six so far – and that of being a self-made construction magnate. He made a special effort for his fatherless niece; his approach was patronising and guileless, always in mock horror at my untoward height, but extracting my affection none the less. His own children were a mob, eating, sleeping, receiving haircuts and treats with no distinctions, no favours, no concessions, no individuality; only the rule of the mob and of Uncle Pat. Aunt Beth had all the weary detachment and patience of a saint towards the wrangling and boisterousness.

More immediately 'Uncle' Peter was all diffidence. He was more relaxed with his son than with me, but like many shy men he was best with very young children. Despite the year-old boy, he was still engaged in post-graduate studies. I found his earnestness endearing. His horn-rimmed glasses and little boy cowlick and soft, brutally barbered neck moved me to protectiveness, an instinct made explicit by 'Aunt' Janet.

Inhabiting the regions between the concrete and the fantastic was the memory of Mr Jansen, the attempted 'Uncle' Jim. Long ago, last summer, he had passed laconic evenings on our verandah, drinking lemonade, the baseball on the radio precluding the need for conversation. I was allowed up late; the heat was such that it would have been unreasonable to expect me to sleep in the airless, sloping-angled room. In any event I would have found excuse on excuse to catch the breeze outside and drink bellyache-making quantities of iced lemonade, crunching the diminishing ice cubes, simultaneously lulled and fascinated by the litany of great baseball names; Yogi Berra, Micky Mantle, Willie Mays. The terminology, like the parroted

Latin responses in church, were touchstones of reassurance: 'top of the seventh', 'three hits, no runs, two errors', 'ball four'. For all the attention I paid to the adults I might as well have been in bed.

Mr Jansen wooed me assiduously in an inept fashion; almond Hershey bars and Wrigley's gum were dispensed with attempted wisecracks and good natured joshing that left me unmoved, implacable. (While my mother remonstrated with him that it was bad for my teeth, that chewing gum was vulgar, I would stolidly consume the offering.) Whether he had already won my mother or had given up trying was in the end irrelevant. I saw it as a matter between himself and me; in the manner of bygone days when propriety demanded that a suitor first apply to parent or guardian, he was seeking my blessing. I would never allow sufficient degree of acquaintance to call him 'Uncle' Jim, despite his repeated urging. Mostly I avoided addressing him or referring to him.

I knew that his somewhat irregular appearances were to do with his job. He was a salesman and drove all over the state, turning up without warning, with chocolate bars and cheeriness, full of praise for home cooking after weeks on the road. Sometimes he would take us out in his car, a big boxlike stately Buick. Such occasions were strained counterfeits of family outings with Uncle Pat where everyone bickered and joked unselfconsciously. His cheer wore thin in the face of my mother's quite resignation and my disdain. My mental picture of him was as almost part of his car, his small pudgy hands tapering into the steering wheel, his shoulders sloping into the back of the seat, his torso spreading to fill the space. I conjured him more clearly from my place lolling in the back seat, his dark curly hair frizzy and thin at the crown, abruptly clipped to a pink neck spilling over the collar of his shiny grey suit with its sprinkling of scurf, than face to face, flabby, thick-mouthed, weak-eyed, blurred. I hated those outings; I could not bear being in public with him.

I could not understand why my mother tolerated him; I supposed it was because she was too timid to send him away. She was not enthusiastic, but she was never enthusiastic. When he turned up she gave him a sad smile and a soft 'Well, Jim', leaning on the screen door edge as if from sheer weariness of life. Her 'home cooking' was basic and uninspired and his extravagant praise a matter of indifference to her. She often said to him 'I don't mind', 'It doesn't matter', 'Whatever you want'. With her effacing manner she fitted in well with the nuns when she went to type in the school office three mornings a week.

Mr Jansen never took my mother out without me, though it would have been possible. She could have got 'Aunt' Janet or 'Uncle' Peter to come up from the apartment below to stay with me. But they merely sat on the verandah or in the living-room until it was late and he went back to his motel. As winter drew in he called perhaps a little less frequently and by Easter I could recall only one visit since Christmas. It was not something I gave much thought to but I was relieved. I didn't know what my mother thought; we did not discuss him, we confided little in each other.

Aunt Janet on the other hand confided in me as an adult; I knew all her worries about her housekeeping money and baby and husband. Soon I was spending more time in her apartment than at home, helping Janet by minding Kevin while she cleaned or cooked, being taught basic cooking skills.

I worshipped Janet. She sought my opinion on recipes and colour schemes. Sometimes she curled my hair in rags overnight. Occasionally I was even allowed to try her jewellery and scent. Always there was something baking, a bowl to lick, something to ice. Together we studied magazines of kitchens and recipes and Janet would plan what they would have when Peter qualified and they had a real house. Her limited budget allowed little for clothes but she and my mother concocted clever outfits for next to nothing on my mother's sewing machine. She always looked very smart and very pretty.

Aunt Janet seemed to like Mr Jansen; always she would have a ready smile and polite chatter for him. It was only I who perceived the unlikely criminality of the man.

2

It was more in embarrassment than in fear that I endured a sudden afternoon interview with the principal, Sister Sepulchre, once it became obvious that I had not been summoned for some misdemeanour. I lost interest and idly noticed the polished wood smell, the perky beruffed wooden Infant of Prague, the starchy black folds upon folds of Sister Sepulchre's habit giving way to thick black stockings as we knelt to pray before the Infant. I surreptitiously examined Sister's red face, scaling on the wings of her nose, round the edge of the gold-rimmed glasses and her red dry hands with cruelly clipped nails. No matter how many times her ugly hands closed abrasively over mine as I struggled with my piano piece I was never inured to squeamishness.

I was lulled by the hypnotic repetitiveness of piano practice in the next room, punctuated by Sister Thomas's exhortations, quellingly more robust than Sister Sepulchre's ever were. Sister Sepulchre was a saint; there could be no doubt. Dwelling on her physical defects made me feel guilty and instead I considered what mechanism attached the black rosary to her waist. It was not until I was dismissed and was dawdling down the stairs that I gave any thought to the imparted news.

The unprecedented appearance of Aunt Janet waiting outside with Kevin in his pushchair made the news far more shocking than the muted interview and prayers with Sister Sepulchre. But we walked back at a leisurely pace and even stopped at the playground. No sense of urgency or desperation was conveyed to me. The prospect of a few days with Aunt Janet and Uncle Peter, the novelty of a folding bed in Kevin's Disney decorated room, excited me. I spared scarcely a thought for my mother, lying resignedly in a dreary hospital room. Even the unorthodoxy of Uncle Peter bathing Kevin, putting us to bed, did not ruffle me. I was enjoying my visit; I knew that there was nothing serious amiss and selfishly hoped that my mother would not be home too soon. I was asleep before Janet returned from the hospital.

I was allowed to stay home from school the next day; it must have been then that Aunt Janet told me. I watched while Janet ironed, followed her closely around as she tidied and attended to Kevin. Watching mother and baby the news suddenly hit me. I slipped upstairs and let myself in with my key to cry in private. The wedding photo of my parents beamed confidently, immortally down from the sideboard; my father laughing indulgently down at my mother, veiled, lacy, eyes downcast with maidenly modesty on the cake they jointly incised. I took the picture down and studied it carefully until it was a blur through my tears.

In the evening Uncle Pat came. He seemed almost angry and his attempts at comforting me were clumsy. His anger was frighteningly unlike his usual roaring outbursts which passed without rancour in a matter of minutes. I felt somehow that it was my fault, that he was displeased with me. I dared not ask what would become of me. Now that it had happened the idea of 'orphan' was not romantic but reprehensible.

I wept a great deal, but my underlying feeling was a well developed sense of outrage. I knew of course that I was a wicked child and that God would punish me, but I also thought that the retribution exacted was in excess of my sins. The reality was mundane; I felt the grown-ups were embarrassed, abashed, even irritated, as though I had been careless. I was not allowed to go to the funeral, although I had attended my grandfather's funeral the previous winter.

I was grateful to be staying with Aunt Janet and Uncle Peter rather than being at the mercy of Uncle Pat's mob. Aunt Beth was awaiting the imminent birth of yet another child and so I was allowed to stay on. It also meant that I did not have either to change schools or face a journey involving two buses each way.

At first I was the centre of attention at school but soon I lost novelty value and was relegated to my former position of little popularity. The nuns were overwhelming in their kindness; it made me squirm as though I had lied to them. Janet's sympathy was the easiest, matter of fact, ungushing. She sat with me in the night when I cried, manufactured treats, invested me with important domestic responsibilities. I assumed that when things were settled I would go to Uncle Pat and Aunt Beth and felt that it was a fate worse than I deserved.

Meanwhile I went for weekends to Uncle Pat and Aunt Beth, hating it, martyred, left out, teased. I revelled in the Saturday confessional and Sunday mass. I was taken twice to see my Grandma but neither time was it a success. She was remote, forgetful, scarcely attending to my presence or to the meal she prepared; the chicken was undercooked, the mashed potatoes cold and lumpy. She ate little herself and said even less. I was glad when Uncle Pat arrived to take me back to Janet and Peter.

I did not brood directly on my loss. I cried myself to sleep every night but by day I did not feel especially bereaved. I was much more apprehensive of my future than nostalgic for my past. I coped as I always had with the business of living; by attending to reality as little as possible. The restrictions of life were transcended by a complex variety of fantasies prompted and expanded by my voracious reading; I read a book almost every day. The resultant imaginings were largely historically based but with more contemporary adventures culled from the Bobbsey twins and other children's series. By this means I had ignored my lack of social life and the exactitudes of my mother's regime. In bereavement my fantasies took on a pleasurably more lurid turn and I would snivel in quiet corners as I conjured ever more dire fates.

My father's brother in England had been written to. Week on week went by; nothing was settled, nothing had been sorted out in the apartment upstairs. I imagined orphanages; wandering the streets in the snow, barefoot, clad in rags, peddling matches; domestic exploitation on a scale to pale Cinderella's into insignificance. Finally a thick cream envelope with queen's head stamps arrived, addressed to Peter and Janet, not myself. The paper was embossed, official, typed, with an impersonal spiky scrawl for a signature. Uncle Pat visited in the evening, irritable, distant, and I was sent to my folding bed while it was still light enough to read.

I was told that the English uncle was coming to visit on my account. I could not conjure any physical picture of him. He would be wicked of course, his own children thin, cold, cowed, his wife dead in suspicious circumstances. More ordinary imaginings were of an excruciatingly jovial man, physically vague, but essentially fat, bald, comfortable, slack-mouthed, smoking interminable cigars as he signed documents consigning me to convents, orphanages, juvenile detention, domestic service, with every indication of generosity and benevolence.

Mostly I daydreamed about being adopted by Janet and Peter. I was not displeased that nothing was resolved; the longer I remained where I was, the more likely that I would continue to do so, I reasoned. Aunt Beth gave birth at last, a boy, but like the death it seemed an almost furtive event, rather than more suitably joyous. But after all, a seventh child was scarcely a novelty.

Shortly afterwards Janet informed me that the English uncle had telephoned Uncle Pat; he was in New York and would arrive in Platea in a few days. Janet planned menus with me, washed and starched the kitchen curtains, took me to buy a new dress.

'What's he like?'

'He seemed very nice from his letter,' Janet improvised.

'But what's he like?'

'I've never met him. He'll be sure to be nice, he's your uncle.'

'Uncle Pat isn't always nice.'

'He's a good man,' she reproved. 'He has a lot of worries right now.'

'He always seems mad at me now.'

'Oh no, Sandy, he's just – well, he has a lot of worries. The new baby is sick,' she confided.

'Oh . . . Does *he* have children?'

'I don't know. I guess so. You mustn't worry, it'll be fine.'

I knew he would be very frightening. But I was not particularly worried in fact; he would have been and gone by the end of the week. I was merely curious. I imagined he would be so old as to look nothing like either his own or my father's youthful photos.

3

The trees lining the road were spaced just too far apart to give continuous shade but it was not inconvenient except for the long clear stretch at each intersection. It was hot for the time of year and the leaves were mature, but still a lurid colour. Women were out on porches with small children. In the narrow gaps between the tall clapboard houses there were glimpses of laundry on clotheslines. The heat invited dawdling, languor, scuffing and stone kicking. The new dress with its lace edged collar and sleeves, carefully ironed down to the tips of its yellow sash and waiting on a hanger on the back of the bedroom door was forgotten, as were the white patent leather shoes polished with Vaseline and the lace-edged white socks and yellow hair ribbons.

In the backyard rows of corner pinned diapers and sheets hung from the upstairs line between the verandah and the tree at the end. But Kevin was not frolicking in the grass attended by Janet. Upstairs, through the screen door, she was mixing frozen pink lemonade concentrate with water. Flowered side plates waited on a tray with Janet's home-baked cookies on a larger flowered plate. Tall glasses rimmed with sugar and filled with ice awaited the lemonade.

Janet was pink with her haste, her careful curls done slightly too tight, her haircut a bit too severe, but looked charming none the less. The checked cloth of her new dress swirled into a wide skirt beneath her neat belted waist.

'He's here!' she hissed in an undertone, too excited to reprimand my dawdling. It would be too late to change; there was no way to the bedroom except through the living-room. Janet fussed at my hair with her fingers and pushed me into the living-room. In the corner Kevin clung to the rim of his playpen, rocking back and forth making a monotonous but cheerful droning noise.

Momentarily his back was presented as he looked down at Kevin, tall, very tall with a dark suit and even darker hair. He turned to greet me. His hand was cool over mine, his voice soft and unintelligible. I didn't know what to say; I had no idea what he had said. He accepted lemonade from Janet and sat down, took a cookie, occasionally, later, eyeing them; perhaps he wanted another one, but I was too shy to offer the plate. He and Janet chatted and I examined him furtively as I ate the cookies, sipped the lemonade, bitter by contrast.

I had not imagined anyone so large; he was far too long to appear at ease in Janet's neo-Colonial armchair with its maple spindle frame and ruffled cushions. His skin was paper-white, faintly moist in the heat. His hands were long and thin and he wore a gold ring on his right hand. His suit seemed very old-fashioned with a vest and watch chain. His nose was long and sharp, his mouth insignificant. His eyes were dark, seemingly lidless like an oriental's. His eyebrows were emphatic, like firmly drawn lines with a charcoal pencil, arching up and away from the bridge of his nose like sideways question marks. But they were neither too thick nor too bushy and terminated un-expectedly in the usual position after their upwards flight. His dark hair was flecked with grey at the sides. He was very old, I knew, older than my father would have been. I was surprised that he was not entirely grey, or at least bald. I was indignant when I realised that he was scrutinising me and fled to the kitchen to make more lemonade.

I could not have hoped to meet with his approval. I was untidy and uncombed, my hand was grimy and sticky in his long clean one. I knew I was an unprepossessing child; even scrubbed and dressed up I scarcely passed muster. At least he could not object to my size, it occurred to me. I thought again of the photographs of the brothers; my father had claimed to six feet and my uncle was the taller.

'Uncle' Peter soon arrived and I remained in the kitchen to help Janet. She was even more animated than usual, going over the afternoon's events, relating how she had dragged a fractious Kevin and wet laundry back from the laundromat and only just got everything put out . . . and by the way, such a nice lady in the laundromat . . . which reminded her, could I . . . As I perilously pulled in the diapers and struggled to drag the sheets over the rail without anything falling overboard, Janet congratulated our foresight in completing so much of the preparation the day before. Just in time she came to help me with the sheets, worrying whether there would be enough food, whether he would approve. After I had changed I was sent out to join the men while Janet bathed Kevin.

They were drinking bottles of beer and my uncle nodded as Peter spoke of his research. He had taken off his jacket now; despite the heat he was wearing long sleeves with gold cuff links. I liked the shiny embossed paisley forming the back of his vest, unexpectedly racy despite its discreet colour. When Janet joined us again he went out to his hired car and returned with packages. There was a stuffed animal for Kevin and English tea in decorative canisters and a linen tablecloth that rendered even Janet speechless and a bottle of whisky. For me there was a doll in Tudor headdress and skirts. It seemed far too ornate to play with. I was aware of my uncle watching me as I examined the doll. Inhibited, and rather intimidated, I put the doll aside.

He did not eat a great deal at dinner, but praised the meal, excusing his lack of appetite as due to travelling through so many time zones that it did not yet seem meal time to his stomach. But I did justice to the chicken and bananas Maryland and candied yams and the salad of celery and carrots and marshmallows suspended in green jello. By then I could understand his accent sufficiently to follow the gist of his conversation. He reminded me of our previous meeting when I was four and still living in Chicago. I remembered vaguely the preparations for the visit but had no memory of him. He abandoned his attempts to converse with me in face of my mumbling embarrassment. Shortly after the meal he took his leave and went to visit Uncle Pat.

Janet put me to bed, telling me that I was lucky, that he was a real gentleman, that we looked alike. I was sceptical. I could not look like that large sharp-edged stranger. My hair was lighter, I would never be that big. I thought also that bland as he seemed, as mercifully unhearty as his manner was, he looked wicked and I was sure that I did not look wicked.

Pulling back the curtain for light I examined my new doll more carefully. She was beautifully made, even the (anachronistic) undergarments finished with lace. The green velvet skirt was slit to reveal a panel of gold brocade. There was gold braid trim and hair underneath the headdress. I had never been given anything so evidently expensive. I decided to call the doll Elizabeth Jane. It seemed both historically accurate and delightfully conventional.

The question of names was to be a bond between us. Mostly I avoided addressing him directly. I was shy of him, and I could not address this larger than average male body by a girl's name. He told me to drop the 'Uncle', as 'uncle' and Evelyn sounded 'ghastly' together. I had always been taught that it was rude to address adults by their first name. He added to my quandary by pronouncing his name in two syllables with a long 'E'.

Later, when he was sorting out the paperwork we discussed my own name.

'Do you like "Alexandria"?' he asked.

'Better than "Sandra".' I made a face.

'You don't like "Sandra"?'

'I hate it.' I screwed up my face again.

'It's pretty awful,' he agreed. 'Common. I suggest we give you something else.' But he deplored my middle name. 'Bernadette indeed! I can't imagine whatever possessed Alec.' He considered. 'What about "Alex"?'

Emboldened, I asked him if he liked his own name. He laughed and said it had been a constant source of trouble.

'Why did they give you a girl's name?'

He explained that in England it was also a man's name but that none the less it was a problem. When I asked why he didn't use his middle name he said it was six of one and half a dozen of the other.

By now I knew that I was not going to live with Uncle Pat and Aunt Beth, but that I was going to England with Evelyn. (I still thought of him as 'him'.) He asked if I would like him to fix my name before my passport was obtained. I would not believe that it was not the conventional feminine of Alexander; it was left like the city in Egypt.

'I can't imagine what possessed Alec,' he said again. I liked his casual references to my father. 'Still, he did enjoy himself there by all accounts.' I did not understand his teasing but his smile was as irresistible as unexpected.

I wanted to stay with Janet and Peter. I wept a great deal and avoided my new uncle as much as possible.

I was told that I could choose what I wanted from the apartment upstairs. Janet helped me to box toys and books, photos and souvenirs, firmly discouraging me from taking too much; old things, outgrown things were abandoned. I pretended

I was choosing a few precious belongings for the trip by wagon train to Oregon, across dangerous river fordings, parched summer prairies, Indian country.

Everything happened quickly now and fantasy had little time to catch up. Evelyn and Janet sorted through the apartment and he insisted that she have the coveted sewing machine and many other things. Uncle Pat had little to do with the clearing out. Aunt Beth had pick of everything remaining after which what was left went to the Church.

Evelyn went to see Sister Sepulchre. I also had another interview with her. She had no doubt that my new uncle was a good man but I would have responsibility for the success of my new life and for maintaining my faith. She explained that my faith would be even more important in the face of my upheaval and said that she would pray for me. Again we prayed together before the incongruously jaunty Infant of Prague, against the background of Exercise Nine, a duet of 'Little Buttercup' which I had failed to execute adequately only the morning before.

I had a farewell meal with my grandmother and Uncle Pat and it was arranged that I would have lunch with Uncle Pat and Aunt Beth before the plane left the following day. At Janet and Peter's I cried myself to sleep, ill-used, unloved, hating both uncles indiscriminately.

In midmorning I was summoned to Sister Sepulchre's office, where she and Evelyn were conversing, balancing cups and saucers. I was astonished; I could not recall anyone ever being offered refreshment before. Evelyn seemed quite out of place, too large, too foreign, too wicked, above all, too masculine; even Monsignor wore skirts.

My eyes went to Evelyn's forehead where a vivid cut over his eyebrow gaped red and raw. His long ringed hand unconsciously covered it as I stared. The wound looked so fresh, so lurid that I had a wild momentary notion that Sister Sepulchre had done it just now. He seemed subdued, certainly. I eyed the things on her desk, telephone, Infant of Prague, metronome, trying to decide what had inflicted the gash.

The inevitable piano practice in the next room ceased and I was seized with the idea that I had been summoned in order to receive my piano lesson early so as not to miss it altogether. But the adults wound up their conversational travelogue, cups were set aside and I was formally turned over. For me there was a rosary and some gilt bordered prayer cards printed with garish saints and for my uncle there was an envelope of documents recording my academic attainments and medical details.

Already nostalgic, I dawdled down the stairs after my uncle, touching for luck the stigmata on the feet of the statue of Jesus that adorned the landing as I had done countless times before, this time for the last time. Evelyn waited on the street, dabbing with his handkerchief at his cut and I shuddered with squeamishness at having touched Our Lord's wounds. Evelyn's car was already stifling in the morning sun and we drove silently to Uncle Pat's for my final goodbyes. I even forgot to be pleased at riding in the front seat for once.

4

I knelt on the radiator cover looking down at the toy cars on 42nd Street; the muted traffic noises just penetrated the hotel windows. I felt alone on the earth; evidence of continuing human existence was reasssuring. I knew that my uncle was still awake in his adjoining room but he seemed no more connected with me than the occupants of the cars eight floors down. It was uncomfortable kneeling on the metal grate but I could not tear myself away.

I felt too weary for my usual marathon of muffled bedtime weeping. I could not even feel guilty that I had no feelings left. Weariness aside, I could feel nothing for my new uncle. The relationship seemed transient, as though he were merely a courier. Despite his low-key manner there was still awkwardness in dealing with him and I avoided doing so more than was essential.

Staying in such opulent surroundings my imagination ran riot, to rather more exalted effect than usual. Gone for the most part was spartan drudgery in austere institutions. Instead the equally dreadful human events were rendered comfortable by the luxurious settings. I fantasised little about my uncle. The reality of his large presence inhibited such mental forays, as if he could read my mind.

On our arrival in New York we took a taxi to the hotel. The hotel itself was more than I could have hoped for. The huge lobby was marble floored, marble pillared, furnished with palms and red sofas. A balcony ran round three sides of the lobby and from this height hung the flags of every nation. At one end of the lobby, which was trellised off, afternoon tea was served at white draped tables with gilt chairs. Inhibition banished by excitement, I pleaded to eat in the lobby. He was amused and said he expected we could in due course. I was wistful that we had to leave the bustle of so many sophisticated and important people to go upstairs when he had registered.

I had my own room, the mirror image of Evelyn's, with two double beds and my own bathroom. I sat in the chairs and looked in the drawers and fingered the stationery provided with the hotel's motif and address and planned to write letters to everyone I could think of. I liked the bathroom best of all. There were tiny individually wrapped bars of soap, dozens of towels and an extra tap at the sink marked 'ice water'. I was instructed to bath forthwith and daydreamed, dawdled, until he knocked and asked if I had drowned.

I thought of all the money he had spent that day, bills – not coins – changing hands for drinks, for luggage being carried, taxis, room service with more drinks. He must be very rich, I decided. I was well pleased, for once, with my fate.

We had drinks before dinner in the hotel lobby. I was too excited to mind that he studied me while I gazed raptly at the world hurrying by. He nodded at my exclamations and diffidently suggested that perhaps it would be as well if I didn't point at people. He called for another round of drinks and I noticed that he left all his change on the serving tray. His own drink was whisky over ice and for me he ordered a drink of ginger ale garnished with cherries and orange slices and red syrup at the bottom.

After that we went downstairs to the hotel dining-room. I had never eaten out in such sumptuous surroundings, nor had I eaten out more than half a dozen times in a real restaurant. I was appalled by the prices on the menu. But my uncle seemed unconcerned and in the face of my uncertainty ordered for me. I was too intent on avoiding some breach of manners to attempt conversation. Beyond ascertaining that I could 'manage', he said little either. I was too surprised to be asked such a thing to be suitably indignant. (It did not occur to me that he was questioning my appetite rather than my prowess with cutlery.) I was offered the choice of a lavish dessert but had to leave half of it. He did not seem worried at such waste, but rather amused. Before bed we had a 'nightcap' in the lobby and he talked pleasantly to me of New York. I gleaned that he knew the city well from frequent business trips. I managed to ask about the cut on his head.

'Oh, someone took exception to my face in a bar last night.'

'What's wrong with your face?'

He had a sort of soft half laugh, half smile that served when he was amused but not sufficiently so to laugh fully that he now gave. I was finding that it also served to close a subject; yet I perceived that amusing him made things easier.

As at bath time and meal time, he asked if I could manage for myself when I went to bed. I supposed his own children were so grown up that he had forgotten how to deal with someone of my age. I resolved to ask him. But his manner, while polite, did not encourage inquisitiveness. I was awed too by his casual dismissal of such an appalling wound. Even brushing my teeth was exciting in the hotel bathroom, unwrapping the glasses from waxed paper bags.

The next morning, Saturday, he picked over my wardrobe. Janet had already omitted the oldest and most outgrown things, intimating that I would get a few new ones. Blouses and nightgowns and underwear faded with washing were set aside, almost nothing was spared. I was mortified to have my things pawed over by a strange man, angry at the implied insult to my mother.

I was torn between revelling in shopping in grand department stores and outrage at his officiousness. Our tastes clashed irrevocably; I homing in on the most extravagantly ruffled and lacy creations in unsuitable pastels, he with an eye to what was simple. He said that I was too old for such frilly fripperies. I was hot and sulky with trying on, with his overmastering will. Usually the saleslady would take my part but she was as easily and blandly outflanked as I. He compromised and all my new night things and underwear were the most fussy available, despite the monstrous extra cost. It was hard to feel ill-used. Finally, laden with shopping, we went to a restaurant at the top of the store. I dreamily ate my way through multicoloured ice cream adorned with syrup and cherries and cream while he drank tea.

In the evening, after my bath, I remembered that I had not thanked him for the new night things in which I was clad, or the new dress I had worn to dinner, or anything. Examining the new things on the hotel hangers I was soon reconciled to their relative simplicity. All the seams and buttonholes were professionally finished, nothing was panelled with contrasting remnants, no rows of braid half disguised the mark of let out hems. I had seldom possessed store-bought dresses, except the yellow dress bought for Evelyn's visit. Awkwardly I thanked him. He gruffly 'not at all'ed and patted my head. I cried myself to sleep. He did not intrude.

Sunday he took me to church at St Patrick's cathedral. I loved the grandeur but was embarrassed by his behaviour. I wanted to sit at the front. He did not and we ended at the side about half-way up. He sat reading a paperbacked book, ignoring the service, neither kneeling nor singing. I was determinedly devout, singing rather than mouthing, kneeling straight-backed, watching him out of the corner of my eye. When I returned from communion, head bowed, hands clasped before me, he was standing, peering about, even more conspicuous. He glared at me. I knelt loftily and lost myself in prayer. He settled with ill grace to his book. Outside, before I could steel myself to reprimand him for his behaviour he pre-empted me.

'That was extremely naughty.' His tone was unaccustomedly sharp and I was torn between self-righteousness and bewilderment.

'What?'

'Running off like that. How was I to –. Besides, you can't possibly have been confirmed.'

'No,' I agreed warily.

'Well then, you've no business taking communion, it was very wicked.' But he seemed almost amused now.

'But . . .' I was at a loss. 'I had my First Communion last year.'

'Your –?'

The misunderstanding was cleared up. I was superior, staggered at his ignorance.

'Aren't you Catholic?'

'Good God, no.'

'So you didn't know any better than to read. You're not supposed to, you know.'

'Aren't I?'

'It was very rude. If you're not Catholic, what are you?'

'I was brought up an Anglican. But I must say all that rigmarole just now puts me in mind of our non-Conformist ancestors.'

'Why didn't we go to your church?'

'My dear girl, the only time I end up in church these days is for funerals.'

'But . . .' I stared at him.

'Mmm?' he prompted.

'What if you go to hell?'

His brows arched. The area around his cut was now raised and purple, quite undignified. He laughed. 'I undoubtedly shall.' After a minute he asked, 'Do you really believe all that?' He smiled at my withering look and said, 'Well, you're very young yet.'

I was so ruffled that I did not think to welcome his good humour. But martyrdom at the hands of heretics could not rival the attractions of the zoo, which we soon reached walking through the park from the cathedral. We passed a playground and he asked if I wanted to play. I was getting too old for such things and anyway was dressed up, but I did not want to hurt his feelings. I went on the swings for a few minutes, wary of scuffing my white shoes while he put my gloves in his pocket and sheepishly held my flowered hat by its elastic. (Earlier he had taken exception to it and tried to persuade me to go to church hatless.) As soon as I felt was polite I asked if we could see the animals now.

Kneeling at the window, looking out at New York, I thought back on the events since my arrival. I thought of my uncle's impassive, incongruously wounded face as he looked through racks of children's dresses, perused menus, viewed animals in the zoo. I thought of his long white fingers wielding his cutlery in that odd way of his, turning over the pages of the orange and black paperbacked book, plucking out the gold watch on its chain. I thought of his fingertips lightly on my arm or shoulder at busy intersections, in crowds. But mostly he seemed to avoid contact, as if it were he who was shy of me rather than the other way round.

I could not tear myself away from looking out at the city. A fire engine went by below. I shifted; my leg had gone numb. My room was scary in the dark, cavernous and high ceilinged. The line of light around the door to my uncle's room was reassuring. A wedge of light appeared on the ceiling as the door opened.

'Alexandria,' my uncle rebuked. I loved the way he so beautifully pronounced my ridiculous name. He crossed to the window and closed the blinds. His hand firmly propelled me to bed. He jerked the covers over me. 'You must sleep now. We've a busy day tomorrow.'

He left me and soon the crack of light around the door had disappeared. All was silent, I was alone in the enormous hotel. He had not seemed really angry at me, he had not shouted. He had felt very strong as he pushed me back to bed. He was a stranger and a foreigner. My knees hurt from kneeling too long on the radiator grate. I longed for my teddy bear. Teddy was totally denuded of fur, copiously mended and so floppy at the joints that he could no longer sit up. He had been banished from my bed when I was seven and was now in a box somewhere between Platea and London. I wept.

5

On Monday I had my first subway ride. The thunderous noise, the rhythmic racketing of the train both soothed and exhilarated me. The noise isolated me from everyone, my journey was solitary. I could pretend that I was alone on my adventure. I liked the maps and the initials of the lines, BMT, IRT. My uncle sat with his eyes closed, peeking at each station. I watched him in the window opposite, large, shadowy, seemingly bisected by his watch chain.

Our destination was an office block downtown, dwarfed by newer skyscrapers. On the fifth floor a plaque announced 'Leibowicz & Stein', underneath, in different lettering, 'USA Distributors for:' and a row of smaller plaques, the first of which said: 'Parrish and Sons Ltd, London and Sheffield'. This did not surprise me. Uncle Pat's three pick-up trucks had 'Mahoney and Bergin' painted on the sides (his own name before that of his brother-in-law's); it seemed obvious that Evelyn's work should bear his – my – name.

In a busy room filled with rows of desks I was seated in a corner and given a rack of rubber stamps and pink paper with printing on one side and coloured pens. Amuse yourself, he told me. I was glad when at last he emerged for lunch from his little frosted glass partitioned corner and admired the intricate designs I had made with the stamps on the clean side of the invoices.

In mid-afternoon Evelyn fetched me into his office. He said we must have a talk and took the multi-coloured phones off the hook. I drank water from a tumbler with matching carafe and tray and made a paper clip chain. He told me that we would go 'home' to London in a week or so when his business was finished. Then he would be able to make proper arrangements and naturally I would go off to school. But while we were in New York we would have to improvise. Did I mind? Had I any questions?

'When do I get to see the Empire State Building?'

He smiled and said we could go now. He lectured me on the perils of New York, I must stay close to him, not speak to strangers. He made me memorise the name and address of the hotel and gave me two quarters to spend and sealed two dollars into an envelope for a taxi in an emergency, warning me to be careful of my purse. At the top of the Empire State he provided coins for the telescopic glasses so that I did not have to spend my allowance. I received change for the subway as well so that I could pay for myself. A stray English sixpence was discovered in his handful of coins and he gave that to me 'for luck'.

On the way to work the next morning Evelyn bought me paper dolls and colouring books and the largest size box of crayons, with a sharpener embedded in the back. In addition there was drawing paper and coloured pencils. I was embarrassed by how much he spent.

I enjoyed going every day to the office. I had no trouble amusing myself with what he bought me. The incessant activity, phones, visitors, provided much scope for fantasy. The women of the typing pool spoilt me disgracefully, chatting to me on their breaks, buying me Coke, taking me to lunch.

At the end of the week he told me that he found himself

'obliged' to go to Toronto in regard to a large potential order. I had never been to Canada. I asked if we could see Niagara Falls.

'No, Alex. *I* am going to Toronto. I've arranged for you to stay with some cousins in New Jersey.'

'I haven't got any.'

'You have, actually.' He told me that I would stay with Gillian, who was his cousin, and her American husband. 'She's Richard's sister,' he explained.

'Who's Richard?'

'Of course, you haven't met him yet, you'll meet him in London.' He added that I would enjoy staying with Gillian; her own daughter was almost my age. I knew that I would not enjoy it.

'I want to go to Canada with you.'

'Well you can't. And I'm not having any more scenes,' he said sternly.

I pushed out my lower lip but did not dare make a fuss so soon on the heels of our previous confrontation. I had not realised how ineptly I was managing my long hair unaided and it was not until several days' tangle lay underneath that he noticed. He said it must be shorn at once, which appalled me so much that I resisted. The upshot of this was an agonising hour while he brusquely worked through the tangle, sipping from a large drink poured from a bottle in his bedroom and ignoring my petulant yelps of pain. Thereafter he brushed it every morning and did it into a clumsy plait secured at both ends by elastic grips. But now I was not sure whether it would have been more prudent to have submitted to the shearing to retain his goodwill.

On the journey to New Jersey I stared with impartial fascination at ugly slums, huge refinery complexes, and later tiny brick boxes surrounded by scraps of lawn. Evelyn slumped in the dusty plush seat, pettish and sweaty, twisting awkwardly with his legs fenced by the crush of commuters. I drank many cups of foetid water from the tank at the end of the car – the cups were absurd, like tiny paper hats – but Evelyn disdained to. I worried about what he would be like in a mood of sustained ill humour. He had been distant rather than short-tempered in our week together, his occasional irritation passing quickly into impassiveness again.

He had soon given up the pretence of reading. His usual freshly turned elegance was crumpled. He looked stern, and, I suddenly realised, weary after his week's work, his week's guardianship. His face was pinched, as if between the thumb and forefinger of a large invisible god.

On the platform a blonde woman flung her arms around Evelyn's neck, kissed his cheek, spoke incoherently at great speed, endearments, news, questions, as he first endured and then gently detached her grip, smiling, nodding. She stood back and looked at him.

'You look tired.' She gestured to his cut head, now mottled green, yellow, maroon around the brown scab. 'My God, what –?'

Evelyn asserted himself, insisted that it was nothing, that he was well, and pushed me forward. I too was embraced and scrutinised as she expressed her delight at meeting her cousin Alec's girl at last.

Her car was new, two-toned with high fins and dozens of lights and leather seats. On the long drive she chattered, asked questions, scarcely awaited Evelyn's replies. The houses became larger, further apart, sidewalks petered out and trees appeared.

'How is Richard?' she asked and attended to Evelyn's answer.

'Much as always, overworked. But well. He sends his love.'

'He ought to take it easier, he's earned it.'

'But he thrives on being overworked.'

'Aunt' Gillian sighed. 'I don't suppose he's found a nice girl to settle down with?'

'No, I don't suppose so. You don't imagine he confides in *me*, surely?'

She quickly began to ask about other people, so many other people that I gave up trying to keep track.

The house was modern, split-level, just like the magazine pictures that Janet so endlessly pored over. Inside there was a huge beige L-shaped sofa in the huge L-shaped, wall-to-wall carpeted living-room. The glossy magazine family were squabbling in the basement family room complete with television and nautical motif. 'Uncle' Ted came forward to shake Evelyn's hand and pat my head. The brothers, eleven and thirteen, eyed me with frank malice as the drinks were handed round. The girl, Angela, had long blonde hair and her nostrils quivered fastidiously like a toy rabbit's. I felt particularly clumsy and overgrown.

Everyone was given Coke. I knew by now that Evelyn's usual evening drink was whisky, over ice if downstairs in the hotel lobby, or neat from the bottle in his room, sometimes both. I was given ginger ale when he was ordering drinks; Coke was bad for the teeth, the ruin of civilisation. I wondered if he would drink the Coke.

The adults adjourned to the living-room. After some aggressive but inconclusive interrogation I was ignored in favour of *The Dick Van Dyke Show* and escaped upstairs. Evelyn gave me a quick look, almost of complicity and gestured me to sit next to him instead of banishing me. The men talked business and Aunt Gillian bore me away to the kitchen.

The meal was strained. The boys, Eddie and Pete, bickered and teased and clowned tiresomely. The elder was finally banished from the table before the dessert. I perceived that the two men did not get on. Uncle Ted forcefully expounded and Evelyn would say something brief, quietly, almost diffident. Uncle Ted would become louder, more insistent. Evelyn would respond with a bland 'Perhaps' and Aunt Gillian would interject brightly with questions or reminiscences about England.

Eventually I was able to snivel furtively into my pillow in the spare twin bed in Angela's room. Her room had gilt trimmed white furniture with a pink frilly skirted dressing table which matched the quilts on the beds. The walls had pictures of ballerinas and horses. She had boasted mendaciously and I had responded in kind. She showed me her own drawings of horses and told me that she was to have a pony for her birthday. My belongings were examined with seeming indifference, but my new underthings were slightly envied, I fancied, with their extravagance of trimmings. (Later, with washing and ironing, Aunt Gillian would say how typical it was of Evelyn to buy such unsuitable things for a child.)

I spent most of my time trailing Aunt Gillian around and avoiding my cousins, deaf to her suggestions that I play with them. I liked Aunt Gillian, envied her pretty stylishness. I could not understand why she was married to Uncle Ted, who was not even handsome. Balding, paunchy, irascible, he was much nearer to my projected image of Evelyn than the reality. He was obsessive about petty disciplines, 'please' and 'thank you' and 'sir', but the real nastiness of his offspring was unchecked, unperceived. The eldest boy was frankly sadistic towards both siblings and the boys ganged up on Angela. I was aloof, on the one hand grimly satisfied to see Angela put in her place, on the other hand certain that intervention would divert their bullying to me. Uncle Ted brooked no tale telling, which I would have predicted; in my own experience Uncle Pat doled out clouts all round if a squabble erupted, impartially, exasperated. I understood clearly that Angela held me in contempt, tolerating me only for want of a more worthy audience.

It was easier in the week. My cousins still had a few more weeks of school but it was not thought worth sending me at such a late date. Aunt Gillian was very nice to me. She talked of the English relatives; her own dear brother; numerous elderly aunts and cousins that I could not keep track of; my Aunt Diana, Evelyn's sister; Evelyn himself. I learned little that was concrete about them; mainly there were anecdotes, often pointless, of family gatherings and other set occasions. I did not think to ask systematic questions.

I hated being there, took gloomy satisfaction in the knowledge that I was not wanted. I retreated into the most dreadful and lurid fantasies of deprivation and ill usage that I had imagined in the interval of waiting at Janet and Peter's. I considered writing plaintively to them but somehow I could not conjure my rescue at their hands. The week that I was to stay stretched into 'another week or so'. The information was delivered briskly by Aunt Gillian; Evelyn had not asked to speak to me.

Uncle Ted made no secret of his impatience with such a cry-baby. Angela nagged her mother to remove me to the guest room. I avoided socialising when Angela brought her friends home from school; if Aunt Gillian remonstrated with her lack of hospitality Angela openly complained of me. The initial immunity from physical bullying from the boys soon passed and Angela egged them on, out of malice as well as a sense of her own reprieve.

Aunt Gillian redoubled her efforts to be nice to me. I enjoyed the day, shopping, helping her around the house, kibitzing her bridge lunches. It was only when the others were there that I was miserable. I did not make it easy for Aunt Gillian. Apart from my unprepossessing appearance, my manner was unforthcoming at best, easily degenerating to sulks. It was difficult for her to make allowances for my bereavement when I was seemingly indifferent to references to my mother and showed no grief.

I did not picture Evelyn in the role of rescuer. I scarcely even thought of him as 'Evelyn'; he was still nearer to 'him'. But I felt increasing nostalgia for our time in New York. I had enjoyed myself. He had not been unkind to me, nor had anyone else. I began to reconsider my impression of him as a transient courier.

Had he not been perceptive enough to choose me Elizabeth Jane, the Tudor doll (albeit now bald, naked, armless at the hands of my cousins – who had for once been hit for their wickedness)? Did we not have the bond of awful names? ('Sandy' had stuck here.) Had he not allowed me to sit up past ten in the hotel lobby watching the world go by? Had he not spent almost a hundred dollars – I was staggered as I considered this – on my new clothes and toys? He had even left twenty dollars with Aunt Gillian on my behalf. I brooded increasingly on this money. She could not possibly have spent it. I plotted how I could obtain enough of it to get back to New York on the train. (It did not occur to me that of course Evelyn would not be there.) In the end I demanded the money aggressively on the grounds that it was mine, Evelyn having left it for me, and was sent to bed early with no dessert or television for my pains.

I was rewarded with Evelyn's appearance on Saturday evening, two weeks after he had gone. His quiet air of authority made my terror seem ridiculous and ill-mannered. I was almost as frightened as I was relieved to see him.

'Well, Alex,' was all he said, his brows rising, his wound now faded to a small pink scar. He did not intervene when I was banished to the rumpus room by Aunt Gillian.

During the last few days I had cultivated total abstraction over a set of jacks from the supermarket, endlessly bouncing the ball and scooping up the metal stars, achieving, by my inept standards, prodigies of dexterity. Now I sat in the hall playing with the jacks instead of going to certain abuse at the hands of my cousins. After a time I realised that I was being watched and found Evelyn standing behind me. I trailed after him into the guest room and timidly asked about Toronto while he opened his bag and found a bottle of whisky from which I was shocked to see him drink. He grinned improbably and said that this time he had come prepared. He spoke amiably of Toronto and other ports of call until dinner was served.

Sunday morning television brought the usual dissent between the siblings over channels and roused Evelyn, who arrived on the scene as Eddie stole my jack set and the boys began to torment me. Evelyn casually gripped Eddie's wrists behind his back with one hand, twisted Pete's arm away from me with the other.

'The very least one would hope for,' he pronounced wearily, 'is a peaceful morning's lie-in after a hard week's work.' He shook both boys. 'If you were mine I'd bang your heads together until your brains spilled – if you've got any.' He stood sternly over them until they had found my jacks and restored them to me, commanding authority even in pyjamas. He went away without attempting to comfort me and television viewing was sulkily resumed as if nothing had happened.

Later, dressed now in trousers and open-necked shirt, he intervened in a battle between Angela and Pete over an English coin he had disbursed on his previous visit by blandly pocketing the coin.

'Has it been like this all the time?' he asked.

'Worse mostly. They're better now you're here,' I said cunningly.

'Well, you're a big girl, why don't you defend yourself?'

Sunday lunch was the worst family meal I had endured so far. Uncle Ted discussed Evelyn's business trip in a tone that even I realised meant that he was suggesting gross incompetence. Evelyn murmured occasional noncommittal monosyllables and pushed his food around his plate. Aunt Gillian gushed at Evelyn in between her husband's griping. The children bickered.

Evelyn attempted to respond courteously to Aunt Gillian's vivacious small talk. The dog, an elderly and smelly schnauzer which I avoided as much as possible, escaped from the basement and was yapping and foraging around the table. A glass of Coke was spilled. Both boys were banished from the table and began to fight. Blows were exchanged, a chair was knocked over. Uncle Ted stood to intervene. A plate of dinner fell to the carpet for the dog. Evelyn quietly folded his napkin and left the table. I followed. In his room he sat on his bed and found what was left of his whisky. Oddly, he seemed in good humour as he packed his case. He sat on the bed again, swigged whisky and looked at me.

'I'd hoped to leave you here another week until I'm ready to leave for London. You do realise, of course, that you've rendered yourself *persona non grata* here?' he said mildly, 'In other words, they don't want you here.'

'Well, I don't want them,' I flashed.

'I can't say I altogether blame you.' He sighed. 'I suppose you'll have to come away with me now. Even if I could prevail upon them to have you for another week that would mean that I'd have to come back again and I don't intend to do that in a hurry.' He pitched the flat empty bottle into the wastebasket. 'I hope you're not going to cause me as much trouble as you're supposed to have caused here.'

We packed my case. Evelyn exclaimed over the defunct doll, castigating my carelessness. I began to cry, I was being blamed for everything and none of it was my fault. I would not be comforted, even by his promise of a new doll. He continued to pack, even my underwear much to my embarrassment, and eventually told me to wash my face, gingerly received back his sodden handkerchief.

Soon afterwards Aunt Gillian drove us to the station, chatting as if nothing was wrong, not quite succeeding. On the platform Evelyn embraced her, said that she must take care of herself, to rely on him if she needed to. She clung to him and cried. He hugged her patiently until she stopped and walked back to the car.

It was a long wait for the train. It was hot and sticky; no air moved. Evelyn bought me chocolate, declined a bite, and said it would have to do until we could have a meal in town. I didn't mind the wait. I was elated to have got away. He did not even seem mad at me. I ran up and down the platform innumerable times until I was red with heat, my fringe glued to my forehead and he bought me a bottle of Coke because it was cold. I sat on the ground with the jacks. He watched, not caring that my dress would be soiled or that I would get germs. I conjured up deathbed scenes, dying with regal resignation, while he, stricken with remorse, blamed his neglect for my fatal illness and begged my forgiveness.

'I don't know what you intend to do, Alex, but I'm getting on this train with or without you,' his voice calmly punctured my fantasy. I scrabbled to pick up the jacks, was on my feet clinging to his jacket long before the train came abreast of the platform.

6

We had different rooms in the hotel, higher up, which pleased me. Evelyn allowed me to sit up late over drinks in the hotel lobby. He was in expansive good humour, unusually forthcoming.

'Why was Aunt Gillian crying?'

'I seem to recall that you were crying today as well.'

'But it was horrible there.'

'Exactly. But you've come away. Gillian can't do that.'

'You mean she doesn't like it there?'

'I think she's finding it . . . difficult just now. I'll tell you one thing; if you show any signs of turning out like those little hooligans I'll drop you straight on the doorstep of the nearest orphanage and that's a promise.'

I pushed my face into mock terror, making him smile. 'Why did she marry Uncle Ted?'

'It's a mystery to me why anyone marries, it really is, Alex.'

I liked him calling me 'Alex'. 'Aren't you married?'

'Good God. Whatever gave you an idea like that?'

'Well, I don't know. You never tell me anything.'

He looked at me sharply, signalled for new drinks, leaned back, still watching me. 'What would you like to know?' he asked dauntingly.

'*Are* you married?'

'No. I'm not married. Whatever has Gilly been telling you about me?'

'Nothing.' It was true; she had recounted nothing I found significant.

'Well what do you want to hear? What do you expect; what do you think?' He prompted me. 'Come, you're an imaginative child. What do you imagine? Blue blood? Blood feuds? Changelings? Sorcery? Duels? Plague and pestilence? Love and death? Well?' He sipped his drink but did not really seem to expect any response. 'What about violence and intrigue, sedition and treachery, transportation and imprisonment? Blots on the family escutcheon, banishment and exile, black sheep, emigration to Australia? Or unrequited love, divorce and adultery, betrayal and shame, depravity and . . . But let's keep this clean. This is your fantasy after all. I think that's about all, I can't think of any more clichés, can you?' He looked at me. 'Well, what would you like to hear?'

Suddenly, inadvertently, he was very close to the usual content of my thoughts. But his tone made me feel ridiculed. I risked my self-respect on eliciting a laugh, usually the best policy with him.

'Orphans,' I said. 'You forgot orphans.'

He did not laugh. He raised his brows. 'Alone and unbefriended, I perceive, at the mercy of the wicked and unscrupulous Evelyn.' He sat back, shaking his head, rueful. 'Is that what you think?'

'No.' I didn't know what I thought; my imaginings concerning him were, oddly, so nebulous as to be scarcely conscious.

'What do you think?' he asked with sudden gentleness, leaning forward.

'I don't know,' I mumbled.

'Allow me' – he took my hand in his large one, bony and faintly dry-skinned, warm – 'to reassure you about your situation. It must be said, I admit, that I have youthful excesses to answer for. But I think that now, in my encroaching old age, I have acquired a reasonable facsimile of respectability. You will, I feel sure, have a quite unexceptionable childhood. You will find your accommodation comfortable. You will receive as good an education as you are capable of absorbing and in due course, no doubt, go to university. You will find the wider family circle agreeable and amiable. In fact, my dear girl, you're in far more danger of being bored silly than ill-used.' He squeezed my hand and released it. His eyes scrunched at the corners, his brows arched. I wanted to cry. It was easier when he was bland. He abandoned the banter in face of my silence, awkwardly saying that it was late, I should be asleep and here he was filling me with absurd drivel.

Although I stumbled in following his soft voice, his staccato accent, for once I felt close to understanding him. I was sure now that I liked him. But the momentary closeness was not re-established. I had made no response to his exceptional expansiveness; he seemed to interpret this as incomprehension or rebuff rather than shyness.

Routine was quickly established. The week until the journey to London again stretched to two. I still went to work every day with Evelyn, which I enjoyed. Sometimes I would lunch with him and the men, the executives. It surprised me that he got on so well with them. They were burly, red-faced, older than him, brashly American by contrast. The men made as much fuss of me as the women of the typing pool and soon I preferred lunching with them quite illicitly in a bar instead of at Chock Full o' Nuts or Schrafft's with the women.

Most of Evelyn's evenings were occupied; I was left behind with a babysitter. When taxed he would say that business was not merely from nine to five; he had obligations, dinners, gatherings, functions of every description in order to gain and consolidate contracts, reward and reassure employees. I was entranced by his tuxedo ('Dinner jacket, Alex, dinner jacket'); I had never seen one in real life.

His days at the office were not long. He seldom arrived before ten and never stayed late. On several occasions he had the afternoon off to take me sightseeing. I climbed up the Statue of Liberty (Evelyn resolutely waited below, refusing to exert himself in the heat), toured the United Nations building, travelled on the Staten Island ferry. We went to the Natural History Museum and the Metropolitan Museum of Art. We ate in the Automat, feeding nickels into slots and removing the food from compartments like post office boxes, and had cold drinks in Rockefeller Plaza.

I became obsessed with the idea that I would lose Evelyn or that he would lose me. When he was out of my sight, in a toilet, at a bar, gone from his office, I was convinced that he had vanished. I didn't credit Evelyn with conscious intent to ditch me; I merely felt that he would disappear, ill, kidnapped, amnesiac or dematerialised, quite impersonally, nothing to do with me; and I would be unable to satisfactorily account for Evelyn's existence and disappearance.

I would sit shaking, interminably waiting, as his unattended glass sweated, rivulets running down the outside, ice melting in swirls in the strong brown liquid. My own drink would dwindle, the red syrup diffusing into watery dregs of golden fizz, orange rind denuded, cherry consumed. Finally, his cubes melted, mine crunched ('I suppose it's essential you do that?' 'Sorry.') there would be questions, endless questions I could not answer. What would be done? What would become of me? Could I recognise him again in a crowd?

And then he would be looming over me, a gulp and a swallow and he had caught up with me. But sooner or later, I knew, the alarm would be real; I would be quite alone on the subway, left unable to pay for the meal we consumed, or abandoned in the office overnight. I began to sleep badly, convinced he would not return, that I would be alone in the hotel. But by day I was content, except for the recurring moments of terror.

It was hot by now, it was high summer in New York. At the weekend Evelyn again took me shopping and bought me a few more suitably summery clothes. He purchased several short-sleeved shirts for himself as well.

On Sunday we went to Coney Island. Evelyn watched while I ate many ice creams (he even had one himself), went on some of the tamer rides, and waded in the sea. It was a very sedate outing and rather constrained. I found myself making an effort to be suitably cheerful and childish, rather than being determinedly sombre as I had done the previous summer when Mr Jansen took us to the State Fair. We were both very sunburnt.

After my bath, he did my hair and rubbed cream on to my face and arms with deft gentleness. (He had gone specially to a 24-hour drug store in Grand Central Station to buy cold cream for me.) I forgot to be embarrassed by his touching me. It was cooler by evening. We had dinner at a sidewalk restaurant in the 60s and sat for a long time over drinks afterwards. At the hotel he again put cream on my sunburn before bed.

For some reason, despite his amiability over the weekend – perhaps because of it – I felt particularly distressed waiting in the dark for sleep and was rather more noisy than usual in my abandonment to grief.

'Alex, what is it?' he asked, standing in the door between our rooms. I lay rigid. He came to the bed. 'Come, I know you're not asleep.' He knelt by the bed and prodded my shoulder.

I was touched. I felt shamed too and hated him for intruding. When he persisted I mumbled that I wanted my teddy.

'Then you must have him. Where is he?' I explained that he was in a box on his way to London. 'We'll get you a new one,' he soothed.

'I don't want a new one, it's not the same.'

'Surely you're a bit old for teddies,' he said gently.

'I don't care. I want him.' I sobbed with renewed vigour.

He did not reply but waited a while longer until I was snuffling and spent and then tucked the covers around me before going away.

The next day he came back from lunch with a large brown teddy bear sporting a lavender ribbon around its neck. It could sit unaided, it was soft and plushy to touch, its face was distinguishable, its ears stood up and I hated it on sight. I sullenly accepted it, forcing out a 'thank you' and immediately setting it aside. I resented Evelyn, resented the toy as we went back to the hotel that evening. I felt silly carrying it in public. I was glad we took a taxi so that I did not have to be seen with it on the subway. (We usually had a taxi in the evening, Evelyn declaring it far too hot for the subway.)

'Don't you want your teddy with you?' Evelyn asked when he came to turn off my light that night.

'Of course not. I'm *nine*,' I said haughtily. I was sure I had hurt his feelings, felt a surge of satisfaction. I wept, hating his clumsiness, longing for him to come and comfort me.

part II

1

Everything was so unfamiliar that nothing, least of all Evelyn seemed real. I did not miss America, and my nightly tears were by now largely habit. On the whole I was pleased with myself for having managed to get to England. I felt very lonely, but I was accustomed to that.

I felt a curious sense of relief at being with Evelyn. He was not forever asking what I was reading, doing, thinking. If he asked about my day, examined my new library books, it was simply politeness, something to talk about. I had never had anything to say to my mother. I had assiduously shielded all my real feelings and views from her relentless scrutiny. Conversation had been mainly around domestic minutiae, padded with intricate future plans mapping out the course of my life and education, and very genteel gossip, mostly rehashing long known and quite unscurrilous snippets in a sort of litany in which I could interpolate expected responses without attending to her in the least.

Evelyn did not gossip, at least to me, took no interest in domestic details unless something had gone wrong and made not the least attempt to question or pry. Silences were long, and at first awkward. But in time we read or ruminated as comfortably as if the other was not there. Conversation improved too; Evelyn could talk intelligently about anything I asked him and began to volunteer information regarding any historical work I was reading. And never did he remonstrate that I was more interested in my book than in talking to him.

Yet his aloofness panicked me. I was incapable of interpreting his actions or characteristics independently of myself. It did not occur to me to wonder what he was like with other people, or whether omniscient surveillance was a necessary component of good parenting. I dared not be naughty and learned instead to say things for effect. He seemed easily amused by the sorts of comments my mother would have punished me for. His smile was sometimes accompanied by a rueful 'Really, Alex,' or 'For God's sake don't go saying that in front of people.' Occasionally, quite unpredictably, he looked outraged and said sternly, 'Alexandria!'

Complicity was comforting; it made me feel less alone. I had always been alone, lacked genuine companionship, but previously I could rely utterly on a set of circumstances and people to behave in prescribed ways towards me, to look after me. Evelyn, by contrast, was wholly unpredictable. I learned swiftly that although domestic arrangements were sketchy, meal times and contents widely variable, I was always provided for on a scale of extravagance far above that to which I was accustomed. I was left almost entirely to my own devices but never neglected.

In the face of my tentative naughtiness, Evelyn's impenetrable politeness gave way rapidly to ruthless firmness. 'Now that's enough,' or 'I won't have it, Alex,' he would say in tones so unpromising that I was quelled at once. It was not so much fright, though his size and his sternness did frighten me. It was the conviction that he would do whatever he thought necessary, banishment to my room, spanking, withholding of treats, genuinely unmoved, indifferent. There was no point.

Despite my enjoyment of life with Evelyn, I was seized by an increasing despair. Perhaps it was merely long-delayed grief. I had consciously, piously tried to feel as I ought at first, but increasingly I felt guilty that I was not more distressed about my bereavement.

The trouble was not being orphaned, or Evelyn, or foreigners. I realised this one morning a few weeks after I had arrived. As usual I waited quietly in my room until Evelyn showed signs of stirring. Presently, while the house filled with the smell of coffee and the voice of the BBC announcer, I was suddenly terrified. I realised that Evelyn could not protect me from the Russians, from airplane crashes, from earthquakes, that he was irrelevant. I was doomed to unspeakable fates. Evelyn could not save me even if he wished to. I decided to die at once, cheat my dire destiny, get it over with.

I lay on my bed to wait for death. I tried to pray but that frightened me more. I had only been to church twice with Evelyn, to confession not at all. Sometimes I was frightened by my lapse and the retribution, especially at night, but mostly I did not think of it. Evelyn seemed devoid of terror at the consequences of his own slapdash heresy and his influence was far closer and more real than that of Sister Sepulchre. Not only did I not die but Evelyn did not come to find me for what seemed hours. I wept as quietly as possible.

'What is it, what's wrong?' Evelyn's light touch up and down my spine, his weight on the edge of the bed inexorably forcing my body towards him embarrassed me. I felt guilty too, I was not ill, there was nothing wrong. I wished he would stop stroking my neck; such unaccustomed tenderness was disturbing. 'Now then, you must tell me.'

'Nothing.'

'What is it, hmm?'

'Nothing.'

'Alex, please, I'm not a mind-reader, I can't guess.' He seemed irritated now. It set off my tears again. I pulled away from his hand at my shoulder.

'Leave me alone. I hate you.' Eventually I peeked and he was watching me. 'Go 'way. I hate you.'

'I had no idea. I'd thought we were getting on very well,' he said evenly.

'I hate you.'

'And might I ask why? Have I been unkind? What have I done?' His voice was soft, his dark eyes intent. I felt merely sheepish now. 'Well?'

'Nothing.' I hid my face again.

'Well,' he said presently. 'It's a great pity. I'd thought since it was such a nice day we could go to the seaside. I thought you'd like that. But if you've taken such an overwhelming aversion to my company I'd better go without you.' Eventually he coaxed me into agreeing to the outing. I sat up and used his handkerchief. He put his arm around me. He smelled of soap and talc and clean ironing. But soon he pulled away.

Evelyn's car was in keeping with the rest of his belongings. It was black and old-fashioned, with running boards and the spare wheel on the outside of the trunk ('Boot, Alex, boot'). He irresistibly conjured the image of an early aviator climbing into the cockpit of a biplane as he eased his too-large frame into the tiny car. This notion was emphasised by the cap he wore, which looked as if he should be wearing knickerbockers to complete the outfit. He bound up my hair with a scarf from the glove compartment, a gauzy square, incongruously feminine. I asked if the car was an antique and he said that he doubted whether it was as old as I was.

I was suitably entranced by the picturesque old world charm of the scenery. I was also both unsettled and exhilarated by landscape so different from any I had known. I was irrevocably beyond familiar territory now. When we arrived at the seaside Evelyn swam in the sea and I paddled at the edge. Then I built an elaborate sandcastle while he sat with an unread magazine. We had fish and chips for lunch, a delicacy I had not previously encountered. I did not care for the thick soggy chips and was disgusted by Evelyn putting vinegar over his portion. In the late afternoon we went for a long walk along the coast until I straggled wearily behind and Evelyn announced that we would take a bus back to the car.

After Evelyn had tidied my hair as best he could with his pocket comb, he found an hotel where we had drinks in the lounge before having a meal. Evelyn lingered over coffee and we set out for home very late. It was cold now but he had put up the roof of the little car. I dozed for most of the journey. Nearing home, waking, I watched Evelyn's big white hands on the wheel, the gear, the indicator. I thought of his fingers touching my neck as he absently fondled the neck of Mrs Carey's cat.

'You're tired, off you go. It's very late,' he said when we arrived home. He removed the elastic bands from my hair as he did every night. 'Did you have a nice day?' I nodded. 'So did I. Good night, pet.' The long fingers gripped my head, brought it into fleeting contact with his ribs and abruptly he moved away.

Not only had I not had a bath. I had not thanked him for the outing. I thought of my mother, driven to incessantly berate my thoughtlessness. 'What do you say? . . . You're the most ungrateful girl I've ever met . . . No one will love you if you behave like that . . . How can you say things like that? . . . I try so hard and all you ever do is complain . . . No one will want to marry you if you're going to be so horrible . . .'

My mother was right. It was no wonder Evelyn didn't care for me. I usually remembered thanks but I was not truly considerate of him. But he did not prompt or seem to expect that I did anything around the house. He never irritably suggested that I assist him instead of uselessly staring if he was preparing a meal or clearing up. No doubt he simply assumed it was hopeless to expect anything of me.

I tried henceforth to be more helpful. He accepted my services but did not seem to take my help for granted. He was a bit more considerate of me since our day at the seaside. He consulted my preferences sometimes. When we were out he would take my hand now in busy traffic or crowds rather than propelling me or restraining me by the shoulder.

2

Aunt Louisa and Aunt Hetty lived in a large Victorian house on a hill in south London. I was too busy noticing the details of the house to pay much attention to my aunts at first. The interior seemed much more old-fashioned even than Evelyn's home. Everything seemed large and dark, the chairs overstuffed, the many plants overgrown.

Aunt Louisa was my great-aunt, Evelyn and my father's aunt. Aunt Hetty was only an honorary aunt, Louisa's first cousin. Likewise, Uncle Richard, who was the other guest for tea, was not a real uncle but only a first cousin to Evelyn. Aunt Louisa was very short; Evelyn had had to bend down to kiss her. Aunt Hetty was taller and unlike Aunt Louisa, thin. Both wore lipstick and powder, not at all what I'd expected of old ladies.

It was a proper English tea, though the sandwiches were jam or 'paste' instead of cucumber. Evelyn ate lots and was teased by Aunt Louisa; if she'd known Evelyn was so fond of paste . . . There was also a rich fruit cake (which Uncle Richard had brought in a tin can) and the chocolate digestive 'biscuits' I was already addicted to.

Over the meal I was asked about the sightseeing we had done, both in New York and in London. Evelyn had taken me to the Tower and the Zoo and the Abbey. We went to the British Museum and the National Gallery and the Changing of the Guard. We had tea in Fortnum's. In Hamley's the unfortunate Elizabeth Jane was replaced without any of the unsubtle prompting I employed when he had said, 'perhaps' about something.

Presently I helped to clear the tea things away. Aunt Hetty asked me whether I was 'managing' all right with Evelyn as I embarrassedly fondled their ugly ginger tom. She asked also what Evelyn fed me and whether he cooked. She seemed nonplussed when I described my first meal at Evelyn's hands: beef in wine sauce and strawberries with cream. In fact Evelyn was surprisingly competent at turning out meat and salad and potato for everyday meals. I felt he shopped extravagantly, real butter, expensive cuts of meat, much fresh fruit.

'Well,' said Aunt Louisa when all the tea things were washed, 'we can have something sensible now. Evelyn, would you be a dear . . .' Evelyn busied himself preparing elaborate drinks from the bottle of bourbon he had brought them from America. Aunt Louisa found glasses in the glass-fronted cupboard in the dining-room and allowed me to wipe them carefully with a clean towel. Each glass was tinted a different colour, its dark stem diffusing into a paler bowl. I was given a matching tall glass filled with 'lemonade'.

As well as the coloured glasses and matching pitcher and the silver cocktail shaker, there was a collection of swizzle sticks which Evelyn added to, souvenirs of New York. The bottom doors of the cupboard hid bottles of every shape and size, more than I could have imagined. 'There's lots more than you have, Evelyn.' The adults laughed.

After Evelyn had mixed something different, served in tall

glasses with lemon slices, we had cold meat and salad and fruit with 'custard' before we went home. I had enjoyed myself, liked the way they spoke of my father, 'Alec', and 'Alec's girl'. I wondered about my father as I waited for sleep, whether I was like him, whether Evelyn was like him. I wished I had asked my aunts. I thought about Uncle Richard too; he seemed even more enigmatic than Evelyn. He did not seem nearly enough like Evelyn to be a cousin.

He had been the first person I'd met after my arrival in London. Waking from an afternoon nap after the long flight, I had heard voices downstairs and slipped down to listen.

'Well never mind about that, we can talk shop tomorrow,' a voice was saying. 'What about the child?'

'What indeed,' said Evelyn feelingly.

'As bad as that?'

'Oh, not really. But I'd never realised how exhausting it is.'

'Is she difficult?'

'No, she's generally very docile.' Glass chinked on glass. 'In fact I often forget she's there. But then I have to keep remembering. I'm really not cut out for this sort of lark.'

'No more or less than anyone else. Is she like Alec?'

'Not really. There's a resemblance, the eyes mainly, but she doesn't really put one in mind of him. I daresay she takes after her mother. Now there's a God-awful mess, poor bloody fool.'

'So it *was* . . .?'

'Mmm. I think that's partly why the brother was so keen to get her out of the way; these things will out in the end. But there's nothing to be done about it. As it was I managed to make an ass of myself before I left Platea, which, incidentally, they can't spell.'

'Is she very distressed?'

'It's hard to say. She cries in the night. But she seems perfectly all right in the day. I really don't know what to make of her. She doesn't say much. I'm told she's very intelligent, which I'd be prepared to believe.' Evelyn's voice moved towards the door. I jumped up and tried to look as if I were just coming down the stairs. 'Well, old thing, did you have a good sleep? I should have woken you, you'll be awake half the night now. Come and meet Richard. He won't bite, you know,' he added as I hung back. He buttoned the middle buttons that I could not do up on the back of my dress.

I was propelled into the dining-room before Evelyn. A man rose from one of the two leather armchairs before the fireplace. He did not look like Evelyn. He had thinning gold hair and a pink complexion. He gravely shook my hand. He was more solid than Evelyn, a bit overweight; his suspenders ('Braces, Alex, braces. Suspenders are for stockings.') seemed to indent his flesh slightly. He seemed very big, like a large, well worn, sleepy teddy bear. I was surprised to realise that in fact Evelyn was the taller of the two. I supposed he was much older than his sister in America, Aunt Gillian.

I laid the table with Uncle Richard's help. Everything seemed old-fashioned, the heavy beaded silverware from felt-lined drawers in the enormous sideboard, the balloon-backed dining chairs. Only the books cramming the shelves seemed modern, paperbacks and bright dust jackets rather than tooled leather. Evelyn carried the food through and poured Uncle Richard a sip of wine.

'Not bad,' he allowed and Evelyn filled their glasses. 'Is the decorating tolerable?'

My bedroom was newly decorated in blue striped wallpaper, though none of the furniture was new.

'Tolerable. It's very sad though, a great loss to posterity.'

'You've left the bathroom?'

'I didn't see why not.'

The bathroom was a big room with a long bathtub on ball and

claw legs and ample room for the towel stand and a large wicker chair. The walls were painted with seaside scenes. Two facing walls were piers, the other two the beach and the sea horizon. There were puppet shows and fairground attractions, snack stalls and deck chairs. Waves broke realistically on the beach and seagulls wheeled in the sky.

'Was my room like the bathroom?' I asked.

'Something like. Rather more excessive.' Evelyn said drily.

'Was it like that when you moved in?'

'Oh, no, a friend of mine was out of work at the time I moved in and had a bit of fun decorating.'

'Would you like some wine, Alex?' Uncle Richard asked. 'It's really rather a nice claret, so I'm not going to spoil it by watering it for you.' He poured a small amount and I sipped, nodded wisely, not admitting my distaste.

I enjoyed my bath, entranced by the people at the seaside, children playing, family groups, fortune tellers. After my bath I was allowed to sit up for a while. The men were playing chess on a board set up between the two armchairs.

'Evelyn.' But Uncle Richard was already explaining to me as Evelyn deliberated.

'Does she call you just "Evelyn"?' he asked when Evelyn had made his move.

'You must concede that the combination of "Evelyn" and "Uncle" is a bit much.'

'Mmm.' Uncle Richard made his move. 'Like "Aunt" and "Blanche".'

'No, damn it, not like Blanche.' Evelyn crossly moved a piece.

Uncle Richard shook his head and took the piece. 'Check.'

'Who is Blanche?' I asked.

'Your grandmother.' Evelyn relaxed into a smile. 'Now there's something for her to conjure with.'

'You mean your mother?'

'Yes, Alex. Incidentally, have you heard from her?'

'No, why should I?' Uncle Richard looked surprised. 'Check.'

'I had a wire with the other post, saying to keep my birthday evening free, but I was away of course. I thought she might have tried the office.'

'Was it your birthday?'

'Several weeks ago.'

'You didn't tell me.'

'By the time you get to be my age, it's scarcely something to celebrate. I was in Canada in any event.'

'How old are you?'

'Oh, ancient, senile.' He made another move. 'Forty-two.'

'Really!' Unexpectedly, the men laughed.

'I'm surprised she remembered to be honest. With any luck she'll have gone back by now.' Evelyn was in check again and resigned.

'Why did you do that?'

'Well, I'm going to lose soon anyway so there's no point prolonging the agony.'

I thought this very poor-spirited of him. Uncle Richard helped me set up the pieces again and then it was bedtime.

3

Mrs Brown came on Tuesdays and Thursdays to clean and hoover and do what washing was not sent out in a washing machine with a mangle attached, as well as to iron and drink endless cups of tea. She told Evelyn that there was now too much work; unlike his shirts, most of my things could not be sent out (why not? I wondered), all the dresses and petticoats were too much extra ironing . . . Evelyn offered her a wage increase which she indignantly refused. If he thought she did for him for the money, it was too much at her age, with her bad feet . . . Besides it wasn't suitable, me there . . . Eventually Evelyn persuaded her that it was perfectly reasonable for him to offer more pay for more work and perfectly in order for her to accept. They resumed their discussion of foreigners, America, diseases and the bloody Government until the tea in the pot was quite cold. Evelyn, in unaccountable good humour, took me to lunch in a dim and tiny restaurant behind Shaftesbury Avenue.

'How did you find this place?' From the outside it was only a door in a dilapidated row of shops. But once my eyes adjusted to the gloom I could see that it was expensively decorated.

'I often come here for lunch,' he said vaguely.

I looked round at the tiny tables, mostly full of intimate couples. I could not imagine his group of jolly bulky red men crammed in, impossibly boisterous in the small space. Perhaps his English colleagues were different. 'What if Mrs Brown had left?'

He smiled. 'She had no intention of leaving.'

'But she said . . .'

'That's just her method of negotiation. I don't see why she shouldn't have more money for more work. Even though she sits drinking tea half the morning anyway.'

'You didn't tell her that.'

'Why should I? Why shouldn't she drink my tea?'

'But it's your money.'

'Precisely Alex. And not for you to criticise how I spend it. Particularly when it's on your behalf.'

'I'm sorry,' I whispered. The iciness of his tone, the knowledge that it was my fault knotted my stomach. I would have left the rest of the prawns had there been any to leave.

'I had no idea how wickedly expensive it is to have children. I can't imagine why people do it. I really can't conceive how I'm going to make ends meet any longer.'

'I'm sorry.'

But he tucked into his entrée in a manner quite unlike that of a man unable to pay for his lunch. Deftly, even before I realised I was in difficulty, his cutlery descended and removed the bone from my trout. He smiled and pushed his wine glass forward like a pawn on a chessboard. 'If you're very discreet you may have a sip." I sipped and he told me about the wine and I sipped again.

'Are you poor?'

'Now really, what do you think?'

'Well, people do live beyond their means sometimes.'

Evelyn laughed. 'I suppose I am rather in danger of living beyond my means, but I'm not in the Fleet yet.'

Back on Shaftesbury Avenue I lingered in front of the theatres with reviews and photographs displayed outside until Evelyn took the hint and bought tickets for a Saturday matinee.

I was too shy to hint that I wanted to see his bedroom and the door always seemed to be closed. The contents of his flat seemed improbable for him to have chosen, simultaneously old-fashioned and outlandish. I had a dim notion that his bedroom would give some hint as to what he was really like, in the way that my cousin Angela's ruffled pink bedroom so suited her.

Finally I peeked in one evening when the door was ajar. It was unlike anything I could have imagined. The bed was covered in a sumptuous spread embroidered in bright colours. Similar fabric embroidered with birds and animals and vines hung on the wall behind the bed and formed a small scalloped canopy. Matching cushions were strewn on the bed. Columns of books were stacked between the bed and the night table. There were even more books than in the downstairs rooms.

'Why have you got such a big bed?'

'I got bored with not having enough room for my feet in ordinary beds.'

I timidly fingered the cloth and asked where on earth he'd found it.

'Perhaps we can find you a few spare bits. I got it in India.'

'When were you in India?'

'During the war.' He turned to the mirror to do his tie.

'Were you in the war? World War Two?'

'What do you think, the Boer war? I'm not that old.'

'I didn't know the war was in India.'

'We retreated there after Burma.'

'Were you wounded?'

'What a ghoulish child.' Evelyn picked up his jacket and waistcoat and shepherded me out. He poured himself a drink and me a lemonade and prepared a Spanish omelette while I teased on about the war, but he would not be drawn. 'It was very boring mostly, waiting for things.'

'Were you very high up?'

'I made Sergeant a few times, but it never seemed to last.'

'Was Uncle Richard in the war?'

'Yes, of course.'

'Was he high up?'

'I believe he was made a Major.'

'Why was he so much higher up than you?'

'Because he's very clever,' he said and settled with his new issue of *Continental Film Quarterly* until the babysitter arrived. I wondered what the Boer war was. I didn't like to betray my ignorance.

I took to waiting in Evelyn's room for him to do my hair in the morning. I admired all his knicknacks; the effect was cosy, cluttered. The surfaces were covered with small ivory and wooden carvings, enamelled and inlaid and brass edged boxes, painted trays and embossed bowls. I had never imagined that men would have so much paraphenalia for dressing; twin monogrammed hair brushes, special trouser hangers, shoe trees, clothes brush. But he was very quick. In Platea, Janet had taken ages preparing to go out. Evelyn perfunctorily brushed his hair in the mirror and tied his tie. Sometimes, if he was in a good mood, he let me choose it.

What chiefly interested me about Evelyn's room was the alcove with the photographs. Over a small chest (infuriatingly locked) frames were crammed edge to edge. There were family groups in absurd old-fashioned dress; groups of men in uniforms; glossy studio portraits of various glamorous men and women; a wedding picture of a pretty woman and a man definitely not Evelyn; panoramic views of exotic places with people posed in the foreground. I studied these whenever I had the chance but I was none the wiser.

I was delivered to Mrs Carey every morning on Evelyn's way to work. Mrs Carey lived downstairs in the basement flat. The morning after our arrival she had buttonholed Evelyn as he took in the milk, all agog at my presence, and invited us to tea that afternoon. She asked in detail of the events leading to my staying with Evelyn. After a day of sightseeing, travelling around on many red buses, I drowsed on her sofa with her ancient and placid cat as the topic turned to her many grandchildren, displayed round the room, many times over, at every age, and back to me again.

'It must be very difficult for a busy man like you.'

'Extremely awkward. It will be easier when term begins, but . . .'

Nothing specific was said then. We went home, up the stairs with half the cake. Later it was agreed that Mrs Carey would be delighted to have me during the day and Evelyn would be honoured to give me into her care.

Every morning I went to the shops with Mrs Carey. I enjoyed the expeditions, enjoyed feeling I was abroad. The transactions were conducted in a foreign language, foreign currency changed hands. The purchases too seemed exotic; in the butcher's the meats were unrecognisably whole and horrible; in the green-grocer's the 'lettuce' was wrapped unhygienically in newspaper. I loved English chocolate and was able to indulge my taste; Evelyn was generous with pocket money and Mrs Carey sometimes bought me sweets.

In the afternoons I helped Mrs Carey in the garden and kitchen. She was very patient about explaining everything and I began to learn a great deal about cooking and housekeeping. Soon I knew all about her two sons and daughter and grandchildren. I sometimes managed to get her to talk about Evelyn too. But she said little, usually evading by saying how nice he was, what a good man, how lucky I was. He had been in the flat for about five years and at first had shared it with a friend. She did not know if he had ever been married; he did not speak as if that were the case. In any event, it was rude to speculate in such a manner, and whatever anyone might say he was a good man, she liked him, I was lucky, even if it wasn't very suitable. Never I mind what anyone might say, it just wasn't suitable, and would I weigh out six ounces of flour.

I liked my days with Mrs Carey but by the end of the day her elderly meticulousness made me fidgety and I was glad to return to the casualness of Evelyn's regime. He arrived back fairly early and worked for a while longer on papers from his briefcase. He would then take a drink to his bath. Finally emerging, he would prepare something for me, eggs or a chop and yesterday's potatoes fried crisp in the glutinous green oil that he used indiscriminately for cooking and salads, while he had another drink and I a lemonade. Sometimes if he was not going out, or going out late, he cooked more elaborately.

I liked it best when he did not go out, unless he was taking me, which happened occasionally. On his evenings in he read, played records, drowsed, and was not too fussy about my bedtime, unless there were people coming round, when I was packed off early. I liked Uncle Richard's chess nights too. He arrived from work and chatted to us while the meal was cooking. On Saturday mornings we shopped for the week. Evelyn was always irritable by the time this was done; we never set off in time to avoid crowds and queues; he was never up in time.

4

'Where did you meet Sophie?' I asked in the car.

'I've known Sophie since before the war.' He glanced at me. 'World War Two.'

Sophie's house was of white stucco with dark beams, bay windows and stained glass. The garden was thronging with people. At the bottom an alarming number of boys were playing ball with an odd flat bat and stakes sticking out of the ground.

'My dear, what a charming picture.' A substantial woman hurried forward and embraced Evelyn, which he returned at inordinate length with mutual exchange of endearments and incoherent phrases. 'You favour Evelyn you know; you're very fortunate,' she told me.

'She favours my brother Alec,' Evelyn said firmly, but allowing her to retain his arm, even covering her hand with his.

She wore many rings and was far too made up for someone so old. But her smile was winning, real pleasure in her eyes as she joked with Evelyn.

Inside, groups of men in ties and braces stood about with glasses in the large hall and spilled over into the rooms, spacious and comfortably furnished. Small children raced on the stairs and groups of women, separate mostly from the men, also milled about with glasses. Sophie's husband was comfortably fat, bald, more evidently accented. 'Uncle' Leo scrutinised me shrewdly and talked to me of London, how strange it had seemed when he had first arrived, how disappointed he had been, while Evelyn fetched a bottle of beer and a lemonade for me.

'She is delightful and you are to be congratulated,' he told Evelyn. 'I've no doubt you are in good hands with Evelyn.' But the look he gave Evelyn was quelling.

In the next room was a large table spread with food. Cold roasts, exotic sausages, salamis and patés were interspersed with salads. There were cheeses bordered with red or brown, streaked with blue, boxed in wood. The bread was seeded and crispy, the cakes and pastries sumptuous.

A man bent over to restrain a toddler pulling books off shelves. He pre-empted the child's squalls by hefting her high in the air, again and again as she screeched with delight. I recognised Uncle Richard. He sat with the child on his knees and wiped his by now bright pink face. He was relaxed, his expression improbably soft and unguarded. I had not imagined he would have such a young child at his age. He greeted me with gratifying cordiality and introduced Vanessa. 'Would you like to hold her?' he offered magnanimously. I declined. I was pleased with this evidence of my maturity, but secretly had little interest in babies. I wondered which of the women was his wife. The toddler wriggled down and wandered away. Uncle Richard asked me how I was getting on. Vanessa, shrieking, was being tossed in the air by Uncle Leo.

'Do you have any other children?' I asked, emboldened by his interest in me.

'Any other . . .?' He was nonplussed, then following my gaze said flatly, 'Vanessa is Sophie and Leo's. I haven't any children.'

'I didn't see you arrive. Are you well?' Aunt Sophie asked him.

'Very well, my dear. And you?'

'All the better for seeing you.' She slipped her arm around his middle. Unlike Evelyn, Uncle Richard had the grace to appear discomfited by the intimacies of a large and middle-aged woman, although he politely responded with his hand on her back. Soon he moved across to talk to a large handsome man with one arm. Aunt Sophie asked me about myself, our domestic arrangements. 'Do you like Evelyn?' I nodded embarrassedly. 'Really, he's a very nice man. Quite unsuitable of course, but very sweet.'

She took me outside to play with her daughter Anita, a slight girl a bit younger than me. Soon I was able to slip away and found Evelyn sitting on some steps with his arm around Aunt Sophie, her head against his shoulder. I sat on the grass behind them.

'Darling Sophie, you're such a comfort to me.'

'It's no good being cross because I give you good advice.'

'But I didn't ask for any, my love.'

'I'm surprised you're managing so well, I admit.'

'I'm not totally incompetent.'

'But this is one thing in which you have no experience.'

'A lot you know,' Evelyn scoffed. Infuriatingly the ensuing argument was conducted in another language, French I supposed. The disagreement was abandoned and they were laughing, each capping the other, setting them to laughing even more.

'Dear love, I have missed you,' he said, in English once more.

'You're a disgraceful flatterer.'

'And you, my darling, are utterly wonderful.' He replaced his arm around her. 'Oh Sophie darling, marry me.' I was rigid with horror but this seemed to set them off quite uncontrollably and Evelyn knocked his beer over. Eventually recovered, Aunt Sophie went to find them more drinks. 'Well, old thing.' Evelyn gestured to the bottom of the garden. 'Why don't you play with the others?'

I ignored this and sat next to him. 'Are you really going to marry Aunt Sophie?'

'It's just our little joke, Alex. I'm sure she's very happy with Leo.'

'But she was hugging you.'

'We're very old friends,' Evelyn said stiffly. 'If Leo doesn't mind I don't see that it's any business of yours.' He attempted to tidy my hair.

'Evelyn? Is Uncle Richard's wife here?'

'Whatever gave you an idea like that? Richard doesn't have a wife.'

'I thought everyone was married but you. People are when they're old.'

'Old indeed. Scarcely middle-aged.'

'Why isn't Uncle Richard married?'

'He has been married. Now look here, you mind your own damned business. Don't you dare ask Richard such prying questions.'

'Why not?'

'Because it's extremely rude and I won't have people think you've no manners or I'll never hear the end of it. Besides, I'm sure it's a very distressing topic for him. You're not to upset him, I won't have it. Is that understood?'

'Mmmhmm.'

'Don't mumble, Alex. How many times do I have to tell you?'

'Yes Evelyn.' I picked at the grass. 'Have *you* ever been married?'

'Don't be absurd.'

'Why is it absurd? Have you?'

'Not that I can recall, no, Alex.'

'Why not?'

'Well . . . I'm not a very serious person, I'm afraid, and marriage is very serious indeed.'

Aunt Sophie returned with some gin and they sat chatting in a mixture of languages until most of the guests had gone and those remaining ate again from the leftovers. Uncle Richard and three other men emerged from the study and I watched as the one-armed man dexterously counted out a bundle of notes and gave them to Uncle Richard. Noticing my curiosity, he quickly tucked half the bills into Uncle Leo's hand.

'Why did he give you all that money?'

'We were uncommonly lucky today; no one usually wins so heavily.'

'You won it! What were you playing?'

'Bridge. Do you play? Perhaps I'll teach you some time.'

'Sophie and Leo seemed quite taken with you,' said Evelyn as he brushed through my hair before bed. 'I can't think why.'

'Do I really look like you?'

'Is that what they say? I daresay there's some small resemblance. But I doubt if you'll be as good looking as I.'

'You're not good looking; you're old.'

'And you are an insolent and very overindulged little brat,' he said mildly and hurried me off to bed.

It occurred to me that Evelyn's bantering manner was most in evidence after he had been drinking. I did not think I had ever seen him drunk, but I was not altogether sure what 'drunk' constituted.

I thought of Uncle Richard dandling Vanessa, improbable

infant of parents far gone in middle age. I deduced that there were two boys as well as the girls. I imagined Uncle Richard's wife, beautiful, ethereal, consumptive, expiring in the arms of her unlikely balding prince. He had such a brave face to his tragedy. I resolved to be especially nice to him.

I remembered Evelyn fussing that morning, ironing a dress with unexpected competence. It mattered a great deal what Aunt Sophie thought; perhaps he was suffering from unrequited love for her. But he had seemed quite cheerful. And how could he love a woman so large and aged? But he was old too. Perhaps she had been beautiful when she was young. Why had not Evelyn married her then? And if she didn't love Evelyn too why did she touch him so much? Poor Evelyn. It was no wonder that Evelyn and Uncle Richard had their chess nights together; they had a lot in common, both broken-hearted.

5

'We really must have a talk about school,' Evelyn said one evening. 'It's proving rather more difficult than I expected. I should have put you down at birth. But there are a few options; I thought if you had any preference . . .' He handed me a folder containing prospectuses and hurried up to his bath. It did not take me long to realise that Yorkshire and Hampshire and Wiltshire were hundreds of miles from London. The brochures were all accompanied with letters; 'Dear Mr Parrish, Thank you for your enquiries concerning your niece . . .' He had obviously been plotting from the start to get rid of me. I had no inkling.

I would not come down to eat. I lay for hours wishing I were dead. I could not even cry. Evelyn brought me a tray with cold chicken and careful triangles of bread and butter and a dainty salad, as if I were an invalid.

'Have you had time to make up your mind where you'd like to go?' he asked when I had eaten.

'I want to stay here.'

'That's not possible, Alex.'

'Why not?'

'It's out of the question. I'm a busy man, I'm away a lot on business. We can't go on imposing on others.'

'You don't want me.'

'Don't be melodramatic. Everyone goes away to school.'

'Everyone doesn't. I don't know anyone who does.'

'I was only seven when I went.'

'Hardly anyone does. Only if they're not wanted.'

'Don't be ridiculous, Alex. I'm far too tired for one of your scenes. You've known all along you'd have to start school. There's no point cutting up about it now.'

'But you never said.' My tears spilled over, rolled down my cheeks. 'You never said I had to go *away* to go to school.'

'But my dear girl, that was understood from the start,' said Evelyn irritably, finding his handkerchief.

'You don't want me.'

'Don't be silly.'

'Why don't you just put me in an orphanage and forget about me?'

'Don't tempt me.' He awkwardly patted my shoulder.

I pulled away and threw myself on the bed sobbing. 'Go away. I hate you.' I threw the plush bear at him. 'I hate you.'

'So you keep saying. I'd have thought you'd be only too glad to get away from me in that case.' He did not go but sat on the chair I had vacated, laid my abandoned cutlery straight on the empty plate. 'Do understand, Alex, this is one thing you're not going to budge me on. No amount of weeping and wailing and hysterics is going to make a scrap of difference.' He picked up the tray. 'Except to wear my patience dangerously thin on every issue. I really can't imagine how I've been so patient with you. It's not something I'm renowned for, quite the reverse.'

Nothing was said for several days about school and I hoped desperately he had forgotten or changed his mind. I was careful to be very good, helpful and conciliatory, not sulking. I could not understand how he could be so nice while all the time plotting to be rid of me. There was ceaseless constraint between us despite the mutual display of good will.

When I asked if I could go to church on Sunday, he merely said of course, that he'd been remiss, I should have reminded him before. He dragged himself up in time on Sunday and drank even more coffee than usual but without reproach.

On Tuesday morning I was dressed in my best dress and Evelyn had the day off work. He told me we were going to Warton in Hampshire for a school interview and that I had better behave myself or else.

'Or else what?'

'Or else everything dreadful beyond your most lurid imaginings.'

The school was a large stockbroker's mansion overwhelmed by later wings and annexes. Evelyn tidied my hair and said, 'Now I mean it, no nonsense, Alexandria.' I knew he meant it; he almost never used my full name.

Miss Favell, the headmistress, was austere and intimidating, like a nun in tweeds. I fancied that even Evelyn was quelled by her. He sat drinking the coffee she poured from a silver pot and saying little. She directed questions at me, my school reports before her. Under the joint scrutiny of her and Evelyn I could barely mumble my responses.

We were shown round the school. The girls seemed cowed, dispirited in their unflattering green pinafores. Everything seemed drab, bedrooms poky, dining-room institutional. The extensive sports facilities did nothing to cheer me.

'Well,' said Miss Favell after we were returned to her book-lined office, with its funereal floral arrangement and antique furniture. 'It's no good pretending that Alexandra doesn't present considerable problems if we're to bring her up to standard for entrance exams. But we do like a challenge here at Warton. It's a pity Mrs Parrish wasn't able to come today, it would have been easiest if Matron could go over the lists with her now.'

Evelyn raised his brows. 'I'm afraid you are under a mis-apprehension. There is no Mrs Parrish.'

'But . . .' Miss Favell rallied. 'Do you mean to say that you are on your own with Alexandra? But that's most unsuitable.'

'Just so. You see why it's imperative that I'm assured of a place for her for the autumn term.'

'I think we will have to say that of course she is welcome here under the circumstances,' she condescended. Evelyn was given lists. 'Some parents seem to think that there is no need for everything, but I do feel we keep within reasonable bounds. You'll find that it's less than many places. And we do like for all the girls to have the same so that no one is conspicuous.'

'Yes, of course,' murmured Evelyn.

'You may settle the financial details with Mrs Jackson on your way out. We shall look forward to having you in September, Alexandra.' She rose and held out her hand regally to Evelyn. 'There is a considerable resemblance between you and your, er, niece.' She withdrew her hand. 'If you don't mind my saying so.'

'So I'm told,' said Evelyn.

Evelyn seemed almost as subdued by the interview as I was. Perhaps the cheque he had written was so large as to disgruntle him. Presently he pulled up at a country inn where we had a large and leisurely lunch. By the end of the meal I was much calmer, allowing Evelyn to beguile me with descriptions of Yorkshire, where he intended taking me on holiday soon.

'Evelyn? Why does everyone keep saying it's unsuitable?'

'What's unsuitable?' He looked suddenly wary.

'I don't know. Everyone says, Miss Favell said so.'

'I suppose they think it's unsuitable that you're with me.'

'But why?'

'Because I'm unsuitable, I expect.'

'But why?'

He attempted to dismiss the subject. 'No doubt I'm considered unsuitable in every particular.'

'But *why?*'

He shrugged irritably. 'I don't know.'

'Is it because you're not married?'

'Very largely, I imagine. Now don't start on that, we've been through all that.'

'Do you think it's unsuitable?'

'Yes, I do as a matter of fact. It doesn't suit me in the least.'

'Don't tease.'

'I never tease. You should know that by now.'

6

Evelyn's idea of a holiday surprised me. There was disappointingly little in the way of plush hotels and lavish meals. Uncharacteristically, he was up fairly early in the mornings.

Equally uncharacteristically he would eat the large fried breakfasts provided, washed down with pots of strong milky tea. His dress was by no means elegant, old flannels and out at elbows tweed jacket, supplemented by garish knitted waistcoats on windy days.

I was much taken, as Evelyn had supposed I would be, with the elegance at Matlock Bath (where we stopped overnight on the way north) and Castle Howard and York. But I was indifferent to the magnificence of the moors. Evelyn seemed quite content to spend the day walking endlessly from nowhere to nowhere in the desolate countryside, unfurling his map and pointing to a path that I could never see.

I sulkily picked my way among rocks and sheep droppings, feet rubbed by new walking shoes, desperate for the loo, pretending that Evelyn had abandoned me to die of exposure, imagining his chagrin when, miraculously, I survived to denounce him. He scarcely attended to me, leaving me far behind as he strode across the moors, conversing little when I caught him up for sandwiches and tea from the thermos flask. He was much more taken up with his heavy camera equipment, crouching, climbing, waiting interminably for clouds or vehicles or people to pass in order to obtain a good shot.

The second day on the moor I flagged before lunch. Eventually Evelyn noticed that I could barely hobble and came back for me. 'Christ! Why didn't you say something before?' he asked as he peeled away my socks and saw the inadequate plasters I had filched from his toilet bag, mangled into a mess of blood and pus. 'For God's sake, do you think I'm some kind of ogre?'

'I knew you'd be mad.'

'Cross,' he corrected. 'Oh God, don't, don't.' He sat next to me on the rock and found his handkerchief. Presently he withdrew his arm from round me and unwrapped the sandwiches.

He had not thought to bring another cup for the flask; at first sharing had made me squeamish, but I was used to it now. He told me about army tea, tinned milk and tea and sugar all boiled up together. He tore his handkerchief and bandaged my heels. 'It's my fault, love, I've had these so long I forgot what it was like breaking them in. They're older than you, my army issue.'

'From the war, you mean?'

'Yes.' He carefully eased my socks back over the bandages. 'I had no end of a row to get these, but it was worth it.'

'Why?'

'Well, I was damned if I was going to spend years doing forced marches in boots too small. I made a fuss, tried on lots.' He laughed. 'I didn't make myself very popular, it took me weeks to live down. Lots of "What, what, I say old chap" and "his lordship". Still, it was worth it, the worst trouble I had was the bloody fungus. Come to think of it, I must have had a new pair of boots after the fighting was over.'

We headed back towards the car as it began to rain. I could hardly walk; in the end Evelyn carried me on his back the last few hundred yards. He dried us with a plaid rug and we ate the chocolate he had stowed in the glove compartment for emergencies.

'I must be out of condition. I shouldn't imagine you weigh more than full kit.' He wriggled his shoulders and grinned. 'Not that I often carried my kit, mind.'

'Why not?'

'Well, it was a question of being in with the lads on the lorries.'

I was little the wiser, knowing only that he was in a good mood despite the rain, despite my infirmity. He drove us to a proper hotel in Harrogate. That evening we had a posh meal and stayed up late in the residents' lounge over drinks. Evelyn appeared reassuringly normal in suit and tie once more. As was his custom, he returned downstairs for a 'last order' after I was tucked up.

I lay, heels throbbing, trying to imagine Evelyn in a khaki uniform, pressed, impeccable as usual, advancing purposefully along tacky tarmac verged with jungle in shimmering heat. I conjured him shot, arms thrown out in astonishment, falling, blood staining his torso, imploring his comrades through thin white lips to go on without him, grimacing as someone pulled his shirt away . . .

But he was being very nice; I didn't wish such a fate. I thought of him kneeling at my feet, bandaging my wounds with no trace of squeamishness, no irritation that the day was spoiled; of how gently he had spread ointment on my feet at bedtime. I remembered the solidity of his back as I clung to his shoulders, nestled my face into his collar against the rain, inhaling the smell of his brilliantine.

In the night he woke me from my nightmare and took me on his lap, methodically rubbing my spine and murmuring softly. Not until I had dozed again did he lift me back to my bed.

It rained heavily, steadily most of the next day. We played chess on Evelyn's pocket chess set, but he won several games easily, even playing without his queen. It was time by then for him to have a whisky before lunch while he read the paper. (As always he travelled with his own bottle, cushioned by socks and pyjamas in his suitcase.) After lunch we played cards and I persuaded him to teach me poker, which he played with Uncle Richard sometimes instead of chess. He advanced me the next week's pocket money and quickly won it back again.

'You're a good loser anyway.' He ruffled my hair and poured another whisky. 'You must never bet more than you can afford to lose. There used to be a lot of that in the Army on pay day.'

'Did you lose all your pay?'

'I was never that green.'

'Were you wounded in the war?'

'Bloodthirsty little beast. Wounds are the least of it. It's the malaria and dysentery that get you. I must have spent a year in hospital all told and I was never more than scratched.'

He tinkered with his camera and posed me in his jacket and driving cap, plait coiled inside to keep it from slipping over my eyes. He entertained himself by photographing me in a variety of silly poses, in various different outfits. He arranged a poker game, emptied his pockets of money and poured a glass of whisky, which he sampled liberally, and posed me with a hand of cards.

'Enough nonsense. That's the roll anyway.' He lay back in the armchair after his frenetic leaping on chairs, turning out props, posing my limbs as if I were a store mannequin. He refilled his glass and caught me unawares in a final photo, consuming the bar of chocolate he'd found in his jacket for me. 'That was very cooperative,' he said conciliatorily.

'If there was a picture of us together, I could see if I really look like you.'

'You look like Alec. Not very like either. I don't know who you're like.'

'What was my father like?'

Evelyn sipped at his drink. 'He was much younger, five years. We were never very close. We were never at the same school at the same time. And when we were older there was the war, of course. Alec was in North Africa . . . a very good natured man, everyone liked him . . . always let me put one over on him as a boy, right gormless. But he never harboured a grudge, told tales. Too trusting, really, always was. He was . . . quite fun to be with, very popular . . . got remarkably silly when drunk though, I've seldom seen the like. No, I suppose I never really knew him or Rose wouldn't have surprised me. I'd imagined something quite different.' He poured the last of the whisky.

'What?'

'Oh, God. Someone bubbly and outgoing, a bit stagey perhaps. Not that I ever imagined anyone intellectual, or even particularly intelligent. I'm sorry, I'm being very rude.' He was inexplicably apologetic. He moved to the bed where I sat smoothing and folding the chocolate wrapper and put his arm around me. 'Do you miss your mummy very much?'

I didn't know what to say and rubbed my face on the knobbly cable stitching of his cherry red waistcoat. I tried to remove his ring. It had an indecipherably elaborate monogram.

'You won't get that off, love, it hasn't come off in years.'

The teasing degenerated into a romp until I was sulky and wheezing with Evelyn's overmastering strength. He coaxed me back to good humour and we braved the drizzle to inspect the Georgian elegancies of the town. Again I sat up late with him in the residents' lounge. At bedtime he even tucked me up.

'I'm sorry it's been dull for you, pet. It should be nicer tomorrow.'

'But it hasn't been dull.'

'I can only imagine that you have very limited expectations in life.'

'Do you think it was dull?'

'I suppose not, actually.' He bobbed forward to peck my cheek, and with equal abruptness hurried off for his last order.

Much later I was woken not by bad dreams but by Evelyn being violently sick. I lay rigid, wondering whether he needed help, what to do. Finally, after another bout of retching, he emerged from the bathroom.

'Evelyn?'

'Go back to sleep, Alex,' he said testily, climbing into bed.

'Are you all right?'

'I'm fine now. Are you all right, pet, no bad dreams?'

7

'Damn it, lad, what's to become of us all?' Uncle Cecil gestured at me. 'It's down to this now. You're not getting any younger, you know. Why don't you do something?'

Evelyn looked down, jingled his change. 'I don't want to rush into anything, make a mistake.'

The old man snorted. 'You've rushed before now. You think I'm too old to remember.'

'By no means. But . . .' Evelyn gestured towards me this time.

'You must be forty if you're a day. I'd had five by your age.'

'Five girls.'

'Tchah.' But he smiled reluctantly under his drooping moustache. 'You could at least show willing.'

'Oh I do, I assure you.'

'You always were impudent. I remember a great deal more about you than you'd like. I'm not senile yet. When I'm senile I'll die. And I shall expect to see you settled by then.'

'You can expect what you like if it pleases you.'

Uncle Cecil damned Evelyn again and chuckled ruefully. He turned his attention to me and exerted himself to put me at my ease. Despite his courtesy, I was intimidated. Dark eyes looked out sharply from under shaggy white brows and his tongue was equally sharp. I had never imagined that anyone so old would be so abrasive. He was eighty-eight, my great-great-uncle. Presently he dismissed us in order to have a rest before dinner.

We unpacked in cavernous bedrooms as antiquated and

threadbare as the downstairs. But the view was spectacular, across fields and trees, hills and moors, depending on the direction of the windows.

'Evelyn? What did he mean about rushing into things?'

'He's very old, Alex, he gets muddled sometimes. I expect he was thinking of something that happened before I was even born.'

This sounded likely; he had addressed Evelyn variously as Sebastian and Aubrey as well as by his own name. 'When he says do something, does he mean having sons?'

'I expect so.'

'But Aunt Gillian has sons.'

'So does Diana come to that.'

I remembered the existence of Evelyn's sister. 'Why won't they do?'

'They're not called Parrish, they're Mackie.'

'I'm called Parrish.'

'Yes, love, I know.'

'Why does it have to be boys?'

'That's how the system works.'

'But it's not fair.'

'I never said it was.'

'Will you have sons?'

'About as much chance of that as my having daughters.'

'But you're not married.'

'We've had this discussion before, Alex.' His tone was discouraging.

'I'm not going to get married either.'

'Aren't you?'

'I'd have to have babies. And cook dinner. And I wouldn't be Parrish.'

'Well it's not something to rush into, certainly. I'm glad you're going to be sensible.'

'Would you rather I was a boy?'

'Good God no, little boys are revolting creatures.'

We stayed with Uncle Cecil in his big decaying house for almost a week. Evelyn took me on several outings, to places like Chatsworth, which was not far. Inevitably there were long walks, through river valleys and woods as well as endless moors. Sometimes we were accompanied by Uncle Cecil's red setter, Lady, but Evelyn always became irritated by her, having to keep her close in fields of sheep and perpetually heave branches for her.

Uncle Cecil seemed glad of our company. He was mainly chairbound and his sight wasn't up to reading very much. He had a housekeeper and a male nurse whose job it was to help him dress and get about. The young man had little conversation and spent much of the day outside with the dog.

I was a fresh audience for all Uncle Cecil's reminiscences of the old days, summers before the war. Then the house had been thronging with children, his own, his grandchildren, nieces and nephews; dogs had been bred; ponies grazed in the paddock for the children and tennis was played on an overgrown plot by the stables; and they sat down twenty for dinner, not counting nursery tea.

The holiday continued to be punctuated by my nightmares, now a regular occurrence. The first occasion I had been awakened by a nightmare it had been one of Uncle Richard's chess nights. I had scuttled downstairs to find them playing cards. They dealt, bet, discarded, bet with lightning speed, exchanging amiable insults and addressing each other formally as 'Parrish'.

Evelyn grudgingly allowed me to stay and watch for a while. Soon I slid from my perch on the arm of his chair into his lap. He did not push me off but patted me. 'Alex has brought me luck.'

I was half asleep by the time Uncle Richard said, 'That's it, you've cleaned me out, Lynnie.'

Evelyn laughed. 'A rare achievement. You could write a cheque.' They both laughed and Evelyn poured more drinks awkwardly across me. But Uncle Richard soon took his leave and Evelyn hastily crammed all the money into his pockets and hurried me up to bed.

'How can Uncle Richard afford to lose so much money?'

'Very easily, I assure you.' He settled the covers around me and left the hall light on for me.

After that I went down whenever I was woken by a bad dream. 'Not again, Alex,' Evelyn would say. 'You're trying it on,' then, relenting he would gesture to a chair. I would tuck my feet up into the hem of my nightgown and listen to the record. Abruptly he would say, 'It's late,' and set aside his book, sometimes soon, sometimes after I had drowsed.

Finding one night that he was already asleep, I stood in his doorway. His breathing, regular, loud, not quite snoring reassured me. Eventually I perched on the edge of his bed to wait for him to wake and cosset me.

I became conscious of Evelyn moving about the room. I could see him in the wardrobe mirror. The startling dark T of hair on his chest, the crossbar wispy, the downstroke as if it were drawn by Evelyn himself with his black filled pen, emphatic, uninterrupted, bisecting his navel and disappearing below his waistband, was even darker compared to the white of his underpants. He donned shirt and socks and selected the rest of his outfit before seeing me in the mirror.

He lectured me on the unsuitability of sleeping in his bed, his irritation sliding quickly into resignation. 'I won't have it, Alex. Wake me up if you need to, but you must sleep in your own bed.' He brushed his hair with one of the twin silver brushes. 'Understood?' he asked the glass.

But I never dared to wake him. Instead I would hunker down on the floor near the foot of his bed with a blanket and pillow from my own bed. (On the first occasion Evelyn just missed treading on me with his full weight in the early dawn and stumbled cursing to the loo.)

This difficulty was alleviated by the holiday. Usually I had a folding bed in Evelyn's room as we had not booked in advance. At Hellisford there was a connecting door between our rooms. I read or fell asleep over my book if he didn't remember to come up when it was time for lights out.

'Alexandria. Do you have any idea what time it is?'

'You said I could read.'

'But it's late now. You should have been asleep hours ago.'

'I didn't want to sleep by myself.'

'Well I'm here now, pet.'

'Where did you go?' I sat up and rubbed against him.

'I went for a pint in the Hellisford Arms but that was rather grim, so I walked into Havering instead and then walked back when the pub closed.'

'Why didn't you just have a drink here?'

'It was a nice walk. And there was a very interesting man in the Crown in Havering, a retired quarryman. No stalling now, I'm very tired, even if you're not.' He squeezed my shoulder and laid me down again.

Evelyn's amiability did not survive his return to work. He was very busy, with long hours and folders full of work when he arrived home. There was no time now for swimming after work as there had been before. He was out most evenings and had little time for me. His patience wore thin with my protracted bed times.

'Evelyn?'

'No nonsense. Good night, Alex.'

'Will you be glad when I'm gone?'

'I can't wait.'

'Don't tease. Will you?'

'I never tease, you know that.'

'Evelyn.'

He relented. 'Don't be silly, Alex. I know you'll be pleased to be rid of me.'

'Would you be sad if I died?'

'It would be a terrible shame now that I've paid for your tuition and uniforms and everything.'

'Evelyn! Stop teasing.'

'I utterly refuse to pander to such a grisly and melodramatic turn of mind.'

'I don't want to go.'

'Alex, don't start that, I warn you.'

'I wish I was dead.'

'I shall lose patience in a minute and wish you were too.'

'Evelyn!' I lashed out crossly and he gripped my wrists.

'Now you go to sleep and stop this ridiculous melodrama. I won't have it.' He released my hands and settled the covers. 'You're being very silly, you know, you'll settle in perfectly well once you're there. It isn't as if you were going to miss me or anything, is it?'

'Of course not.'

8

Evelyn had been sanguine in his supposition that I would settle in perfectly well. I had never been in the slightest doubt that I would loathe it. I had enjoyed the steady diet of school stories that Evelyn had calculatingly supplied all summer, Malory Towers, the twins at St Clare's. But I had never supposed that the reality would be anything like the fiction (although I was disappointed that there was never a Midnight Feast, something much nearer a necessity than a treat under Miss Favell's regime).

The only particular in which reality overlapped with fiction was the emphasis on games. Naturally, I fulfilled the role of the unsportsmanlike and sly foreigner. I was only sorry not to be able to fiendishly plot the downfall of the school at some vital sporting event and regretted my lack of dastardly adult accomplices.

In addition to my spectacular ineptness on the playing fields, I was much behind the standards of work expected and had no French at all. My traditional reliance on sheltering behind academic superiority was at an end. My adherence to the true faith isolated me further. The three other girls with whom I journeyed to confession and Mass were much my senior and ignored me. My background rendered me beneath contempt socially.

I started off badly, castigated before the class on my first morning for vanity, the plain silver ring Evelyn had bought me in York confiscated. My reputation for affectation was sustained by my dogged insistence on the 'i' in my name.

Miss Favell herself, presiding over the prep session devoted to letters home, singled out my letter as a shining example of illiteracy. Grammar, spelling and content were inextricably linked, as she criticised each sentence with her ponderous, carrying-voiced sarcasm. Left behind alone as I frenziedly scribbled a new letter and began the 100 lines she had set incorporating all my American spellings, she modified her approach. Her homily, delivered with a perfunctory veneer of cosiness, enumerated the advantages of endeavouring to put aside my slovenly Americanisms and the unsuitable influence of my uncle. She contrived to make 'uncle' sound as if he were something that had crawled from under a stone.

In such circumstances, it was difficult to remember that I hated Evelyn. Even his crowning iniquity paled by comparison. On my last day in London he had finally persuaded me to allow him to trim the tiniest bit from my hair. He spread newspaper on the kitchen floor, found good scissors, combed my hair across my back.

'Only a tiny bit. Promise,' I said urgently.

'For God's sake be still.' I felt his hand against me, heard the scissors rasp on my hair and was filled with a dreadful suspicion. 'Perfectly still, Alex, if it's uneven I'll have to take more off.' When at last he finished I whipped round and looked at the long mousy strands heaped on the newsprint. He had cut a good six inches, right up to my shoulder blades. 'I'm sorry, pet, but it had to be done, it was ragged all the way up. Besides, you'll have to manage your hair by yourself at school.' I would not speak as he folded up the newspaper and my hair. 'Now really, Alex, it's for the best. If they'd cut it at school, they'd cut it right off, it's still quite long really.'

That was undoubtedly true. I was angry at myself for being foolish enough to trust him. I alternately nurtured my grudges against him and felt wistful for our time together. I would lie snivelling as quietly as possible in the night thinking of him. Sometimes, sentimentally twisting his ring (restored to me at the end of the week and worn surreptitiously in bed), I longed for Evelyn's company.

But more often I hated him, endlessly imagined my revenge: Evelyn, cowering at my mercy, pleading, begging . . . Evelyn splayed, bleeding, terror in his eyes as his life drained away . . . Evelyn thrashing desperately, unavailingly as waves engulfed him, filled his lungs . . . I gloated over his enormous limp corpse.

In less vindictive moments I conjured him weeping and remorseful at my implacable death bed; distraught, tearing his hair at my disappearance; kneeling in supplication at my repudiation; rag-clad, humbly petitioning for a portion of my untold riches. I decided to run away and began to save most of my pocket money.

In more vulnerable moods I would remember the solid warmth of his lap with the conviviality of his and Uncle Richard's manic card game lapping over me. I thought of his generosity with treats and presents and clothes. I remembered the rainy night in Harrogate, nestling against him, his bristled chin catching on my hair, and the odd, disembodied quality of his voice as he murmured soft endearments above my head: 'It's all right, darling, I won't let anything happen to you.'

But he had. It was all his fault, he had done it on purpose. He would not even be sorry if I was dead. As half term neared I rehearsed the scenarios of my reunion with Evelyn, myself aloof, dignified, icy in the face of his bogus charm.

But on the day, without thought, script forgotten, I hurled myself at him, rubbing against his suit as he indulgently patted my head. His good mood did not outlive the interview Miss Favell had unexpectedly, and ominously, written to request.

'They seem to have formed the curious notion that you're not very bright,' he said in the car. But his irony rendered the entire business beneath consideration. I felt the absurdity of weeping over such trifling discomforts as I had undergone.

Evelyn mellowed over drinks and dinner. He took me to a restaurant I had not been to before and I found it satisfactorily opulent. Even when, inevitably, I was spectacularly sick in the night he was not cross. He jollied me gently as he changed my sheets, clad me in one of his undershirts and tucked me up again.

In the morning he took me shopping for another nightgown and a winter coat. This seemed extravagant in addition to the jacket he had bought for the holiday and the green cape that went with the school uniform. It had been the one thing that I liked about the uniform, but I hated it after a few days wear. There was no fastening except for the chain at the neck so the cold flooded in. It was awkward to carry books under the cape and there were no pockets. The more I considered it the more impractical the gesture seemed. I would only be able to wear the new coat for a few weeks at Christmas and by Easter it would be too warm. Nor would it do for next year. Upon offering to have the next size up he had replied, 'We'll worry about next year when it comes. I won't be seen with you looking as if I dressed you from jumble sales.'

I puzzled over Evelyn's motives as I unpacked the boxes that had arrived from America while I was away. I was disappointed with them. The games and toys and books seemed shabby and juvenile in comparison with what Evelyn had bought. The winter clothes that Janet had tucked in to wedge the contents were likewise almost outgrown.

'Now look, let's get this out of the way and I shan't mention it again,' Evelyn said abruptly when I came downstairs. He gulped his drink and regarded me. 'You're doing very badly at Warton, you know.' He continued mildly that he was a busy man, worked hard, had many worries, surely I must realise how awkward things were for him ... He broke off and leaned forward, pulling out his handkerchief. 'All right, never mind. I'm sure you'll do better next half, hmm?'

'I'll try,' I snuffled.

'You'd bloody well better,' he said with sudden grimness. He fetched another drink and settled next to me before the fire to look at our holiday photos. There were endless spectacular skies over moors, quaint villages and many of me, whimsically posed, frolicking unawares and the whole roll that Evelyn had taken when it was too rainy to go out. He watched me, his arm around my shoulders, pulling me near to warm me. (It had not occurred to me that I could run the fire in my bedroom.)

We had unexpected company, a man in uniform. It was an inferior sort of uniform, like that of a postman or bus driver. Oddly, he wore no tie with it.

'I'm sorry. I thought Mr Parrish lived here.' The voice was that of a native Londoner, the face round and anxious looking down at me. He followed me up as I speculated on what Evelyn could have done to incur visits from such arcane officialdom.

Evelyn was off the floor and on his feet in one movement. 'Good God!'

Both laughed as they thumped each other on the shoulder and the man disclosed in eager half sentences that he'd arrived from Copenhagen, had meant to ring, was on the Scandinavian run. He found a bottle in his case, I fetched glasses. 'You're supposed to knock it back in one.'

'Oh aye?' I now recognised that Evelyn's typical expression of scepticism had been acquired in Yorkshire.

'Skol.'

They drank, the uniformed man choked, Evelyn hit him on the back.

'I'm not anyone's bloody uncle,' he balked at Evelyn's introduction of him. 'I'm Tim.'

Soon Evelyn sent me to my bath, turned on the electric bar in the bathroom, lit the fire in my room. In answer to my questions he told me that Tim was a steward on a passenger ship, that he had not seen Tim for ages, had no idea Tim would visit, that we would still go out that evening.

Tim was looking through Evelyn's photographs when I hurried down again, but Evelyn was dismissive of Tim's praise.

'Now let's be serious.' Evelyn topped up their glasses. 'Let's see what you've been up to.' He allowed me to choke on a fiery sip of the Danish drink before examining Tim's folder. 'Now be careful, don't make any marks. Tim has to sell these,' he adjured me.

There were several dozen sketches; shipboard scenes, passengers, crew, family groups, sailors at their ease, diners, bar patrons. Evelyn spent a long time going over them, returning to several again and again.

Tim changed into a cheap crumpled jacket and trousers with a tie of Evelyn's. While Evelyn changed he asked me about school and I poured out my heart.

'It's bloody barbaric if you ask me,' Tim said firmly. 'Only the ruling class pack their children off like that. It's just typical,' he rounded on Evelyn, 'typical of you to be so hypocritical. We all know how much you enjoyed your school days.'

'For God's sake,' said Evelyn irritably.

'You're a dreadful callous brute, you are. Shocking I call it, poor motherless mite and you such a terrible scoundrel. A wicked shame, that's what it is.' Tim winked at me.

They looked funny together, Evelyn tall and well turned out, Tim small and creased, both giggling uncontrollably. On the street I tucked my hand in Evelyn's and he squeezed it, retained it instead of pulling away. Tim took my other hand and I skipped and skittered along between them. We had a Chinese meal and I marvelled at Evelyn's prowess with chopsticks. He had learned 'out East'.

'In the war?'

'No, Alex, after the war. I travelled a bit before . . .'

'Before you sold out to the bosses,' finished Tim.

'Did you go with him?' I asked Tim.

'I was still in nappies then. How old do you think I am?'

Evelyn snorted. 'A two-year-old able seaman, no doubt.'

'How old are you?'

'Old enough to know better than answer questions like that. Thirty-two,' Tim conceded.

'The same as Uncle Pat.'

'Pat is Alex's maternal uncle. He has seven children, another on the way by now, no doubt, and looks far older than I,' Evelyn explained.

'Christ! At least I haven't got seven children.'

'Have you got any?' This set off their giggles again.

'No, not a one. Thank God.'

'And no, Alex,' intervened Evelyn, 'Tim isn't married. Unless it's of recent duration?'

Tim grinned. 'You want a white wedding, with bridesmaids, do you?'

I shook my head vigorously. 'But everyone's supposed to be married. I think that's why they get cross with Evelyn, because he's not married.'

They looked at each other. 'Do you think so?' Tim asked gravely, but they were laughing again.

I could not remember Evelyn being in such a cheerful mood, giggling childishly with Tim, egging on his absurdities, joining in his comic turns in funny accents. The mood infected me. But in the night, waking from my nightmare I sobbed and sobbed, all the pent up terror of night on night huddling alone in the dark overflowing. I could not stop, would not be reassured that it was all right.

Tim, unexpectedly sturdy in pants and singlet, face puckered with concern, fetched me a drink of water, pulled funny faces and I allowed myself to be soothed, pointedly ignoring Evelyn. I was fascinated by the blue and red and green dragon that coiled over the space from shoulder to elbow, undulating realistically when Tim flexed his muscles. He settled me under the covers with my plush bear. I did not think of my old bear, unpacked in the afternoon.

Saturday we went to the zoo. Tim did many sketches, swift, unerring, reproducing any animal to order until at last Evelyn told me to let Tim have a rest. In the evening Evelyn took me to Crystal Palace for a meal with Aunt Louisa and Aunt Hetty. Tim came back to the flat in time to tuck me up.

When I woke in the night I did not even go down, simply wailing for Evelyn until he came. I refused to be comforted by Evelyn's endearments and assurances and sobbed on and on, choking and gasping and bawling. But he would not concede that I would not have to go back to school.

'Don't make me go back. Please Tim, don't let him make me.'

Eventually Tim sat on the bed and pulled me inside the blanket-as-dressing-gown he was wrapped in, telling Evelyn angrily to 'sod off'. He sang to me softly, breathily, off key and when I was calmer tucked me up, promising to stay until I was asleep.

'Do you always have bad dreams? What do you do about it at school?'

'Wait for it to be light.'

'Christ.' At such close quarters he was older, lines at the edge of his eyes. His eyes were yellow-brown, like a cat's, flecked with glinting specks of green and maroon. Even in the small hours he did not look dark-jawed as Evelyn did in the night. 'What do you dream about?'

'Different things. It depends.'

'Big monsters and things?'

'Don't be silly. Only babies dream that. Do you have bad dreams?'

'Sometimes.'

'What?'

'Oh, storms at sea. Being caught. Don't you ever have nice dreams?'

'No. Do you?'

'Often.'

'What?'

'Now that would be telling.' His grin was irresistible.

On Sunday morning Tim and I were again up before Evelyn.

'I tell you what you ought to do, is run away from school. Lyn's dead soft really.' Tim gave me the toast he'd done for himself.

'I'm saving up. It will be expensive to run away.'

'You don't miss a trick, do you?'

'Can I run away to sea with you?'

'I don't think you'd need to go that far.'

'Oh please, I want to!'

'We'll see. Do you want to take Lyn up some coffee?'

'Why do you call him "Lyn"?'

'That's what he said to call him when we met.'

'Where did you meet him?'

'He came to an exhibition of my pictures and bought one. Rather a rare event in those days. I thought if I buttered him up he'd buy some more.'

'Did he?'

'Oh yes.' Tim smiled.

'Have you known him for years and years?'

'Not really. Six or seven.'

'Why did he tell me to call him "Evelyn" instead of "Lyn"?'

'Evelyn's for when he's being respectable.'

'Where are you going?'

'To see my mum and dad. And nan. In Walthamstow. You'll be gone when I get back, so cheerio.' He gave me a swift hug and advised, 'Don't take any nonsense from Lyn, stand up to him.'

'But he's bigger than me.'

'He's bigger than me too, but I don't take any nonsense.'

I wished I had wheedled Tim into taking me to his parents

instead of being taken to Sophie and Leo's by Evelyn. No one attended to me.

'What's the matter?' Uncle Richard sat next to me on the stairs.

'They won't allow girls.' Prowling up a second flight of stairs, I had been repulsed by a boy at the top, stern and supercilious.

'That's not very nice. Have you had lunch? Will you come and have lunch with me?' He served me to food and drink, sat with me and asked about school.

'It's horrid.'

'Well, you've quite lost your accent anyway.' I was pleased that he had noticed. He asked what I had done over the holiday.

'Evelyn took me shopping and we went to Aunt Louisa and Aunt Hetty for dinner and Evelyn and Tim took me to the zoo.'

'Tim?'

'Don't you know Tim?'

'Yes, I know Tim. I haven't seen him for some time. I didn't realise Evelyn was still in touch with him.'

'He drew a picture of me but it wasn't very good.'

'That surprises me.'

'Uncle Richard, if Evelyn died, what would become of me?'

'Well . . .' His eyes were wide and startled, very blue. 'I expect you would continue at school.'

'So it wouldn't make any difference if he died?'

'I'm sure he won't, he looks very healthy to me. Aren't you being a bit morbid?'

'I wouldn't care if he did die.'

'That's not very nice. What's he done to deserve that?'

'He's making me go back.'

'Well, everyone has to go to school, it's the law.'

'I didn't have to go away before.'

'I went away to school when I was younger than you.'

'Did you like it?'

'It gets better as you get older. Would you care for some cake?'

'Tim didn't go away to school.'

'I don't suppose he got such a good education.'

'But it doesn't matter for girls.'

'Of course it matters.' He stacked our used plates. 'Your Aunt Diana went to Oxford and did very well. I'm sure Evelyn intends you to go to university.'

'Did you go?'

'Yes, I went to Oxford too.'

'Did Evelyn?'

'He went up but he never finished.'

'Why not?'

'You'll have to ask him.'

Evelyn seemed in no hurry to take me back to school. He even endured my climbing on his lap. I listened drowsily to the arguments about the election, hoping desperately that he had forgotten, or changed his mind. Despite my extravagant scene in the night he had not relented.

Inevitably, Evelyn finally said it was time to go. I peeked round at the audience, Uncle Richard, Sophie and Leo, a room full of adults.

'I'm not going. I don't want to go back.'

Evelyn stiffened and gripped me tight in both his arms, brushed his face against my hair. 'Now look here, are you going to get up quietly and say thank you to Sophie for the party and say goodbye nicely? Or am I going to have to throw you over my shoulder and drag you away?' he murmured.

I jerked away and glared at him. I looked at his empty supper plate on the table next to him, had a momentary vision of driving the knife into his heart, twisting the fork in his entrails. But of course the cutlery would be too blunt. He pulled me close again, smoothed my hair. His breath, smelling of beer, was moist against my ear. I looked around at the idiot adults gazing benevolently at the tableau.

'Make no mistake, Alex, I can carry you if I have to. And you'll look damn silly if you're dragged kicking and screaming. Are you going to come quietly?' he asked softly. 'Now you'll get up and mind your manners.'

9

I did not like the only friend I had. She was skinny, with glasses and thin lank hair and an infuriating gasping laugh. Laura had little to say for herself but followed me about, ran errands for me. I was incessantly rude at her expense and fantastically untruthful about my background and home life but she hung on my every word. Fortunately she did not share my room, so that I could keep a distance. She was generous at tea time with jars of jam, so I was resigned to eating with her.

In the swimming bath Laura squealed desperately and clutched at me, unable to see anything without her glasses. I too was inept, but never timid, though I received no credit for fearlessness. Evelyn, although he had not really succeeded in teaching me to swim, had convinced me that I would always float and need not be frightened. I had enjoyed swimming with Evelyn, frolicking at my own whim rather than struggling lap after lap. The bigger children had never bothered me either in Evelyn's company.

Games were even worse. I was never allowed to be unobtrusively surplus on the sidelines but was singled out time and again to rehearse various motions, receive lectures on letting the side down through my lack of application. Wheezing, muddy, purple knee'd, I would fight back the tears as the games mistress's booming berations were carried on the wind and the other girls nudged and whispered and giggled.

I was outraged to realise that the staff perceived me as a trouble maker. But I had no following, nor did I answer back or clown in class. My disruptiveness was more clandestine, avoiding games and homework. These lapses were increasingly less possible as I was ever more closely supervised. I was given additional prep, purportedly to catch up with the others, and arbitrarily enrolled for every conceivable extra-curricular activity – mostly games – and soon had almost no time to myself.

I was told that the burning rash on my hands was caused by hanging about on radiators and thereafter severely reprimanded any time I was discovered anywhere in the vicinity of any of the few functioning hot pipes. Anyone discovered lurking indoors with anything less than a cast iron excuse was herded outdoors for yet more sporting activities.

I prayed very hard in church each Sunday, lingered lighting candles in the side chapels until Miss Griffiths would hiss irritably that I was holding up the others. The Sunday after half term she unexpectedly detained me when we tumbled out of her elderly Morris Minor back at school and invited me up to her room.

The living quarters of the staff were as much an object of speculation as that of the nuns had been at Sacred Heart. I avidly drank in the details of her small room, books, photos, plants. Unexpectedly I felt sorry for her as she attempted to put me at my ease, chattered of her family, showed me a jumper she was knitting for her sister.

'You don't have any brothers or sisters, do you?'

'No.'

'It's a pity, it's lovely having a big family.' She offered another
biscuit. 'And your uncle, he hasn't any other children?'

'No.'

'It must be difficult, coming to a new country, getting used to
being without your mummy?'

I made a non-committal noise in my throat.

'Still, I suppose it helps to have such a strong faith. It's very
important to you, isn't it?'

'Mmm.'

She loomed confidingly close and I tried not to look at her
large-pored shiny face. 'It's a great pity you seem to have got off
on the wrong foot here.' She nibbled her biscuit in a rabbity
fashion, breathing hard through her large nostrils. 'Still, I expect
things are better this term, hmm?'

I took another biscuit. I might as well eat something nice
while I was stuck here.

'Did you have a nice time at half term? What did you do?'

'Evelyn took me to the zoo and we went swimming and he
bought me a winter coat.' I knew that evening meals out and
Tim were not appropriate.

'Evelyn's your uncle? And is he nice? Do you like him?'

I nodded and squirmed embarrassedly.

'And you don't have any problems at home, with your uncle?'

'No.'

'Did you know him before? I mean before your mummy passed
on?'

'No.'

'It must have been exciting to meet him.'

'Mmm.'

'And were you excited to come to England?'

'No.'

'Your uncle's not married, is he? Wouldn't it be nice if he
was?'

'No.'

'But you could have brothers and sisters.'

'He says he doesn't want to be married. He said he always gets tired of people too quickly to get married.'

'Does he say things like that to you?'

'I asked him. I'm glad he's not married, it's much more fun, just us.'

'I fear he spoils you a great deal.'

This was patently ridiculous. I was heartily bored by now and there were no biscuits left. I endowed Evelyn with an irrevocably blighted life, a fiancée who had died only a week before the wedding, health broken by the war, elderly mother in a wickedly expensive lunatic asylum, unscrupulous business associates.

'Poor man. I had no idea. You must be a great comfort to him.'

I was fearful that I had overplayed my hand. The following Sunday I was again invited for elevenses but carefully confined my reminiscences to more or less truthful accounts of life in America and Uncle Pat's large family. Miss Griffiths asked with many embarrassed euphemisms about my mother and how I was coping with her death which I answered in grudging mono-syllables until she began to talk of her own family instead.

After that the sessions metamorphosed into what was billed as a religious discussion group which took place in one of the music rooms in the dead interval between dusk and tea, without the tea and biscuits. It was also made interdenominational. I did not bother after the first meeting.

Evelyn's weekly letters, each on a single sheet of stiff company stationery, as if he dashed them off in his tea break, were supplemented by lurid postcards of German cities. Before his trip, he had commended me to Uncle Richard in the event of emergencies. Uncle Richard sent me a postcard of the municipal buildings of Sheffield, where he himself was away on business.

Belatedly, almost after I had given up hope, there was a card of the mermaid in Copenhagen harbour. 'Terrible crossing, everyone sick' – a line of faces at a railing – 'even me' – dejected face of Tim – 'but weather lovely now. Wish you were here' – Tim with a mug of beer, arrow to an empty café chair in front of an enormous dish of ice cream – 'Love, Tim.'

Since half term Evelyn put some tentative XXXs at the bottom of his letters but signed, 'as ever, E'. Not even I could read between his bland lines the smallest hint of reprieve. But I kept the letters all the same.

I fantasised a great deal about Tim rescuing me, running away to sea with him. I did not think that Evelyn would mind. I knew that Evelyn scarcely thought of me when I wasn't there. He could shut the door of my room, forget I existed. It frightened me to think of my empty room, of Evelyn relievedly reverting to the life he had lived before I came. It was like being dead, unmourned, unregretted, leaving no trace except a few toys and ornaments to be jumbled.

In my more down to earth moments I counted my money and plotted how to run away alone. This scheme was soon abandoned after the theft of my money. In what even I recognised as a put-up job one of the prefects confiscated my sweets and savings for insolence. My silence was ensured by threats to produce witnesses to my purloinment of the sweets and money from the prefect's own locker.

I had never paid much attention to the three other girls in the tiny bedroom but realised that one of them must have seen me counting my money. They began teasing me, hiding my belongings, making apple pie beds, taunting me after lights out. The protection money now extorted from my weekly pocket money protected me from nothing.

Assaults during sporting activities were commonplace. One Saturday, sliced viciously across the back of the knees with a hockey stick, I fell face down in the mud. Winded, frozen, giddy, I would not get up. There seemed little point; I would only be attacked again.

Eventually I was carted to the sanatorium. Once there, cleaned, ensconced in bed, for once with enough bedding in a warm enough room, I realised that I really felt very ill. Presently I was sick and repeated this throughout the evening. I was better on Sunday, but evidently suffering from a virus that was going round.

Luxuriating in the warmth and solitude, I realised that I could not bear to return to the routine, cold, ostracised, robbed. I would rather die. I prayed hard to die and was peeved to wake from a nap alive. A tray of invalid's dinner was brought, bland, lukewarm, not remotely tempting. I left it, resisting attempts to make me eat anything. The solution was obvious. The more I considered, the more attractive it seemed.

If I did not eat for long enough I would die. I could be dead by next weekend, or shortly thereafter. It would cause the maximum of fuss and inconvenience for the school and strike Evelyn with remorse. Being ill, it would be easy to reject food for a day or so until my scheme was well advanced. I soon gave in and drank water, but resolved on no other concessions. Matron impatiently coaxed me to eat from the evening tray but it was so unappetising that I wasn't even tempted.

I had not bargained on how hungry I would be by Monday. Matron bullied me at lunchtime so that I could snuffle feebly, insisting I wouldn't eat instead of giving in and picking surreptitious bits from the tray. It was only then that anyone admitted that I was wilfully not eating.

Laura visited after school and brought some sweets; fortunately I couldn't bear liquorice and left them without a qualm. In the evening Miss Griffiths administered my tray. I lay feigning sleep until she went away. Later she visited again and left half a packet of chocolate digestives. After lights out I ate them all and was sick.

There were no more lapses after that. Laura came at lunchtime to eat her meal with me. The food actually looked nice, white chicken meat and smooth mashed potato. But I felt too ill to eat. In the evening two of the girls from my bedroom came, awed, curious, bearing a bar of Cadbury's Dairy Milk and a slice of tinned fruit cake, assuring me that it was all right, that they wouldn't tell anyone. But I knew they would and turned my back.

Miss Favell herself came the next morning, her charming concern soon yielding to sharp exasperation. 'It will be the worse for you if we have to involve your uncle. I've no doubt he'll be very angry indeed.'

'I don't care.'

She swept away. I snivelled piteously, feeling very frail. But I knew it could not be long now and longed for death more than ever. I was scarcely aware of the arrival and removal of several meal trays and Laura's visits. I dozed a great deal.

'Well.' Evelyn was drawing up a chair. He held out a large box with a lush Alpine scene, gilt edges and a large ribbon. I tried to look at his face, gauge his mood, but I could not think. He opened the box himself and urged the chocolates on me.

My mind cleared. 'You think I'm stupid.'

'No, that's one thing I don't think.' He set the box aside. 'Now what's all this in aid of?'

'All what?'

'I'm not stupid either, Alex. Why aren't you eating?'

'I don't want to.'

'Why don't you want to?'

'I just don't, that's all.'

'All right then, what's your negotiating position?'

'How do you mean?'

'What are you holding out for? What do you hope to achieve?'

'I shall die.'

'Don't be ridiculous. What do you want out of this? Come, I'm not stupid.'

'I want to die.'

'Alex, you won't get what you want if no one knows what it is.'

'I want to be dead.'

He leaned forward. 'Don't you think that's a bit melodramatic?'

'I don't care. I'm going to be dead.'

He sat back again, fingered his watch chain. 'You're not joking, are you?'

'I told you.' I turned over and burrowed under the covers.

Presently he said, 'I don't suppose it matters if I mind if you're dead?'

'But you don't! You couldn't care less!'

'But of course I do.' He touched my shoulder.

'Go away. Leave me alone.' And when I looked he had gone. I wondered if it were a dream. But the box of chocolates was still there. I dozed again.

'Now, Mr Parrish, let's not be hasty, I'm sure we can work out . . .' Miss Favell was saying with unaccustomed conciliation.

Evelyn jerked the covers off me. 'Get dressed. We're going.'

'. . . most unwise . . . the child's extremely ill . . . cannot be answerable for the consequences . . . most ill advised journey . . .'

'I'm not asking you to, you've more than enough to be responsible for already,' Evelyn snapped. I got out of bed and immediately gave way at the knees. Evelyn gently sat me down. 'I want the child's things packed and ready to go in ten minutes.'

'. . . most unreasonable . . . shocking lack of sensibility and restraint . . . small wonder the girl is such a disruptive influence . . .' But as Evelyn took out his watch and looked at it, she huffily went away.

'It's all right, pet, we'll be home in no time.' He sat on the bed and supported me against him. He asked the other girls if they didn't find it cold. By now most were hanging off the end of their beds so as not to miss anything.

'It's much warmer here than the rest of the building, sir,' an older girl ventured.

While we waited Evelyn interrogated Matron, who mendaciously asserted that I had been eating contraband food incessantly. Laura, however, did not corroborate this. Evelyn turned his attention to putting Laura at her ease, asking her about herself.

Miss Favell returned to inform Evelyn frostily that my belongings were in the foyer. She threw discretion to the winds with face to save in front of her girls. 'Never before in a long and not undistinguished career . . . disgraceful lack of parental discipline and control . . . deplorable attitude . . . uncouth and dimwitted child . . . sly and unpopular . . . the sins of the fathers . . .'

'Jesus Christ, let's go,' Evelyn murmured. But I couldn't stand up. He pulled a blanket from the bed and draped it round me before scooping me up in his arms. He swept out of the room and shifted me up against his shoulder as he urgently demanded instructions on the way out. I looked over his shoulder at Miss Favell, crimson-cheeked, still recriminating, and Matron, sullenly bringing up the rear, and put out my tongue.

'Put your arms around my neck and don't move or we'll both end up arse over tip,' Evelyn hissed. He managed to sail grandly down the stairs as the girls came from their rooms to watch. Laura materialised to hold the front door for Evelyn, who issued a regal command to 'Bring the cases' to Miss Favell.

My slippers scuffed the gravel and then I was tucked up in the passenger seat with the box of chocolates on my lap. Evelyn climbed in and we roared away in a satisfactory spray of gravel. He cursed exhaustively, repetitively in a variety of languages, but it was all Greek to me. Soon he pulled over and gave a long series of shuddering sighs, slumped over the wheel.

'I'm just going to nip across the road for the loo. Shan't be a minute,' he said and eased out into the rain.

I rubbed the steamy glass and saw him disappear into a pub. I resigned myself to a long wait and opened the chocolates. As I hoped, the foil wrapped one turned out to contain a cherry. It was too dark to read the crib sheet so I ate my way stolidly down the row until Evelyn returned, not all that long.

'Christ!' He snatched the box away, put it in the back. 'You'll be sick as a horse.'

'No, I won't.'

part III

1

Neat rows of soldiers advanced unflinchingly, fife and drums, muskets and cannon, mounted officers, like a swarm of red beetles through puffs of smoke. Firing downhill on the redcoats were variegated rows of men, homespuns, buckskins and blue coats interspersed. At the edges of the field, wounded were attended to with jugs of water, tourniquets, amputations.

I had worked most of the day on the drawing, taping on more sheets of paper. The red pencil was worn almost to a stump by all the red uniforms and blood. Evelyn gave me a lesson in drawing horses by making a series of circles and connecting them up and abandoned a discourse on perspective to attend to his own work. His secretary had arrived after lunch and their work was spread across the other end of the dining-room table. I spent as much time watching them as on my own drawing.

But I was none the wiser. Evelyn was being very nice, but that didn't mean anything. Without reproach he had stopped for me to be sick on the drive home, sat with me as I bawled in the night, had even given in to my demands that I be allowed to sleep in his bed. (He did not seem to have slept at all in the night.) In the morning I had easily extracted his solemn promise that I would not return to Warton.

Later Uncle Richard came and Mrs Deveraux took shorthand notes of what they said. He did a stint of signing the stacks of Christmas cards with the company motif while Evelyn prepared the meal. I was allowed to seal the cards into their envelopes under Mrs Deveraux' direction.

Evelyn was on terms of easy familiarity with Mrs Deveraux, addressing her as 'Lesley' and persuading her to stay for dinner. At tea time he had ignored her protestations that she ought not and cut her a generous slice from the cake that Mrs Carey had sent up. When she went up to the loo, he said, 'Do have a look round while you're there, I'm sure Connie will be dying to have all the details.'

'Who's Connie?'

'Mrs Crawford. Richard's secretary. They're like that.' He held up crossed fingers. 'Still, I mustn't complain. They contrive to let us think we run the place.'

Mrs Deveraux marvelled over the seascaped bathroom. 'Was that your friend Tim?'

'Mmm.' Evelyn spread a sheaf of graphs.

'You never said it was Tim. When is Tim coming again?'

'I don't know, Alex. Now I really must get on if we're to finish this.'

'I didn't know that you were – I mean, that Alex knows Tim.'

'He stopped by once while he was in town. Now the whole thing would make a lot more sense if this graph were plotted the other way up,' Evelyn said firmly.

Evelyn made me sleep in my own bed that night but came to tuck me up.

'Are you going to marry Mrs Deveraux?' It seemed very suitable. She was an appropriate age, a little younger than Evelyn, I judged, and still pretty despite her slight plumpness.

Evelyn laughed. 'I'm sure that's the last thing she'd want. She knows me far too well.' He settled the covers around me. 'Why are you so obsessed with me marrying? Would you like me to marry?'

'No!'

'I assure you, Alex, it's most unlikely. I'm far too set in my ways. Besides, who would have an old boy like me?'

'You're not that old.'

'Well, thank you.'

'Evelyn? Why haven't you got married?'

'Because I didn't want to. Now go to sleep, Alex.'

'But why not?'

'Because it's much more fun not to be married.'

'Does Uncle Richard think it's more fun not to be married?'

Evelyn sputtered. 'I've no idea. And you're not to ask him.'

'I don't want to be married either.'

'Don't you? Why not?'

'I don't know. You have to keep having babies if you're married.'

'Only if you're Catholic.'

'You mean you don't have to have babies if you're not Catholic?'

'Not if you're careful.'

'How do you mean?'

'Oh Christ! I mean very careful indeed. Now you must sleep, it's very late, pet.'

On Sunday we went to lunch with Aunt Louisa and Aunt Hetty. I was relieved that Uncle Richard was not there. He had admired my epic drawing of the battle of Bunker Hill. 'I take it the British lost,' he had said with an unexpected smile that made his blue eyes glisten. But I had heard him say to Evelyn that he thought I looked very well pleased with myself. I did not suppose the rest of the family would approve of my behaviour either. I was dreading the meal.

Aunt Hetty took me into the kitchen to help with preparations. But I managed to overhear part of Evelyn's row with Aunt Louisa by fussing over the indifferent tom outside the living-room door after I had laid the table.

'It's no good expecting us to bail you out,' Aunt Louisa was saying.

'I'm not asking you to. I'm just asking your advice.'

'Well, I'm very flattered, dear. The last time you asked my advice was in 1932.' She sounded suddenly amused.

'Good God! What about?'

'I never discovered. You were far too embarrassed to say enough to give me any idea.' They both laughed.

'What do you think I should do?'

'I think you should act your age for once.'

Evelyn muttered irritably.

'Do you want the child with you?' Aunt Louisa asked.

'It's a question of what's best for her.'

'Exactly. Do you want her with you?'

Evelyn's silence lengthened unbearably. The cat struggled away. Woefully sucking my clawed finger I went back to the kitchen. Aunt Hetty was beginning to dish up the meal.

We sat down and I watched Evelyn's long hands carve the meat. I could not look at his face. He had tried to fob me off on Aunt Louisa and Aunt Hetty and even they did not want me. Aunt Louisa did not seem any longer to be cross and did not even seem especially formidable as she organised the handing round of the vegetables. Evelyn directed a small private smile of encouragement to me as I squared up to my plate.

I was staggered at the ease of his duplicity; no furtive embarrassment in case I could read his perfidious intentions, or shy abashment at the scale of his betrayal. I concluded that if no one wanted me I would be sent away to somewhere else. I could not eat.

'You must make an effort, pet.'

'I can't,' I whispered and felt rather than saw the adult glances exchanged.

'Now really, Alex.' But Evelyn's tone was gentle and he crouched by my chair.

'May I be excused now?' I did not wait for consent.

As we tidied the kitchen Aunt Hetty coaxed me to confide in her. It would be ridiculous, melodramatic – I could picture Evelyn's ironic look – to announce that I was upset because no one wanted me. She changed tack. Had something happened at school that I could not talk to Evelyn about? Was I sure? Had Evelyn upset me? Was I unwell? Her eyes, soft, brown, compassionate, were like Evelyn's, I suddenly realised, and equally untrustworthy.

On Monday I was delivered to Mrs Carey for the day. It was not a success; I was weary, unwell, petulant, certain now that she did not want me either. I was glad of Evelyn's less exacting indifference in the evening.

It was perfectly simple. I had been a fool to start eating again when my scheme had already been so far advanced. I had not eaten much since the awful Sunday dinner. It would not be too difficult. I rejected breakfast on the grounds of not feeling well. After much cajoling to tell him what was wrong, Evelyn stomped away to drink his coffee and hear the news in the living room.

He said blandly as he pulled on his overcoat, 'You know about the suffragettes, don't you?' I shook my head. 'They refused to eat.' He held out my coat. 'They were taken to hospital and a tube was forced through their noses into their stomachs and food was pumped down.' He jerked the coat over my shoulders. 'I'm not joking, you know.'

'You're making it up.'

'Ask Mrs Carey,' he said wearily.

Mrs Carey was very busy so near Christmas. She talked of her family, of the journey to her son's, what she would buy, prepare and take to them. In the afternoon I broke a china box on one of the occasional tables cluttering the room. When Evelyn came I was sent upstairs to put the fire on while they talked about me. I forestalled Evelyn by going to bed.

'I don't feel well,' I whimpered when he came to find me. He lit my fire and said that if I wasn't better in the morning he would take me to the doctor.

Evelyn had summoned the doctor on my first morning back. After I had been examined I eavesdropped on the stairs. Evelyn and the doctor were arguing about me, the doctor seeming reluctant to leave me with Evelyn. So if I went to the doctor, he would arrange for me to be taken away from Evelyn. Probably there was an orphanage somewhere in the area. And Evelyn would have me off his hands. I wept and eventually dozed.

Later Evelyn brought me a drink of lemonade. 'How are you feeling, pet?'

'I don't know.'

Evelyn sighed and perched on the edge of the bed. 'This really isn't working out, is it?'

'You're going to send me away again.'

'I don't know what on earth I'm going to do with you.' He put his head in his hands, did not look at me as he spoke. He'd thought it was all settled, that I was home now. But if I wasn't happy, didn't like being with him . . . 'Do you want to go back to your family in America?'

'No.' They did not want me either, had sent me away to Evelyn. I was scarcely even outraged. I realised it was just like Evelyn to accuse me of not wanting him when the truth was exactly the opposite.

'Well, what do you want?'

'I want to stay here,' I mumbled.

'Well, here you are. You don't seem very enthusiastic.'

'Neither do you.' I terminated the proceedings by turning

over and pulling the covers over my head. Presently he removed his weight from the bed and when I peeked he had gone.

2

'You haven't eaten.'

'I'm not hungry.'

'Shall I put out some cheese?' I coaxed.

'Not on my account. You have your bath now.' Evelyn scraped our half-eaten meal into the bin and began to wash up.

'Are you getting a cold?'

'I'm fine. Off you go, pet.'

I dreamily considered the seaside panorama through the steam and puzzled over Evelyn's listlessness. The previous week Evelyn had given me a little talk on how I must co-operate if I was to remain with him; he worked long hours, would sometimes have to be away on business, I would have to make things easy for him. Having mumblingly agreed to this, we had an expensive meal out to seal the bargain.

Evelyn was carefully considerate and attentive to me. At the same time he seemed remote, preoccupied, weary. I tried to be helpful and thoughtful. But we had little to talk about. Evelyn soaked long in the bath after work, topping up the hot water several times. After dinner it was my turn. Eventually Evelyn would remember to call me and I would emerge with hands and feet shrivelled like dried fruit.

The impasse was punctuated only by my tenth birthday. Evelyn's presents were lavish and satisfactorily adult, a small inlaid chest not unlike one I admired in Evelyn's bedroom and a shiny oriental dressing gown like the one Evelyn wore in the summer. I was touched too at Aunt Louisa and Aunt Hetty's efforts. There was a birthday cake and a meal as well as a new set of coloured pencils, bubble bath and fleece-lined mittens. Uncle Richard gave me a gold 'A' on a chain to be stored in the new red lined box.

Evelyn always tucked me up now and when I had bad dreams in the night he comforted me, sat with me until I slept again. But his morning manner was brusque. I could not reconcile the two men into one. I knew his moods and whims but from this I could predict nothing.

About a fortnight after Evelyn had fetched me home he took me to visit friends one evening, a long drive through interminable streets of grey semi-detached houses. Ben was almost as tall as Evelyn and even thinner, with the sorrowful, stoical face of a saint. He would have looked more in character in sandals and a coarse robe tied with rope than in black trousers and turtle neck. His tonsured head was much greyer than Evelyn's. Molly was younger, small and plump, fadingly pretty.

They did not gush or patronise me. Ben's deadpan irony was reassuringly like Evelyn's and his soft Scottish accent appealing. The men drank the whisky that Evelyn had brought and Molly drank bottles of black beer, saying perplexingly that she ought not, the baby would be drunk.

The baby was called Helen and was three months old. At Molly's urging Evelyn gingerly held the infant and watched its tiny fist clutch his finger. He handed the child back and winked at me.

Molly took the infant away to feed it and invited me with her. It had never occurred to me that babies could be fed like puppies or kittens; my cousins were all bottle fed. I was fascinated and more than a little disgusted but mostly embarrassed. Molly chatted to me quite normally, about the baby, about her little boy asleep in the next room, about Evelyn. He had been best man at their wedding, he and Ben had once worked together. She managed also to get me to tell her a great deal about myself.

'And you're getting on all right with Evelyn?'

'Mmmhmm.'

'He's an old softie really.' She shifted the baby on to her shoulder and patted its back. 'He was very upset about your school fiasco. He had a terrible time at school himself, so now he feels very bad about sending you.'

'Is that what Evelyn said?'

'He came round one lunchtime last week. He was in a right state, didn't know what to do for the best. For God's sake don't tell him I've told you!' The baby, now satisfactorily burped, was laid in her cot and Molly readjusted her clothes.

Evelyn and Ben argued on and on; Khrushchev, Nixon, Bevan, Gaitskell, elections, Hungary, Castro, CP, ILP . . . I drowsed, roused intermittently by their increasingly acrimonious voices. At some point Molly went to bed. Finally, the whisky drunk low, it was time to go home.

Evelyn frowned, blinked, stretched as the engine warmed. 'Well, pet?' His big hand clumsily smoothed my hair.

'I want to have a house like that when I grow up.' I was entranced by the bay window and stained glass and half timbered frontage. 'I'd have different furniture though.' Evelyn laughed. Ben and Molly's furniture was a hotch potch. Nothing matched, there was no colour scheme, no pictures, only a chaos of toys and books and unmatching glasses. They had not apologised, had not even seemed to notice. 'Ben's awfully old to have a new baby.'

'How old do you suppose he is, for God's sake?'

'I don't know. A bit older than you?'

'A bit younger than me. Do you think I'm too old to have babies?'

'You'd be very very old before it was grown up.'

'I shall be decrepit enough before I get you off my hands.' He was laughing again, put his arm around my shoulders. 'Oh love,' he said into my hair and pulled away to put the car in gear.

I scrutinised Evelyn as he perched on the edge of my bed, settling the covers around me, his movements measured, his eyes glistening. 'You're drunk,' it dawned on me.

He smiled ruefully. 'Do you mind?'

'You'll have a bad stomach in the morning.'

'Mmm.' He bobbed forward to peck my brow.

'Poor Evelyn.' Impulsively I returned his kiss and he kissed each cheek before he went away. I lay wiping my hand on the covers where his brilliantine had rubbed off. By his own admission he was drunk. But at what stage did having some drinks become drunk? He did not behave badly or create disturbances. I could remember no instance of being previously aware that he must be drunk. If anything I preferred him drunk. He was more relaxed, more easily amused, more demonstrative.

Try as I might I could not conjure the concatenation of circumstances which would inevitably result in Evelyn's final degeneration into a down and out and my admission into institutional care. Nor could I imagine him being upset at my unhappiness at school. I was not at all sure I believed it. I wished I had thought to ask Molly more about Evelyn's previous visit.

The weekend brought the long hoped for return of Tim. He patiently endured my excited prattle and allowed me to clamber on to his lap. (It was not very satisfactory; he was much smaller than Evelyn and I soon slithered off.) When we went out for a meal I held his hand and sat next to him in the restaurant. At bedtime I insisted on Tim tucking me up. He suggested after I had slurpily kissed his cheek that I should have Evelyn come and say good night as well so that his feelings would not be hurt. I was surprised by the idea but acquiesced to Tim.

On Sunday Tim went to lunch at his family's. Evelyn and I went to Aunt Louisa and Aunt Hetty's. In the evening I'd scarcely seen Tim when Evelyn sent me to bed. Tim quelled the rebellion by taking me up.

'Are you going away tomorrow?'

'I'll come again some time.'

'I want to come with you. You said I could before.'

'I said we'd think about it.'

'Please Tim. Please take me with you, please.'

'There's no point now, is there?'

'I want to come with you.'

'What would I do with you? I work very long hours on duty.'

'I could help you.'

'Now don't be daft, you're much better off here.'

'You don't want me either.'

'Now what's all this? There's nothing to cry over.' He found his handkerchief and held me against his shoulder. Eventually he coaxed me to tell him in a garbled fashion of how Evelyn didn't really want me at all, of how even my aunts had refused to have me. 'I think we'd better sort this out with Lyn now,' he decided and bundled me into slippers and dressing gown, ignoring my pleas not to make everything worse.

'Alex wants to come away to sea with me tomorrow,' Tim told Evelyn.

After a long silence Evelyn said, 'Well, I've no objection. It seems an excellent suggestion. How do you propose to support her?'

Tim made a rueful open palmed gesture and looked at me enquiringly.

'You can give him some money, Evelyn,' I said.

'I see. You want me to give Tim money so he can take you away from me.'

'It's a bit of cheek, Alex,' Tim said.

'It wouldn't cost you any more than it does anyway,' I assured Evelyn.

'That's not the only difficulty.' Evelyn drained his glass and held it out to Tim. 'The matter is out of my hands. I'm only a joint guardian, you know. I can scarcely make you over to an impoverished and rather dubious young man without your Uncle Pat's consent. And in all conscience I couldn't recommend him to do so. Tim has no wife, no money, no home to take you to. I'm afraid we must be practical, Alex.'

Tim gave me a drink of Ribena and lemonade. The men sipped whisky.

'The thing is, Lyn, Alex thinks you would prefer her to be away somewhere,' Tim said apologetically.

'She knows perfectly well that's not true,' Evelyn snapped.

'Does she?'

Evelyn drank his whisky and fetched the decanter from the dining room. 'What it comes down to is that Alex doesn't really want to be here.'

'Well?' Tim said gently. 'What would you like, hmm?'

'I want to be where I'm wanted,' I said eventually, faintly.

'That seems reasonable,' Evelyn said after a moment. 'I wish you'd tell me what I've done to make you feel unwanted.' He came and sat next to me and enumerated everything, purchases, treats, outings, all the nice times we'd had together, how much he had enjoyed our holiday. He smoothed loose wisps of my hair back as he spoke, asked again what he'd done wrong.

I felt even sillier now, but with the conviction that I had once again been outmanoeuvred. Finally I mumbled that he had sent me away to school.

'Well it was a mistake. I admit it. I was idiotic enough and, you must allow, inexperienced enough to listen to a lot of well-meaning advice about how I couldn't possibly manage on my own. But you're back now, hmm?'

I nodded warily, looked at Tim. He turned his glass, coating the sides with whisky, not looking at either of us.

'Now really, Alex. Surely you don't imagine you've out-jockeyed me, do you? If I didn't want you here I'd be making arrangements to send you somewhere else next term. And you know full well what arrangements I've made.' He referred to an appointment in the offing to visit the head of the nearest council school.

'I think you should give it a go, Alex,' Tim said. 'You've not really had time to settle in again. It's not that bad, is it?'

I smiled feebly. There was no point in holding out if Tim wouldn't stand up for me. Evelyn squeezed my shoulder and pulled me to him. Tim prepared us all hot chocolate and discovered a packet of chocolate digestives.

Eventually when I drowsed Evelyn said, 'I'll take you up, pet.'

'No, I want Tim.'

'You're not bloody giving him much of a chance, are you?' Tim sounded stern as he pulled the covers up.

'How do you mean?'

'You seem to be sending him to Coventry half the time.'

'I'm not.' I had learned the hard way what that meant at school.

'Well you're bloody hard. Why are you being so unkind?'

'I'm not.'

'It was pretty rude just now, telling him you didn't want him.'

'I didn't say that.'

'As good as. How do you think he must have felt?'

'He doesn't care.'

'But he does. Do you know, we talked until three in the morning last night. And most of it was about you. He's been worried sick.' Tim continued that I did not make enough allowance for Evelyn's inexperience with children, his tiredness after a day's work. He thought Evelyn was making a good go of things. So would I try and be nicer to him?

'I don't think you realise how shy Lyn is.'

That was too much. 'Don't be silly.'

'I think you're on to a very cushy number here. Lyn lets you get away with murder and indulges you something chronic if you ask me.'

'Don't tease.'

'Tease! My old man would of tanned my hide if I was still awake at this hour when I was a kid. Don't tell me your Mum let you sit up past midnight.' He settled me under the covers and said, 'Now shall I tell Lyn you want him to come and say good night?'

'All right.'

Tim left early in the morning and I snivelled interminably, refusing breakfast, enduring Evelyn doing my hair.

'Now really, love, it's not the end of the world.'

'I want Tim!' I pulled away from his tentative pat.

He gathered up the bedding Tim had used and said, 'I've no doubt a lot of people want Tim. Come and wash your face. I don't know what Mrs Carey will think.' He firmly propelled me upstairs before him.

3

The boardroom was dominated by an enormous table of gleaming yellow wood like slices of amber symmetrically pieced together. There were matching chairs upholstered in a nubby grey and similar shining panels of wood on the walls. During the week before Christmas I was settled in the boardroom while Evelyn worked. I was abstractly aware that Uncle Richard and Evelyn worked together, but I was still surprised on Monday morning when he entered the boardroom. His surprise equalled mine.

'Mrs Carey is away so I had to come with Evelyn,' I explained.

'But I thought . . .' He opened a large chest, took out a silver box. 'Are you the chairman today?'

'How do you mean?'

'Usually the Chairman of the Board sits there. Will you be chairman today?' He settled in a chair halfway down the table and I nodded dubiously. 'Excellent. I can let you worry about exchange rates today.' He took a cigarette from the silver box.

'I didn't know you smoked,' I reproved.

'Only once in a while when I have a problem to work out.'

'Are you the chairman?'

'For my sins. But I'd much rather you were chairman today.' He explained the pictures on the wall. There was the founder, my great-great-grandfather, his offspring, their offspring. There was a photograph of Evelyn's father, Aubrey, a bony-faced man of rigid bearing with abundant grey hair and sad dark eyes.

Aubrey's younger brother Theodore had a proper portrait in florid oils. Uncle Richard drew a diagram of the relationships for me on a blackboard behind one of the wall panels. Suddenly he looked at his watch and hurried away. I looked at the stern faced men in old-fashioned clothes. It made Uncle Richard seem very old.

He came again in the afternoon, pacing up and down and smoking, nervously jingling his change. I did not interrupt but presently he chatted with me, admired my drawing of an epic sea battle with sailing ships, cannon and a storm brewing.

'Why isn't there a picture of you up there?' I asked.

'Nobody goes in for that sort of thing anymore. It's a bit silly really, don't you think?'

He taught me how to play shove ha'penny on the glassy table. A formidable woman in glasses looked in. Furtively, like a schoolboy, he wiped away the chalk marks he had made on the amber wood and stuffed his handkerchief into his pocket before his secretary returned with two cups of tea and biscuits.

'Is the table antique?'

'Hardly. Our Uncle Theodore spent a great deal of money in the thirties having the place done out. Pickled wood was all the rage then. Evelyn says it's hideously vulgar.'

He was being very nice; I was grateful for his forbearance in not mentioning the original plan for me to stay with Aunt Louisa and Aunt Hetty for the week. But at the last minute I took exception to the scheme. Already I had vetoed a stay with Laura and her family in Buckinghamshire and an overnight visit to Sophie and Leo's.

'I knew you would send me away again.'

'Don't be ridiculous. A few days with Louisa and Hetty is hardly packing you off. No doubt you'll be disgracefully indulged.'

'You don't want me.'

'Now don't start that again. Really love, it's only for a few days.'

'And next time it will be for a few more and then more. I knew you'd do this.'

'Now that's enough. I can't ring them now and say you're not coming after all. They've made plans, it would be very rude.'

'I didn't say I wouldn't go. I don't want to stay where I'm not wanted.' I ran away to my room.

Evelyn did not come to find me until much later. 'You're frozen to the marrow, you'll catch your death!' He lit the fire.

'Good!'

'Then I'll be sorry.' He laughed infuriatingly and said we would go out and eat as we weren't going to Crystal Palace.

'We're not?' I felt a surge of triumph.

'Certainly not. How can I foist you on Aunt Louisa and Aunt Hetty if you're going to sulk all week? It's too much for them at their age. Besides, I'll never hear the end of it if they realise how ill mannered you are.' But having vented his sarcasm, he exerted himself to be entertaining over the meal out.

I saw very little of Evelyn at work; mainly I was looked after by Mrs Deveraux. Uncle Richard took me to lunch once and sometimes had his break with me. One afternoon I was taken Christmas shopping by two previously unencountered relatives, Uncle Theodore and his brother Uncle Sebastian, Evelyn and Uncle Richard's uncles, my great-uncles.

Uncle Theodore and Uncle Sebastian came to take Evelyn and Uncle Richard to lunch and took me as well. I enjoyed being the only child amongst the smartly suited men. Uncle Theodore was not unlike his portrait, fat and rubicund, with protuberant pale eyes. He seemed uneasy with his nephews, joking and hearty, showing his teeth a lot like a nervous horse. Uncle Sebastian was taller and cadaverous with sternly set face. He walked with a bad limp and used a stick, the result of a war wound.

Evelyn shamelessly persuaded the old men to take me off his hands for the afternoon, much to Uncle Richard's amusement. I had already been taken shopping with Evelyn the afternoon after our interview with my new headmaster. Evelyn had bought most of his presents, which were to be from us both. In addition I had new patent leather shoes (black for winter) and several new dresses, including one in dark red velvet for Christmas wear. I had never had anything so splendid before. Evelyn brushed aside my thanks, saying he was damned if Louisa was going to be able to criticise him.

But my current dilemma was what to get Evelyn for Christmas. (I had a respectable sum to spend, the stolen running away fund having been reimbursed by Evelyn.) After much deliberation between my uncles a bottle was chosen on my behalf for Evelyn and they took me to tea at Fortnum's. I declined Uncle Theodore's offer to take me to see Father Christmas.

'I'm *ten* now.'

'Really, Teddy,' Uncle Sebastian remonstrated.

Uncle Theodore solemnly begged my pardon.

Neither uncle seemed inclined to interrogate me about our domestic arrangements, what Evelyn fed me. Uncle Theodore genially imparted a fund of incomprehensible puns and jokes and Uncle Sebastian talked to me about Italy, where he lived for most of the year. I liked being made a fuss of and felt pleased that I would see them again at Hellisford over Christmas.

But I heard Uncle Richard say irritably to Evelyn, 'Why didn't anyone tell me Theodore was coming to Hellisford? I thought he was going away with Mrs Keppel again.'

'Who's Mrs Keppel?' I asked.

'It's a joke, Alex. A private joke, so don't go blabbing,' Evelyn said firmly.

Christmas was on a Friday and we were to drive up to

Hellisford on Thursday afternoon. Little work was done Thursday. The floor below the top floor, which held Evelyn and Uncle Richard's offices and the boardroom, was also given over to the company. The space was open with rows of desks, and offices at one end, the whole festooned with decorations. Food and drink was arranged on a desk and the women sipped martini from tea cups while they desultorily typed memos. Evelyn had a word for everybody and most of the women made a fuss of me. When he retreated upstairs with a full cup of drink, Mrs Deveraux, heroically at her post, gloomily informed him that he'd missed Mr Parrish.

Evelyn fetched another drink from the locked chest in the boardroom and sent me to the loo before our journey. I found Evelyn hugging Mrs Deveraux, his bottom resting on the edge of his desk, her head on his shoulder. He gently eased away and held the glass for her to drink, coaxing softly. He set aside the empty glass and squeezed her shoulders. He did not even have the grace to appear embarrassed. I pulled away when he took my hand and ran ahead to the lift button. But he looked so sad in the lift that I relented and slipped my hand into his.

'You are going to marry Mrs Deveraux.'

'Don't be ridiculous.'

'But you were hugging her.'

'She's very upset. Her mother is very ill in hospital.'

He gave the man on the door a Christmas envelope on the way out. Then we went to a florist's. The young assistant bantered with him and an older woman hurried forward. He sent flowers to Mrs Deveraux at home and her mother in hospital, and as an afterthought to someone else as well, signing a slip 'on account'. He took his time, discussing the relative merits of various blooms.

I stood inhaling the scents, astonished by so many flowers in winter. Before I realised what he had done the manageress was leaning forward to pin white rosebuds to my coat. The tidemarks of her orange foundation were visible at such close quarters and the line of her eyebrows below the thin pencilled arches. She asked rhetorically, gushingly what a nice daddy I had, simpering at Evelyn as she spoke. Evelyn's expression was amused, conspiratorial. I did not repudiate him.

In the car he transferred the corsage from my coat, folded in the back with his, to my dress. As he fumbled with the pin I studied the lines around his eyes, the grey hairs over his ears. He gave the flowers a final adjustment and smiled at me. I could not look at his face. I watched him furtively as he drove, turning away at the little smiles he gave me when he realised I was looking.

I thought of his large hands, startlingly white on Mrs Deveraux' navy suit, his cajoling murmur. His kindness was nothing to him. There was nothing special at all about his soft endearments in the night when I had bad dreams. His easy careless comforting signified no strength of feeling on his part. I glowered at him in the foggy dusk. I could sense his tense tiredness and quashed my sympathy. When he stopped I feigned sleep and he gently tucked the plaid rug around me before he drove on. I tried hard not to cry. I dared not ask after having missed the opportunity, and my desolation soon yielded to increasing desperation for the loo.

4

The speech was finished, prayers commenced, then the drums rolled. Thwack! The head flew sharply up from the block and bounced into the crowd.

'Alexandria! What on earth do you think you're doing?'

'You told me to play quietly,' I said sulkily.

'I didn't tell you to play with knives.' Evelyn tied his dressing gown closer around himself and ran his hand through his hair.

'It's not a knife. It's a sword. The king gave permission to send to France for a swordsman,' I explained. I laid the corpse in the waiting shoe box and retrieved the head. (The doll broken by my cousins often came in handy for more violent enactments.) My other dolls were ranged round the improvised scaffold, supplemented by my stuffed animals and china figures off the mantel.

Evelyn was clutching his hair again. 'Give me the knife.' His tone was weary, long-suffering. It would be no use arguing with him now. He went back to bed, emphatically shutting his door, not quite a slam. He was not the most stoical of patients, irritably spurning my ministrations and insisting I leave him alone. But he had attended to me assiduously, sitting up all night when my flu was at its worst. Now I was on the mend and he was in the grip of the virus.

Later he found me a carved letter-opener to use as a sword and admired my drawing. He had given me a roll of wallpaper lining with my Christmas stocking. I was planning to draw something big enough to go around my entire bedroom, but had not yet had the right idea. Meanwhile, my drawings reflected a widening range of reading. Bunker Hill and Bull Run and wagon trains gave way to Bosworth, Hastings, Florence Nightingale at Scutari. I was bogged down in an interminable Waterloo, heartily sick of the hundreds and hundreds of tiny figures, the difficulty of drawing horses.

'I'm not surprised you've had enough. All that blood and gore. It's not normal,' Evelyn said.

'Didn't you have soldiers when you were a boy?'

'That's different. I preferred my train set anyway.'

'I haven't got a train set.'

It was William who initially weaned me off epic battle scenes. He was at art school and under his auspices I began to turn out bowls of fruit and flower arrangements. He gave me more futile lessons on drawing horses and people, divided my paper with faint pencil lines into proper perspectives, taught me to blend colours in crayon or pencil.

Mrs Carey accepted my new floral studies with unaffected delight. 'How lovely! I knew you could draw *nicely*.'

We first met William one Sunday at the Royal Academy. He was with Tim. We had not seen Tim since before Christmas and I was torn between excitement at seeing him again and pique that he had not let us know he was in town. They came back to the flat with us. William and I made rounds of buttered toast and tea while Tim and Evelyn caught up on all their news. Evelyn treated us all to a Chinese meal in the evening.

The result of this meeting was that William became my regular babysitter. Previous arrangements had been precarious and ad hoc, Evelyn or myself usually taking exception to them. William took to arriving early to have earnest intellectual discussions about Art with Evelyn while he was preparing to go out. This also meant that he ate with us, or with me if Evelyn was eating out. He ate ceaselessly the whole time and soon we began to lay in extra stores of bread and cheese, biscuits and fruit for William's nights.

He looked hungry, ragged and bony, always in the same paint-spattered corduroys and turtle-necked jumper. I liked him. He imparted his knowledge without condescension, nor was he hearty or gushing. Also his game of chess was not very much better than mine, so that I could sometimes win. He could never make me go to bed – he never tried very hard – but would diffidently suggest when it was late that it might be as well as for both of us if I was in bed when Evelyn got home.

It was not surprising that I was heartily bored in school art sessions. My opportunity for protest came one afternoon when the usual coloured paper and paste and paper doilies had been distributed for the making of Mother's Day cards. I did not participate but sat idly waiting to be noticed, announcing calmly that I did not have a mother when rebuked. My insouciance of manner goaded the teacher into brusquely telling me to make a card for an aunt or grandmother instead. With a sense of ill usage I toyed with scraps of paper and suddenly I recalled constructing just such a card with paper lace the previous year for Mother's Day. Overcome by tears I slipped away.

I found my coat and ran across the playground, expecting momentarily to be noticed and apprehended. My only thought was to get to Evelyn. I sniffled interminably throughout the bus journey, in the lift up to his office. I burst into his office without going through Mrs Deveraux' room but no one was there. I was beginning to feel silly now and decided to wait in the boardroom to avoid the secretaries.

Serious men in suits sat all round the big table, which was almost hidden by blotters, documents, ashtrays. Evelyn was standing at the blackboard giving a talk. They all looked at me. I fled.

I was surprised when Evelyn hurried after me, even more

surprised that he wasn't angry. In his office he gave me his handkerchief, tidied my hair, took me on his knees. He coaxed from me how I had been reprimanded for not making a Mother's Day card, how unsympathetic the teacher had been, how I had made one last year, destined never to be given. I had not started the escapade with a scrap of grief but now had worked myself into such a state that Evelyn did not question my interpretation of events. I was allowed to sit on his lap for a while and then we had tea and biscuits before he went back into his meeting.

Evelyn was sufficiently moved by my distress to rearrange his evening. William was put off and I joined Evelyn and his European representative for a meal out. We went back to the flat first for drinks and I changed from my uniform to my red velvet dress. Evelyn came up to do my hair.

'Evelyn, is he the biggest man in the world?'

'Don't be rude.' But he was laughing.

'Uncle' Dieter was as tall as Evelyn and twice as wide. He was swathed in yards of pinstripe and his tie looked like string against the expanse of white shirt front. My hand had disappeared in his handshake as he congratulated Evelyn on my acquisition.

More and more whisky disappeared down his throat as he regaled Evelyn with anecdotes about their customers, their competition. Sometimes he was laughing so much he could scarcely deliver the punch line.

At last I whispered to Evelyn, 'I'm starving.'

We went out and ate a lavish and interminable meal. More wine, more bread, more coffee was called for. Uncle Dieter, abandoning his tales of men he had met on his travels, assumed a soft and persuasive tone, describing at length the benefits that would accrue to Evelyn and to the firm if only Evelyn would authorise something or other.

Evelyn laughed and cut him short. 'Dieter, we've been

through all that. I don't think we can swing it yet. You must learn to bide your time.'

'Time! It will be too late, I tell you! If you would only . . .

'Now that's enough. I know perfectly well you could sell me my own watch. I'm too tired to go into it all again.'

'But Evelyn, look here.' Carefully he calmed his voice.

'Not tonight, Dieter.'

'Yes, now, *now*!' His face grew redder, he pounded the table with his fist and the coffee cups jumped. 'You never take me seriously. I will resign!'

'Whatever you like, my dear fellow. But not tonight. The poor child's asleep on her feet.'

He glared at Evelyn with bulging pale eyes, drained his glass. When Evelyn had paid he said sullenly, 'Tomorrow I get work with the Americans. They appreciate get up and go.'

'It's up to you,' Evelyn said indifferently, helping me with my coat, fussing satisfactorily over me. I rubbed against Evelyn, disquieted by Dieter's ill temper.

In the taxi Uncle Dieter was unaccustomedly silent and in the light of the flat I realised he was crying. He begged Evelyn's pardon again and again, told Evelyn that he was his only friend in the world, lapsed soon into his own language. Tears coursed down his face, he trumpeted into a large handkerchief. Evelyn hurried me off to bed.

'Is he drunk, Evelyn?'

'I daresay. It's late, you must sleep at once.'

'Then you must be drunk too.'

'Of all the cheek.'

'But you've drunk as much as him. Why is he sad?'

'Well, he's had a trying time with the Board today.'

'Will they fire him?'

'Of course not. He's very good. He wants to expand his

territory too far too soon and the Board won't agree. He thinks if I would back him more clearly they would.'

'Would they?'

'It's nothing to do with me. It's up to Richard.'

'Evelyn, men don't cry.'

'Don't be ridiculous. Everybody cries sometimes.'

Evelyn overslept in the morning. Eventually I dressed and ate breakfast, washed the glasses and plates, put away the cheese board.

'Alexandria. Why aren't you at school?' Evelyn looked ill and seedy in his dressing gown.

'You didn't wake me up. I can't go in late.'

Evelyn drew his mouth in but said nothing. He began to make coffee.

'Poor Evelyn. Have you got a bad stomach?'

After lunch he took me to school himself and saw the headmaster to complain about the incident the previous afternoon. Not only had I been treated with shocking callousness, but no one had appeared to realise I was missing. I begged Evelyn not to complain. I knew it would only make matters worse. I knew too that the whole mess was my own fault.

That night William came to mind me. I had not been in bed long enough to fall asleep before Evelyn returned. I could discern the ringing voice of Uncle Dieter as well as other voices. I rumpled my hair, rubbed my eyes vigorously and went down. With Uncle Richard and another man, Evelyn and Uncle Dieter were settling down to play cards. I sat on Evelyn, kibitzed Uncle Richard and drank Ribena with lemonade, watching the stack of money in front of Uncle Richard growing steadily. Evelyn slept even later the next morning but it was Saturday.

It was not long after the visit of Evelyn's European representative that Evelyn undertook another trip to the United States. Our final days together were strained. My tears, entreaties, threats were all useless. Evelyn would not take me with him.

'Now enough nonsense, Alex. It was agreed that I would have to be away sometimes. It was part of the bargain. You're not keeping your end up.'

'I don't care. I wish I was dead.'

'You're being quite absurd. It's only for a few weeks.'

On the morning of his departure he held me firmly by the shoulders and looked at me with stern eyes. I wasn't to give Aunt Louisa and Aunt Hetty a hard time, they were old and frail. I had given my word and must keep it. He softened, cajoled, embraced me.

'I hate you,' I said calmly and he was gone before I could unsay it. I knew I would never see Evelyn again. My last words were irrevocable. I imagined his plane plummeting into the sea, his mangled corpse under the wheels of a yellow taxi, his hired car concertina'd against a truck. I sobbed myself to sleep each night, each night woke screaming from nightmares. My aunts could not console me.

But on the whole I enjoyed myself staying with Aunt Louisa and Aunt Hetty. The journey to school was interminable but after the first week it was the Easter holidays. One of their cats had a litter of kittens I spent hours with. I helped them with cooking and baking, and every night we had a pudding with our evening meal. (Evelyn never bothered, but provided fresh fruit.) I was allowed to have the tom cat on the end of my bed at night. We went on picnics to Box Hill and Hampton Court and the seaside in their little round car.

I received three post cards and two air letters from Evelyn, each signed 'all my love'. I awaited the inevitable telegram announcing his death with resignation. He arrived back in due course, seeming genuinely pleased to see me. I wondered if he had cried in the night as I had during our separation. I could not imagine it. It seemed my due therefore that I should be allowed to have one of the kittens. But I was surprised at the speed of Evelyn's capitulation.

5

I did not meet any paternal grandmother until almost a year after I had arrived in London. She lived most of the time in the south of France and made one or two trips a year to London. Evelyn had not intended that I should meet her even then, but I wore him down with wheedling and sulks. It was too unjust for words that I could not see my own grandmother.

We met over tea in a sumptuous hotel, far grander than the hotel I had stayed at in New York. The waiters wore tail coats, the musicians wore dinner jackets and the tea service was silver. It did not seem possible that someone so tiny had given birth to a giant like Evelyn; she was not much taller than I in her high court shoes.

I could not help staring as the fuss over what to order, how I was to address her, was settled. She was nothing like my Grandma Mahoney or indeed any other grandmother. Her hair was an improbable shade of dark red and her face elaborately made up. The jaunty hat matched her bag and shoes and the piping of her suit. I was bidden to call her 'Grandmère'. (Subsequently, with Evelyn, I called her 'Grandmother'. Evelyn always referred to her as 'Blanche' or as 'your grandmother', never as 'mother'.)

'It hardly seems possible,' she said herself. 'Of course I was very young when I married poor dear Aubrey. What a pity she's so tall. I suppose you picked that dowdy frock, Evelyn.'

'Now Blanchie,' said her husband peaceably, leaning forward to light her cigarette. He smiled at Evelyn in mute conciliation. I supposed he must be younger than her, but he was still quite old and looked most odd.

'My poor baby, you really don't know about women's things at all, do you? Why don't I take Alexandria shopping? Wouldn't that be lovely, darling?'

'Don't be ridiculous, mother, you'd be bored silly,' Evelyn said sharply.

'You could do with some sprucing up yourself, darling, you're letting yourself go shockingly.'

I scrutinised Evelyn in bewilderment. He was impeccably turned out, pressed and polished, as he always was. She could not possibly be suggesting that he was running to fat either. I stolidly ate cake as my grandmother chattered on, making a noncommittal noise in my throat when she asked me if something wouldn't be lovely, darling, shopping, a visit to her in France, a meal together.

Evelyn was increasingly irritable and attended as little to his tea as his mother. She stubbed out half smoked cigarettes in the middle of the dainty cakes abandoned on her plate and prised out the ends from the ivory holder with long red nails, shiny as fresh blood. Only my step-grandfather, Larry, was unruffled, attending assiduously to his wife, always with his lighter ready. For Evelyn he had a running commentary of mime; raised brows, shrugs, gestures and many conspiratorial smiles. Evelyn seemed uncomfortable with his height for once, like a boy, twisting in his chair, hunching sulkily when he stood.

'What a pity she's so tall,' my grandmother said again as we were leaving.

'No taller than Diana at that age,' Evelyn said. 'Aren't you going to ask after your daughter?' I knew that Evelyn had a sister who lived in Hong Kong and had three sons. I supposed vaguely that both these circumstances had prevented her from inviting me to live with her upon my bereavement.

'Yes, of course, how is she, darling?' I suffered her to kiss the air near my cheek. 'So like poor dear Alec. He was my favourite, you know.' Evelyn bent down and they both kissed the air. She retained him by the lapel, looked at his face for a moment. 'You were such a beautiful little boy.' She sighed and her husband smirked. 'It's been lovely, darling.'

Outside Evelyn strode away so quickly that I could not keep up. Presently he waited for me and held out his hand as I drew near.

'Poor Evelyn. You need a drink.'

'Yes, love.' He squeezed my hand hard. 'I'm sorry. I knew I shouldn't have let you come.'

'That pub is open. I can wait for you if you want.'

He laughed. 'I'm not that desperate. But it's very thoughtful, love.'

At home Evelyn drained off his glass at the sideboard and refilled it before he sat down.

'It must be incredibly expensive to stay at that hotel.' I had been horrified at the amount Evelyn had put down, at the waste of such costly cake.

'Undoubtedly. But I'm sure they're not staying there, she'd just like me to think so.'

'What for?'

'To impress me.'

'How silly. Evelyn, his hair didn't look real.' I had finally worked out why Larry looked so odd. His hair was like patent leather on top, with frizzy grey bits emerging at the sides.

'That's probably because it isn't real.'

'How does he keep it on?'

'With a drawing pin through the crown of his head.' Evelyn indicated.

I considered this, looked at Evelyn's impassive face. 'Don't tease.' He relaxed into a smile and allowed me to perch on his knees. 'Do I really look like my father?'

'Not very. There's a certain family resemblance. Not that Blanche would know anyway. She only saw him twice after he was two.'

'What do you mean?'

I was staggered to learn that Evelyn's mother had left when he was seven, my father only two. 'Poor Evelyn.'

'Don't be absurd, chimp. We did very well without her. My father was a very nice man, and we had Aunt Louisa, and, really, I'm sure we were much better off.' He pulled me against him. 'It wasn't the same as it was for you.'

Not long after this meeting with Evelyn's mother, his sister and her husband came back to England on long leave. (Uncle Gordon was with the Colonial Civil Service.) Aunt Diana had very much Evelyn's looks but was ample, matronly, with more grey in her hair. She was cross with Evelyn over the business. 'How could you, Evelyn? You know I don't let her see the boys.'

Evelyn shrugged. 'She wanted to see her grandmother. I thought she might as well see for herself.'

Embarrassed under my aunt's scrutiny, I cuddled my sturdy adolescent kitten more closely, kissed it. Uncle Gordon turned his attention to me.

'It's a lovely cat. What's its name?'

'Berengaria.'

'That's a big name for a small cat.'

'She's called Berry for short.' I allowed him to hold the animal.

He stroked her, asked all about her, let her get away as she'd been trying to do for ages. Uncle Gordon benevolently watched the reunion of brother and sister as he chatted to me.

Despite her disapproval, Aunt Diana asked all about her mother, extracted every detail of the meeting from Evelyn.

Evelyn took a great deal of care over the meal, brought out the best china and glasses and linen, polished the silver, deliberated on wines.

'Why don't we just go out, Evelyn?' I'd asked as he rushed around, home early from work.

'Well, in their job they're out all the time. I'm sure they'd rather eat here.'

But I perceived now that they had arrived that Evelyn was making a point. Aunt Diana could comment on the shambles of my state schooling, wonder that Evelyn should allow me to have a kitten or see my grandmother but she would be left in no doubt as to Evelyn's ability to provide meals for me. Nor, to be fair, did she remark on my outfit or appearance.

'Shall I tell her I get this to eat every night?' I asked Evelyn as I put the vegetables into serving bowls and he attended to the salmon steaks.

'Don't expect a taste of wine,' he said sternly, but grinned and patted my shoulder.

The meal passed off without a hitch and soon I was sent to bed. I made a fuss about finding Berry to take up with me, having Evelyn tuck me up.

'You're not very alike,' I told him. 'Except for looks.'

'I never supposed we were.'

'Does she not like Grandmother because she's divorced?'

'I don't suppose that has much to do with it.'

'Then why?'

'You mind your own business. And you're not to ask her,' he added hastily.

'I don't think I like Grandmother much either. Are divorced people not very nice?'

'Alexandria! What a dreadful thing to say. Divorce is a private matter, it's nothing to do with whether people are likeable or not.'

'Well I don't know. I don't know any other divorced people.'

'You do as a matter of fact.'

'Who?'

'It's not your business. Enough stalling, it's time you were asleep.'

'Are you divorced?'

'No, I am not divorced, nor married, nor anything except thoroughly out of patience with impertinent little girls.'

Evelyn's levity over such a shocking matter was not surprising once I had thought it over. His views on religion seemed equally flippant, and the two were not unconnected. In my experience, the most scandalous and unimaginable depravity that one could conceive was summed up in 'divorce'. It meant roasting in hell for all eternity. But then, Evelyn didn't appear to believe in hell either.

6

Diana and Gordon's long leave provided Evelyn with an easy solution to arrangements for the summer break. A week after the end of term Evelyn drove me up to Hellisford, old Uncle Cecil's large house outside Sheffield where we had spent time last summer and at Christmas and Easter. Aunt Diana and her family were already there. Uncle Cecil was in good spirits with his house so full. In addition, his daughter Hetty, and niece Louisa came for a visit. Evelyn and Uncle Richard came for weekends and Uncle Richard spun out his business in Sheffield.

Diana's sons and Norman, Uncle Cecil's attendant, desultorily bowled and batted on the overgrown lawn and rigged up a net for tennis. (The original tennis court was too rutted and weed-choked to use.) There was not much else to do. The books were too grown-up. Uncle Richard took me up to the old nursery with tales of splendid train sets and Victorian dolls' houses, but the toys were long gone. All that was unearthed was a stack of yellowing *Gems* and *Magnets* which Uncle Richard and Uncle Gordon spent the rest of the weekend reading. I thought walking over the moors monotonous and the ground was treacherous, soggy and honeycombed with hidden holes.

My cousin Christopher was thirteen and solidly built, not quite fat, but not much taller than me. He resented this and made constant remarks about my size. He was a bully as well, with cunning methods of pinching and twisting that left no mark. With the adults he was obsequious. It amused me that his attempts at being ingratiating with Evelyn merely irritated him. He complained a great deal about his elder brothers' treatment of him while stigmatising me as a tell-tale and cry-baby.

Nicky appeared only occasionally for weekends. He was at medical school. John was seventeen and easygoing, usually to be relied on to clout Chris if I complained directly to him, and to dispense money for sweets. But sometimes he was exasperated and vanished on long walks or told us to clear off.

Uncle Gordon, as was to be expected, adjudicated diplo-matically, but his wife had less patience and little sympathy. Uncle Cecil would usually take my part, working himself into a rage, summoning Diana and saying he would not have me bullied in his house. But Evelyn told me I must not upset him all the time, he was very old; I must try and get my difficulties resolved myself.

In short, I was suitably martyred, crying every night for Evelyn and Berry, unloved, ill-used. I lurked near the adults, avoiding Chris as much as possible, ignoring suggestions that I run along and play. When Evelyn arrived for the weekend I would hurl myself at him exuberantly and fawn on him.

'Really, Evelyn, she's too big for that,' Aunt Diana would say.

Evelyn never said I was too big for his lap. He would say that it was hot or late, that he was old or tired, but he never blamed me. He always settled me more securely or stroked or hugged me in response to her remonstrances.

The variant was, 'It's time she grew out of that.' Diana advocated leaving me to myself if I had dreams in the night. 'We were always left.'

'Not by Daddy,' flashed Evelyn.

It was always Uncle Gordon who came in the night when Evelyn wasn't there. In the evening when they played bridge Uncle Gordon let me see his hand. Chris and John played if there were no other adults. Uncle Cecil said he was too old and watched the family tableau benevolently until he dozed. Uncle Richard too was very helpful about teaching bridge.

'Evelyn, do you play bridge?' I asked when he arrived at the weekend.

'Not if I can avoid it.'

The adults laughed.

'Why not?'

'Because he's no good at it,' grinned Uncle Richard.

It was much better with Evelyn there. No one bothered me and Evelyn attended to me more than anyone did when he was away. He shielded me also from Aunt Diana. While he was there she never told me not to whine or to act my age. I made a point of making Evelyn fuss over me and he played up to it. I always had Evelyn do my hair though my aunt insisted I was old enough to manage for myself. In fact, I did mostly now, but Evelyn still did it for me a few times a week to be sure it wasn't tangled, when I was unwell or if the occasion was important.

'You should never have let her have the animal,' I heard her tell Evelyn once when there was difficulty about arranging feeding for Berry one weekend that Mrs Carey was away too.

'It was nothing to do with me,' Evelyn said irritably. 'Louisa painted me into the corner. Besides, I can't see it does any harm.'

'That child has you wrapped round her little finger.'

In the afternoons the Mackie males and Norman and Uncle Richard played cricket while Evelyn dozed with a book. Eventually Gordon and Richard would join Evelyn on the sidelines, Richard bright pink, Gordon wiping his gleaming bald head and spectacles with a handkerchief. Once we went to a neighbouring village for a proper cricket match. Uncle Richard, immaculate in white, played intermittently, ambling up to the stumps to bounce a ball off the ground, or standing about in padding with a bat. It was very slow and quite incomprehensible.

I was impatient with attempts at explanation. Aside from the slowness, any game that allowed bouncing the ball was contemptible. 'It's silly,' I said firmly, and as I had half suspected, that made Evelyn smile. 'You don't play.'

'I was never any good. I've never been much good at games.'

This staggered me. He was large and strong and never clumsy. What really awed me was his supreme indifference. It was of no consequence to him. I thought of the interminable games at my boarding school, how miserable my life was made by my incompetence. Perhaps, I thought doubtfully, it was different at Evelyn's school. Or, more probably, he had been clever instead.

'You spoil her,' Aunt Diana told Evelyn when I sat up late in the evenings.

Evelyn would shrug and say, 'No doubt she'll be sent to bed early enough in the week when I'm not here. It's not as if she has school in the morning.'

Evelyn went away on business and did not come up to Hellisford for a while. Uncle Gordon too was away and I could not bear being at the mercy of Chris and Aunt Diana. I snubbed her attempts to be nice to me; I would not forgive her.

It was true that I was to big for Evelyn's lap and for having nightmares and for telling tales. It was true too that Evelyn spoiled me. But she did not understand. I did not have Evelyn wrapped around my little finger at all. That was the whole point. Evelyn indulged me because it was my entitlement, my compensation for not being wanted.

It occurred to me that I had no need to endure such persecution. I counted my money, the pound Evelyn had given me for emergencies, the ten shillings that Uncle Richard had tipped me, assorted similar gratuities from the others, my mainly unspent pocket money. I wheedled further final coins from John and Norman and Uncle Cecil.

The next market day I caught the bus into Sheffield from the village and got a train to London. I was prepared with suitable lies if anyone challenged my travelling alone, but no one did. I walked home from St Pancras and let myself in with my key, planning how I would manage without being seen until Evelyn came back from his business trip.

But he was already back. Wet headed, fresh from his bath, he sat drinking beer. He jumped up, tying his dressing gown and exclaiming angrily.

'When did you get back?' I managed with a semblance of casualness.

'Never mind me. What's the meaning of this?'

'They were horrid to me,' I mumbled.

'Well I don't blame them,' he retorted and stomped upstairs.

I picked up the sleeping tabby and fondled her, trying not to think about Evelyn's wrath. Soon he was dressed and came down again. He poured a glass of whisky to have with the beer.

'How many times do I have to tell you not to maul that poor animal? You can see perfectly well she wants to get down.'

'She's pleased to see me. *She's* missed me.' But I prudently set Berry down.

Evelyn made me tell him how I'd run away and sat silently, frowning. He looked at me with a measuring look that I knew meant I was to be outflanked.

'Does it never occur to you that you always think everyone is being horrid to you?'

'Well they are.'

'Why should they be? Don't you think you inflate things out of proportion sometimes?'

After a long silence I warily whispered, 'No.'

'I know perfectly well Diana can be overbearing but she's certainly not unkind or vindictive. You're being quite absurd.'

'I'm not.'

'She's quite right, I've spoiled you shockingly. I don't know how you had the cheek. I suppose it didn't occur to you that they would worry at Hellisford?'

'They won't. They'll be glad to be rid of me.'

'Poor old Cecil, an upset like this could kill him.' He fetched another bottle of beer. 'And what the devil am I supposed to do with you? I'll have to cancel my evening. Who's to look after you with William and Mrs Carey away?'

'I can come with you.'

'No, you can't.' He was still very angry, more angry than I could remember. I wondered if he would hit me. I began to cry. He did not relent. 'You're filthy. Go and get in the bath.'

I escaped gratefully upstairs. It was true. Everyone was always horrid to me. No one loved me. I cried and cried. Tim's handiwork around the walls was no comfort. Tim never came now I was here.

Still damp, I crept down to the bend in the stairs to listen to Evelyn on the telephone. He was chatting inconsequentially to Diana and presently asked if he could have a word with me. After some evasion he said bluntly, 'In other words, here it is tea time and no one's seen her since breakfast? . . . Well I would be worried if I was you . . . I'm not overreacting, I assure you . . . Your parental supervision and responsibility is such that Alex has got a bus into Sheffield, got a train to London and reached home without any of you at all even noticing she was gone. If you think . . .' Battle was joined and they argued furiously, '. . . and if you ever dare give me another syllable about irresponsibility and tell me how badly I've managed . . . And what about your little thug? . . .' Soon he hung up on his sister and I heard the chink of the decanter in the dining-room.

'Evelyn. I'm sorry,' I said piteously.

'All very well to be sorry now,' he said severely. The phone rang. 'No, leave it. I can't face her going on at me any more.'

But Aunt Diana was persistent, ringing back repeatedly, letting it ring for ages. Soon Evelyn said we would go out for a meal as he hadn't anything in. I had left my things behind and Evelyn did my hair with his own silver-backed brush. I watched him in the wardrobe mirror, his fingers jerking at my hair, looked at his stern face, his mouth vanished to a slot. It was worse than I could have imagined. Tears started. He set the brush aside and adjusted his tie in the glass.

'All right, chimp, all right.' He hugged me from behind and groped for his handkerchief. But I couldn't stop weeping. 'Never mind, you're here now.' He patted me. 'Oh God, don't, it's all right, love.' He managed to turn me against him and I clung to him, wishing desperately that his comforting was any more significant than the soft absurdities he murmured when Berry greedily received his stroking. But he did not impatiently move away, and when at last the renewed ringing of the telephone impinged, he gave me a tight hug before he released me. He tidied my hair and kissed the top of my head, smiling cajolingly at me in the mirror. As soon as I had washed my face we hurried conspiratorily away, hand in hand, my summer weight cardigan with imitation pearl buttons over his arm like a ladies' fur stole, leaving the telephone echoing in the empty hall.

7

In the early days, apprehension of Evelyn's unpredictability had overshadowed my life with him. But I learned that he was easily got round, and far too fundamentally easy going to sustain a mood of ill humour. I recovered quickly enough from my very real fright at his anger over my running away from Hellisford to create a scene when he drove me back there at the weekend.

His abstracted moods I found more difficult. Sometimes the weekends would slip away, nothing accomplished, as Evelyn slept late into the afternoons, eventually rising to lie on the settee, desultorily drinking and listening to his old jazz records. Neither my presence nor my promptings would accomplish the organisation of grocery shopping or even an outing.

My evident invisibility on such occasions panicked me far more than his anger, often exasperatedly roused in the end by my crude stratagems to draw his attention. But usually he was contrite, commended my foresight in having slipped out early for bread and a few staples, treated me to a meal out. He would then make an effort to be better organised for a few weekends before lapsing again into indolence.

After the holidays Evelyn seemed a bit more energetic, but this meant that he arranged his weekend evenings without me, summoning William to come and mind me.

In that autumn, just before I turned eleven, Joe, George and Matthew arrived in London. They all had rooms in the same house as William. With unerring instinct they gravitated to Evelyn at the housewarming party that William insisted Evelyn attend. The sedate tea Evelyn provided in return degenerated into a long drinking session as soon as the mounds of sandwiches and cold chicken and potato salad, trifle and walnut cake had been disposed of. Thereafter it seemed at times as if they never went home.

Evelyn adjudicated their intense arguments about Marx and Mao and Maynard Keynes. But it was a thankless task and they would usually round on him in the end. Often he would provoke them, throwing an incomprehensible name or slogan like a hand grenade into the debate and sit grinning at the babel of dissent as they harangued one another or angrily denounced him.

The crate of bottled beer that Evelyn kept in and occasionally changed at the off licence was now changed almost weekly and supplemented by an additional crate. He ordered modestly priced wine by the dozen, cheaper than he was accustomed to buy, for them to wash down the Sunday dinners they began to show up for regularly.

'Don't they ever eat at home?' I grumbled.

'I don't suppose so. They haven't really got cooking facilities, just a gas ring.'

'They should eat out.'

'Well, I don't imagine they have much money. It gets very depressing eating in cafés all the time.'

Evelyn was happy to pay for meat and drink, but he organised the young men into doing the menial work. Early Sunday afternoon found them peeling potatoes with their first beer; later they washed up and dried everything before Evelyn handed round whisky. Evelyn was an unexpectedly genial host, giving every indication of enjoying a mob eating him out of house and home.

As winter came on it seemed that they had moved in. More often than not at least one of them would come round in the evening, punctilious about refusing to scavenge a meal, but eager to turn the gas up and crouch before the fire with Evelyn's beer, and invariably persuaded to decimate the cheese board later in the evening.

They paid little attention to me and I ignored them, scarcely troubling to distinguish them at first. Joe was the charmer, witty and winning, better looking and better dressed than his compatriots. George and Matthew were taller, almost as tall as Evelyn. But George was awkward and gangling, hiding timidly behind his black-rimmed glasses while Matthew was much beefier than Evelyn. All had the decided opinions of very young men.

'Who is Marx?' I asked Evelyn. Even not attending to the conversation I could not be unaware of the name.

'He wrote the *Communist Manifesto*.'

'*Communist!* ' I was appalled. 'Are they communists?'

'It's part of the syllabus. If you read Politics you do Marx.' Evelyn was amused. 'Anyway, why shouldn't they be communists?'

'Well . . .' I was flummoxed. 'It's wicked.'

'Who tells you that? I thought you said you might be communist.'

'I did not! I never said anything like that!'

'You said you were thinking about being socialist instead of Liberal.'

'That's different!'

'No, it's not, it's all in favour of the same things.'

'Don't tease, Evelyn.'

Matthew was something of a loner, what social life he had revolving around political and church activities. Joe quickly found his feet in London and did not often have time for us. But George relied heavily on Evelyn. Evelyn would be asked to look at his draft essays, recommend books, criticise his arguments in advance of deadlines and tutorials.

I resented George. I seldom had Evelyn to myself any more and we entertained in more instead of Evelyn taking me out. I felt too that sometimes Evelyn would have preferred him not to come if he was too tired or in too frivolous a mood to read George's cramp-fisted discourses on Smith and Ricardo, or Weber and Hegel, or hear the latest instalment in the sagas of his landlord's disobligingness over the broken window in his room or the faulty geyser or the noisy neighbours.

'Why does he have to come all the time?' I grumbled.

'Why not? It's not easy settling into a new country, making friends.'

'Joe says he's too busy to come.'

'Well Joe has rather more money to spend on going out than George.'

William was also was busy with work and socialising and increasingly often George would turn up instead of William to babysit. Sometimes we didn't know who would come but Evelyn didn't mind as long as someone did, and he was never let down. George was diffident about telling me what to do, but if I refused to go to bed he would threaten to tell Evelyn I had been naughty. He didn't care whether I read until all hours in my room.

Evelyn dismissed my pleadings that I preferred William, lectured me on my rudeness, reiterated that I had no idea what it was like to be alone in a foreign country. I did of course; it was plain that there was no reasoning with him. I tried to be nicer to George. He was always polite but was quite indifferent to me. And I still resented him. Sometimes he would come on outings with us so that I was wedged in the back of the car. George came swimming with us a few times but that was not a success. He disliked the chlorinated institutional pool and was helpless without his glasses. Afterwards he huddled miserably in front of our fire so that there was not even space for me to edge in to dry my hair.

Often he would keep Evelyn up after he returned from his evening out, putting the world to rights until the small hours before finally settling down to sleep in a mountain of blankets on the armchair and sofa cushions in the living-room. Evelyn never had the heart to send him home in the rain.

In the end George too began to find his feet. He had more confidence in his abilities after months of encouragement and criticism from Evelyn. He looked smarter too under Evelyn's direction. Evelyn gave him quite a few shirts and ties, and some jumpers and trousers, and all Evelyn's clothes were well made. They were almost the same height although George was thinner. Evelyn advised George on the purchase of shoes and a good suit.

George and Matthew came regularly for Sunday dinner, and Joe too often turned up later, when the meal was nearly ready and the vegetables long since prepared. I liked having the opportunity to make cakes or lavish desserts for a large enough and suitably appreciative audience.

Uncle Richard came sometimes on Sunday too and the young men would try their arguments on him, attacking capitalism and imperialism. Uncle Richard was unpredictable; he might equally defend his position as a factory owner so deftly that they were sometimes outflanked or tell them blandly that they were perfectly right, the British had used their country abominably, as the mood took him. He encouraged their visionary discourses on the imminent independence of their country, which seldom failed to degenerate into a heated debate on the finer points of future policy.

I was astonished at Evelyn's patient hospitality, and more than a little jealous. Aside from my hitherto undisputed proprietorship, I felt obscurely that Evelyn's kindness to others devalued his kindness to me. Generally he allowed my displays of possessiveness, but could be merciless in publicly repudiating any gesture that he felt was intended as a slight to anyone else present.

Verbal reprimands were more private, not, I supposed sulkily, to spare me, but to save George any embarrassment. It was in vain that I protested that I was not prejudiced. Evelyn was implacable that I certainly acted prejudiced and that was how I would be judged. It was a typical outflanking manoeuvre on Evelyn's part, I felt, that I was being blamed for not liking black people, when it was only a question of not liking George, which was really quite reasonable.

Yet it was difficult to nurse these very legitimate grievances. I had no real reason to suppose I was not, so to speak, in full possession of the field. We were conspirators, partners. As Evelyn would inform George regretfully that we were just going out, I would hurry to change so that we could give verisimilitude to the lie by leaving the house as soon as George had consumed a quick drink. I had only to draw in my mouth disapprovingly for plausible previous arrangements to spring to Evelyn's lips in response to unwanted invitations from zealous mothers of schoolmates. The lateness of my bedtimes, the number of Evelyn's evenings out, went unmentioned at Crystal Palace.

If Evelyn stayed out late in the evenings, returning redolent of alien smells like Berry returning after a nocturnal prowl, he always peeked in at my door, sometimes looking for ages. He would sit on the edge of the bed to talk for a few minutes if he knew I was awake, just as Berry returned to curl at my feet after her adventures in the night.

8

Nocturnal life seemed oddly disconnected with the mundane routine of the day. It was not merely the contrast between Evelyn's curt, almost edgy early morning manner and his gentleness in the night when I had bad dreams. Events themselves often seemed implausible; expansive conversations about the state of the nation or unexpected reminiscences of Evelyn's childhood were not unknown. With Berry free to come and go, I was often vaguely aware of her snuggling into the bend of my knees, or assiduously licking herself, sleepily reassured that Evelyn was still up by faint sounds of music or conversation. I was not surprised that he slept so much at the weekends; it sometimes seemed as if he never slept at night.

On occasion the night noises were anything but comforting. Once I was awakened after midnight by the persistent ringing of the bell. There seemed to be an interminable altercation and I set aside the book I had dozed over and went downstairs. George was vehemently insisting to an irate taxi driver that he had never seen the passenger before, that it was nothing to do with us, while the passenger drunkenly propped the doorway.

'Tim!' I ran joyously down. He attempted a wan smile and edged past George to collapse on the stairs. I was terrified to realise that his face was covered in blood. 'Tim!'

'It's six and eight on the clock, *and* all the trouble, and blood all over my cab. If I have to fetch a copper . . .'

'Don't be so *stupid*, George, pay him!' I crouched anxiously by Tim. 'Idiot! Evelyn will pay you back.' I watched as George reluctantly counted coins. 'Tip him for God's sake, don't you know anything!' I plucked a ten shilling note from his fingers and held it out to the taxi driver who grudgingly accepted it and went away, muttering angrily.

'Alex! Ten shillings, really, there was no need . . .'

'Stupid! Never mind that, help me with Tim.'

'I really don't think you should have let him in. What Evelyn will say I don't know . . .'

'He'll say you're a bloody arse and never trust you to look after me again,' I squealed. 'If you're not going to help me then get out of the way.'

George helped Tim upstairs to the living-room, and having settled him in a chair hovered about uselessly. I shouted at him to make some sweet tea and frantically ransacked the bathroom cabinet.

'I'm sorry, love,' managed Tim faintly as I gingerly attempted to wipe his face with a tea towel dipped in water diluted with Dettol.

'Are you drunk?'

'I don't think so, just foggy. I didn't think, I thought Lyn would . . .'

'It's all right Tim, it's all right.' I smoothed his hair. I realised it looked worse than it was, but I had no real idea how badly Tim was hurt. George was being no use at all, sulking now at my peremptory manner.

'Oh fuck!' said Evelyn wearily in the doorway. My school friend Bobby had told me this swear word. Evelyn took off his coat and jacket while I brought him a large drink. 'I think one for George too, love.'

Tim refused whimperingly to be taken to hospital. Evelyn deftly cleaned and anointed him with antiseptic, coaxed him to drink some sweet tea and helped him up to bed. Evelyn sent George home and bustled about making Tim comfortable, hearing how I had managed everything.

'You've done very well, chimp. Now you must put on a clean nightdress and get to bed. I'll come and see you in a minute.'

I peeked into Evelyn's room to say goodnight. Tim was shivering convulsively. I called urgently down to Evelyn, who was making up a bed downstairs for himself. He put more blankets over Tim, took his hand, told me sharply to go to bed at once. Eventually he looked into my room.

'He's not going to die, is he?'

'Of course not, it's not as bad as it looks. He's not peeing blood.'

'He won't be scarred for life?'

'Not so you'd notice. He might need some stitches. Perhaps he'll be sensible about going to hospital in the morning.'

I slept very late and when I got up, Evelyn was already up. Tim was in his underwear perched on the edge of the bed, weeping as Evelyn attempted to help him dress. I was very frightened; I had never seen a man cry before, except 'Uncle' Dieter, and that was because he had been drunk.

'Is Tim going to die?' I asked when Evelyn came downstairs with a tea tray.

'Don't be ridiculous. There's something wrong with his hand; it's quite swollen. So naturally he's convinced he'll never be able to paint again.'

'Was Tim robbed?'

'That too,' he said as he hurried back upstairs.

We went with Tim to hospital and he was admitted overnight for observation. George had informed the others that there would not be a Sunday meal, but we had to cook the meat anyway. Evelyn spent the rest of the day stretched on the sofa listening to old blues records, his book unread, a sure sign he was not in a good mood.

Tim was discharged the following day and came to stay for a while. He was not fit for work and did not wish to upset his family by turning up in such a state. His face was adorned with stitches here and there over the bruises and his bound hand was in a sling. He had been assured his hand would recover fully; nothing had been broken, but he moved stiffly.

I was glad of Tim's presence, but he was very depressed and had nothing to occupy him while his hand was useless. After school we talked over pots of tea. Tim told me of his travels, of his shipmates, of his National Service in the navy, of his youth roaming blitzed London with a sketchpad instead of going to school, of his student days at Art School. He smoked a good deal, which he did not usually. I wished he wouldn't.

'Tell me about Evelyn.'

'Well, you know about Lyn. You know him as well as I do, better these days.'

'I don't know about Evelyn at all. I know what he's *like* but I don't know *about* him.'

'I don't see the difference.' Tim fetched a beer and awkwardly opened it, snapping when I attempted to open it for him. 'If there's things you want to know about Lyn's past you'll have to ask him. It's not for me to say.'

'Tim,' I protested.

'You seem to be getting on all right here with him now.'

I nodded. 'It's most agreeable.'

Tim laughed a great deal at this, a phrase Uncle Richard was given to using, and coaxed me to show him my drawings. Soon the table was strewn with scrolls of epic battles, medieval coronations, Venetian religious processions, as well as flower arrangements and pictures of Berry on ordinary paper. I was a trifle jealous at how much she favoured Tim, always going to him rather than to me.

'What's this?'

'Nothing. It's not very good. I had to do it in school, so I didn't have enough time.'

'But what is it?'

'It's the execution of Connolly. They had to shoot him in a chair because they broke his ankles.'

'They?'

'The British.'

Tim laughed and laughed. I waited, undecided whether to take offence. He asked me to tell him about Connolly.

'Don't you know anything!'

'Well, it's not the sort of thing you get in school. Not that I went much anyway. I'm not really very clear about the details.'

I explained at length about the abortive uprising, regurgitating every lurid detail fixed in my mind by my maternal grandfather's recitals.

'What did your teacher say?'

'She said it wasn't very nice, and she wouldn't ask me to show everyone my picture anymore if I didn't draw *nice* things. She took it away to show the headmaster.'

'The headmaster? What did he say?'

'I don't know. He gave it to Evelyn on parents' evening.'

Tim was grinning now, for the first time in days. 'What did Lyn say?'

'He said it was better not to draw too much attention to myself if I didn't want a lot of busybodies interfering with us. He said I'd better draw *nice* stuff if it's just for school.'

'It's a pain, innit? Keeping your head down, being ordinary all the time, it's bad enough people knowing you're an artist.'

'Poor Tim.'

'Are you going to be an artist?'

'I don't know. I don't think I'm good enough; I can't do people very well.'

Tim avoided looking at me, opened another beer. 'There's not much money in it. If I were you I'd do something with more money.'

'Do you think Uncle Richard would give me a job?'

'You'll have to ask him.'

'I bet they don't take girls. Just for secretaries, typing all day.'

'Not much money in that either. But I don't think Richard would mind that you're a girl, he's quite open-minded really.'

'How do you know?'

'Well ask him.'

Tim stayed for almost a fortnight. I was overjoyed to have his constant company, infinitely preferred him to either William or George as a babysitter. But somehow, he and Evelyn did not seem to be getting on so well. Evelyn would be irritable after work, several times made sarcastic remarks about Tim starting on the beer so early, although I knew that Evelyn would have no compunction about drinking just as early as if he was not at work. There were no outings of the three of us as there had used to be, although Tim took me to the National Gallery on Sunday. I wept and wept when he left, but I was relieved too.

The sombre circumstances of Tim's visit left their mark. My nightmares, seldom for many months, returned almost nightly. I was terrified to be out after dark, or in poor areas such as where Bobby lived. I kept close to Evelyn and made an increasingly elaborate ritual of goodnight kisses, prolonged greeting and parting hugs.

'Where are you going, Evelyn?'

'Just out to a pub.'

'Be careful, Evelyn, don't get robbed.'

'I won't, love.'

'You might if you're not careful.'

'Well, I'll be very careful indeed, I promise. Oh love, is that what's worrying you?' He smoothed my hair. 'You really mustn't worry about such things, pet. It's most unlikely. Tim was very unlucky. And I don't think he can have been very careful either. Besides, I'm much bigger than Tim; if someone wanted to steal they'd probably look for a small man instead.'

Tim's assault reminded me uncomfortably of another violent incident that had occurred the previous spring, when I was still ten. Very late, after I had a nightmare, I had been sitting on Evelyn's lap when two men had arrived. I had only a shadowy recollection of the taller man. The shorter of the two, plump and pink, squeezed Evelyn's hands, patted his shoulder. Evelyn brusquely bade me to run along back to bed. The effusive greetings were broken off and the man turned his geniality to me, forcing Evelyn to perform a perfunctory introduction. The man laughed heartily and said something that made Evelyn grab him by the collar. I stood on the bottom step transfixed as Evelyn banged the man against the door frame, the impact of his head on the wood making a sickening repeated thud, as the taller of Evelyn's guests tried ineffectually to pull Evelyn aside. Finally freed, the man slithered down the wall to rest in a heap and his companion hurried him away. Evelyn followed them down to slam the door after them, elaborating on what would happen if the man were to show up again. I scurried up to bed. It seemed a very long time before Evelyn came to tuck me up and turn off the light. I had not dared ask him what had really puzzled me about the business; I could not imagine why anyone would call Evelyn 'Johnny'.

Other nocturnal events were merely inexplicable rather than violent. Once I had gone downstairs after a bad dream to find everything so dark I was frightened that Evelyn had gone to bed.

Unexpectedly, sinister in the gloom, I heard Evelyn laugh and murmur. Bravely peering round the door, I discerned him lying before the gas fire, his trousers faintly illuminated by the green glow of the radiogram, the skin of his long bare back gleaming orange from the gas fire, with disturbingly too many arms. Evelyn murmured again, shifted, received an answering murmur. I had not been seen yet and carefully backed out, pulling the door to. The record finished and I froze. Another dropped and when the music started again I crept back to bed, my distress forgotten in bemusement. I lay listening to the rain, considering what I had seen. As I dozed there were whisperings on the stairs, movement between Evelyn's room and the bathroom and then all was silent.

In the morning, the episode seemed so improbable that I was almost convinced I had dreamed it. Evelyn did not look as if he would ever do such a thing as lie in the dark with no shirt on. But before we left, he fetched his briefcase from the living-room and hurried upstairs with a crumpled ball of white cloth that trailed a cuff with cuff-link.

Usually though, evening signified treats, meals out or a film or a play. Sometimes we would take Aunt Louisa and Aunt Hetty to the theatre. Such occasions seemed much more festive than when we went on our own. Aunt Louisa would always have her hair freshly done, her best jewellery, incongruous court shoes. Aunt Hetty blossomed forth in beaded evening coats, pendant earrings, large rings of silver swirls or semi-precious stones, her straggling knot of hair unaccustomedly restrained by heavy ornamental combs and clips, her eyelids daringly tinted. I tried not to be jealous of how dearly Evelyn cherished them and perceived clearly that the bracing tone adopted between Evelyn and Aunt Louisa ill concealed a marked favouritism.

Occasionally we had them come to us for dinner, an

innovation since my time, usually when Evelyn felt the impulse to cook one of his lavish curry meals, an undertaking requiring several days preparation and frantic ransacking of the Cypriot shops for the requisite spices and vegetables. No one expected Evelyn to have such talents and he enjoyed, as always, revealing unlikely accomplishments. It was, he said, one of the few useful and reputable skills he had acquired out East.

Always late nights had a conspiratorial quality to them, a tacit understanding that outside perception of our nocturnal activities would be censorious. Meals out, late bedtimes, hot chocolate as a remedy for nightmares would be regarded as spoiling me disgracefully. Evelyn's evenings out, his choice of babysitters would be considered ample illustration of his unfittedness to have charge of me. It was by unspoken agreement that such unsuitable topics were little mentioned to others. But regardless of outside opinion, it was my firm conviction that we looked after each other very well.

part IV

1

The festivities surrounding the centenary of Parrish and Sons Ltd culminated in a party in Sheffield for all employees and retired employees and a guest of their choice. I had not been allowed to attend the formal dinner given for leading local and industrial luminaries, much to my indignation. The party, with buffet and dance band was held in the social club of one of the larger steelworks, hired for the occasion. The entire family was present.

Uncle Richard was everywhere, with a word for all the older folk, dancing at least once with every female of importance. The buttons on his ill-advised double-breasted dinner jacket were strained and his face pink as he laboured to ensure that no one was overlooked. His secretary, Mrs Crawford, whom I regarded as a dragon far gone in middle age, was transformed. Her tight black dress, low cut front and back, was amply, though not excessively filled. Her discreetly lightened hair was pulled on top of her head and she was lavishly made up. Her glasses were discarded for the occasion.

'Do you think she's Uncle Richard's mistress?' I asked my cousin John.

He contemplated them as they glided professionally round the dance floor. For reasons best known to himself, John had deigned to stand at the edge in my company. I was happy to allow his twenty years to add consequence to my thirteen. Also, he kept me supplied with martini and laughed at my quasi-sophisticated attempts to amuse him. 'I doubt it. She's too young for him,' John pronounced.

'Young!'

'Well, she doesn't look much over thirty.' Uncle Richard's forty-ninth birthday had occurred in the midst of the celebrations. 'Still, that doesn't seem to stop Evelyn,' John grinned. 'Or him.' He jestured to our great-uncle Theodore, much fatter and redder than Uncle Richard, jocularly chatting to several young women. He was evidently enjoying himself immensely and had already danced with most of the youngest females. The presence of his sister Louisa and his niece Diana in no way seemed to cramp his style.

I ruffled at John's comparison of Evelyn to Uncle Theodore's deplorable drooling and groping. Evelyn was distinctly ill at ease, and for now, having been endlessly civil to employees and dignitaries, was standing with Lesley, his secretary. She was overwhelmed by her red dress and, unlike Mrs Crawford, did not appear to be revelling in the event. They looked serious, not in the least flirtatious. Evelyn was doing his usual trick of perching on the edge of a table so that she didn't have to crane her neck to talk with him.

As always, I felt large and ungainly compared to Lesley. John was reassuringly taller than me, even in my evening shoes. Evelyn had disapproved of the spiky heeled shoes, castigated Sophie for allowing me to purchase them. But as I already took a women's size seven, there was little else to choose from. I was even more self-conscious of my black dress in the face of Mrs Crawford's stunning appearance. I was the wrong shape in every direction and despite Aunt Louisa's alterations, the dress was quite unflattering. Sometimes I worried that I would never stop growing. Evelyn said I was the same height as Aunt Diana at the same age, but she denied it strongly.

At this point Evelyn came over and dragged me on to the

dance floor. 'You've had quite enough to drink,' he said sharply.

'So have you.'

I was still sulking from our earlier confrontation. Foreseeing his reaction, I had not come downstairs at Hellisford until the last minute, so that there would be no time for me to remove the eyeliner and mascara and eyeshadow and lipstick I had applied ineptly. We then had a hissed row in the back of Uncle Richard's car, Evelyn insisting I must clean my face as soon as we arrived. I hid in the Ladies for a while and repinned my falling hair, but there was nothing I could do with the make-up, although I was taken aback to see the results under fluorescent light. But fortunately, the main hall was fairly dim.

'Don't push, Evelyn!'

'Well, then bloody well go where you're supposed to.'

'It's not my fault if you can't dance.' This further provocation was ignored. 'You shouldn't have asked me if you can't dance.'

'I thought you would prefer to be rebuked in private,' he said stiffly.

I was then claimed by Uncle Theodore, who remarked with laboured joviality on the fact that I was taller than him. I insisted that it was merely because of the evening shoes, and passively endured being shoved around the floor. He did not cling, but his hands were clammy and his breathing laborious. I was frightened that he would have a heart attack before the number was finished.

Uncle Sebastian smiled sympathetically as I was relinquished into his care. 'You know, that's one good thing about this wretched leg of mine. I was never much one for dancing, even before that. It makes a convenient excuse anyway.' (He had been wounded in the Great War before he was twenty.) Evelyn was now dancing with the wife of the works manager, a matronly woman scarcely reaching his shoulder. 'Evelyn was never much one for dancing either. Not his sort of thing at all. Richard was the great dancer.'

'Uncle Richard!'

'Certainly. He and Angela were out dancing every night by all accounts.'

'Angela?'

'His wife. Remarkable woman, very striking, beautiful dancer. Do excuse me, someone I must have a word with. Haven't seen them in years.'

I tottered back to where John was disdainfully propping the wall and stepped out of the shoes.

'Mum said I wasn't to let you drink anymore. So I got you that.'

The baleful look I directed at my aunt was wasted; her resplendent purple back was to me. I sipped. It was a double. We grinned.

'Look at that little creep,' John said in disgust. His brother Christopher was being feted by all the old retainers, explaining to the old dears that he would in due course inherit the mantle. I remarked bitterly on this to John.

He snorted. 'I bet that's news to Uncle Richard.'

'Why aren't you going into the firm?'

'Well, it's boring. Besides, no one's asked me. And I'm sure they'd ask me before they'd ask him!' John was doing an architecture course, rebelling at following his father into the Civil Service.

'I think they should have me instead of him. At least I'm a Parrish.'

'At least you have a few brains.'

'Did you know Uncle Richard's wife?'

'No.' He drained his drink. 'Which one did you mean?'

'How many did he have?'

'Two. His first wife died in the war. Angela. I must have met the other one but I don't remember, I was very little.'

'What happened to her?'

'She went off with another man. I don't think they were married long.'

'No one ever told me that.'

'Well they wouldn't, would they?' He elbowed me. 'Get it?'

'How did you find out?'

'I worked it out. I don't think it's any great secret they're divorced.'

'I never knew he had two wives.' I was indignant I had not been told. I watched him talking with some employees. He did not look like a ladies' man. But it wasn't his fault, after all, if he had not kept his hair and his figure as Evelyn had.

'Mum said I ought to dance with you. You don't want to dance, do you?'

'You'll only stomp all over my feet like Evelyn.'

John grimaced as the orchestra launched into a sprightly rendition of the recent Billy J. Kramer hit. 'Do you want to know a secret? This is the worst one all evening. It beats me how anyone can dance to crap like this anyway.' He spotted some empty chairs and loped over to claim them.

I was glad to sit down. I had only once before worn the shoes, for our friend George's graduation. George had asked Evelyn and myself as his guests for the ceremony. He had been grinning, uncharacteristically chirpy after the ordeal of Finals, surprised he had obtained an upper second, sneakingly miffed he had not got a First. His compatriots, Joe and Matthew, also got upper seconds. Although Matthew and George had been treated to a sumptuous celebratory meal out by Evelyn, Joe had been too busy to come. Evelyn had taken many photographs of the three in caps and gowns for the families back home.

The centenary party finally finished. The jollifications of my elders had been distinctly unedifying. I knew that I would never be seen bouncing about undignifiedly, unseemly amounts of exposed sagging flesh quivering, red-faced under thick foundation, flirting excruciatingly with equally red and flabby old men. The younger women had been distinctly vulgar too, snogging in corners with uncouth boys, or playing up to Uncle Theodore with no hint of distaste.

Despite myself, I had been flattered by the attentions of some of the apprentices. But soon they were mimicking my accent. Uncle Richard took me away to meet some people, without seeming aware of any difficulty. It did not occur to me that it was the realisation of my age as much as any haughtiness of demeanour that had caused the teasing.

'Thank God that's over with,' said Evelyn in the car. 'Don't blame me if you have a hangover in the morning.'

'Don't blame me if you have a bad stomach,' I retorted. But it was very cramped between him and John in the back of the car and much more comfortable to snuggle against Evelyn with alcohol-induced sentimentality.

It seemed pointless to have given such an expensive party. Uncle Cecil had been taken home very early by one of his married daughters. For Uncle Richard it was a chore and for Evelyn an ordeal. Still, Uncle Theodore hadn't found it a duty. I thought about the revelations about Uncle Richard. I wondered what else no one had told me about.

2

My adolescent sophistication owed little to Evelyn, who was discreet to the point of being secretive about his private life, as well as adroit at turning away awkward questions and avoiding unsuitable topics of conversation. It was my school friend Bobby who proved so usefully informative, making up in luridness for what was lacking in accuracy. I made friends with Bobby shortly after changing from the boarding school, and although by the time of the company centenary we had almost completely drifted apart, his influence lingered.

Our relationship was a strange one, in that we never acknowledged each other's existence in school. Bobby's reputation for toughness and trouble making would have suffered irrevocably, as would mine for meek academic superiority. While at school I endured, as I always had, the company of the other assorted outcasts but rejected closer involvement with such bores.

For a time, various schemes for holidays spent with Laura in Gerrard's Cross had been put forward. (She now attended a day school, having been removed from Warton at the end of the same term in which I had been triumphantly borne away by Evelyn.) But I had refused the invitations and Evelyn did not press, though it was much less convenient to have me at home for half terms. One of the mothers of my breaktime associates had been persistent about Girl Guides at first.

'Do I have to, Evelyn?'

'No, of course not. I just thought you might like to.'

'Yuch!'

'Alexandria.'

'No, thank you, Evelyn.'

'All right, chimp. It really wasn't my sort of thing either.' He laughed. 'There was no end of a row when I wouldn't do the OTC.'

'What's that?'

'Officers' Training Corps. It was compulsory. Marching, drilling, playing soldiers.'

'Why wouldn't you do it?'

'Well, it was a dreadful bore. I decided to be a conscientious objector.'

'What's that?'

Evelyn never rebuked me for failing to feel as I ought about conventional niceties. He found it perfectly reasonable that I did not like organised activities such as Guides and parties, that I had no interest in my schoolmates.

I knew that for a variety of reasons Evelyn would not approve of Bobby, and for some time managed to keep our friendship secret. Mainly, he would be very angry at the nature of our association, which took place entirely out of school; we played truant together. With increasing temerity I had begun to miss games afternoons, and then whole days, and I soon encountered Bobby similarly unoccupied. He caught up with me walking west, away from school one morning, making me jump, unceremoniously demanding to know how much money I had with me.

'One and six,' I said stiffly, on my dignity. In fact I had rather more but thought it prudent to keep some back.

Bobby sniffed with dissatisfaction and asked how much pocket money I received.

'None of your business.'

At his instigation we descended into the Underground. He had it all worked out, how to travel to the ends of the routes, change lines, avoid barriers, enter down fire stairs.

We ate my makeshift packed lunch on the Piccadilly Line. At Earl's Court he took Aero bars from a kiosk for our dessert and dragged me between the closing doors of a train in a neat get-away.

'My mum and dad are divorced,' he boasted after he had ostentatiously balled up his sweet wrapper and bowled it the length of the carriage.

'My mum and dad are both dead,' I said. 'I'm an orphan.'

'Coo!' He was impressed despite himself.

Eventually I insisted I must go home. Mrs Carey was expecting me. Bobby, as he now conceded I could address him, was at liberty until his mother returned from her secretarial job in the evening. He arranged that we should meet the following Wednesday and instructed me to ignore him completely at school so that no one would suspect our conspiracy.

I managed to contrive a larger lunch the next week and although I brought some money I was by no means foolish enough to bring it all as he had instructed.

Bobby was full of clever schemes. We travelled all the way across town on buses without paying by jumping on and off platforms at traffic lights. We got into movies free through fire exits. He schooled me as decoy while he took sweets, although I refused to steal anything myself; I was too timid. He extracted chewing gum and cigarettes from slot machines without coins and coaxed telephones to yield up their treasures, money cascading out as from a fruit machine.

On nice days we did the buses, on rainy days we kept dry on the Underground. Often we played 'Spies', earmarking some innocent passenger and tailing them to their ultimate desti-nation, fabricating the most lurid details of their espionage. My voracious historical repertoire coupled with Bobby's exhaustive high tech Bond-style invention made London Transport exciting beyond the wildest imaginings of the commuters.

Bobby was frankly nosy and asked in the minutest detail about my domestic arrangements, about Evelyn's personal life, marital status, war record, employment history.

'I don't know,' I had to keep saying. I began to resent his interrogation and would not be drawn any further.

'Well, it's obvious. He's a Russian spy,' Bobby concluded excitedly.

I denied this hotly, threatened to go home before we had spent any of my money.

Disgustedly Bobby allowed that Evelyn probably wasn't a spy, or that he might be a spy for our side. 'Does he have lots of girlfriends?'

'Of course not.' I was indignant.

'Well, my dad has lots of girlfriends. You should of seen the one he had last time I stayed. Talk about knockers!' He nonchalantly lit up a stolen cigarette, managing not to cough. 'What is he, a bloody pansy or something?'

'Of course not.'

'Well he's got to be something.' He attempted to blow smoke rings. 'Stupid!' he said crushingly at my bewilderment. He began to talk of his mother's boyfriends. He had no high opinion of any of them, but they were a useful species, always to be relied upon to disburse generous sums in exchange for Bobby making himself scarce.

'Don't you know *anything*?' he said exasperatedly on another occasion. Magnanimously he gave me a lurid, detailed and inaccurate account of what he described as 'the facts of life'. I didn't really believe him. We both lied to one another outrageously and were well aware of this.

Beyond a bored display of his prepubescent equipment in an

alley by way of illustration neither of us experimented further. It was true that he made a half-hearted attempt to make me show him mine, but when I refused he contemptuously said he'd seen better, mine wouldn't be anything much anyway.

I really couldn't imagine any person carrying on in the manner he described. Certainly I could not believe that anyone would ever do so with Bobby. He was an unprepossessing boy, with sticking out ears and freckles, never very clean or tidy. His straight hair fell in greasy spikes over his forehead and he was half a head shorter than me.

That persons as elderly as Evelyn or Uncle Richard could indulge in such senseless acrobatics without injury or rupture was out of the question. It never occurred to me to connect the activities that Bobby described with the unspecified wickedness condemned by the Church. But I had known instinctively that it would be a mistake to apply to Evelyn for illumination or correction on 'the facts of life'.

Now that I was older I presumed urbanely that Evelyn and Richard had mistresses, but it was no easier to consider the actual details, conjure any image of them behaving so undignifiedly. Nor was my assessment of Bobby's charms remotely altered by increasing maturity. He had, much to my surprise, managed to do well in the eleven plus, but our paths increasingly diverged. His interests developed into unhealthy obsession with unlocked cars and surefire methods of besting fruit machines in amusement arcades. It was as much boredom as timidity that made me distance myself, and he was relieved to be free of a girl it did him no credit to be seen with, having neither looks nor accessibility.

It was Bobby who made me consider Evelyn's private life. Always, precariously, there had been a string of babysitters. (Not until the advent of William were the exigencies of evening childminding resolved.) My early notion that Evelyn spent several evenings each week entertaining clients was not discouraged. Gradually I came to realise that in fact such duties were infrequent. But if I asked what he had done, he would briefly describe a meal or film, party or play. If further pressed, he would allow that he had been in the company of a friend, occasionally plural, and would never be drawn further, brushing aside my inquisition on the grounds that I should have been asleep hours since.

I didn't like to think of Evelyn having a good time without me. And often enough he would take me for a meal out or to the theatre, but he kept me quite separate from other evening companions. Sometimes there were long phone calls, and he would pull the flex to its full length so that he could sit just inside the dining-room, leaning against the door, the soft cajolery of his tones scarcely audible. I began to realise too, that despite his advanced age, some of the girls at the office made up to him quite blatantly. But his response was diffident, even embarrassed. Occasionally he would bring me flowers, small and modest selections suited to my age, freesias or pinks. But Bobby spoiled my pleasure in these posies. After his inquisitions I would involuntarily recall Evelyn signing an 'on account' slip, and wonder who had received what superior, grown-up bouquet.

My own secret life was revealed to Evelyn long before I was much the wiser about his. Mrs Best disclosed Bobby's existence to Evelyn by the simple expedient of ringing to invite me to tea. I had been to Bobby's house before, although I doubted his mother realised it.

He lived in a dark and narrow flat above a row of shops, reached from a frightening passage round the back shadowed by brick walls, fire escapes, warehouses. His flat was always untidy, the small living-room displaying evidence of previous meals; his mother's room completely filled by a double bed covered in feminine garments; everywhere an obstacle course of ironing, shoes, dirty cups.

Bobby's own room was scrupulously tidy, stacks of comic books under the high lumpy bed, the models displayed on every surface adjusted at precise angles, clothes put away. Unexpectedly, he was lavishly provided with expensive toys, boxes full of Meccano, board games, soldiers, racing cars, microscope.

Occasionally in the most inclement weather we adjourned there. But it was seldom. Bobby was annoyed, possibly ashamed of his mother's improvidence. Often there was nothing to eat in the house and no clean crockery. He would eat cereal or make fried egg sandwiches without attempting to clear the mess or assist domestically in any way.

Mrs Best had made touching efforts for the occasion. All the laundry had been shut into her bedroom, the front room tidied with a jug of flowers on the table. She fed us Bobby's favourite meal of egg and beans and chips, and had prepared a trifle, jelly and tinned fruit, with custard and Nestlé's cream over the sponge.

The evening was not a success. Both Bobby and I were angry at being pushed into the situation, increasingly irritated by her coyness in the face of her son's first romantic interest. But I felt sorry for her, tried to be helpful while Bobby was scathing, countering her every action and remark with reproach or ridicule. I was glad when Evelyn came to fetch me.

Evelyn seemed too big for the room. Politely he accepted the gin he was offered and perched on the floral-covered austerity settee. Mrs Best was flustered as she had not been by her son's unkindness. She smoothed her bright wispy hair and smiled sidelong at Evelyn through a lopsidedly applied red gash, smoking daintily, overlaying the fried smell of the flat. Evelyn vaguely countered Mrs Best's friendliness, committing neither of us to the delightful social schemes she vivaciously outlined, displaying no emotion at being told of my romantic attachment to such an unprepossessing urchin. Soon he took me away.

'Why didn't you tell me you have a boyfriend?'

'I don't! He's not!'

'There's nothing wrong with having a boyfriend.'

'*Yuch!*'

'Are you suggesting that Mrs Best is labouring under a misapprehension?'

'Evelyn! Don't tease.'

Evelyn poured a drink and gulped to eradicate the taste of the orange squash that Mrs Best had mixed with his gin. That was the only drink she had in, except for some Coke for us. 'What an enterprising young man,' Evelyn said mildly.

'How do you mean?' I was wary of his tone.

'You know very well what I mean. If you let him get you into trouble there'll be even worse trouble with me.' Evelyn drank. 'And you can save that wide-eyed innocent gaze. If you think I haven't a pretty good idea what boys his age get up to running loose round London without any supervision . . .'

'What things did you get up to?'

'Not very much. I was at school in the country.' He smiled,

almost ruefully. 'I must say, I'm surprised at you. He's not at all the sort of friend I would have expected of you.'

'Just because he's not as affluent as you.'

'Don't be ridiculous, Alex, you know perfectly well that's not what I'm talking about. I can't imagine his mother exercises the least control over him, poor woman. What do you think will happen if you get into a mess?'

'I won't.'

'You'd better not. I'll never hear the end of it from Louisa and Diana and Sophie if you get into trouble. Everyone will feel entitled to poke their oar in and we'll never have a moment's peace again.'

I took his glass and refilled it. But he did not ask what we did get up to, and he did not say anything about school, neither interrogating me about past attendance nor threatening future penalty.

Evelyn reciprocated Mrs Best's hospitality by taking Bobby with us for a Chinese meal. Bobby was freshly scrubbed and on his best behaviour. I was bored to tears as they discussed cars and Evelyn allowed him to look under the bonnet and sit in the driver's seat of his car. The evening ended badly when we took him home. There was no one there and Evelyn insisted on waiting for his mother to return despite Bobby's urgent urging that he would be fine, he was used to being left. Evelyn took a high hand and managed to restore Bobby to good humour by playing poker with him, teaching him some finer points and allowing him to win one and six.

Mrs Best returned at last, tottering on absurdly pointed heels, supported by a beefy red-faced man. In shimmering evening wear, elaborately coiffed and made up, she was almost pretty. Evelyn indulged in a bout of dry sarcasm which made Mrs Best flinch and her companion turn purple, and regally bore me away before the purple man could come to blows with him.

'I'm sorry, Evelyn.'

'Why should you be sorry, chimp?'

'You're cross.'

'It's not your fault, love.'

'He's my friend.'

'It just annoys me. Whatever faults I may have I manage better than that, and do I ever get any credit for it?'

'Mrs Carey says you do very well, all things considered.' I knew too that I made it much easier for Evelyn than Bobby did for his mother. I was helpful around the house and my behaviour was acceptable when I was being looked after by others. My aunts or Sophie would no doubt have washed their hands of Bobby.

'Well, they don't know what an appalling boyfriend I let you have.'

'Evelyn! Stop it!'

He squeezed my shoulder. 'All right, love, I know.'

'I'm never going to have a boyfriend.'

'I'm sure you will. But you're far too young to think of such things for a long time yet.'

'I won't. Never ever. I'm going to stay with you for always and always.'

'A fate worse than death. I'd planned on being rid of you in another few years. Now enough, you must sleep at once.'

Sometimes Bobby came round for Sunday dinner but he was bored with the conversation and with my female toys. We played cards though, and Uncle Richard taught him some superior card tricks. Uncle Richard was very good at the sort of conjuring tricks that appealed to the little ones at Sophie and Leo's gatherings, but he never bored the older children with juvenile pastimes in an excruciating hearty manner.

Evelyn would suggest sometimes that Bobby accompany us on an outing in the car, or swimming or for a meal. Usually I would veto this firmly. Bobby was not unamusing, but I would infinitely rather have had Evelyn to myself. But occasionally I would agree magnanimously to the invitation. Mrs Best was always pleased for Bobby to be invited out, but she was shy with Evelyn since the occasion when Evelyn castigated her for leaving her child alone late at night. I thought that Bobby was much better left alone at night than during the day when he was at liberty.

'You didn't tell me your old man had a girlfriend,' Bobby reproached me.

'It's not like that. It's like us,' I insisted.

He made a vulgar exclamation of derision. 'With knockers like that? Don't be stupid.'

It had not occurred to me that Evelyn and Jean were anything other than good friends. They were not soppy or romantic together and Jean had a healthy disrespect for Evelyn, teasing him forthrightly.

At first I had not liked her. It was true that Jean was decidedly pretty in an overblown sort of way, but she was improbably blonde and quite definitely – no euphemism such as 'generously proportioned' or 'plump' would do – fat. Her manner of conversation was disconcertingly blunt and she did not try to tone down her Australian accent. (I thought resentfully of the cruel mimicking I had endured at boarding school until my accent conformed.) She won me over by her unaffected interest, her treatment of me as an adult. But even someone as elderly as Evelyn should surely be able to find a more attractive lady.

Bobby made me reconsider the possibility of a romantic involvement. The more I thought about it, the more fantastic it seemed. But the fact remained that Evelyn had never introduced me to a lady friend before. And sometimes latterly he allowed that Jean had been his companion on an evening out.

I surreptitiously began to observe Evelyn, but he did not betray any signs of a man in love. Aside from evident sentimentality I didn't have a clue what to watch for. I could not ask Bobby; he would be distressingly crude, and probably unreliable. They were an ill-matched pair, Jean dumpy and short, not even reaching his shoulder. Evelyn was much too tall to kiss her easily; I could not imagine it. Also, Evelyn was really too old for her. But perhaps with all her shortcomings, he was the best she could do. And surely, old as he was, Evelyn could do better.

I was not so tactless as to question Jean. I thought of asking Uncle Richard, but never managed to do so. And somehow, I dared not ask Evelyn directly if he was going to marry Jean. I was afraid of the answer.

4

Although the family assembled every year for Christmas at Hellisford, and often there were groups at other times of the year, it was seldom that there were so many as for the centenary party. Celebrations in London had tended to centre around Uncle Richard, little though he seemed to relish it, but in Sheffield he made sure that Uncle Cecil received the laurels.

I revelled in the sense of history, one hundred years, whole, complete, rounded, so unlike the unsatisfactory fragments of my maternal family history, its very incompleteness redolent of the failure that had dogged them. The Parrishes had clawed their way up from the ranks of craftsmen, had managed to look after their own; all were accounted for. But the very obscurity of the Mahoneys bespoke persistent disappointment.

I was by now familiar with the litany. Uncle Richard was rather more forthcoming than Evelyn on such matters, and as a child I had never wearied of asking again and again for his anecdotes. The stories became ritualised, and he would not be allowed to deviate from them. Yet often new stories, additional information came to light.

It became custom for Uncle Richard to have me to stay sometimes when Evelyn was away on business. He lived much further from work than Evelyn, near the river, in a flat on the fourth floor. He was much fussier than Evelyn about domestic arrangements and bed times. I could not imagine him sprawled on the floor in front of the fire, or even with his feet up on the sofa.

I always enjoyed my visits; he devoted all his attention to me and arranged everything as he thought it would please me. He took me to the theatre and out in the car at the weekend. He showed me his photo albums without demur and was much more informative than Evelyn. Many of the pictures, especially of childhood, were taken on the same occasion as Evelyn's or were duplicates. His albums finished with the youthful Richard in cap and gown, with his family and alone.

'Is that all?'

'I believe there's some in a box somewhere.' But he would never be coaxed to find them.

I always wanted to see the pictures of his wife, but had never asked. I felt a stab of resentment at Evelyn's assumption that I had no tact or manners. Uncle Richard had been handsome as a youth, slim and luxuriantly blond-haired. Evelyn looked much the same in all the pictures, not so skinny as in his youth, but always languid and detached, never laughing or eager, even as a child.

Uncle Richard was also helpful over other matters. Evelyn would give an opinion if asked, but I could never be sure of the strength of his convictions, whether he was merely being flippant or provocative. Early in my acquaintance with Ben and Molly I was exposed to many socialist arguments. I found them sensible, and not especially contradictory to my hazy political notions regarding liberty and democracy.

'Are you a socialist, Uncle Richard?'

'No, of course not. What do you know about socialism?'

'Evelyn says he's a socialist.'

'I expect he was teasing you. You know what he's like.'

'He said he was. Is he not really?'

'Well, he certainly used to be when he was young. But he doesn't take much interest in politics these days. I didn't suppose he has such decided views any more.'

'What are you?'

'I'm a Liberal. We've always been Liberals in our family. As a matter of fact I did vote Labour in 1945, but that was exceptional.'

'Is Evelyn the only socialist?'

'I believe so. He was very forceful about it in his youth. It didn't go down very well. I used to think he did it for effect, but that wasn't really fair.'

'Do you mean his father didn't like it?'

'Oh, Uncle Aubrey never minded about things like that. But some of the older folk ... You know what families are, "When I was your age ..." and "No respect for your betters ..." That sort of thing. Evelyn was always chafing against that.'

'Weren't you?'

'Certainly. But I went about it more circumspectly and Evelyn drew all the fire. They all said he was very bolshie.'

'Was he?'

'I don't know. It certainly seemed so compared to everyone

else. He didn't settle into a regular job; he went off to Spain instead. But it didn't really matter, we could all see the war coming.'

'Did you have a job?'

'Oh yes, I went straight into the firm from Oxford. I hated it. Uncle Theodore and I didn't exactly see eye to eye. He had notions about starting me at the bottom, working my way up. But I don't think he had any intention of ever letting me have any real responsibility.'

'But you stayed.'

'Not at all. I asked for my wage to be doubled from £4 a week to £8 when I wanted to get married.' Uncle Richard smiled reminiscently. 'He said he'd never heard of such impudence and that I was far too young to be thinking of marriage and that he flatly refused his permission for me to marry. So I went downstairs to Stone and Hawkings on £9 a week and married forthwith.'

'Didn't they stop you?'

'I was twenty-three, there was nothing they could do. Poor Theodore, I didn't give him an easy time. One knows it all at that age.'

'When did you come back to Parrish's?'

'I went back in after the war, as soon as I was demobbed. The terms were rather better then.'

'Why hasn't Evelyn ever got married?'

'I think you'd better ask him.'

That was often what Evelyn said if I asked him about Uncle Richard, or about other family members. But I had learned a great deal from Uncle Richard. He talked about his grandfather and the history of the firm. He talked more about his boyhood, summers at Hellisford, older relatives than Evelyn would. Like Evelyn, he had had a nanny until he went away to school. I tried to imagine what it would have been like. I supposed it would

have been like having the nuns at home as well as school. I felt
very sorry for the young Parrishes. Uncle Richard didn't seem to
have had a happy life at all. He bore his sorrows bravely, never
self-piteous or resentful.

'What's a Liberal?'

He explained about the history of the hitherto unknown
third party, its great days in the last century, its decline at the
hands of Lloyd George. I decided to be a Liberal too; it seemed
eminently satisfactory to both embrace family tradition and
extend my potential as a martyred underdog. Sometimes I flirted
with socialism, but I would never give Evelyn the satisfaction of
persuading me irrevocably.

A sense of history had always pervaded family reminiscence. I
knew from my mother's father that we had come to America in
the 1880s, not during the Great Famine. His narrative was
always truculent and I knew by heart all his set pieces; the
interminable saga of the wrongs of the English against the
Irish; the vicissitudes of his father in becoming established in the
New World; the hardships of the Great Depression; the
marvellous career of the great saviour of the nation, Franklin D.
Roosevelt.

In old age he had struggled as fiercely, and as ineffectively,
against the regime of his wife and daughter as he had against
landlords and bosses and unemployment in his prime. He had
never really recovered from our move from Chicago, instigated
and implemented by his children, so that my mother and myself
and my grandparents could live near Uncle Pat, away from
urban squalor and violence. I knew all about his old tavern
cronies left behind in Chicago, their stories, their capacity for
drink.

I thought of his small, wheezing frame, sipping a surreptitious
Guinness before supper and drawing on a clandestine cigarette
in quick avid puffs as he told me of youthful shifts to make a few

pennies, the pranks to alleviate the monotony of production line working, the savagery of Pinkerton men. There were few photos of the old days; no one could afford them. But his words conveyed the past far more vividly than pictures of men and women posed formally in old-fashioned dress.

Uncle Richard's family history was interesting, but bloodless. There was no self-righteous indignation at the injustices of life, no crowing triumph at victories over powerful adversaries, no lectures on historical wrongs. Everything was prosperous, cosy, well-regulated, inviolable. I felt detached in a way that was never allowed by Grandpa's emotive discourses. In any event he had explicitly discouraged me from valuing my English ancestry.

'It's not your fault. Not even your father's. He was okay, he couldn't help being English.'

'What was he like?' I sometimes asked Grandpa.

'Pretty full of blarney for an Englishman. I guess the English are like that on the sly, they talked people out of a whole Empire.'

'But what was he *like*?'

'Everyone liked him. Even your Grandma liked him. And he had an English accent. The ladies really seemed to go for that.' He chuckled. 'He didn't really care about background, he didn't mind that your mother comes from an ordinary working background.'

'Why should he mind?'

'Well, the English are funny that way, snobbish, I guess you'd call it. But he didn't care about the Irish either, about history. You mustn't forget about history. There's history in all of us.' He drew heavily on a forbidden cigarette, and coughed a long shuddering cough. "I guess you could say he wasn't an intellectual man. But then, most of us are too busy working to be intellectual. Now if I had my time again I'd finish High

School, no matter what, at nights, anything. You get your schooling. I'd like you to go to college, have better opportunities than I did.'

I had missed him when he died, wished him back again, imagined conversations.

Evelyn would no doubt have preferred a more passionate history, struggles and blood, oppression and vindication. But if his privilege embarrassed him, it was not sufficiently for him not to avail himself of it. While he distanced himself, he was inextricably bound up with the family, not merely in his work, but in his leisure moments. He and Richard socialised often outside of work. However much he and Diana were at odds when they met, they corresponded regularly, voluminously. If Evelyn's letters were rather more erratic than the fortnightly letter from Diana, they were also longer, many pages requiring expensive air mail postage.

Regularly each month we went to Crystal Palace for Sunday lunch with Aunt Louisa and Aunt Hetty and stayed late. Early on I lost the feeling that the visits were on my account, that we were summoned for succour and scrutiny; Evelyn would have gone alone if I had not been there.

Evelyn did not appear a sentimental man, but his very forbearance belied him. His pigeonholed life, our unspoken complicity in keeping things from Louisa and Hetty, was as much to avoid causing distress as to deter criticism. I thought of all the photos displayed in his bedroom, of the boxes of pictures on the bottom shelf of his bedroom bookcase.

For a long time he had evaded my inquisitions, did not get out the boxes; it was too late, he was not in the mood, perhaps at the weekend. But eventually, in my leisurely convalescence from the rigours of boarding school, he had let me look through them. There were interminable pictures of his childhood, the children overdressed, the women in large-brimmed hats and witches' shoes. The baby pictures were indistinguishable except for neat writing on the back; 'Diana, Summer 1916' or 'Lynnie, Easter 1918'.

There were wedding photos too. Blanche, astonishingly pretty, with a white square shoved on her head, gazed into the distance as my grandfather, uniformed, splendidly moustached, looked protectively down at her. Aunt Diana was improbably slender and beautiful for her wedding, Uncle Gordon painfully earnest and even then rather bald.

'Who's that?' A glamorous man and woman stood together on some steps.

'That's Richard and Angela's wedding.'

'Uncle Richard?' I scrutinised the picture incredulously. He looked very young, grinning jubilantly. The woman was laughing and holding her hat on. 'Why hasn't she got a white dress on?'

'It was a registry office wedding. Angela was married before.' Evelyn shuffled away all the wedding pictures and then there were interminable army pictures; studio portraits of all the cousins including Uncle Sebastian and Uncle Theodore's dead sons; groups of young men in uniform against tropical backdrops; snapshots of skinny young soldiers on leave, convalescent on hospital terraces, at tables in front of tents. Evelyn took advantage of my flagging interest to put the pictures away. It had made him moody and irritable and I did not protest.

Thereafter it was a recognised invalid's privilege to look through the photographs, which I never tired of doing. This could take up an entire afternoon if I could wheedle Evelyn into going through the bundles of his own photos. His own photography was distinctly 'arty', with shots invariably taken from an unexpected angle and lots of light and shadow. I was not sure I cared for it but William was grudgingly approving. Only in my most determinedly pettish moods would I persevere to the end of these.

I searched for photos at Hellisford, but found none. I pumped Uncle Cecil for details of the old days, but his discourse was more disjointed than it had used to be (he was ninety-two now). While I enjoyed hearing his pieces, I learned little that was new, little about Evelyn.

5

While it was true that I had not behaved very well over the centenary party, I was quite clear that Evelyn's annoyance was disproportionate. He seemed to be irritated by the least little thing, making much more fuss about make-up and hem lines than he had ever had about far worse things. Even the crisis precipitated by my truancy reaching such levels that it could not be disregarded when I was eleven, had provoked Evelyn far less than any thoughtless remark seemed to lately. Nor did he have the provocation of Bobby coming round any more.

Aunt Louisa attempted to have a cosy chat with me at Hellisford, but her assurance that I mustn't worry, it was only a phase I was going through, terminated the dialogue. It was not me, it was Evelyn, and a man of forty-six was too old for phases.

Evelyn had been, as usual, subject to a great deal of well-meaning advice during the centenary celebrations, much from peripheral relatives, such as Uncle Cecil's married daughters. If he seemed a bit irritable, it was scarcely surprising, it occurred to me, given the amount of advice he had been forced to listen to over the years.

This year there was no summer holiday, although Evelyn promised instead to take me to the States in the autumn when he had to go on business. In previous years we had gone abroad, to Aunt Louisa's brother, Uncle Sebastian in Italy, or to France. I had always loved having Evelyn to myself for several weeks, no rival work or social claims on his time. But his mood was such at the moment that I did not resent being left at Hellisford nearly as much as I might have done.

Evelyn's intermittent moroseness, manifest in heavy drinking and much playing of Billie Holiday records, was lately oddly intermingled with uncharacteristic manic flashes. Impulsively he would decide to tidy his wardrobe or rearrange all his books, or we would go for a meal or a drive at a moment's notice, even if there was food prepared, or it was raining.

Most marked was the diminution of his social life. For a time it had been a positive relief when his young African friends had finished their degrees and gone home. I knew that Evelyn was almost as weary of them haunting the house as I was; it was not a question of basic hospitality, but the incessant emotional and intellectual demands, especially from George. I found it difficult now to imagine Evelyn having such patience as he had for so long with George.

Now that George and Matthew and Joe had gone home, the Sunday dinners were no longer given. Richard came in the week if he came at all these days and I had not seen Jean for many months. Jean had often presided over the Sunday salon, coaxing George into a sociable manner, flirting desultorily with Joe, talking financial investment with Richard. But it was always Evelyn who oversaw the preparation of the meal and attended to the drinks, never allowing Jean to do anything.

I had long since ceased to wonder if Evelyn would marry Jean, or anyone else. There were often lapses in their association of many months' duration. Bobby's prying had made me alert to clues to Evelyn's private life, phone calls and messages, half overheard joking and endearments. His various friends came and went, my own situation unaffected, and I grew used to the idea that I had nothing to fear from these desultory involvements. It seemed obvious what was troubling Evelyn now. He was not seeing anyone at all. He was too old and resented the fact that no one was interested any longer.

Either that, or he was in financial difficulties. He complained a lot lately about the cost of everything, about my increasing demands on his purse. I wondered if perhaps we couldn't afford a holiday. But when he returned to London after the centenary party, leaving me at Hellisford for a few weeks, he left me five pounds.

At Hellisford I read a great many crumbling leather-bound novels, plowing stolidly through the fat volumes, indiscriminately absorbing Ouida and Mrs Humphry Ward, Trollope and Mrs Gaskell. It exactly suited my mood and the setting. I was surprised at how much I missed Evelyn, as if I were a small girl again, wanting sometimes to weep at bedtime. We did not correspond, but he telephoned most evenings.

I had not been able to talk about Evelyn to Aunt Louisa, and I had been unforthcoming to the point of rudeness when Aunt Diana tried to ask me about him. Perhaps it was true that it was my fault. What was needed, I realised, was Tim. I could talk to him, and he would sort things out. No one else was capable of making Evelyn pull himself together. But Tim did not come very often these days.

As a child I had pestered Evelyn frequently with a plaintive, 'When is Tim coming again?'

'I have no idea, Alex. I wish you wouldn't keep asking.' Evelyn was more easily irritated by this than most of my inquisitions.

'I want to see him.'

'He's very busy, Alex, and he's not in England very much.'

'He's in England every week. He said so.'

'Only for a day or so. I daresay he's usually so tired he has no time left after he's had a decent sleep and seen his family.'

'I wish he'd come.'

But things had changed with Tim in a way that I could not quite put my finger on. Was it that I was older? Had he and Evelyn fallen out? Was he too taken up with new friends to spare us the time? Tim had done a centenary portrait of Richard, informally in ink and chalk. The unveiling had gone quite well, and Evelyn had then commissioned a drawing of his sister for Uncle Gordon. But there had been so much going on we had not had Tim much to ourselves, and Tim's clandestine drawing sessions for the portrait while Richard and Evelyn played chess had necessarily distracted Tim's attention.

After much scheming as to how I could get in touch with him I arrived at the conclusion that it would not do after all to involve Tim. If he and Evelyn were not getting on so well these days it would not help matters for Tim to lecture Evelyn. And it might hurt Evelyn's feelings if I turned to Tim. My childish difficulties, hoarded and poured out to Tim, had not infrequently prompted Evelyn's wistful reproach, 'Why didn't you tell me? What do you think I am, some kind of ogre? Am I always so cross with you?' Remorseful, sheepish, I would hide my face against Evelyn as his long fingers methodically smoothed back my hair or stroked my spine.

Besides, I realised in a sudden access of maturity, Tim might have enough difficulties of his own. It was not unknown. He was frequently despondent about the lack of advancement of his aristic career, correspondingly fed up with his job on the ship.

And that was not the least of the troubles he had known. I remembered the frightening circumstances of a visit long ago, when I was eleven. Tim had arrived on the doorstep late at night, beaten and bloody.

Evelyn had unhestitatingly taken him in, looked after him. But it seemed in retrospect that there had been an underlying unease between them after that. Yet there had been no row. Always they argued fiercely about matters artistic and political, but the only personal disagreement I was aware of was over myself, Tim disapproving of Evelyn sending me away to school. No doubt Tim was simply too busy to visit often. It was a pity though; I felt that more social activity might be good for Evelyn.

I could see no way to help Evelyn. I was no longer childish enough to imagine that I was sufficient solace to him to render additional companionship redundant. He did have friends, seemed perfectly capable of making new friends. Rather he would make no effort at the moment. Even I had been abandoned at Hellisford instead of being taken back to London with him. It would have been no trouble to him now that I was older; there would be no child-minding problems and I could make sure the evening meal was prepared when he returned home.

I toyed with the idea that he wanted me out of the way while he conducted a passionate affair or attempted to launch an involvement with someone. But he had seemed much too despondent, indeed indolent for anything so exciting. I wondered if he had suffered a disappointment of some sort. I knew that Uncle Richard was happy with Evelyn's work; he had praised his contribution fulsomely in several speeches during the celebrations, much to Evelyn's mortification. I could not imagine him suffering from unrequited love, could not conjure the sort of woman that would disturb his peace of mind to such an extent. He simply did not want to be bothered with me, with anyone.

I even wondered whether his difficulty was simply that he was drinking heavily, rather than that he was drinking more because he was upset. I was used to him consuming a great deal of alcohol, but I was not accustomed to the sharp sarcasm that seemed increasingly characteristic of his drinking sessions, instead of his easy expansiveness after a few drinks. Certainly I thought he drank more and did less at the weekends than ever before. But perhaps it was just that I was older and more observant, or that he was less careful to guard his tongue than when I was little.

I tried not to worry too much, to cultivate a sophisticated cynicism. But steeped in Victorian tragedy, long-lost heirs, unrequited love, foundlings, ruined mill girls, workhouses, Sacrifice, it was fatally easy to weep for Evelyn, for Tim, for my lost childhood.

••••••••••••••••••••••••••••
                           •
                           •
6 •
                           •
                           •

Surfeited with melodrama, I began to entertain anew a clichéd fantasy that Evelyn had firmly quashed years since. Bobby had originally put the idea in my mind in the first weeks of our acquaintance. I had nurtured the thought for many months, increasingly convinced, desperate for its truth. Finally I had picked a propitious moment when we were on holiday in Italy, two summers before, when I was twelve. Judging Evelyn sufficiently mellow from a week's rest, an evening's wine, I had blurted, 'You're really my father, aren't you?'

Evelyn choked on his wine, bent over his handkerchief,

eventually pouring more wine and drinking it before replying. 'There really is no limit to the luridness of your imagination, is there?' But he had not seemed angry. 'Now really, you know me better than that. Don't you think I would have told you if that were so? Don't you think I'd have told everyone?'

I considered my choice of words. 'But if you're not married . . .'

'Oh, Alex.' He shook his head ruefully. 'I assure you, such a trifling consideration wouldn't have weighed with me. If you were my daughter I would certainly have told you at the outset. But the fact is that I only ever met your mother once, and you were four years old by then.' He summoned the waiter and helped me to order an ice cream.

'It would be much better if you were my father.'

'I've been looking into it as a matter of fact, chimp. It's perfectly true, it would be much better.' I knew that there was something in the offing. Evelyn had had several private conversations with his lawyer at Sophie and Leo's on Sundays, and I had become convinced it was to do with me. Evelyn now explained that he had been investigating the possibility of formal adoption. But he was not optimistic. The law explicitly excluded single males from adopting females unless there were exceptional circumstances. And while Evelyn had been advised that the chances were good, it was by no means certain that the judge would accept his case. And once proceedings were set in motion, nothing could be undone. Council investigators would be appointed, school and neighbours and relatives interviewed, everything scrutinised. And if the case went against us, it was unlikely that the court would allow me to continue living in an unsuitable environment. 'So you see, if I were your father, it would make everything much easier for me to admit it.'

'You could pretend.'

'I don't think that would do, love.'

'Will they take me away from you?'

Evelyn shrugged. 'Probably not. But if we lost the case . . . Donald's suggested I need more specialist advice before I decide.'

'You could get married.'

'I could. Would you like that?'

'I don't understand, Evelyn. Why shouldn't men get to adopt girls?'

'We've been through all this before, love. People don't think men make suitable parents on their own.'

'If they take me away from you I'll run away.'

He smiled. 'You always do. But I don't think that would help.' He said that it was his view that we should wait. Once I was old enough to leave school the whole business was much more of a formality. And in the meantime his will accounted for me amply without further legal niceties. 'Anyway, I have no intention of dying yet.' He smoothed away the face I pulled.

'We could pretend.'

'Pretend?'

'Pretend you've adopted me now.'

'All right then.' The waiter came with my ice cream and Evelyn ordered some spumante to celebrate the adoption.

I preferred it to champagne; it didn't pucker the inside of my mouth. 'Evelyn? Does this mean I get to call you "Dad" now?'

'No!'

Evelyn's further enquiries convinced him that it would indeed be rash to proceed with official adoption. But the whole exercise was extremely useful to him. It was not necessary for him to use his anger to control me. The threat of social workers, truancy officers, police all delving into the details of our lives; served easily to contain my escapades with Bobby within reasonable bounds, particularly as I had already been badly caught out over a forged sick note.

Occasionally now in public I addressed him as 'Dad' when I

wished to tease him, and always I referred to him at school with Bobby's phrase as my 'old man'. I had believed his denial of paternity, and at heart still did. But I toyed with the possibilities. Perhaps his form of words disclaimed not my paternity but maternity.

I was clear now that my mother had been a very boring and rather tiresome woman. Magnanimously I felt compassion for her. She had not had an easy time, struggling to make ends meet, trying to maintain exacting standards. I realised I had been an unrewarding child. We had had little in common, nothing to talk about. I had been obstinate and contemptuous, without even the compensation of looking a credit to her. She had toiled to dress me exquisitely, but although I was neat and ladylike, I was not pretty and much too big to show off to advantage the ruffled and lace-edged frocks she made for me. My retrospective image was of a dainty little woman trailing her sulky overgrown child by the hand in uncomplaining bewilderment, like a sparrow with a fledgling cuckoo in tow.

Unlike my mother, Evelyn did not get round my wilfulness by tears and deviousness. His approach was direct. Sometimes there had been confrontations, more usually I was blandly outflanked, but openly, without guile or blackmail. Now that I had learned most of his ways, it was less easy for him to outmanoeuvre me and there were more head-on clashes. But generally, we got on very well simply because differences didn't all that often arise. Evelyn displayed no emotional possessiveness about my life and would not allow any from me.

But he was neither cold or unfeeling. My original impression had been of immense dignity; it seemed inconceivable that Evelyn would laugh, relax, romp as Uncle Pat did with his children, tried stiltedly to do with his fatherless niece. Evelyn was a great deal more indolent than Uncle Pat and I was much too big to be thrown in the air or ride on his shoulders, but

Evelyn had not been not above some playing, jumping me off walls, sparring, tumbling, although I was too old for that now.

Of course I was much too big for his lap long since, and I wasn't tucked up any longer. But it was not just that. His abstracted smoothing back of my hair, rubbing of my spine, as he did with Berry was also past. Good night kisses no longer came with a hug, walks were not hand in hand. It did not occur to me that Evelyn was being careful to adjust to a growing female, merely that things weren't the same any more.

Evelyn seemed more relaxed after my return home from Hellisford and made an effort to be congenial. We went out fairly often, albeit just to the cheap Italian restaurant around the corner or an even cheaper Chinese establishment. He revived our weekend photographic expeditions, as always patient about advice and direction, continuing invariably to pay for my film and developing. I was allotted a clothes allowance separate from my weekly pocket money. Increasingly he would take me to the theatre, evening instead of matinee, listening seriously to my opinions in the interval. Evelyn's private concerns, however, defied close scrutiny. It was impossible to say whether he was more circumspect now that I was older or simply that he had nothing to hide.

I liked to think Evelyn was my father; my own seemed devoid of interest, my mother dull. I preferred to have a more exciting background. It was true that Evelyn was only a businessman, but there were many blanks in his life, travels abroad, unspecified employments, vagueness as to his war that I could embroider at will.

I dredged up instances from my childhood, the many times that strangers had supposed us father and daughter, more sinister allusions. It was clear now that at boarding school I had been universally presumed to be Evelyn's own child. I did not suppose it had helped my situation, but I didn't imagine it would have been much improved without the misapprehension. On other occasions too there had been enigmatic looks when Evelyn spoke of 'my niece', which I now realised were expressions of scepticism. I had joyfully marked Evelyn's increasing tendency to refer ambiguously to 'my little girl' as evidence of affection but now I considered whether it was more pragmatic.

'Don't be so bloody melodramatic,' was all he said when I confronted him again after I returned from Hellisford.

'But I want to know.'

'Well, I've told you.'

'Evelyn!'

'For God's sake, what difference does it make? You're here, aren't you?'

'Does that mean you are my father?'

'No, I bloody well am not. Thank God. I've enough to be answerable for in this life without having foisted you on the world into the bargain.'

'Are you sure?'

'Quite positive. Now what's all this in aid of?'

'I just wanted to know, that's all.'

'You read too much rubbish.'

'I read *improving* works. What else have you got to be answerable for?'

'It'll be bloody murder in a minute!'

But later he said, 'Does it really matter, chimp? Do you think it would be any different if you were mine instead of Alec's?'

'I don't know. I just thought it would be nice.'

'Well, I can't do anything about that,' he said brusquely, and hugged me as if I were little again.

7

In the autumn after the centenary Evelyn was away for a protracted trip to the States. I split my time between Crystal Palace and Uncle Richard. I liked staying with him. It was much nearer to school than Crystal Palace. Usually he would take me out for a meal at least once to an establishment where we could indulge our mutual passion for potted shrimps. There would generally be a visit to the theatre as well; when I was younger it was an excuse for him to see a Gilbert and Sullivan. Now my secondary school was conveniently close to the office so I could get a lift back with Uncle Richard if I wished.

Uncle Richard's flat was more conventionally appointed than Evelyn's. He had an accumulation of family china, silver and glassware, but his furnishings looked as if he had bought the contents of Heal's window. Only the piano was old, and the books. Neat stacks of music filled the lowest shelves of the fireplace alcove, and each evening he played for a while, with a drink perched on the candle sconce. Stylised Scarlatti smoothed away his temper, thundering Grieg proclaimed his good humour.

'Uncle Richard, have you ever been in love?'

He blinked characteristically in a rapid spasm, and I relaxed; he wasn't going to be cross. 'Well, I've been married twice,' he temporised.

'Twice? No one told me that,' I said deviously.

'It's not a secret. What have they told you?'

'Nothing. Only that you used to be married.'

'Well my first wife died in 1943 and my second wife and I are divorced. All right?' He topped up his drink.

'Why are you divorced?' I remembered John's theory.

'We found we didn't suit. These things happen, you know.'

'Were you married long?'

'Not long. I was away most of the time, in Germany. And when I was demobbed it was evident it was a mistake.'

'But you were in love?'

'Whatever that means.' He looked at me, brandished his reading glasses by the stem. 'You needn't melodramatically imagine me pining away all these years from a broken heart either.'

'But you haven't got married again.'

He shrugged, gestured with folded spectacles. 'I'm not opposed to the idea. Perhaps I've been overcautious. What do you want to know about love anyway?'

'I don't know. Everyone at school talks about love all the time. Always going on about some dumb boy. It seems silly to me.'

'I'd have thought you were a bit young to be worrying about love.'

'I mean, what's the point? Worrying all the time about what some cretin thinks about you, getting all upset because they're not interested. What a waste of time.'

'Just so.'

'It's not funny. They all laugh at me because I'm not interested in boys. Yuch.'

'I really don't think you should worry about such things yet.'

'Were you in love when you were my age?'

'My dear girl, you must remember that I went to a single sex school.'

'Not all year round.'

'It's so very long ago I can't really remember. I'm quite sure girls my own age were never interested in me. Boys are much more juvenile than girls at that age, you know.'

'Perhaps you're right. Maybe I need to meet some older men.'

'Maybe you should help me with getting dinner,' he said drily. But when the casserole was in the oven he said, 'I can tell you what Evelyn would advise you. He would tell you that interest in the opposite sex seldom has very much to do with love, and life is much easier if one avoids confusing the two.'

'Is that what you think?'

'I think there's something in that, it may be an overstatement. But then Evelyn has always been rather pessimistic.'

'You mean cynical.'

In the wake of our discussion, I wanted to ask Uncle Richard to see the photos of his wives, but I felt it would be tactless to ask. I poked thoroughly around the guest room in hope of clues. The bottom of the wardrobe contained wine racks and there was nothing in the drawers except spare blankets. The pictures were some of Aunt Hetty's watercolours of the countryside around Hellisford. Unlike Evelyn, Uncle Richard had no photos of family or friends displayed.

The bookcase was more interesting. Hitherto I had attended only to the row of P.G. Wodehouse volumes, many of which I had not found elsewhere. It had been Uncle Richard who had introduced me to them, reading aloud to me sometimes when I was ill as a child. But underneath the yellow Gollancz whodunnits were Marx and Engels, Penguin Specials and Left Book Club volumes. It was much more unexpected than finding Lady Chatterley openly on Evelyn's shelves with the rest of D.H. Lawrence.

I looked through the bottom shelves, *Unemployed Struggles, Black Man's Burden, I Was Hitler's Prisoner*. Earlier volumes were inscribed in a bold hand, 'Angela Mayhew', later ones 'Angela

Parrish'. I wondered about Uncle Richard's marriages, regretted having asked if he had ever been in love, hoped I had not upset him. He had not seemed upset as he admonished me not to imagine him brokenhearted.

'I don't feel well, Uncle Richard.' I announced a few mornings later.

He looked up from *The Times*, eyes magnified behind his glasses. I wondered what Evelyn had told him, whether he had been warned not to let me skive off. He said I looked all right, and I gave in. But I was much worse by the end of the day and went to bed with a severe headache after school.

'How are you this morning?' The enlarged eyes scrutinised me, his look softened. 'Tea?'

'Horrible.' Half smug, half embarrassed I said, 'I'm bleeding.'

'Bleeding!' He set the pot down. 'It's not the first time?'

I blushed and nodded.

After a pause he asked, 'Is there anything you need to know?'

I shook my head.

'Are you sure?'

'Sophie talked to me. She gave me a pamphlet as well.'

'Sophie?' He frowned. 'Well then, I daresay you're all right.' He clicked his pen and confidently began to ink in boxes on the puzzle.

'Uncle Richard.' I nerved myself. 'I'm afraid the sheet's ruined.'

'Well, it can't be helped. Take a clean one from the airing cupboard.' He patted my hand. 'There's no point in being embarrassed about it. I've been a married man, you know.' He told me I could stay at home if I liked. In the evening he brought me a large parcel. 'For God's sake open it in the bathroom,' he said irritably. He had even remembered the little belt to go with the sanitary towels.

I felt despicable now. I had whiled part of the day nosing in his bedroom. The books were fewer than in Evelyn's, a mixture of more recent purchases and old favourites, Austen, the latest Michael Innes, Tibullus in Latin. His drawers and wardrobe were neatly ordered. I had dared not disturb the contents. The only discovery of interest was in the night table drawer, a large framed studio portrait of a woman, half obscured by spectacle wipes and pharmaceuticals, which I had not the nerve to take out.

He offered me a sherry when he had his drink.

'Does it mean I'm grown-up now?'

'Well, it's a milestone, certainly.'

'Don't you think, if I'm grown-up, I should be told things?'

'Probably not. What do you think you should be told?'

'Evelyn didn't go to the States by himself, did he?'

'What do you mean? We haven't sent a colleague with him.'

'But he didn't go by himself.'

'I don't know why you should say that.'

'He said I could come this time. It was all planned, he promised. He was going to take me to Platea. And then at the last minute he said he would be too busy and I couldn't miss school anyway.'

'Well that's certainly true. But it doesn't follow that he took someone else.'

'He did though, didn't he?'

'What makes you say that?'

'You haven't denied it. It's true isn't it?'

Uncle Richard poured himself another drink. 'I have no idea what Evelyn's private life involves. But I would be very much surprised if he'd done such a thing. I'm sure he hasn't.'

'Well I'm sure he has.'

'Really my dear, I'm sure you're mistaken. Why should you think so?'

'Different things. He had two plane tickets.'

'He has to come back, you know.'

'That's all in the same booklet. I've seen them before.'

'I'm sure you're mistaken.' He looked both weary and stern.

'I'm sure I'm not,' I muttered. There were various overheard phone calls as well, but I could not admit eavesdropping to Uncle Richard. I was deeply hurt that Evelyn had taken his mistress instead of me. I wondered how many times he had done this before.

I was confounded to encounter Jean in the foyer of the building a week before Evelyn's return. She worked for a firm of accountants below Parrish and Sons Ltd. I had not seen her for ages, and it transpired in the conversation that she was not even aware that Evelyn was away.

8

'Evelyn, I don't think I should go to Uncle Cecil's funeral.'

'Why not?'

'Well, I don't believe in God anymore.'

'Neither do I. It's nothing to do with God, it's a question of courtesy to Hetty. Now go and pack.'

It had been a long time since I had consciously thought about religion. I had never arrived at the point of deciding that I didn't believe in God, but having made my announcement to Evelyn, I had no qualms, no second thoughts. I scarcely even recollected what a dreadful burden it had been to believe in God, live in constant dread of transgression, retribution, damnation for eternity. My preoccupation must also have been a trial to the grown-ups.

Evelyn had tended to avoid discussing religion, but often he was caught unawares, as on the occasion when he had insisted that the pubescent Berry be 'done'.

'Evelyn, can they do that to people? Take out bits to stop babies coming?'

'They only do that if there's a disease. It's not ethical otherwise.'

'How do you mean?'

'Ethical. E-t-h-i-c-a-l. You know where the dictionary is.' He lay back in his chair and closed his eyes.

I looked. 'Evelyn.'

'Later, Alex.' He refilled his drink and loped up to his bath.

That night Berry, shaven and stitched, was tenderly ensconced as usual at the foot of my bed.

'Don't kiss her like that, you don't know where she's been.'

'She's been at the vet's. It's antiseptic there.'

Evelyn smiled reluctantly and simulated boxing my ears.

'Evelyn? Can people stop babies coming?'

'It's no good asking me. I'm not married.'

'Don't tease.'

'You know perfectly well I'm not married.'

'Evelyn!'

'Now that's enough. It's time you were asleep.'

'Is it really true that you don't have to have babies if you're not Catholic?'

'Yes, perfectly true. But you don't have to worry about babies until you're grown-up anyway.'

'Why is it different if you're not Catholic?'

'I've no idea. All religions are different.'

'Maybe I should change. What are you, Evelyn?'

'Not much these days. I was raised Church of England.'

'Do you think I should change?'

'I'm not a theologian, Alex. You must suit yourself.'

'Why aren't you religious?'

'I don't know. I just grew out of it I suppose. You haven't been to church in ages anyway.'

'You haven't taken me.'

'You haven't asked. It's up to you if you want to go.'

'You don't like me to go.'

'I've never said so,' he said emphatically. 'Now say your prayers and go to sleep.'

I knew he was teasing. He never suggested I pray. On Saturday he asked me if I wanted to go to church in the morning.

'Mmmhmm.'

'You don't seem very enthusiastic.'

'I haven't been to confession.'

'Well, you didn't ask to go,' he said exasperatedly.

'Doesn't the Church of England have confession?'

'Good God, no.'

'Supposing if we go next week,' I said feebly.

My church attendances had petered out, so that now I only went at Christmas, at Hellisford with Uncle Sebastian to midnight Mass. Evelyn had neither reminded me nor ridiculed my beliefs, but his vagueness was in marked contrast to his clear views on impersonal issues.

William had been much more forthcoming than Evelyn. He never told me to mind my own business, or evaded by teasing or insisting that it was bedtime.

'Are you religious, William?'

This made him pause in his systematic demolition of a packet of biscuits and a block of mousetrap. 'Of course not. How bourgeois.'

'What's that?'

'Middle class. Reactionary,' he said through a mouthful of apple.

'Is that bad?'

'Terrible. Look at Sargent. Look at John or Lavery or Whistler.' His bony shoulders shuddered, his large nose quivered. 'Ugh! All those awful Impressionists. Renoir. Degas. Disgusting.'

'Oh.' Of course, he was not necessarily more illuminating than Evelyn.

'Don't you think it's time you were in bed?' he suggested when he had finished his snack.

'No.'

'Okay.' He tidied the kitchen and went to fill the bathtub to the brim with hot water, taking sustenance in the form of a banana. But a long wallow in our bath did little for the ingrained paint on his hands and he cheerfully put back on the same smelly paint-streaked clothes when he was washed. He said he liked looking at Tim's work while he bathed.

'Have you known Tim for a long time?'

'Not really. He came back to the college for an open day last year. He thought one of my pictures was interesting and we went for a drink.'

'Do you see him very often?'

'I haven't seen him for ages.'

'I wish he would come again.'

When I was able to consult Tim, he said firmly that he wasn't in the least religious.

'Why not?'

'Well,' he floundered, before saying that God had nothing to offer him.

'How do you mean?'

'Well, it's in the Bible. He has nothing to do with the likes of me.'

'Don't be silly, Tim. Jesus was poor too. Much poorer than you.'

I was offended at him laughing and did not think to question him further.

I once asked, "Are you religious, Uncle Richard?"

He considered his response. 'Not especially. Why?'

'I was just wondering.' I suddenly felt it would be impossible to talk to him about babies. 'Why doesn't the Church of England have confession?'

'Well . . . there's not really any need for an intermediary. One's conscience is a private matter between one's self and God.'

'Oh.'

'Are you having religious difficulties?' he asked gently.

'I was just wondering. English people aren't very religious, are they?'

'I don't know why you should say that.'

I knew that Aunt Louisa and Aunt Hetty went to church and had the Vicar to tea regularly. Mrs Carey also went to church sometimes, but she was only a Methodist. Religious observance at school was perfunctory, with a hymn at the end of assembly and a sentence of grace before the institutional lunch. Matthew was very devout, deeply involved in church activities, and sometimes George accompanied him to church before coming to lunch, but it was only some obscure evangelical sect and they weren't English.

'Well, the ladies and children are more religious,' I qualified.

But he too seemed to find my theological thoughts amusing.

Philip, of course, went to church every Sunday, in the company of his mother. Dr Marigard was content to leave religion to the women and children, perhaps exhausted by the inevitable call-out in the small hours.

I had only recently been made aware of Philip Marigard's devotion, when he had summoned the courage to leave a Christmas present in my desk, a bracelet accompanied by a card inscribed with a poem of his own devising, an ode to my crowning glory. It was true that my hair was now almost to my waist and reasonably abundant, but it was boringly straight and mousy. Only the most idiotic or besotted could find anything remarkable about my hair. Despite his manifold shortcomings, not least his lack of inches, I was flattered.

Uncle Cecil's funeral oration seemed to last forever as the mourners shivered and huddled in their coats. I pondered with sophisticated amusement on my childish religious difficulties. If some of the recollections of how I had plagued adults made me cringe, they did so rather less than the encomiums on the deceased.

Uncle Richard was fixedly entranced with the beamed ceiling, Evelyn with flexing and smoothing the leather gloves that he'd got that Christmas. The vicar eulogised at length on Uncle Cecil's virtues, his sense of duty, his concern for his employees, his charitable works, his patriotism, his goodness as a husband, father and Christian. Aunt Hetty created a welcome diversion in the midst of a convoluted period on the fortitude of Christians in the face of illness and debility; collapsing and being assisted to the vestry by Uncle Sebastian and Aunt Louisa.

After perfunctory graveside prayers in a blasting gale, much needed drinks were dispensed back at the house. I watched apprehensively as Uncle Richard saw to everyone's needs. But at last, after everyone had been served, he gave me a sherry. The vicar, balked of more eminent prey, began to chat to me. I considered his unctuous smile, his bobbing conciliatory head. I could not imagine any of the relatives requesting, or even acquiescing to such a eulogy as had been delivered.

Aunt Hetty had now recovered, and was in fact apologising for being so silly, while Aunt Louisa insisted that the perishing cold was enough to overwhelm anyone. I wondered what Aunt Hetty had thought of the panegyric to her father. She had seemed very fond of him, and he of her. He had hated her doing anything for him, and had always tried to hold out for the services of Norman, or anyone else available, even though this made him appear cross with her on occasion.

The vicar evidently preened himself on his ability to relate to young people, as he tried to get me to talk about myself. I marvelled at the effrontery of his service; at the complacency that could allow his self-congratulations on how the relatives were moved, comforted, gratified by his performance.

I managed a sketchy smile. 'Actually, I'm an atheist,' I said and moved away.

'Alex,' reproved Evelyn mildly.

'If that's the sort of person God calls, then I'd infinitely rather roast in hell for eternity.'

'Really, Alex.' But he laughed. Deftly he reached across for a new drink and topped up my sherry. 'I flatly forbid anything like this when I go. You can put me out for the bin men.' He filled his sister's glass.

'The clergy are not what they used to be,' pronounced Diana.

Evelyn shrugged. 'I don't think he's any worse than the others used to be.'

'Really, Lynnie. Such presumption.'

'Poor old boy. He'd have been livid.' Evelyn smiled ruefully and unexpectedly hugged his sister's shoulders. I was rivetted by her hat, small, black, netted round the edge, but irrepressibly jaunty on her regal head. It was a perfectly ordinary hat and there was no reason why it should appear so sprightly. It had not been perched at a daring angle or lavishly trimmed. As if aware of my scrutiny, she unpinned it and took it upstairs.

Aunt Diana remained in England for a further week after the funeral before returning to Uncle Gordon. Evelyn took her to dinner and to the theatre. I was surprised that they seemed to be getting on so well. It occurred to me that the siblings got on better without Uncle Gordon. But relations between the brothers-in-law seemed unaffectedly cordial, with no evident undercurrent of antipathy. Nor did it seem that there was any strain between husband and wife, so that Aunt Diana would be more relaxed on her own.

Philip was pronounced a very nice boy by Aunt Diana, as if surprised that anyone reasonable would be interested in me. Philip was insufferably nice and I endured him only so that it would not be remarked by my contemporaries that I had no suitors. He always looked almost unnaturally clean, scrubbed glowing pink, the wave to his hair meekly damped down. I always felt he should come with the laundry's cardboard collar insert and paper band around him.

He was rather shy and deferred always to my opinion. His respectfulness goaded me constantly to unkindness in the hope of any display of spirit. Evelyn was much more tactful with Philip's obsequiousness, talking to him man to man in a way that disguised the useful hints that Evelyn imparted, about wines, clothes, books, taking out a lady. Evelyn sometimes chided me for my abuse of him.

'But he's so *boring*.'

'Well then I don't see why you bother with him.'

'I've got to have some friends.'

'If he's a friend you shouldn't be so horrible to him.'

'Well, he shouldn't be so pathetic.'

Philip was wary of Evelyn, as if supposing Evelyn would not approve of him. But Evelyn was always nice to him, and never teased me about him. Perhaps he was merely relieved that I had acquired such an unexceptionable friend. Evelyn's own private matters were elusive as always. He still went out several evenings a week, though not as frequently as he sometimes had. It had been thrashed out that I was too old for a babysitter now, but I don't think he was altogether easy about leaving me. And for all my protestations, I was glad not to be left too often.

Uncle Cecil's death seemed to increase Evelyn's irritable contrariness and moroseness. His usual easy-going indifference was much less in evidence. Sometimes now the entire weekend lapsed in a continuous drinking session. I avoided the living-room where he lolled on the sofa with endless blues records. With astonishing resilience he would pull himself together for Monday morning, but I could interest him neither in going out nor in eating anything. Often he did not bother to shave at the weekend and his beard showed pathetically grey. He did not seem to sleep well, often up and about no matter what hour of night I chanced to wake, not even lying in late invariably anymore.

Now that George and Matthew had gone home, we seldom had visitors except Uncle Richard, and even he seemed to have chess evenings with Evelyn less frequently. I liked to think of Uncle Richard's time being taken up by a torrid love affair. But he always seemed as stolid as ever, not remotely lover-like, aside from being almost fifty. We still went to Sophie and Leo's monthly gatherings, and sometimes to Crystal Palace, but that was all. We hadn't seen Ben and Molly for ages, nor had Jean been at all in evidence.

The disposal of Hellisford, the unfashionable Victorian

furniture and ornaments, took ages. Sorting through everything, clearing out, was a major task. Only one of Cecil's married daughters was left alive and in England, and was in poor health. Effectively the job was left to Aunt Hetty, his youngest daugther, but we all helped, and Evelyn and I spent Easter at Hellisford to lend a hand.

Evelyn was subdued and spent most of the time at Hellisford taking long solitary walks. Not even the dogs were left to run out with him. Lady was long dead and Uncle Cecil's attendant, Norman, had taken her successor. Uncle Richard occupied himself with an inventory of the remaining contents of the cellar.

Tangible evidence of the decline was melancholy. From impoverished beginnings, Cecil's father had acquired a country house, too new and too ornate for a gentleman's, but large and hospitable. Lavishly appointed in the fashion of the day, his son had filled the house with guests. From the heyday of open-handed open house, when the attics had been filled with servants and the cellars with wine, only the trappings were left, decayed, unwanted. All of Evelyn's generation, and that of his father's, had spent halcyon childhood summers here and now it was done. The history weighed on me with pleasurable poignancy. Wistfulness for the lost era was inextricably mingled with nostalgia for my own lost childhood. It never occurred to me that Evelyn, and the other adults, were taking things much more to heart than I possibly could.

part V

1

Contrary to my melodramatic forbodings, the death of Uncle Cecil had marked no evident downturn in our fates; the ensuing year was uneventful and indeed rather cosy. For my part, I found that I was enjoying school rather more, both because the work was increasingly interesting and because of my acquaintance with Christina. Evelyn seemed better too, making more of an effort, picking up the threads with old friends like Ben and Molly. His work seemed to be going well, and he had a series of trips to the Continent. (I suspected that he enjoyed going on the razzle with Dieter was much as the business dealings.)

In the summer we went to visit great-uncle Sebastian in Italy. I had been several times before. Last time we had gone at Easter, flying to Rome and spending only a few days in Padua. But this time we were based there in the usual *pensione* near Uncle Sebastian's flat. It had suited Evelyn very well when I was little. Uncle Sebastian called for me in the mornings and I went with him to have chocolate and rolls at the café where he always had his breakfast, while Evelyn had a lie-in. In the evenings I could sit with Evelyn while he had drinks, unlike English pubs. Sometimes Uncle Sebastian would take me to friends or relatives in the evening, leaving Evelyn to his own devices.

Uncle Sebastian's married daughter had three sons, the eldest now aged ten. Her circle of in-laws seemed boundless and there was often a large gathering to which we were invited, with gargantuan meals, pasta, roast meats, salads, sweets as well as limitless local wine. Despite having little Italian I was always made to feel part of the proceedings. Evelyn's Italian was serviceable and he was able to converse, joke, flirt with plausible fluency.

This time Evelyn was more energetic about expeditions to outlying areas. Usually he would borrow Uncle Sebastian's car and drive us up into the Dolomites where it was cool in the heat of the day. Walking was rather more ambitious now that I was older. We would buy bread and cheese and olives in the marketplaces for lunch. Evelyn allowed me more than token libations of wine this time, I stayed up later, met Uncle Sebastian for breakfast less often than I had as a child.

One night we were on our own, late, after much wine had been drunk. Evelyn broke the companionable silence. 'I owe you an apology.'

'What for?'

'Well.' He was intently regarding a group of youths clustered around a motor scooter on the opposite side of the square. 'It can't have escaped your notice that I haven't been very easy to live with lately.'

'Don't be silly,' I said without conviction. In fact it seemed that he was much better in the last few months than he had been at Christmas.

'Diana thinks I have a drink problem.'

'Do you? Think so I mean?'

'Not really. I know I drink too much but it's not generally a problem. It's a question of, well, being depressed.'

'Oh.'

'I go through low phases, quite badly sometimes.'

'Why didn't you say if you were feeling down?'

He shrugged deprecatingly. 'The point is, that's when . . .' He raptly read the label on this bottle of acqua minerale. 'When I'm most likely to allow the drinking to . . . to get out of proportion. You've been very good about everything, I do realise that.'

'Don't be silly,' I said again, more warmly and patted his hand.

He smiled ruefully and filled our glasses. 'I've never regretted it, you know.'

'Now stop. You'll be weeping into your wine in a minute and telling me I'm your only friend in the world, just like Dieter.'

'I'll spare you that, I promise,' he said drily.

'Why do you get depressed, any special reason?'

'I don't know, not really. There have been times when there's a good reason. I was intermittently ill for years at the end of the war, and that was very depressing, I thought I'd never get well.'

'What did you have?'

'Oh, some sort of dysentery. It kept coming and going, I couldn't throw it off. And I daresay I was quite low anyway, shell-shocked, or whatever.'

'Did you do a lot of fighting?'

'On and off. They'd never pull you out until you were too sick to walk at all, everyone was in the same boat. And when you got sent back in you were still weak as a cat.' He gulped. 'When you know what you're in for, then it's bloody awful, the anticipation. If you have any respite it's worse going back in. That sounds cowardly, doesn't it?'

'Of course not. It sounds intelligent.'

'I remember when I told Daddy I was going to Spain he said I had no idea what I was doing, it wasn't playing soldiers. I'd never seen him so angry.'

'Did you go to Spain?'

'There was the small matter of a civil war. I had no end of trouble over it later. "Premature anti-fascism" they called it.'

'I know about the Spanish war.'

'Do you?'

'There's lots of books at Richard's. Left Book Club and stuff.'

'Not really!' Evelyn was amused.

'I think they were Angela's.'

'Ah,' said Evelyn. 'Mind you, Richard wasn't too bad over Spain.'

'Why did you go?'

'Well, I thought I was a good communist.' He laughed. 'Harry Pollitt told me I was a jumped up little public school turd. Quite true. But they took me in the end. Daddy was perfectly right too, I hadn't really got a clue. I had no excuse either, years of reading. But it was the obvious way out.'

'How do you mean?'

'Well, I wasn't getting on very well at Oxford. I didn't like the course, or the tutors. I wasn't doing any work. I was too busy being involved with all sorts of nefarious activities, politics and clubs. I was tipped off that there was going to be investigations into various things and I thought it would be much simpler just to leave. I didn't want to upset Daddy. So I went off to get killed instead.' He signalled for more wine and watched the youths riding round in turn on the motor scooter. 'It still surprises me sometimes to wake up alive at such a great age. I never supposed for a moment I'd see thirty.'

'Is it true, what Orwell said, about the anarchists and things?'

'Certainly. Some of us weren't very happy about it, we were lucky to get out alive. Angela could never understand why I wouldn't go on the homecoming march of Brigade survivors. Lots of us didn't.'

'What was she like?'

'Oh, well . . . I had a great deal of respect for her. She spent all her time working for Spain, anti-fascism, the unemployed. Her family washed their hands of her, very county, Richard wasn't considered at all eligible. I found her rather formidable at times, but I was very young.'

'She doesn't sound like the sort of wife for Richard.'

'Nonsense, they were having a wonderful time.' He smiled. 'They argued all the time, but I'm sure they did very well really.'

'Was she very beautiful?'

Evelyn considered. 'No, not at all. She just made everyone think so.'

'What was his other wife like?'

'What do you know about that?' he asked sharply.

'Nothing. I'm asking you.'

'She was very amiable. Quite young, rather pretty.'

'She sounds boring.'

But he would not be drawn any further, said it was depressing thinking of wars, of all the people he knew long dead, said it would give him bad dreams.

'Do you have bad dreams about the war?'

'Sometimes. It goes in phases. You used to have bad dreams.'

'You must wake me up if you have bad dreams.'

'Oh, love.' He squeezed my arm and invitingly held out the wine carafe.

Another motor scooter putted into the square, and soon the two were competitively revving, while the youths squabbled over who was to get rides, run a race. It was too noisy to converse any more. I knew that he was thinking of the conversation we had had here, in the same square, three years before, about adoption.

It had been much hotter on that visit and I had lived on ice cream. At last the motor scooters left the square, the cater-wauling fading in the distance and the waiters began to stack the tables and chairs. I could not remember now whether it had been this café, or another in the square. We stood to go and I found that I was unsteady. Evelyn's smile was good-naturedly mocking and he took my arm. I resolved to get him drunk every night while we were here; he was much more forthcoming drunk and I had hardly asked him anything yet. I hadn't even asked about Love. And if I had known then about Kaye, I would not have even considered asking him either.

Love was by no means my main preoccupation. I was too old to worry about Religion, and had more or less exhausted Death; now my main worry was Destiny. I had no idea what to do with my life. Evelyn was not very helpful; while he did not ridicule my grandiose notions, he tended to take the line that I was too young to have to worry about such things yet.

What I really wanted to do was be a great artist of some sort. But I knew I had no talent for drawing, and even less for music. There was no point in trying to act; I was evidently not going to be attractive and would be taller than the leading men. I secretly wrote poetry, but I had insufficient interest in reading poetry to have any hope of being good. Besides, there was no money in poetry. Other types of writing lacked sufficient grandeur. I worried a great deal about my dilemma. I really needed to talk to Tim, but he seldom came, and I never saw him alone. It did not occur to me to ask him to meet me somewhere else.

My friend Christina was very clear on the solution to this difficulty. She was clear about most things. It was this firmness of purpose that had distinguished her from most of our contemporaries. Her determination and ambition amused me; I supposed it was my delightful unconventionality that interested her. She had not deigned to notice me until the previous academic year, but by the summer I had the honour to be her principal school associate.

Christina intended to go to Oxford or Cambridge to meet rich and upcoming men. She would be able to pick and choose and end up with a future cabinet minister, or possibly a title. She was contemptuous of an Oxford graduate like my Aunt Diana settling for a mere Colonial Civil Service man.

We planned how she would run her salon; what refreshments

would be served, how the establishment would be decorated, what guests admitted. The guest list was subject to almost daily revisions and additions, depending on what we were reading, who was in the news. Our arguments over the appropriate literary, artistic and political figures to be favoured were endless. Christina was an admirer of Macmillan, and not really an intellectual, despite her pretensions. I was able to feel superior in this respect, although I never dared accuse her outright of being lowbrow. In turn she often condescended to allow my pronouncements on literature and art; it saved her the fatigue of reading things herself.

Christina, of course, had decided views on Love. She believed utterly in Grand Passions, La Dame aux Camélias, Anna Karenina, Cleopatra. On the other hand, Mary, Queen of Scots, was not in the same league, had botched it sadly in her view. But she was also firmly of the opinion that love was a mug's game, only a fool would be taken in.

'The secret is, you see,' she revealed magnanimously, 'to *inspire* Grand Passion, *not* to be the victim of it. If you can do that, Alexandria, you can have anything in the world that you like, fortune, fame, fun.'

It did not seem to occur to her that this wouldn't work if one didn't look like Elizabeth Taylor or Marilyn Monroe; but then, she didn't seem to realise that she didn't look like a film star. What irritated me is that no one else seemed to notice that either.

When she wasn't planning her own triumphant career, she speculated endlessly, gleefully on the particulars of the private lives of others. She devoured fan magazines, endlessly rehashed the romances of the stars. She was no less avid about lesser humans. I was privy in excruciating detail to her mother's pedestrian affairs. She was persistent in trying to extract information about Evelyn. I was generally unforthcoming, partly from scruple, partly, I realised, because I knew very little. But her incessant badgering eventually put her in possession of most of what I knew.

Her conjectures about Evelyn seemed as wildly improbable as the lurid fantasies she weaved around anyone else. Despite not having met him, she had very clear notions of what he was like, ruthless, unscrupulous, a hardened rake, never so gullible as to fall in love.

I certainly had no image of Evelyn as a man susceptible to romance. Nor could I imagine him as a man of savage passions, a Gothic hero accustomed to having his wicked way, loving and leaving, until hauled up short by the inevitable spirited but chaste governess (Christina favoured the violet-eyed, raven-haired version), destitute, at his mercy. I presumed that Evelyn discreetly maintained a succession of involvements, but his approach seemed desultory, indolent, never driven, desperate, violent. I was not aware of him ever having suffered in the slightest over his affairs; either he was very adept at concealing his emotions, or he had nothing to conceal, I supposed.

2

The Italian holiday had been successful in several respects. Not only did we have a good time, Evelyn and I got on much better than for many months. The rapprochement showed every sign of continuing after our return. A major bonus of the trip was the amount of ammunition it gave me against Christina. She had been sent to her grandparents near Eastbourne. They were very strict and buried in the middle of nowhere.

By contrast I was able to talk glibly of the sights of Venice and Milan, the liberty Evelyn allowed me, the alcohol I had been permitted to consume, the string of eligible and handsome young men I had met through the auspices of Uncle Sebastian's daughter Theresa. If Christina suspected my veracity, there was sufficient element of truth, more than ample plausibility, for her to be distinctly subdued for several days.

I spent a great deal of time at Christina's. I did not bring her home at first. I knew Evelyn would not like her. While I was not averse to provoking Evelyn, the bound of his reactions were unpredictable. Despite his care to be kind to Philip, I felt he would be perfectly capable of being so withering and sarcastic as to put my friendship with Christina beyond salvage.

On the whole I was careful with Evelyn, clandestine with make-up and clothes of which I felt he would particularly disapprove (he actively approved none of my purchases), ringing up scrupulously to inform him of changes of plan, keeping to the curfews he set.

After continuing unsubtle hints from Christina, and in compensation for her dull summer, I decided to risk a meeting between her and Evelyn and invited her to dinner. I knew Evelyn would have no objection. He liked filling up the flat with guests, and had frequently extended his hospitality to Bobby with forbearance.

Christina was on her most demure behaviour at first, and meekly, under my meaningful glower, Evelyn offered us a drink. When I suggested that he should see to the wine, in a manner calculated to imply that we had wine every evening, he gave me a sardonic look and went to select a bottle. He urbanely offered Christina a choice of bottles and she immediately plumped for the one he manipulated her towards choosing.

'Oh no, Evelyn, I'd much rather have the St Emilion.' But I was pleased to realise that I knew more about wines than she did.

'Alex, really. Where are your manners?' He smiled engagingly at Christina. Her choice uncorked to breathe, Evelyn went to his bath with a very large whisky.

'You didn't tell me he was good-looking,' reproached Christina.

'Evelyn? Do you think so?'

'He's a very attractive older man.' She recrossed her legs and took out a cumbersome gold-plated cigarette case and matching lighter. I fetched us new drinks while the bath water was running, so Evelyn wouldn't hear the bottles rattle.

'Anyway, he's not rich enough for you,' I said.

Christina looked around the room, the comfortable plush suite that had been Evelyn's parents', the overflow of books, the worn patches in the bordered carpet. 'No,' she agreed pointedly.

She was at her most vivacious over the meal. I brought in the starter, and Evelyn seated her, poured wine, mercifully without remarking on my appropriation of the Christmas Fortnum's paté.

'Do you believe in Free Love, Mr Parrish?'

Evelyn finished his toast triangle, sipped the wine. 'Well, it's a nice idea. But you know, by the time you've had as much experience as I, you'll find that there's no such thing as Free Love, there's always a hidden cost.'

'You must be very experienced by now.'

'Very,' said Evelyn.

'Alexandra Kollantai said it should be as natural as drinking a glass of water.' She unaesthetically heaped more paté on her plate.

'But water is so boring, don't you think?' Evelyn smiled

beguilingly. I wondered why I'd never noticed before; he was really very nice-looking, even for someone so old.

'One can always drink champagne.'

'If one can afford champagne.'

'A cynic,' explained Christina to me kindly, 'is one who knows the price of everything and the value of nothing. I'm so glad you invited me tonight; Thursday is Mummy's lover's night.'

'You find yourself, er, *de trop?*'

She gave Evelyn a perfunctory smile, tossed back her long blonde hair and confided the excruciating details of Mummy's lover, leaving us in no doubt of the tension between mother and daughter as a result of the man's inclination to admire Christina.

'And does Mummy's lover have a name?' enquired Evelyn dulcetly.

'I call him "Gerald". Mummy always tries to make me call him "Uncle Gerald". But I'm much too old for that sort of nonsense, don't you agree – Evelyn?'

I was glad when the meal was over. Evelyn cleared away our simple midweek cheese board of six cheeses and Bath Olivers. Christina took out a cigarette and toyed with the lighter in a meaningful way, with sultry, sidelong looks at Evelyn.

'Why don't you kids run along upstairs and leave the washing up to me?' he suggested thoughtfully, going through to pour himself what Uncle Richard referred to as a post-prandial. We had been given only one glass of wine at the meal; it was rare, even on holiday, that I was allowed more than one drink, even now that I was older. Multiple drinks invariably meant smaller measures.

When Christina had gone Evelyn said, 'Don't you ever see anything of Bobby anymore?'

'*Do* you believe in Free Love?'

' "Believe" is a bit strong. But I'm not married, and I'm not a bloody monk.' After a pause he said, 'And you needn't think that gives you licence for that bloody brat to egg you on. I should have known you'd turn up with more friends that need watching.'

'I don't know what you mean.'

'Don't say I didn't warn you.'

I attempted to divert him. 'Have you ever been in love, Evelyn?'

'Why? Is there something you need to know?'

I shook my head. 'I was just wondering.' Last year, on his return from America, in the wake of my first period, he had given me an embarrassingly blunt talk. He had disregarded my protestations that I knew all about 'that', saying that if I had my information from the likes of Bobby it was guaranteed to be wildly inaccurate. This was true. He finished his explicit discourse by adjuring me to come to him at once if I was in difficulty or needed further information. He said he would be very angry if I got into trouble, there was no excuse now I'd had full information, but none the less he hoped I knew I could rely on him and would do so.

'Are you in love?'

'Of course not,' I said indignantly. '*Have* you ever been in love?'

'If I tell you to mind your own bloody business I suppose you'll just harass Richard or Louisa instead.'

'Evelyn!'

'I know you better than that. You're not to mention such a thing to them, is that understood?'

'I won't if you tell me.'

'Well, get me another drink.' I fetched the decanter through. 'The fact is, I'm not remotely convinced there is such a thing as being "in love".'

'Evelyn.'

'Well, there isn't. One can either care for someone, love, if you like, or want them, I mean physically, but I don't believe that either constitutes being "in love".'

'What about both at once?'

'I don't suppose that happens very often.'

'So what you're saying is, that when most people think they're "in love", they just fancy someone?'

'Well . . . yes.'

'That's awfully cynical, Evelyn.'

He laughed. 'Shocking, isn't it?'

'So you're never been "in love"?'

'Oh, well, I suppose when I was very young I must have imagined myself in love a few times. Nothing to speak of. Look here, are you luridly imagining my solitary state is the result of a broken heart?'

'Of course not. I can't imagine you being in love."

'Ancient and decreipt as I am. Well, thank you.'

'That's not what I meant at all.'

'Cold and unfeeling as I am.'

'Evelyn.'

'Now that's enough. Unless there's anything else you need to know, can we consider the subject closed?'

'That's very helpful. I'm sure I won't make the mistake of imagining I'm in love with anyone.'

'But you have been hitherto?'

'Evelyn!'

'You mean that abominable girl has encouraged you to think so?'

'Evelyn!'

'Now really, Alex, I'm not stupid.'

'I was just wondering. Everyone at school goes on about being in love all the time. I wondered if there was something wrong with me.'

'Nothing but an excess of the prosaic. The fact is, Alex, that you've outgrown that sort of schoolgirl nonsense.'

'You mean I missed it altogether.'

He bit his smile and topped up his glass.

'Evelyn!'

'Well, love, if you think I can't remember what a crush you had on Tim, days of weeping every time he left, talking of nothing but Tim, pestering him, really, Alex.'

'It wasn't like that at all, we're *friends*.'

He raised his brows and shrugged. 'Evidently I've been labouring under a misapprehension all these years. My apologies, my dear.'

His views, in fact, were much what Christina had predicted. But I did not tell her what he had said, did not even mention that any such discussion had taken place. I knew that she would not rest until she was in full possession of all the details, had embroidered them satisfactorily out of all recognition. Increasingly I resented her prying, kept more and more to myself. Her sordidness was entertaining, but not when it extended to Evelyn.

In retrospect I was outraged at the perfidiousness of this discussion. What he told me seemed to bear no relation to the truth of his situation. It appeared that during all that time, he had been languishing after Kaye. And if he had not been pining, why on earth did he allow her to invade our lives so comprehensively?

The first I knew of Kaye's existence was several months after this conversation, shortly after Christmas, our first Christmas since Uncle Cecil had died and Hellisford put up for sale. I had returned home from school, long before Evelyn was due back from work, to find the hall filled with baggage. As I edged past the suitcases, my first thought was that Evelyn had not mentioned that he was going away on business. And he certainly wouldn't take nearly so much luggage. Moreover, his suitcases were much more expensive, and there were some boxes and bundles tied with sheets. In the living-room Evelyn perched on the arm of the chair by the fire and a woman sat in the chair, huddled forward over the blaze.

'Alex, this is Kaye. She'll be staying for a few days.'

3

'I suppose it's too much to expect an uninterrupted night's sleep,' I said sarcastically. Kaye had been staying for over a week, and although I resentfully kept a balance sheet of every inconvenience or slight, real or imagined, I had not hitherto been awakened by them at four in the morning.

Evelyn was dressed willy nilly, unshaven, car keys in hand. 'This is no time to be giving yourself airs.' His voice squeaked with anger. 'Go and sit with Kaye while I get the car. And try to be civil. She's having a miscarriage.' He was running downstairs before I could say anything.

Kaye was perched on the edge of the bed, half-dressed, spinelessly sniffling. In a feeble voice she refused my offers of assistance, thanked me, apologised. I found some shoes for her and a coat. It was left to Evelyn to finish dressing her, drape the coat over her shoulders.

'Now stop that,' he said sternly. 'It's no good being hysterical.'

For a moment I thought he would hit her. She cowered and drew long hiccoughing breaths. 'There now.' He put his arm around her and helped her downstairs. He told me to set the alarm, that I wasn't to miss school.

But I could not get to sleep. I changed Evelyn's sheets. There was blood on the sheets and the underblanket, blood tinged the mattress beneath. Squeamishly I bundled up the bedding, threw away Kaye's ruined nightdress. Feeling quite unwell, I huddled in front of the living-room fire with a pot of tea.

Everything was much clearer now. If her husband took exception not merely to infidelity but to the paternity of the child, his behaviour was, if not justified, at least explicable. It was no wonder that Kaye needed refuge at short notice, that Evelyn had felt bound to provide it, after such a savage beating. I tried to reason myself out of being surprised at Evelyn; I knew perfectly well that he had no respect for conventions. But I couldn't help being surprised that he hadn't been more careful; that he was in difficulties over such a commonplace girl.

I had not done my French homework; I didn't know whether I would copy someone's at break, or brazen through the lesson without it. Now, perversely, with a ready-made excuse to hand, I tried to avoid thinking about Evelyn's situation by doing the exercise. Besides, we hadn't been taught anything useful. I didn't know how to say 'the mistress of my uncle' or 'miscarriage'. Not, I supposed, that I would be believed anyway.

I did not like to think of Evelyn's private life. But I worried at the thought, furtively, like a tongue on a toothache. I could not imagine, however improbable Evelyn's tastes were, that he could find a nylon baby-doll style nightie erotic, not *pink*. Aside from anything else, Kaye would be all gooseflesh beneath it, unless the fire was kept running all night.

He was very late back after work, and looked so weary that I forebore to harangue him. I fetched him a drink, asked politely after Kaye.

'Oh, she'll be all right. They'll keep her in for a few days.' His face set grimly. 'I'd forgotten what it's like in hospital. Bunch of sadists.' Initially Evelyn had been assumed to have himself inflicted Kaye's beating, but when he had overcome the hostility and put them straight, only an articulate display of upper class officiousness had prevented them from ringing Kaye's husband, revealing her whereabouts.

'Did you send her some flowers?'

'Yes, of course.'

I organised a meal. It was no doubt unfair to judge Kaye by what I had so far observed. She would certainly be lively and interesting once she was over the shock of what had happened to her. And probably, once her bruises faded she would be very attractive, although perhaps not pretty. I wondered if Evelyn still had an account at the florists' around the corner from his office.

Evelyn spent most of his time the next few evenings reorganising his bedroom. Many of his own belongings were packed away, hung in the hall cupboard to make space for Kaye. There was no question now but she would have to stay a while longer. She was ill and frightened, in no state to find a job and a bedsit, for a month or so anyway. I knew perfectly well that she would never go, just as I had known that the show of Evelyn bedding down on cushions downstairs the first few nights after her arrival would not last. With calculated goodwill, I cooked and arranged flowers in all the rooms for her return. Deliberately I lingered at Christina's after school to give them time together, returning only in time for dinner.

'Evelyn!' There was blood on his shirt, he held a tea towel to his head.

'Would you believe it,' he said in disgust. 'An old boy like that.'

'Old? Is her husband old?'

'No, no, her father.' It transpired that Kaye had felt lonely, rung her mum. She had been persuaded to discharge herself into her parents' care, but her father had then rung her husband to come and collect her. Fortunately, Evelyn, missing Kaye at the hospital, had gone to see if she was really all right. He had had to force his way past the door, there had been a fierce altercation and Evelyn was assaulted. Kaye had come away with Evelyn, his coat over her nightdress, in great haste, before the wronged husband arrived.

'But does he want her back? Her husband?'

'Evidently. He probably intends to kill her this time, now he knows she's been here.' He put the cold cloth aside and gulped at a large drink. 'Oh God. No, don't go, it'll only be him.' But eventually he could endure the leaning on the doorbell no longer and went down.

'. . . purely routine, sir.' The voice was deferential. Filling the hall, hats in hand, were two policemen. I offered tea, which was accepted with anticipatory rubbing of hands, remarks on the remorseless rain.

The other one was brusque. goading Evelyn with Kaye's father's version of events, insisting that Evelyn had started the affray, pointing out that he had no right to abduct Kaye.

'I didn't hit him. I was particularly careful not to. And I didn't abduct her, she came willingly. One could say eagerly. If that bloody husband of hers had got there first *he* would have abducted her.'

'But as you're not her husband this *is* a police matter.'

'Are you suggesting that if her husband had taken her you'd have done nothing?'

'That's a domestic matter.'

'Domestic! He put her in hospital. I suppose if it was murder it would be bloody domestic!'

'Look, sir,' jollied the deferential one. 'If we could just see the lady, have a quick word.'

'I'll go up and see if she's awake,' said Evelyn sulkily.

'Now really, sir,' said the brusque one sorrowfully, catching Evelyn by the arm. 'If you don't mind, I think we'd better see the lady alone.'

When they had satisified themselves that Kaye was not being detained against her will they went, leaving her sobbing on Evelyn's shoulder, cursing her father. I was quite sure I had never seen Evelyn so angry.

'Call yourself a bloody socialist,' he rounded on me. 'Refreshments! Why not a drink? I don't mind, keep the whole force pissed as rats.'

'Don't be ridiculous, it was only a cup of tea.'

'It's only the bloody principle of the thing. If you'd ever told me I'd see that lot drinking my tea in my house . . .'

'You're being melodramatic. Take up Kaye's milk before it gets cold.'

He stomped upstairs. I could hardly blame him for being so furious at not being believed, but I was surprised by his over-reaction.

It was not the first time he had been hurt. He was merely annoyed that he had let it happen. He didn't seem worried about the threat of Kaye's husband, except in so far as it distressed her. He showed no fear of being hurt, being worsted. I remembered the cut on his brow on my first day in his care. I wondered what had really happened. I thought of Tim arriving on the doorstep, covered in blood.

I thought of another occasion, long forgotten. Two men, whom I had supposed were Evelyn's friends, had visited late one night but soon Evelyn picked a fight with one and had banged him repeatedly against a doorway before throwing the pair out. The next morning I had noticed a brown smear and some hairs on the door jamb. But Evelyn had been younger then, and younger than his opponent. I was worried what would happen if Kaye's husband were to find them. I knew Evelyn was very strong, but he was quite old these days. He was really much too old to be making such a fool of himself over a woman in her early twenties.

As I had suspected, Kaye was not much use. She kept out of my way, and was always conciliatory, but she did nothing. She didn't help around the house, or cook or shop or even wash up and Evelyn invariably countered any half-hearted offer of help by insisting that she was a guest.

Kaye's routine was to get up after noon and have a long bath, with Radio Caroline and magazines. By the time I arrived from school she would be engrossed in getting ready for Evelyn's return from work. She would take the rollers out of her hair and fill the flat with the smell of hairspray. Then she would do her nails, sometimes her toenails with new varnish. Thick foundation covered her face, even after there was no need for the disguise of her bruises; her eyes were painted with black liner and framed by false lashes, highlighted with shades of purple or green; her lips coated with 'Baby Pink' or 'Winter Blossom'.

Even so, Kaye was very striking looking, with a square face and high cheekbones. Despite the rollers and hairspray, one side of her fringed brown bob turned obstinately outwards after a few hours, so that she was always licking her fingers and pulling at the ends of her hair. The deceptively wilful set of her chin, the forceful look of her deep set eyes were out of keeping with the docile passivity of her personality.

I supposed that it would only be a matter of time before Evelyn was heartily bored. But he had persevered this far. I began to realise that I really didn't know him very well after all. The question was whether he would become bored before Aunt Louisa and Aunt Diana got wind of the affair.

I was surprised to find that I had no temptation to bear tales. My rage had died with Kaye's miscarriage. I was still very angry with Evelyn, but there seemed little to be gained from making an adversary of Kaye. There would be scant satisfaction in besting someone so pathetic, and it would not help matters with Evelyn. I made myself as scarce as possible, at Christina's after school, at work on Saturdays.

4

Mr Wainwright, of course, never spoke of Love, and it would certainly never have occurred to me that he would have anything useful or interesting to say on the subject. But he saw himself, and was, an essentially Romantic character, despite his absurdity. He cultivated a formidable veneer, but that had never intimidated me, even at the outset. No doubt it was because I was in a blaze of fury at the time, but my indifference to his scathing tongue, my bold replies, served as no calculating stratagems could have done to commend me to him.

Christina, I felt, had not been sufficiently helpful about the Kaye situation. Her proposed solutions were inadequate, or merely melodramatic. It seemed also that she was deriving no little enjoyment from the misfortunes of her friend. I decided that offensive action was required, but nothing that would smack of childishness, histrionics or sulking. This narrowed down the field considerably. In this frame of mind, wandering piteously around the West End, driven from my home, I had seen the card in the window. After toying with the idea overnight, I had rushed home from school, pinned my hair up and ironed a black dress. It had not been an auspicious interview.

'You?' The bearded man behind the counter glared at me and changed his glasses. 'What do you know about books?'

'My dad collects books,' I produced.

He asked a great many questions about what Evelyn had, what I'd read. I was able to turn my browsing of the old books at Hellisford to good account. Then he had me do some mental addition of prices and calculation of change. 'Well.' He chewed the stem of the spare spectacles. 'How old are you?'

'Sixteen,' I said too promptly.

'And so am I.'

'Fifteen. Practically sixteen.' Only another ten months to go.

'You won't get very much. It would suit me, really. Less since you're under sixteen, you know.'

'That's all right.'

'Well, we don't usually take people like you.' He swapped his glasses, and turned back to a tray of papers. 'All right then. You can start tomorrow.' He had not come from behind the counter or offered me a seat, conducting the whole interrogation as he served customers.

'I've got a job,' I announced provocatively to Evelyn.

'A job?' His brows drew together. 'What sort of job?'

'A Saturday job. In a bookshop. Off Charing Cross Road.'

'Well, that sounds very interesting.'

I had expected remonstrance, remorse, apology, or at very least, acrimony. I flounced to my room, not even having the satisfaction of being able to break off the discussion in a huff.

I lay on my bed, again and again going over the scene confronting me on my return from school that fateful Monday, wishing with single-minded intensity to eradicate it from our lives, put the clock back. I remembered that I had been cheerful, that I had planned to cook for Evelyn, never dreaming that my life, Evelyn's life was already ruined forever, that my thoughtfulness was to be repaid by such perfidy.

Now, after more than three weeks, it seemed an eternity since Kaye had come. I kept to my room, answered in civil monosyllables, and by superhuman effort managed not to say the hateful things that filled my mind. I contrived to notice Kaye as little as possible without evident rudeness.

'He meant girls. Mr W. never has girls,' Hillyard explained kindly the next morning. 'But he's in a bit of a jam, what with one thing and another. He's too mean to advertise in the *Standard* or something.'

Mr Wainwright seemed satisfied with me. I was enthusiastic, and did all the boring things that hadn't been done for months, dusting the window displays, scourging all the tea cups, filing letters. I did little till duty. Much time was taken up with making tea, the junior's job. I also made up mail order parcels, receiving a rare encomium on the neatness of my work and ensuring the task now wholly devolved to me. It was me that was sent to the bank for change, round the corner for pints of milk.

Mr Wainwright spent his day on a stool behind the counter, answering letters and pricing secondhand stock. Lots of people tried to sell books, and he enjoyed haggling for hours. The most favoured runners got a stool and a cup of tea. When he was bored, Mr Wainwright would offer resumés or unsolicited testimonials of whatever book a customer was perusing. He was mordant at best, malicious not infrequently. One reason he liked me was that I never took umbrage at his sharp tongue, sometimes retorting wittily if I thought of something.

'I wish you wouldn't be so bloody keen,' Hillyard grumbled. 'He'll start getting ideas about the rest of us. Besides, it's so *fatiguing*.' Hillyard looked as if just getting up in the morning had almost finished him off, indeed, he hadn't got to work on time. He had straight pale hair, straggling spikily on to his grubby collar, and a sickly complexion, greenish, sometimes purple under the eyes if he'd had a late night. He was very slight, and staggered pitifully under stacks of books. ('Well, you look big and strong,' Mr Wainwright had allowed on the first morning, evidently on the verge of changing his mind and sending me away.)

I had only been sorry to go home at six. I kept to my room for the rest of the weekend. The enormity of the disaster prevented me from running to Crystal Palace or Uncle Richard with the news. I had no desire to be the messenger of such tidings. I wanted very much to visit Uncle Richard, to be suitably cossetted, but it was not just the news of Kaye that prevented me. I was convinced that he would not regard my job as showing initiative, but rather think that shop work was a sad comedown from my exalted ambitions.

Uncle Richard had rescued me from my dilemma over a career in a characteristically pragmatic fashion, suggesting that I do Law. Initially I had, with some trepidation, consulted him about the possibility of entering the firm. He seemed so surprised at the idea that I was offended.

'Just because I'm a girl. It's not fair!'

'It's nothing to do with you being female, really, my dear . . .'

'But you're going to have Chris. Why can't you have me? He's not even a Parrish.' The more I had considered it, the more I had resented that my cousin Christopher might be given a position.

'I have no intention of taking on Christopher, I assure you.'

'He said it was all settled.'

Uncle Richard looked thunderous. 'Well, that's simply not true. This is the first I've heard of it. I can't imagine why he should suppose I'd rather have him than Nicky or John. Or you. Or my nephews. When did you hear this?'

'He was telling everyone at the centenary party.'

'Was he, by God! Just wait until I . . .' He jumped out of his chair and prowled round the room, hitting a few resonating bass chords on the piano. 'To be perfectly honest I had no idea that you had the remotest interest in the firm.'

'Well, I have.'

He sat down again and sceptically drew in his mouth. 'But you've seldom asked about anything. And don't dare tell me how exciting you find engineering.'

'I've talked to Evelyn a lot,' I said sulkily. 'I know lots about what he does.'

'Then perhaps you should be considering going into sales. Evelyn is really sales, not engineering. Or management.' He talked fluently on the limitless possibilities for a career in sales, especially with a product not rooted in an entirely male industry.

'Yuch! Demonstrating make-up in Selfridge's. There's no money in that.'

'Now really. What about Evelyn's friend Ben? He's doing very well; I believe he started as a rep in publishing.'

I was revolted. 'But they're *poor*.'

'Alexandria, no one is going to hand you a sinecure on a plate. The sooner you realise that the better.'

'You got one. Just for being a boy.'

'Let me assure you I got nothing,' he said stiffly. 'Do you have any idea of the mess this company was in by the end of the war!'

'I thought everyone made money out of the war.'

'Not Theodore.' With controlled patience he reminded me that he had left the firm before the war, and that he had no intention of returning. His position had been held for him in his other job; everyone had also assumed that Parrish's would be nationalised by the Labour government. He had been appalled to find that there would be no nationalisation, that Cecil looked to him to sort out the mess, and had taken a great deal of persuading to take on the task. He insisted that he would have had an equally remunerative situation with far less worry if he had stayed where he was and he felt no one had done him any favours.

'You gave Evelyn a job.'

'If you'd been party to the interviews, you'd have been in no doubt he was the best man for the job, I assure you. And he didn't get a directorship on a plate. He earned that, he got results.'

'But someone will have to come in when you retire.'

'Whoever's up to it. I certainly don't intend to throw everything away just to keep it in the family. There's no room for any dead wood.'

'But I wouldn't be dead wood.'

Uncle Richard sighed. 'Oh God, you make me sound just like your Uncle Theodore.' He poured drinks. 'I sometimes think it was a mistake to allow myself to be talked into coming back. There was the possibility of going back to Oxford, a fellowship. I'd have liked that.' He handed me a sherry. 'If you want my advice, you'll do whatever it is that you really want to. It's not worth wasting your life drudging away at something that bores you silly, believe me. I'm sure Evelyn would tell you the same.'

'Poor Uncle Richard.'

Unexpectedly he grinned. 'It's not all been bad, I really can't complain.'

But in the end, from Destiny, to Career, it was down to a Job, for all Mr Wainwright's fluency about Dedication, Service, a Way of Life, especially when the question of wages arose.

5

I spent as much time as possible away from home. Evelyn was suddenly amenable to whatever I suggested; where previously objections and protracted negotiations attended my requests for later curfews, overnight stays with Christina, extra spending money, he now meekly acquiesced to most schemes, with a token face-saving grumble. My main difficulty was where to go.

Christina was having similar domestic problems with her mother; she preferred to make herself scarce when Mrs Schaffer was entertaining gentlemen callers. On evenings when Evelyn was taking Kaye out, she came round to see me. Often though, we nursed halves of cider in pubs, both parents supposing we were at the other's. I found it gratifying that we were almost invariably served without challenge but Christina was blasé. It would in fact have been impossible to tell whether we were thirteen or thirty beneath the elaborate make-up we applied at Mrs Schaffer's three mirrored dressing table before going out. (I could never manage to call her 'Desirée' as Christina repeatedly urged me to do.) Arriving home, I would bolt up to my room, avoiding Evelyn until I had cleaned my face with cold cream.

Increasingly I wearied of Christina. I was fed up with being patronised. I knew that I had no looks, but I was sure that I wouldn't imagine that long blonde hair would disguise the fact that I was dumpy and broad-bummed if I looked like her. She was no more pretty than I was, and her hair was so dark it could only just be considered blonde. But we always considered her conquests, her opportunities, her success, seldom my own.

I found her advice regarding my changed situation unpalatable. It was true that I turned matters to good account. But her calculating the gains so coldly gave me real qualms of conscience. And I felt somehow that there was a qualitative difference between extracting concessions such as an extra hour on weekend evenings and a leather jacket, and planning a campaign of intimidation against Kaye. I wasn't very nice to her, scarcely concealing my contempt, but I wasn't actively rude either, and I quailed at the idea of a war of attrition. I felt that Christina had no idea of what Evelyn was really like if she supposed he would tolerate such behaviour, that he could not easily beat me at my own game.

'Really Alexandria, don't you know anything about men! You take my advice.'

I wondered why she should suppose that I knew any less than her about the manipulation of men, having lived six years with Evelyn, having had a succession of male babysitters. I remembered her last encounter with Evelyn, what I hoped would be her only encounter with Uncle Richard.

It had been one of Christina's regular Thursday evenings, and Richard came from work with Evelyn. Inexorably she unleashed her charms on Richard. I was astonished when he leapt forward with suitable deference to take her lighter, offer one of his own cigarettes. She smiled flutteringly up at him, gleaming with self satisfaction as I waited in vain to be offered a cigarette too. In fact, I had persevered for several weeks under the spur of Bobby's ridicule, but had never managed to get over feeling horribly sick.

Christina ran through her repertoire of sophisticated gestures, wry faces, leaning forward, crossing and recrossing her legs, as she chatted to Richard about herself.

'And are you going to read for the Bar, like Alex?'

'Oh, I don't think so, it's so terribly dull. I'm going to be a world-renowned courtesan.'

'How very interesting. I've always wondered, how does one get started in that line? I mean, what's the career ladder, does one need qualifications, is there an exam, that sort of thing?'

'You girls run along now,' said Evelyn firmly. 'Richard and I have business to discuss.'

'What a poisonous child,' Richard said audibly in our wake.

'He's not nearly as attractive as Evelyn,' Christina retorted.

'But he's much richer,' Evelyn pointed out as he closed the door.

'Really, my dear Alexandria, you haven't got them very well trained.'

The purchase of my leather jacket marked a period of coolness. I had been longing for one in emulation of my cousin John, but Christina disapproved, both of John and of the image. '*Not* sophisticated, Alexandria.' I wore the jacket all the time in an attempt to wear it in. John's jacket was a veteran, collar moulded to his neck, arms creased, skid marked. I looked forward to riding pillion looking the part.

The first time John had stayed with us was on his way back from Europe. He had taken a year out after his 'A' levels, travelling abroad. He had gone to Sicily and Tripoli, as well as all the usual places. He had arrived back late one evening, looking very thin and brown, his head shaved, his glasses mended with a sticking plaster. Evelyn had plied him with food and drink. John showed his sketch books of architectural drawings, talked until the small hours. He stayed for a week, before setting off to his paternal grandmother's with clean laundry, new clothes and a respectable, if unflattering, crew cut.

He had fitted in easily with our routine, got on well with George and William. He enjoyed Evelyn's sophisticated treatment of him, talking as with an equal, offering him drinks. I knew too that Evelyn had cabled him some money once while he was away, as well as tiding him over on his return. In his first year at the School of Architecture John had frequently come to London for the weekend. After that it seemed to go in phases, depending on the other friends he could stay with in London and how much was happening in Oxford.

Now I was older he sometimes good-naturedly suffered me to accompany him if he went to Eel Pie or the Craw-dad. He would bike down from Oxford on his Bantam and take me on the back wherever we were going. Evelyn raised no objection to where I was going if I was with John. For his part, John liked having a companion who could be relied upon not to be demanding or expect romantic attentions. Although I was awed by him, and had been chagrined that my billing of him as an eligible older man had failed to impress Christina, I no more expected or wanted romance than if he had been my elder brother.

'I don't know what Mum's going to say.' He gulped at his pint. Instead of getting half cut at Evelyn's expense before the gig as he normally did, he had dragged me away as soon as decently possible to a pub.

'That's not true. We know exactly what she's going to say.'

He smiled ruefully. 'We'll never hear the end of it.'

'Are you going to tell her?'

'Alex!' He was horrified. 'It's nothing to do with me.'

After I had poured out all the details about the affair with Kaye, complained at length, it was time to go. Neither of us, nor Evelyn, thought anything of his riding the bike after he'd been drinking. He was never foolhardy and sometimes at the end of the evening he would say that if I didn't mind he'd take it slowly.

John was nice to Kaye, made a point of talking with her; probably, I thought viciously, because he fancied her, she was his own age. But he did not come for the weekend again for a long time.

Increasingly I fell back on the company of Philip. He was now as tall as me and filling out nicely. About every fortnight or so I had dinner at Philip's. Invariably the meal would be punctuated by someone ringing to call out Philip's father. He was a GP, nearing retirement. I thought he was bracing to the point of rudeness with the patients, but I supposed a lifetime of cold dinners and false alarms had engendered a healthy callousness. Philip's mother looked forward wistfully to rural retirement, half apologetic about being in town, as if she would be accused of wilful maltreatment of her children.

I felt that the Marigards did not approve of me, although they were always unfailingly polite. They made allowances for the fact that I had an unsuitable home life. I did not try them nearly as far as I might; even that wasn't entertaining, damped as it always was by the doctor's wide experience of humanity. Often Philip's sister would be there as well. She was some years older than him and married to a man who travelled to the Middle East a lot. Her refinement was even more oppressive than her mother's. Philip seemed to have no other friends and was always available at short notice if I rang him up.

I was mortified that no one else displayed any interest in me. I supposed it was because I was too tall. It was grossly unfair that I should have an aunt who was an accredited Beauty, an uncle still attractive enough to appeal to a woman like Kaye, who was scarcely older than me, and have inherited nothing from them except too much nose. But other girls with little looks received attentions. I realised I needed advice.

'Richard? Do you find me attractive?'

'Certainly not. If you think you're going to play off all the tricks you've picked up from that appalling girl on me.'

I squeezed out a few tears. 'It's all right. I didn't think you would. Nobody does. It's not your fault I'm so ugly,' I said bravely.

'Don't be ridiculous. Now what's all this in aid of?'

'I thought you'd be honest with me at least. I want to know what's wrong with me.'

'My dear child, there's nothing wrong with you. Why on earth should you think such a thing?'

'Nobody's interested in me. I'm the only one without a boyfriend.'

'What about Philip?'

'Philip!' I scoffed. 'Yuch. Besides, that's *platonic*.'

'So I should hope at your age. Do you really suppose Philip is any different from any of your friends' boyfriends?'

'It's because I'm too tall, isn't it?'

'Too tall for what? Don't be absurd. When you're older you'll find things like that aren't the least important. Look at your Aunt Diana, she's taller than Gordon. Sophie's taller than Leo. Angela was almost as tall as me, quite a few of her shoes made her taller. I really do assure you it doesn't matter, my dear.'

'Then what is wrong with me? Why isn't anyone interested in me?'

'I should imagine it's chiefly your age. I'm sure we were all interested in older girls at that age. And older boys aren't likely to attend to a girl your age either. You're really much too young to be worrying about these things.'

'It's not fair. I wish I was pretty.'

'Like Blanche? You're being quite silly. There's nothing wrong with your looks. I daresay you'll be very presentable in a few years, and you'll have the sort of looks that last; you won't be a faded flower before you're thirty like your grandmother.'

Unexpectedly it was Richard who filled the breach. He was the first of the family to become aware of Kaye's installation in the flat. I was taken aback when I realised that they already knew each other. Evelyn had dallied not merely with a married woman, but with one of his own employees. I was not aware of him having done so before; it would be characteristic of him to keep his private life carefully separate from work. Kaye was horribly flustered by meeting Richard again under the circumstances but he was very kind about putting her at her ease.

I took to visiting Richard at the weekends. He seemed to be working very hard, even over the weekend. But he always appeared glad to leave his work, turning off the lamp on his desk in the little office that had originally been a maid's room, behind his kitchen. There was barely room for the desk and filing cabinet between all his wine racks. He would make tea and later on, if he wasn't playing bridge in the evening, he would take me out for a meal.

Gradually we fell into a routine of an evening out most weekends, a meal or a show, or even both. I would pin up my long hair, worn in the week hanging straight down from a centre parting, find one of my more demure dresses, leave the leather jacket at home. If I was finding it particularly difficult to cope I would invite myself to stay for the weekend. When the weather was nice he would take me out in the car on Sunday. It was comforting being with Richard, it was like it had been when I was a little girl.

6

It was to be expected that somehow Aunt Louisa would get wind of what was going on. I arrived from school one afternoon to find her and Aunt Hetty having tea with Kaye. Kaye appeared so agitated that I could almost feel sorry for her, and I exerted myself to smooth things over. I could tell that Aunt Louisa wanted me to leave them, but I knew Kaye would much prefer I didn't. But mainly I knew that Evelyn would be back from work any time, and I had no intention of missing his reaction.

He stood in the doorway, putting his coat on a hanger, looking so utterly weary that I felt compassion for him for the first time in weeks. I could not help admiring his act, jaunty, chirpy, pleasantly surprised, as he kissed the old ladies, chastely pecked Kaye's cheek, poured drinks.

'We despaired of you ever coming to see us, so we decided to see you while we were in town,' said Aunt Louisa.

'You should have rung me to give you lunch.' He sounded admirably contrite, and in the dining-room drank off several fingers of whisky before refilling the glass and joining the company.

But Aunt Louisa rapidly reduced Evelyn to a shuffling schoolboy under her unflinching scrutiny. 'You should have come down one weekend, brought Kaye down to meet us. Really, Evelyn, one might suppose you're ashamed of the girl. It's not very flattering to her.'

Evelyn muttered some disjointed phrases about Kaye not having been well.

'You really must forgive him, my dear.' Aunt Louisa smiled kindly at Kaye. 'He's not accustomed to courting young ladies. I'm sure he'd have brought you to meet us in due course.' With ill grace Evelyn leaned forward to light her regally waved cigarette. 'Kaye's been telling us all about how very kind you've been. I'm so glad you've been looking after the poor child so well.'

Evelyn lit Kaye's cigarette and took one for himself. My aunts exchanged glances as he coughed. Evelyn almost never smoked. I remembered my shock as he had cadged one of Tim's cigarettes on the first occasion that Tim had turned up, how primly disapproving I'd been. Evelyn unbuttoned his collar and pulled off his tie with a violent tug, lashing it like Berry's tail as she watched birds in the garden from the fire escape landing.

At last they went, Aunt Louisa deftly manipulating Evelyn into seeing them to their car, no doubt in order to give him a piece of her mind. Kaye and Evelyn then had a row, and I hastily left the flat. Christina was out, Richard's number rang unanswered. Philip was dragooned into meeting me in a pub, my change conveniently running out before he could demur. Much to my annoyance, no one would serve us. I was surprised; had never had any difficulty before. It was Philip; he looked all of fourteen, despite having turned sixteen.

In the icy spring dusk we wandered along the Embankment, around the West End, Philip ecstatically clutching my hand. Eventually, to keep warm we nursed cups of cappuccino in Mario's until Philip insisted that he would have to go.

'Will you turn into a pumpkin?' I said viciously.

'You don't understand.' He looked pained. 'Just because *he* doesn't care where you are. It's different for me, my dad isn't too busy cavorting with his mistress to care about me.'

With satisfying melodrama, I slapped him across the face and ran out. The truth was that Philip was revelling in the whole business. He was flattered by my recourse to his company. His ego expanded visibly as he expounded on Evelyn's unsuitability, planned how he would cherish me and look after me when we were married. His complacent proprietariness grew apace, goading me to increasing outrageousness. And he liked the salaciousness, thrilled to say words such as 'mistress' in a blasé adult manner, blushed in the company of the fallen woman.

Philip trotted along next to me, doggedly determined that I could not go home unescorted even if I never spoke to him again. Indeed, I could hardly be blamed for being upset by his unkindness. He would not say another word, would never bother me again, but must insist on seeing me to my door.

'You may kiss me goodnight,' I relented. I endured his mouth brushing my cheek, saw his cheeks shining with tears. 'Idiot.' I made myself kiss his mouth. Emboldened, he embraced me, put his mouth against mine.

'Really, Alex.' Evelyn's reproof was unexpectedly mild. Philip retreated in incoherent disorder, edging round Evelyn on the pavement as if he anticipated being hit. I was relieved by such a timely interruption. I did not even wave at Philip as we went inside.

'He's not very good at it,' I placated.

'It's a question of practice. You'd be well advised to let him practice on someone else.'

'I don't usually let him do anything. Not that he even usually *asks*.'

'He evidently knows what's good for him.'

'I think the whole business is vastly overrated anyway.'

'I'm sure you're right.' Evelyn poured a drink, stacked Jelly Roll Morton records and found a new magazine from his briefcase. Kaye had gone to bed. He didn't seem in the least distressed by his altercation with Kaye, nor remotely concerned to go up to her. His choice of music didn't suggest a bad mood either.

I considered the visit of Louisa and Hetty. They had been dressed for battle, not shopping. Aunt Louisa had been wearing her church coat and hat, her feet spilling over her Sunday court shoes like loaves in tins. Aunt Hetty too was dressed to impress, in a multicoloured velvet jacket, her hair restrained into a precarious French pleat instead of straggling in its usual knot at the nape of her neck. If they had seriously been 'doing' Oxford Street they'd have worn sensible shoes, workmanlike tweed suits. They had come up to town specially.

Their kindness to Kaye was unexpected, but I found that I was relieved. I had felt momentarily sick, waiting for an unpleasant scene to break over Evelyn's head. But there had been no ultimatums, no threat of a breach. I realised that they had even less stomach for a confrontation with Evelyn than I had. They could not approve, nor could they stop caring for Evelyn.

It was my impression that part of the settlement in the wake of Hetty and Louisa's visit was the reciprocal presentation of Evelyn to Kaye's family. Certainly it was not long after that Kaye's mother and sisters came one Sunday evening. Kaye gossiped and giggled with the girls in the kitchen. Mrs Cooper's help had been refused, Kaye insisting that she put her feet up and have a nice chat with Lyn.

Evelyn plied her with sherry, encouraged her to talk about her grandchildren and her garden. She blossomed under Evelyn's attention, laughing at the liveliness of her daughters, confiding in him all her worries, consenting to having her drink topped up yet again. Kaye too seemed much more animated than usual, joking and cheerful, enjoying playing hostess.

'Oh Lyn, you're so good,' Kaye said when they'd gone, putting her arms around him, hugging him hard.

'Don't be absurd, my dear.' He responded with his hands on her bum.

'But you are. I haven't seen Mum enjoy herself so much in ages. You were so nice to them all.'

'Really, Kaye, what did you expect? Did you think I'd watch telly and shout for more beer?' He slid her to arms' length to look at her face.

She flushed and hid her face against him. 'Oh Lyn, you're so wonderful.'

I clattered the supper dishes into a stack and hurried out to the kitchen. I didn't think I would be able to take much more of Kaye's hero worship. Besides, I thought it was extremely bad for Evelyn to be made so much of. He was taking it modestly so far, but I felt he was sufficiently arrogant already. I couldn't bear their physical displays of soppiness. Despite Christina's comprehensive Freudian analysis, I did not suppose for a moment that I was jealous. Any rational person would have been equally embarrassed.

Several evenings a week they would go to the pub after dinner. Evelyn was teaching Kaye to play bar billiards, and occasionally I would accompany them. I was always asked but would usually excuse myself. The spectacle of Kaye picking Evelyn's pocket for change, nestling up to him with coy meaningfulness when her choice, 'My Guy', was played was bad enough. But Evelyn's sheepishess was unendurable.

Kaye's father accompanied his wife to visit Kaye for Sunday tea the next time. Although the younger sister didn't come, the elder, Vivien, brought her children. Mr Cooper gave Evelyn a grilling, unceremoniously demanding details of Evelyn's work record, army career and general background. It was plain he was enjoying tripping Evelyn up, exposing his imposture.

'Sergeant? I'd have thought an Oxford man would certainly have been an officer?'

'Well, there was rather a bottleneck for commissions, if you remember. I was in a hurry to see some action, so I enlisted.'

'And you weren't put in for commission later?'

'Turned it down. I thought I was doing more good where I was. I didn't really feel easy about pulling a nice billet at Officer Training when all my comrades were stuck in the field.'

Mr Cooper gave a perfunctory smile of disbelief and allowed Evelyn to pour him more Glenmorangie from the decanter. 'Killed a lot of Nips, then?'

'Yes. Rather a lot, actually.' Evelyn topped up his glass. 'Some of ours too. Couldn't leave them, you know. Had to finish them off ourselves.' He sipped whisky. 'And what was your war like?'

Meanwhile, his grandchildren, Kaye's nephew and niece, were engaged in jumping off the back of the sofa on to a heap of cushions, smearing everything they touched with traces of the food they'd eaten. Kaye's mother silently sipped her sherry and ate the buffet Evelyn had prepared, evidently not noticing the look her husband gave her whenever Evelyn offered her more drink. Her early attempts at conversation withered by a robust 'Nonsense, Muriel' from Kaye's father, she now seemed perfectly content to watch her family gathered together.

Later, in the kitchen, Evelyn intervened as she attempted to wash up. She obtained his recipe for the Coronation Chicken, what had gone into the salad, allowed Evelyn to give her a second portion of trifle. Evelyn had told Kaye to for God's sake splash out a little this time, or her people would think he was a shocking miser. Kaye sulkily asked what had been wrong with the food last time, and the disagreement terminated with her shouting, 'Well, you do it then, if you don't like my cooking.'

'All right then, I will,' Evelyn had retorted, refusing Kaye's apology, her offers of assistance. Aside from the cold chicken, he had bought real ham, not what he stigmatised as 'slime', prepared several salads without beetroot and a proper trifle, with lots of sherry and real cream.

Kaye was an indifferent cook, but had little faith in the ability of the male in the kitchen. Evelyn's competence belittled her. His robust style, his universal reliance on costly olive oil, exotic vegetables and spices, far too much garlic, baffled her. She fell back on the irreproachably English, heavy pastry, leaden Yorkshire pudding, glutinous white sauce. Evelyn usually unhesitatingly perjured himself, expressing suitable appreciation, which I judged an ominous indication of besottedness. Gratified by his appreciation, Kaye began to be more useful around the flat.

I couldn't help reflecting as I swabbed at the cushions with a damp cloth after everyone had gone, that it was a good thing that Kaye had miscarried. I could not imagine Evelyn enduring a houseful of recalcitrant toddlers with good grace for more than a few hours. I was sufficiently surprised at how well he behaved with Kaye's family, how punctilious he was about taking Kaye to Crystal Palace.

Kaye, however, complained that Evelyn never allowed her to meet his friends. Evelyn's invariable reply that hadn't got any friends for her to meet did not, on reflection, seem as flippant as it sounded. It was true that he had not introduced her to Ben and Molly, or Sophie and Leo, but I was not aware of anyone else he could introduce her to.

This in itself seemed odd when I thought about it. Uncle Richard had a very wide circle of friends, business and bridge, which he kept up with assiduously. Most of these were married couples, and he was the eternal spare partner for dinners and cards. I knew too, that in regard to his bridge, he moved in very exalted circles, although he was never above enjoying a few rubbers with less challenging opponents, perpetually ready to oblige suburban hostesses such as his financial director's wife.

Evelyn did not play bridge if he could avoid it, and was perhaps not very reliable as a spare man, likely to drink too much or indulge himself in the wrong sort of wit, if not precisely ill-mannered. His business contacts remained more strictly business, and he tended to lose track of married friends.

Ben and Molly were exceptions. He seemed close to them both, and not infreqently would visit for the evening, and they would argue late into the night about the most arcane permutations of the Popular Front, or colonial independence or the Labour Party. But they had nothing in common with Kaye; I could not imagine how she would react to hearing about marching to Aldermaston with the children in pushchairs. Even less could I imagine what they would make of her.

Evelyn still dutifully replied to George's sporadic letters, polemic and personal items illegibly crammed on a single sheet airletter. But he had not again undertaken the onerous responsibility of having a protegé. Certainly none of his private involvements had ever required so much time and energy as George had demanded of Evelyn.

Evelyn did not keep up with old girlfriends, as far as I could work out. Most of his male friends were scattered across the world, in transit, lost track of. I knew he had men friends I hadn't met, occasionally names were mentioned, phone messages left, but perhaps the acquaintancce was too fleeting or insufficient to invite them home, be invited.

Sophie and Leo were even more puzzling as friends of Evelyn. They were originally Evelyn's friends rather than Richard's, but Richard fitted naturally into the circle of professional married people and high powered card games, seemed to belong much more than Evelyn. I thought Evelyn was right to hesitate to thrust Kaye into the middle of one of Sophie and Leo's monthly gatherings.

As for Tim, it was a question of waiting for him to turn up; one did not summon him. And if Evelyn had any sense at all, Tim's reaction to Kaye would not be something that he was looking forward to, I thought.

7

I was not surprised when Kaye accompanied us to Sophie and Leo's next do. Evelyn prevented Kaye from squashing into the back of the car, giving me a quelling look I could not ignore. Although Kaye was not small, she was not so tall as I. It made me feel particularly juvenile to have to squeeze behind and it was much more uncomfortable than when I was little.

I did not enjoy the spectacle as much as I imagined I would. Kaye was overdressed in shiny pink, much more appropriate for the evening. Despite her tartiness, it was clear to me that Evelyn was being censured rather than Kaye. Everyone was very polite to Kaye, but she stuck close to Evelyn and seemed lost when Sophie unceremoniously dragged Evelyn aside to give him a piece of her mind. I vanished to the attic where the sons of the house, David and Lennie, held court.

Additional clandestine stocks of beer and wine were usually to be had, and everyone lay around on the floor discussing existentialism and attempting to smoke with sufficient panache to imply a twenty a day habit. Presently, intellects drained, we would listen to the Stones or the Yardbirds and someone would be sent to raid the food and drink downstairs. David's side of the

room was adorned with Raquel Welch pictures, Len's with
Diana Rigg.

David thought Kaye was scraggy. 'Not enough tit,' was his
verdict. His brother concurred. In fact, Kaye had an excellent
figure, but the style she favoured didn't do much for her. The
halter neck made her wide shoulders look like those of an East
German swimmer, and tailored darts highlighted her slender
bosom. She bought a great many clothes, which I presumed
Evelyn uncomplainingly paid for, but she had no taste. The
shorter the skirt, the higher the heel, the more exposed the
shoulders, the better. She favoured fashionable daffodils and
salmons, but Evelyn, generally so compliant, balked at this. She
confided in me that he told her she looked much sexier in black
or white. Certainly, in the garments she purchased thereafter,
she looked much less jaundiced.

Increasingly Kaye was inclined to confide in me, consult me
about Evelyn's preferences, pump me for details about his past,
request advice regarding differences between them. I found it
much easier to be on good terms with her. It was useful to be
able to borrow clothes from her, have spare stockings to hand.
Several times she spent the afternoon making me up as
elaborately as she did herself for important occasions and
showing me the best way to use various cosmetics. One of her
old flatmates had been a hairdresser and knew all the tricks.

I did not like hearing about Evelyn from Kaye. I didn't want to
know about the private jokes they shared, their secret pet
names, what really excited Evelyn. Her coyness, her revelation
of only tantalising tame snippets made everything seem even
more tawdry than it was. She was filled with self doubt as to her
attractiveness, her worthiness, of Evelyn's love for her. Yet at
the same time, never did she doubt that he would do the decent
thing, that she had made him very happy, that they loved each
other truly.

Once, when she was newly back after the miscarriage, she had complained to Evelyn that there was nothing to read. Evelyn had hurried meekly off to buy a bundle of women's magazines and a Mars bar for the invalid. While she respected the fact that he read, was an 'intellectual', she didn't seem to feel the need to try and keep up with him. And yet, she perceived it was more of a gulf between them than their disparity of age and class.

Now Evelyn took her home from Sophie's fairly early, leaving me to be delivered by Richard later. He was in an animated mood, having won handsomely at bridge.

'I do wish you'd stop referring to poor Kaye as Evelyn's mistress,' he admonished.

'Well, she is.'

'It's not very polite. Besides putting me in mind of how Diana will take it.'

'Does she know?'

'I have no idea. One can only hope not.'

'Do you have a mistress, Richard?'

'How dare you!'

'There's no need to be stuffy. I mean, it's not as if you were married.'

'That will do, Alexandria. If I were you, I'd be rather more concerned with my own affairs.'

'How do you mean?'

'I don't suppose that Evelyn will remain so preoccupied indefinitely that he won't notice that young David is paying you, er, marked attentions.'

'Why should Evelyn object if he is?'

'Perhaps he won't care for the nature of David's, er, attentions.'

'You don't know anything about it. It's none of your business.'

'My dear, you do realise that David has an, er, official

girlfriend? Leo was telling me only this afternoon that she came to dinner last week.'

'I know all about that. You think I'm stupid, don't you?'

'No, love. I just don't want you to . . . to take things too much to heart.'

'Well I won't. You don't suppose I'm in love with a pathetic child like that do you? Really, Richard, if one can't even indulge in a little innocent flirtation.'

'Innocent flirtation?'

'Most boringly innocent, I assure you.' The clandestine groping was certainly boring and fairly innocent as well. I was under no illusions as to the nature of David's attentions. David's official girlfriend was a nice girl who went to St Paul's, had ash blonde hair and never let him kiss her. She did not come from any of the families that made up his parents' social circle, and never came to the Sunday parties. I did not suppose that David loved, or even fancied me. I pragmatically accepted being used, but I wasn't prepared to allow such an unflattering estimation to become general currency.

'What's all this rubbish about selling the firm?' I diverted him.

I was shocked when he told me that it was perfectly true. Several of the directors and managers were retirement age. An extremely favourable offer had been made, and was being considered.

'But you can't do that. It's been in the family for a hundred years!'

'I don't see what that's got to say to anything.'

'But what will you do?'

'Well I won't need to do anything once I have my share of the proceeds.'

'But – but don't you care, don't you mind if it goes out of the family?'

'Really Alex, there's no point in being sentimental. I thought you'd read Marx.'

'What's that got to do with it?'

'Well,' he temporised, 'If you're a Marxist you should know all about concentration of capital. If we don't accept an advantageous offer now, we may well be forced to take much worse terms at a later date. The boom won't last forever, you know.'

'You're not a Marxist.'

'Marx was a perfectly sound economist. Much of what he says is valid regardless of political outlook.'

I complained to Evelyn. It was all very well for him and Richard, they were almost retirement age anyway. But what about me? It wasn't fair. Didn't they care at all for the long tradition, the family connections?

'The vanguard of the revolution. La Pasionaria,' jeered Evelyn.

'It's all very well for you to laugh. You never did anything much until you wheedled a job out of the family. Where would you be now if you hadn't?'

'You sound just like your cousin Christopher,' he snapped. 'I don't know why you should suppose you aren't going to have to work just as hard as the rest of us have. I'm sure I've never given you any reason to expect any favours.'

The news was new to Kaye too. 'What will you do, Lyn? Can you get another job?'

'I daresay I could. But I've a fancy to travel again.'

'I'd like that. I've always wanted to travel.' She snuggled against him. 'It's fun travelling with you. Darling Lyn.'

'Darling.' Evelyn put his arm around her.

Kaye was soon to have her wish. It was arranged that we would have a holiday in France. I was not looking forward to it.

'It will be horrible,' I confided in Richard.

'Do you and Kaye not get on?'

'Oh.' I shrugged. 'It's all right. It's just so embarrassing. Kaye will be fawning on Evelyn all the time and telling him how clever he is because he can order a meal in French. And they'll be all soppy and romantic and they'll never get up until lunchtime and I'll be in the way and it will be horrible.'

'I take your point. Evelyn's not really "soppy and romantic" is he?'

'Well ... She is and he puts up with it. She calls him "Tigger".'

'Really, Alex, you have no right to tell me such things.'

'Well, she does. Not to mention other things. It will be awful. I'll have to put up with all that the whole time we're away.'

'I'm surprised Evelyn hasn't thought of it that way.' He deliberated. 'Would you prefer to come on holiday with me?'

'With you!'

'It wouldn't be that bad, would it? I just thought you might prefer it to tagging along with Kaye and Evelyn. I'm sure I should enjoy having you come with me.'

'Where would you go?'

'Wherever you like, my dear.'

He argued persuasively. He would much prefer my company to going alone. It seemed increasingly tempting. We got along very well together on the occasions I stayed with him. And it would certainly be better than going with Evelyn and Kaye. Evelyn didn't like the idea at all, flatly refused permission. But whatever Richard said to him privately carried the day. I was to split my time between Richard's and Crystal Palace while Evelyn and Kaye were away, and at the end of the summer Richard and I would have a holiday together.

Meanwhile, over the summer I worked three days a week in the bookshop. I loved the job, regarded it as a civilised oasis. Mr Wainwright's florid histrionics, archaic declamations and stoical fortitude enacted with all the subtlety of a nineteenth-century provincial touring company, appealed exactly to my fifteen-year-old taste. In truth I found him more amusing and more sympathetic than Christina, with her cynical broadsides and relentless sophistication. His astringent tongue didn't worry me in the least, nor did the odd behaviour of Mr Bassett and Mr Kirkup, his stalwarts, who had been there forever and scarcely deigned to notice my existence.

They manned the rooms upstairs. Mr Bassett's desk was at the back of the first floor. He was a vaguely military looking man with a stubby moustache, who always looked much smarter than the others, despite his worn garments. He never said a thing to me in all the months I was there except 'Good morning,' or 'Good evening,' or 'Ta, very much,' when I had toiled up the narrow stairs with tea. Once he almost smiled at me when he noticed the biscuits on the edge of the saucer, another of my innovations.

Mr Kirkup was mad, He muttered to himself all day in a grumbling way. He was engaged in constant warfare with the leaky skylight, fussing with stepladders and rags and buckets. He didn't notice me at all for the first month or so, until one morning he suddenly shouted, 'What the hell do you want?' I stammered that I had just brought some tea and he had waved me away with an irritable headmasterly gesture, as though he had not, after all got one of the troublemakers in the back bang to rights *this* time. Later he had demanded aggressively of Mr Wainwright, 'What's that?'

'That's our new Saturday, Miss Parrish. I trust you'll make her welcome.'

'We've never had anything like that before,' Mr Kirkup barked. 'In all the years . . .' He gave in his notice. He gave notice at least once a week, which was always accepted, but he never left.

Both men were supposed to be mainly occupied with

preparing new catalogues. We worked with catalogues long out of print, the most recent having been sent out in 1961. They always looked busy, poring over drawers of index cards, but there was no indication when a catalogue would be ready. Mr Wainwright didn't seem in the least perturbed. He had a very cavalier approach to the clientele and had been known to ball up a letter and toss it away, or hang up on a telephone customer if he was tried too sorely. Of course, he was more sinned against than sinning, beset by cunning rogues, scheming scoundrels, base villains, surrounded by dull-witted simpletons and perfidious ingrates.

Hillyard and I became friends, very soon 'Missy' and 'Hillyard' instead of the more formal 'Miss Parrish' and 'Mr Hillyard'. We giggled together over Mr Wainwright's vagaries, mimed behind his back as he warbled 'Oh, for the wings of a dove,' or 'Pale hands I loved beside the Shalimar' in his occasional cheerful moods.

Hillyard confided increasingly less censored details of what Mr Wainwright termed the primrose path of dalliance. I reciprocated with the meagre details of my own love life, and bemoaned at length my domestic difficulties. Hillyard was never shocked, never appeared bored, never sneered or condescended. He treated me as an equal, took my difficulties as seriously as his own. Incapable of sorting out his own affairs, none the less he counselled wisely, invariably encouraging me to go easy with Evelyn.

8

Tim's reaction to Kaye was to begin drawing her at once. She was flattered, disarmed. I had been astonished at her stiffness. Generally she was complaisant to whatever situation Evelyn threw her into. I knew that she felt ill at ease with most of Evelyn's small circle; the visit to Sophie and Leo's was never repeated. But always she was eager to please, longed to be approved. I had not supposed that Tim would approve, but presumed that he would blame Evelyn rather than Kaye. What I never imagined was that Kaye would not take to Tim at once; I could not believe that anyone wouldn't.

I realised that Tim's constant sketching, although in no way an affectation, served as a defence against awkward silences, inopportune remarks. Evelyn seemed pleased to see him, relieved to be over the initial difficulty of presenting Kaye. Her frostiness was all the more evident in the face of Evelyn's expansiveness. I became aware that Tim was working on one large picture rather than the swift doodles he usually indulged in socially. Before it had been decided whether Tim would have a meal with us, he signed with a flourish, 'T.T.' and the date, presenting it to the happy couple.

Tim gave his cheeky grin and said, 'Well, I'd better push off now, Mum and Dad are expecting me.'

'I'm going for a drink with Tim,' I said and ran out after him.

'This is a bit of a laugh. Pub crawling with little Alex.' He smiled again, much less successfully and gulped at his pint.

'That was horrible, Tim. How could you?'

'It just came to mind. I suppose I've got a nasty mind, that's all.'

'I thought he was going to cry.' I drank half my cider in one go.

Tim's picture was a caricature of an official portrait of the Kennedys, with Kaye, square face emphasised, sitting on the sofa, Evelyn posed behind, with unnaturally too much hair, his hand on her shoulder. Even Kaye had perceived the parody at once. Evelyn had said nothing at all, his initial thanks dying away as he viewed Tim's handiwork. Neither goodbyes to Tim nor remonstrances to me had been forthcoming.

'Give over, Alex.' He fingered my jacket. 'That's nice.'

'Evelyn got it for me.'

'What did he get her?'

'Tim. Stop it. If I don't mind, I don't see why you should.'

'Never been my sort of thing, leather. But it's very nice.'

'What is your sort of thing?'

'Do you really not mind about her?'

'Well, not much. It's quite useful really. I can't have him poking his nose into my affairs all the time.'

'Your affairs?'

'Really, Tim. Not love affairs. You're worse than he is.'

'So you're . . . you're not in love then?'

'Of course not. There's no one worth bothering with. Besides, look where it gets you.'

'Do you think he's in love with her?'

'I don't think so. But I sometimes wonder how he can put up with it if he isn't.'

'He has no business inflicting his tarts on you.'

'It wasn't like that, Tim, you don't understand.'

'It seems to me I understand only too well, knowing Lyn.'

'Do you mean he's had other girls living with him before?'

'Not in my day. But he's always been, well, suggestible.'

'You mean randy as a stoat.'

'Alex! Any more talk like that and I'm off. And buy your own fags if you want one.' He got us another round and I gave Tim all the gory details of how Kaye had come to be living with us.

Kaye had confided the excruciating details about her affair with Evelyn. Although she had been involved with him before her marriage, she insisted that she hadn't seen him at all since before the wedding until the day she had left her husband with no money and nowhere safe to go.

'Well what else could I do? I mean, I'm quite tough really, but I had to think of the baby. I couldn't let it go on.'

'Do you mean he'd hit you before?'

'Well.' She looked embarrassed. 'Just a bit of a knock. Not like that before. I don't think Nigel really wanted the baby. We hadn't intended to start just yet.' It transpired that she had left him on an earlier occasion and gone to her parents. Her father had summoned the erring husband and made him apologise to Kaye, told Kaye she was a bad wife if she had to be chastised physically, dispatched them back to the marital home.

She was really, despite her glamorous appearance, and the circumstance of living with a man not her husband, an extremely conventional girl, easily shocked, evidently taken aback by her current situation. Christina's usual outrageous dialogue for effect for the first time had found a worthy audience. Kaye had endeavoured diffidently to suggest to me that Christina was a bad lot and would get me into trouble, implied she felt responsible. It was her fault that Evelyn was not in a position to take a firm line on my association with Christina. I was astonished that Kaye had broken her engagement after meeting Evelyn, and then married Nigel after all.

'How could you go back to him?'

'Well . . . It was different then. Nigel was keen to have me back. He could be dead sweet when we wanted to. And Lyn, well, he's never married in all these years. I thought at first he would ask me, but . . .' She looked defiant, flicked her lighter like a flamethrower. 'You've got to look after yourself. I didn't want to type letters all my life. I'm twenty-six.'

This surprised me. I had supposed her several years younger.

'Anyway,' she waved her cigarette in a philosophical sweep, 'it's all worked out for the best in the end.'

'Do you think so?'

'Well, I suppose I'd never have realised how much I love Lyn if I hadn't gone through everything with Nigel.'

'Do you?'

'Yes, of course. Oh, Alex, you don't realise. He's so kind and dear. And he always understands. He's a gentleman, Alex, that's the point.'

'He's the ruling class, Kaye. A bloated plutocrat.'

'You're always so cynical, you'll learn one day. He – he just knows how to treat a lady, that's what it is.'

'He seems quite rude to you sometimes.'

'You don't understand. Some day when you're in love . . .'

'Is Evelyn going to marry you?'

'You don't understand at all.' Her eyes filled with tears. 'How can he ask me a thing like that the way things are now? He's much too tactful to say anything until I'm free to marry.'

'But you said yourself . . .' I pointed out reasonably.

She jabbed out her cigarette. 'I'm very sorry if you don't like it. But Lyn and I happen to love each other,' she said with careful dignity.

'As long as you're both happy, I don't mind at all. I just worry about Evelyn, that's all.' I watched her carefully tissue the tears from the corners of her eyes. 'After all, he's all I've got.' Her reflection in the glass looked even guiltier than I'd hoped.

Kaye stared in to the glass for the insertion of her contact lenses before she commenced making up. This delicate operation terminated our chat. She was very embarrassed about wearing glasses, but she could not keep the lenses in all day or her eyes became sore. When Evelyn was about she would sit blindly incapacitated rather than put her glasses on. In the mornings she would run her hand along the wall to the bathroom. If she was out without her lenses she would flutteringly ask Evelyn to order for her in a restaurant, cling to his arm for guidance on the street.

'What I don't understand about the whole thing is, she's so *boring*,' I said to Tim.

'Well, I don't know. I just don't know him any more. It happens all the time, you're best mates with someone for ages, and then, all of a sudden, you wonder whether you were ever on the same planet.'

'But you've never lived with anyone *boring*, have you?'

'Well, I don't usually stop around long enough to find out whether they're boring.'

'Tim!' We laughed immoderately.

'I'm not really in a position to talk to him now, I suppose.'

'You really did put your foot in it. They were in New York when he was assassinated, you know.'

'Oh shit.' He offered his Players. 'Well, how was I supposed to know that? Do you mean he took her to New York?'

'She told me.' I inferred that the trip had not been a success, for it was not long after that she had broken with Evelyn and resumed her engagement. 'I was rather annoyed about that. Evelyn was going to take me, so I could see my mum's family. And right at the last minute he changed his mind. I thought he'd gone with Jean.'

'Jean?'

'She's great, lots of laughs. If Evelyn had any brains he'd marry her.'

'How many others are there?'

'Oh, I don't know. Lots I suppose. He's always gone out lots in the evening. They all slobber over him at work. It's disgusting.'

'Yeah. Got a big head, has our Lyn. That's always been his trouble. Bloody New York! He never even took . . .' He savagely clicked at his lighter.

'That's new.' I admired the silver lighter.

'Flash, innit?' He grinned. 'It was a present.'

'All those rich widows on the boat. What else have you got?'

'Alex, give over. You're a big girl now.'

'Maybe I should get a job with the line.'

'I shouldn't. Not what it used to be. I was thinking of moving on myself. Long distance. Australia, America. It's time for a change.

'I'll come with you.'

'Run away to sea. Yeah.' We laughed. 'I'd like to break his neck, giving you a bad time like this.'

'It's not that bad, Tim, really. Besides, someone's got to be on hand to pick up the pieces.'

'Someone always is with him. Takes it for granted.'

'I don't know why you should be so bitter. I'm all right, really. I can handle him.'

'That's true. You're as bad as he is. You always were a horrible little brat.' He squeezed my hands. At closing time he walked me back, although he would not come in. He gave me his address, both care of the shipping line and his parents. He had never done that before. 'You get in touch if Lyn gives you a hard time. I've had a go before now.'

We stood in the doorway drunkenly clinging on to each other. He very gently kissed my cheek, then the other before hurrying away. I felt I should have been seeing him home. I was bigger than him now. I was shocked by how old he looked. There was no grey discernible in his light hair, and he didn't seem markedly more wrinkled than I remembered, but somehow, the set of his face seemed harder, the bearing of his shoulders wearier. I thought of all the nice times we'd had, the three of us, when I was little, and cried myself to sleep as I had then whenever Tim went away.

9

Troubles, as Mr Wainwright was wont to observe, came not as single spies but in battalions. This was certainly true of Evelyn's troubles. On top of all his other difficulties, Uncle Richard had a heart attack at the most crucial phase of negotiations for the sale of the firm. It was soon clear how much extra work this made for Evelyn, but my own initial fright and upset was such that it did not occur to me that he must be far more distraught than I could possibly be.

'I'm sure it's not that bad,' comforted Philip inadequately. Regardless of the scale of the disaster, a failed French paper, the loss of a ten bob note, the introduction of Kaye into the household, he invariably assured me that it wasn't that bad, really, and prosaically undermined my dramatics. But in this case, I knew that it was far worse, and specifically my fault into the bargain. I was ludicrously seized with the idea that the evening's misdemeanours had invoked the disproportionate retribution of Uncle Richard's heart attack.

I had browbeaten Philip into agreeing that we should see an adult film with subtitles in order to practice our French, and heartily repented it within the first ten minutes. The film was unbelievably silly. There were a few shots of a woman in a slip, putting on stockings at one point, and a scene with two lovers talking in bed, the covers up to their armpits. Philip, however, was suitably embarrassed, and had not even attempted to hold my hand. Usually he got at least that far, though his advances could never be regarded as anything so ungentlemanly as a grope.

It seemed an opportunity too good to be missed. I snuggled up to him, eased his arm around me. He gasped when presently I unzipped his trousers. Somewhat to my surprise, he did not stop me. He didn't take nearly as long as David. Too late he fumbled for his handkerchief. 'Idiot!' I hissed. He hugged me tightly for some moments afterwards, a few tears slipping from his closed eyes. Presently, regaining some composure, he began his usual ritual toying with my hair, smoothing, twirling, running his hand through it. But he seemed still in a state of shock, even more reverential than usual on the way home. I almost felt remorse for unsettling him so much.

At home Kaye told me that Richard had had a heart attack and Evelyn was still at the hospital. It made me feel quite wicked, washing traces of Philip from my hand, reflecting that all this time Richard lay dying. Mercifully, Philip had gone when I finally went back down to wait for Evelyn. I could see that Kaye had been crying too.

Philip was right; it was not as bad as I had luridly imagined. Richard was expected to make a full recovery, but it would be some weeks before he was back at work. I tried not to resent the loss of my holiday. Already it had been put back to half term. Richard had been extremely apologetic, and even got Evelyn to agree that I could have an extra week off school so that we could have a fortnight abroad. Instead I resented Philip, loathed him for his calm assurances that his father was a doctor, he was destined to be one himself, so he must know what he was talking about, everything would really be all right.

When I visited Richard in hospital, he looked much less ill than I had supposed he would. He was wry, matter of fact, resigned. In due course he was discharged and went to stay at Crystal Palace for a few weeks until he could manage on his own at home. Once he was back in his flat, his recovery seemed to lose momentum. He was dispirited, at a loose end, fretting over the projected sale, ringing the office often. Mrs Crawford always took a firm line and told him bluntly that if they needed him they would ring, to go away and rest.

Between us, we made sure that Richard was visited daily by one of the family. I would sometimes go after school and stay for an evening meal. He had been put on a strict diet, which he followed meekly, his confidence seeming to deflate as he shrank. He also gave up smoking. His occasional habit had increased in the last year or so to the point where he carried his own cigarettes instead of raiding the board room supply at work. Evelyn sorted through his books and lent Richard a stack that he thought he would enjoy. But it was my impression that Richard spent many hours at the piano, took the gentle walks he was prescribed and was at a loss. He always appeared pathetically grateful for my visits; apologising inordinately for being so out of the way, so far from the tube. He was touched also that Kaye visited regularly when he was first home, in case he wasn't up to getting his own shopping.

An energetic attempt at turning out and sorting all his sheet music petered out on the first afternoon, and for days afterwards the room was unaccustomedly untidy. He rifled through various stacks, began sorting everything into categories, and slid soon into desultory, wistful tinkering at the keyboard with variations on the popular tunes of his youth. After a week or so the chaos was added to with old correspondence and then boxes of photographs.

I was frightened by Richard's lack of direction, his dabbling ineffectually at various tasks, so at odds with his usual determined purposefulness. The longer he convalesced, the less well he looked. Partly it was the loss of weight, the babyish round pinkness of his face giving way to innumerable lines and sags. He looked older, and much sadder.

I did my best to jolly him along, making a joke of laborious duets at the piano (it was many years since he had spent long futile hours helping me with lessons); accompanying him on his walks; reading whatever book he was reading so that we could discuss it; looking through his photos with him.

'I never knew you had an older sister.' Gillian was younger than Richard.

'There's no secret about it. I supposed you knew.'

'Is she illegitimate?'

'Of course not. Really, Alexandria, you should endeavour to curb your imagination. As a matter of fact, she's my half sister. My father married twice.'

'Nobody ever told me that. Was he divorced?'

'No, no. His first wife was an invalid for many years. He married my mother when he was almost my age.'

'She must have been a lot younger.'

'Half his age. I don't believe it was very successful.' He watched me stack up the tea things without protest. 'Mother and Isabel didn't get on at all. I'm sure it couldn't have been easy, stepmother to an adolescent girl much accustomed to having her way with her father.' He looked flustered as I blushed, and said hastily, 'But I don't think my mother was very ... well, wise about dealing with her. And my father didn't make things any easier. He wasn't ... wasn't an easy man.' He showed me a picture of a woman swathed in white lace, a man in a morning suit. In front of them was a small blond boy in a velvet Fauntleroy suit. 'I was page at Isabel's wedding.' Involuntarily I looked from the boy to Richard, and was relieved to see he was laughing. 'I was sick over the bridesmaid later. An obnoxious child with ringlets. I wasn't a bit sorry.'

'Richard.' We both laughed. 'Didn't you get into trouble?'

'I think nanny took me away early and dosed me with something nasty. She wasn't at her best when we were ill. Poor nanny.' He found his parents' wedding portrait, then laid over it a young man in a Sam Browne belt. 'There's Arthur.'

'Arthur?'

'Isabel's brother. My half brother. I suppose he'd be Managing Director if he'd lived. He was killed on the Somme when I was a baby. It seems strange to have a brother one never knew.'

'I don't suppose it's any different from not remembering one's father.'

'I'm sorry.' He squeezed my hand.

I shrugged, smiled. Having the advantage, I asked, 'Are your wedding pictures here?' I had seen some of Richard's first wedding before. The second wedding wasn't in church either. 'What's her name?'

'Megan.'

'She's very pretty.' She looked much smaller than Angela, very young, and somehow familiar. I had seen other pictures of her, at Hellisford or Crystal Palace, I supposed, without realising who she was.

'Very,' agreed Richard, almost rueful.

I sympathetically rubbed his arm. 'Is it true that she ran off with another man?'

He jerked back. 'Who have you been talking to?' I perused the pictures intently. 'In a manner of speaking. She did go off with someone else, but we'd already agreed in principle that we'd made a mistake.' He laughed softly. 'The war did funny things. The whole thing was quite idiotic.'

'How do you mean?'

'Well, I'd only known her for three weeks when I proposed.'

'Richard!' I scrutinised him with awe. I could not conceive of him doing so, even on his own admission.

'Well, she accepted me.' He started to gather up the pictures. 'But it must be said that I at least was old enough to know better. You see, I was being shipped overseas, for the occupation. It . . . forced my hand.'

'You don't look old.'

'I was thirty. She was only nineteen. Ah well, it wasn't as bad as Aubrey and Blanche.' He resolutely set the pictures aside. 'I find I keep thinking about all those things just lately. I don't care for it. It's very morbid. I thought perhaps if I looked at the pictures it would exorcise the ghosts.'

'And has it?'

'That remains to be seen.'

'Poor Richard. Was it very awful?'

'It's not something I would care to go through again. But everyone's been so kind. It's quite overwhelming. Evelyn . . . I couldn't have managed without him. He's been . . .' He trailed off inarticulately, his blue eyes glistening with earnestness.

'I know.'

'I suppose you do, my dear. Are you going to stay and share my lettuce leaves?'

I tried to explain to Evelyn my amorphous worry over Richard. He agreed wearily, said he didn't know what to do for the best. In the end he arranged with Aunt Louisa and Aunt Hetty that they should all three travel to Uncle Sebastian in Italy, to give Richard some company and take his mind off work until he was well enough to take up the reins again.

It was only latterly that I began to grasp how much Evelyn was upset by Richard's illness. He had known Richard all his life. I never got the impression that they had been particularly close when young, but these days they were good friends. They worked closely and socialised regularly. Much of their conversation was cryptic, half sentences, allusive jokes, shorthand, like a comfortable, long married couple. The additional work was the least of his concern.

I worried over Evelyn as well as Richard. He too looked very old and tired. I wondered if his heart was all right, whether he was up to the burdens of Richard's illness. In fact, predictably, it was his stomach that packed in on him. I had always known that he was prone to vomiting if he had too much to drink, and his hangovers generally affected his stomach rather than his head. But under the additional strain he tended to be sick in the night several times a week, although he was drinking quite moderately. (It was my impression that Evelyn and Kaye had rowed over his drinking and that he was being very carefully restrained on this account.) There was little I could do for him without usurping Kaye's self-appointed role, except make myself scarce and avoid upsetting him.

10

'He threw you out last time.' I gripped the door firmly and filled the gap. Last time he had been sleek, pink, scented. I was surprised to recognise him at all, shrivelled, yellow, bald. I had only met him once, years before; he had turned up late one evening and picked a row within minutes, angering Evelyn to violence. I had been terrified by the display of Evelyn's temper, by the easy strength with which he banged the smaller man against the wall. For some time afterwards I was unsettled, apprehensive at the memory of Evelyn's rage. I was well aware that he could be firm, even stern, but had never dreamed that he could be moved to such exertion, so seriously agitated.

The man glared, threw off some of his decrepitude. 'Well, tell him I'm here. Jamie Robertson.'

'Did you over as well.' I carefully closed the door before I went up.

Evelyn looked grim, went down hastily, and after a very long time came back for his coat, told Kaye he was going out for a drink.

'You might have taken me,' she reproached when he arrived home at closing time.

'You can't have it both ways, Kaye. You've asked me not to introduce . . .' He looked at me sharply. 'Is there a good reason why you aren't in bed?'

Things were not going well between Evelyn and Kaye. Evelyn had borne the brunt of coping with Uncle Richard's heart attack. All the details of the sale of the firm, of keeping things ticking over, fell on Evelyn. He was not qualified to make many of the crucial decisions. I did not understand the intricacies, but it was a labyrinthine transaction, involving all sorts of distribution agencies and a myriad of financial holding companies (which had been the original reason for splitting the headquarters between London and Sheffield in the early years of the century). Only Richard was clear as to what was to be disengaged and retained, what wound up, amalgamated or sold. Evelyn had to keep the buyer interested while avoiding decisions on the most complex issues until Richard was well again.

In fact, Kaye had uncomplainingly bolstered Evelyn through all the trouble, making a big effort domestically, providing meals, and generally cosseting him. But now Richard was back at the helm and the pressure had eased off a bit, she accused Evelyn of neglecting her, taking her for granted. She complained that they never went out any more, never had any fun. They had many rows, Evelyn at his most viciously sarcastic, Kaye hysterical and tear-sodden. But always they were noisily reconciled in Evelyn's large bed late at night.

A phone call from Evelyn at work the evening after Robertson's visit left Kaye in tears. 'It's just like with Nigel. Out drinking with the lads.' She didn't even care that she was ruining her make-up. 'He'll come home at God knows what hour, drunk and revolting, expecting me to . . .' She broke off embarrassedly and defiantly mixed herself a gin and it. She was not a big drinker and I had never known her to drink alone before.

'Don't be ridiculous, Kaye. I'm sure he's not *violent*.'

'No,' she conceded, snuffling. 'Oh, no. I'm being silly. It's just,' she blew her nose, 'it frightens me.'

'Really, Kaye. How can you be frightened of Evelyn?'

'I'm sorry. But he can be so, so – difficult if he's been drinking.'

'Well tell him to piss off and sleep downstairs. That'll make him grovel soon enough.'

'Do you think so?'

'Do you think he means to scare you? Do you think he wants you to think he's like Nigel? He hasn't, he's never hit you, has he?'

'Of course not.' Her indignation gave way to a feeble smile. 'I shouldn't be drinking alone. Will you have something, Alex?'

Acting on my advice, she went to bed at eleven, locking the bedroom door and leaving Evelyn's pyjamas and a heap of bedding on the sofa. I went to Christina's after school the next day and stayed until late, but I didn't avoid their row.

'Do try, Kaye, just try to exercise a little imagination,' Evelyn was saying through his teeth. 'He's *dying*, Kaye, do you have any idea what that means?'

'I bet he's just saying that?'

'Have you ever seen anyone die, Kaye? Well, I have. More deaths than you've had hot dinners. And he is, all right. No doubt about that. Have you ever thought about what it's like to die, Kaye?'

'Well, that's his problem. You said yourself you don't even like him.'

'I don't dislike him so much I'm prepared to cut him loose to die on his own in a place where he doesn't know anybody. Besides, I owe him one. Very likely I'd be dead right now if not for him.'

'I don't see why he can't go back to Saigon or wherever it was.'

'There happens to be a war on. Why do you think he's here now?'

'You always make it sound like I'm being horrible. Don't you think I've put up with enough? I've hardly seen you for months, done everything for you, and Alex, been nice to that bloody pansy . . .' She shrieked and glass shattered.

I hurried upstairs. In a moment Kaye followed and threw herself on Evelyn's bed, sobbing. I went back down. Evelyn took a glass from the sideboard and poured a big drink.

'Did you hit her?'

'Of course I didn't bloody hit her,' he snapped. 'But some people aren't too old to spank.'

'It's not my fault she's upset. I thought something broke.'

'I threw a glass. *Not* at Kaye. Now mind your own business and go to bed.'

'That's bloody prize. The pair of you shouting half the night. And if you're not shouting you're having it off loud enough to hear her at the end of the street. How do you expect me to get any sleep? It'll be all your fault when I fail my 'O' levels.'

'I don't have to take that from you.' He was absolutely white. He stomped up to his room, ignoring Kaye's apprehensive squeal. He banged doors, slammed drawers, packed a case and flounced out, shaking off Kaye, deaf to her entreaties. 'I wish you the joy of each other.'

It took me hours to soothe Kaye, get her off to sleep. After an exhaustive bout of weeping, she had been sick, retching and heaving over the toilet for ages. The broken glass had sent shards across the living-room and there was nothing for it but to get out the hoover. The room badly wanted doing anyway.

Mrs Brown had grimly given notice after Kaye was installed. Evelyn had blamed Kaye for getting her back up, but Kaye was hardly aggressive. I thought it more likely that Mrs Brown had been morally offended. Evelyn had managed to make her take a golden handshake and the official story was that she had retired. Kaye had been charged with the task of replacing her, but I suspected she felt both timid of hiring someone, and embarrassed by her own ambiguous status in the household. Sporadically she cleaned herself, but lately her zeal for the duration of Richard's illness had quite vanished.

Kaye continued to wear her wedding and engagement ring. She said she couldn't get them off. It may have been true. She had unexpectedly broad hands with large knuckles. Evelyn was evidently not sufficiently mortified to buy her a ring himself.

Evelyn was back from work the next evening as if nothing had happened. I avoided being at home as much as possible. At some point Evelyn and Kaye resolved things sufficiently to be sharing a bed again. On Sunday I went to Crystal Palace.

'All alone, Alex?' Aunt Louisa stood on tiptoe to kiss my cheek.

'Evelyn and Kaye were busy having a row, so I came on the bus.' I kissed her and Aunt Hetty, pecked Richard's cheek. 'Kaye's period is late.' Aunt Louisa sat down hard and Richard gripped my arm painfully in rebuke. 'But I don't suppose it'll come to anything, she's probably lost count. That would be just like her.' It wouldn't, in fact. She was unexpectedly quick with calculations.

Christina was very sanguine about the news. 'I shouldn't worry. He'll know how to arrange for her to get an abortion in Harley Street.' Her voice dropped to a whisper. 'I know all about that. It happened to Mummy a while back.'

'I'll tell Evelyn to contact your mother for details.' I said sardonically.

'Really, Alexandria. Do think, my dear, this could be the answer to all your problems.' She fiddled with the flame adjustment to her lighter. 'People *die* from abortions some-times.' She inhaled deeply. 'Bleed to death,' she said with relish.

Somehow I could not feel that Kaye's death would let Evelyn off the hook. Richard's heart attack had made me worry a lot about death. I had irrational moments of terror that something had happened to Evelyn, as I had when I was little. I worried for Richard too. I was surprised by how upset I had been. I worried about being dead myself. Evelyn was right; I could not imagine it, and I was sure I had a better imagination than Kaye.

I thought of all the blood there had been when Kaye miscarried. Often I fantasised about Kaye leaving. When I was angry I conjured horrible fates for her, pictured her death. But thinking about her bleeding to death made me shudder. I was especially nice for a few days, and then her period came after all.

11

Evelyn's troubles were legion. On top of Richard's illness and the deteriorating relationship with Kaye, Jamie Robertson died shortly before Christmas. Evelyn was extremely rattled to have the police come round to inform him of the death. Robertson had given Evelyn as next of kin on his hospital forms.

Robertson had in fact caused Evelyn an incredible amount of trouble. Having run up a series of unpaid bills in middle range hotels around Hyde Park, he had then spent almost a week at the Savoy, making lavish use of room service and other extras. The night before he was due to be readmitted to hospital, probably for the last time, he had taken an overdose of sleeping tablets. Evelyn had to give evidence at the inquest, and fend off irate creditors. Although I had reason to believe that Evelyn paid for the funeral, he saw no reason to be responsible for Robertson's debts.

In the weeks between Robertson turning up on the doorstep and his death, Evelyn had spent more evenings than not with him, and several times at the weekend took him out in the car. After her initial objections, Kaye put up with the situation, but Evelyn was sufficiently guilty about this further neglect to provide astonishingly lavish Christmas presents. I was irrationally annoyed that Evelyn's presents to Kaye and myself had been evidently carefully considered for scrupulously equal expenditure on us both.

Jamie Robertson's funeral was at Golders Green Crematorium

shortly before Christmas. Evelyn had put a notice in *The Times*, and there had been a few sentences about the inquest in the *Evening Standard* under the heading of 'Suicide at the Savoy', but he was the only mourner. At the last minute, having ascertained that Kaye had no intention of going, I had gone by tube.

'Alexandria! What the hell . . .' he hissed under the organ music. He looked most annoyed.

'I'm sorry. I don't have a hat for funerals. Shh.'

The service took less than ten minutes. There was no eulogy, and Evelyn did not even pretend to sing the only hymn that was played. Afterwards there was a delay while Evelyn repudiated any claim on the ashes and explained that he had already arranged for the remains to stay at Golders Green. Then he drove us to a pub. At the bar he drained his whisky and had it refilled before paying.

'Anything to get out of school, hmm?'

'I didn't want you to be the only one at the funeral. You said you didn't expect anyone else.'

He smiled apologetically and squeezed my hand.

'I thought Kaye was going to come,' I said censoriously.

'She didn't even know him.'

'You didn't introduce him.'

'To be perfectly honest, Alex, he wasn't the sort of man I wanted to introduce to her. Or to you.'

'How do you mean?'

He shook his head and chased his whisky with a draught of beer.

'Anyway, she could have given you a bit of moral support.'

'I've asked far too much of her already.' He looked guilty. 'I think she's a bit jealous really.'

'Jealous!'

'Well, she doesn't like to think that there's anything about me that she doesn't know about, isn't part of.'

Kaye was certainly very possessive. If Evelyn was reading, she would interrupt to ask what he was reading, if he still loved her. She was unhappy at Evelyn's continuing association with old friends with whom she did not fit in, although she behaved irreproachably. She devoured mundane details of his post and phone calls, pried into his past in a way that I had never dared, resentful when he was unforthcoming.

Something about the relentlessness of her demands reminded me very much of George. He had never asked about Evelyn's life, of course, but he had the same need for incessant reassurance. With Kaye, Evelyn did not even have the intellectual stimulation that had been integral to all his long discussions with George. But perhaps Kaye was less wearing than George had been; she never argued with his pronouncements on world affairs or required long essays to be read and amended before the next morning's tutorial.

I had never heard Evelyn say anything so private about Kaye before and he looked very much as if he'd thought better of it. I thought of how much Kaye confided in me about Evelyn. He would be mortified if he realised I knew so much. I thought of how she was trying to arrange Christmas, tie up her family with his and realised that his reluctance sprang as much from his dislike of being discussed by them, of anyone revealing anything about him, however trivial, as from his distaste for most of Kaye's family. (He had never criticised them in my hearing, but it was plain to me that he had little liking for any of them save Kaye's mother.)

'Why did Robertson call you "Johnny"?'

'How do you know that?' He frowned. 'It started in the army. I mean, it was bad enough being posh, without admitting being called "Evelyn". It was worse than school.'

'Poor Evelyn. It gave you a bad time, didn't it?'

'It's all of a piece with Blanche. I was supposed to be called

"Alec" after an uncle who was killed, but she named me after Sebastian instead and only for a middle name. It's fortunate I've always been big, it might have been much worse.'

'Where was your father?'

'I believe he was in hospital. He wasn't well, bad nerves, shell shock, he'd been gassed too. I can't imagine Blanche being the least use to anyone in that situation.'

'Did you know Jamie Robertson in the army?'

'Good Lord, no.' The idea seemed to amuse him. 'It was when I was travelling after the war. I washed up in Saigon with no money. I'd got through what Daddy left, which wasn't much. I was looking for work and he insisted I stay with him until I was sorted out, got me a job with a friend. There's wasn't much to do, I don't know what pressure was brought to bear to get me on the payroll.'

'What did Robertson do?'

'Business man. They all were.' He grinned mischievously. 'That covers a multitude of sins. Mostly I had to take a parcel to Bangkok or Singapore every now and again, documents, gems sometimes – I wasn't supposed to know that. God only knows what sort of a mess I might have got into.'

'I'll get this one, Evelyn.'

He was laughing when I came back from the bar. 'I never managed to get away with that when I was your age.'

'I think it's a question of make-up. Besides, I'm sixteen now.'

'I haven't been a very good parent, have I?'

'Don't be silly, Evelyn. What was it like in Saigon?'

'I loved it. It reminded me of being in Paris before the war. Not that it was really the least like Paris; it was very restful.'

'Were in you in Paris? I thought you were in Spain.'

'Well they threw us out a year or so before the war. I was called up in the spring of '38, but they turned me down flat. I don't know why. I know I wasn't all that healthy after Spain. I think it was more to do with politics. They didn't want bolshie conscripts.' He sipped his beer more moderately now. 'So I thought "sod them" and went to Paris. I stayed until the German advance, so I didn't enlist until Dunkirk. I got a lot of stick about that. No one ever seemed to allow that I'd already been fighting the Nazis. And then it took me ages to find a regiment that would take me.'

'Why?'

He shrugged. 'Too old. Too posh. Not posh enough. Not healthy enough. Premature anti-fascism.'

'Too old?'

'I was twenty-three by then. Old and bolshie.' He grinned. 'It's a pity about Saigon. I can't bear to think of what's happening out there, it was such a nice place. What beats me is how Jamie came to be on his uppers. I'd have thought the war was a licence to print money.'

I remembered a conversation with Richard some months before. 'Really, Evelyn. I thought you'd read Marx. Concentration of capital.'

He looked at me with respect. 'Mmm. Cartels. Mafias. Probably the protection got too expensive. And his Vietnamese was never up to much. He never bothered. He . . . I didn't like his attitude, very colonial, Empire holdover.'

'But you said it was French.'

'Didn't hold with that either. But it looks like it got him carved out in the end. He may have been losing his grip for some time by the look of him. Poor old boy. I hope I don't go like that.' He smiled again. 'I underestimated him. Dangerous thing to do. I never thought he'd have it in him to do that. I hope I'd have the nerve.' He drank. 'I forgot how ruthless he could be when he was up against it. He sent me a letter. Said he calculated it would all be out of the way in time so as to not ruin my Christmas.'

'I think it's funny, going round all those hotels.'

'You would.' He laughed. 'I suppose it is really. Look what he gave me.' He pulled back his jacket sleeve. The cuff-links were chunky, gold encrusted with diamonds.

'Are they real?'

'Certainly. He didn't see any point hocking them for his bills. But what he thought I could do with his ID bracelet I don't know. Never been my sort of thing.'

'Well, those aren't your style either. You could sell it.'

'It's a lot of gold, might fetch a few bob. But I'm sure the watch is a fake. Just like him not to give me a straight answer.'

'You told Kaye he saved your life.'

'Did I say that?' He looked at me sharply. 'Well, it's a moot point. I was very sick. Someone fetched him to my lodgings and he paid my debts and got me on a flight to Hong Kong, wired Gordon to collect me. It must have taken some doing to get someone delirious with fever taken on the plane. Mind, he drugged me to the plimsoll line.'

'Gordon and Diana must have been pleased to be landed with you.'

'Scared the life out of them. Gordon got me a job in a bank when I was better.'

'You? In a bank?'

'It was awful, nothing had changed in a hundred years. I didn't last long. No one could pigeon-hole me in the hierarchy. And I was much too friendly to the natives.'

These rivetting reminiscences were cut short by Evelyn looking at his watch and recalling a meeting at work. He dropped me at school on the way. I had intended to miss the rest of the day. It was undeniable that the new car was much more comfortable in the winter, but I still regretted the MG, resented Kaye for occasioning its sale. Evelyn had bought Richard's car when Richard got a new one. When I was little I had loved the silver cat leaping off the end of the bonnet that Richard always had on his cars, the pickled wood of the dashboard like offcuts of the boardroom panelling. But I had enjoyed even more riding in Evelyn's sports car.

'Thank you for coming, love. It was very thoughtful.'

'I couldn't let you be the only one.'

He should have known I would come, I thought resentfully. The previous summer when my grandmother was in London, he had said, 'I don't suppose you want to see Blanche.'

'You don't want to go by yourself.'

He had not demurred, but squeezed my hand gratefully. He had not asked Kaye to accompany us, nor, much to my surprise, did she press to come.

I had been fascinated in a macabre sort of way. I effectively quelled the old lady with my glare, fixedly staring, not at her eyes, but at the bleeding bright lipstick on a withered mouth that had never been generous. Nothing had been said about my height, my adolescent plumpness, Evelyn's undyed grey. It occurred to me now that there was something in the obsequiousness of my step-grandfather towards Evelyn that put me in mind of the deceased.

Evelyn said, 'I wasn't expecting anyone else.' He hugged me and laughed. 'After all, I don't suppose for a moment that Jamie died with the name he started with.'

part VI

1

On a particularly cold day not long after Christmas, I arrived home after school to find the hall stacked with suitcases and boxes.

'Kaye, what the . . .'

'I'm leaving Lyn,' Kaye announced dramatically.

'Oh.' This was one thing they had not rowed over. 'What does he say?'

'I haven't told him yet. I'm waiting for him now.' She looked guilty.

It transpired that Kaye had obtained a job and a bedsitter. I was relieved, but I thought that it wasn't very nice of her to have gone behind Evelyn's back. She felt badly about this, but half frightened of him, half convinced that any attempt to leave would have been thwarted by another torrid reconciliation in bed. (She was not so blunt, but allusively coy in her usual excruciating fashion.) This was probably true.

'But I think he'll be upset you haven't said anything. Really, Kaye, it's not as if he was likely to beat you up.'

She began to cry. 'I can't keep on like this. It's no good. I've tried so hard, really I have.'

This was also true. Her assiduous attentions while Evelyn had been under great pressure at work were irrefutable. But Evelyn had not seemed especially grateful. I supposed he didn't like being fussed by Kaye any more than he did by me when he was tired.

Kaye had even gone blonde in an attempt to revitalise the relationship. I had been half admiring, half appalled. It had been done very expensively but I had not felt that it flattered her. Evelyn had stood speechless, before eventually managing to inject the right note of astonished delight into his 'Oh, Kaye!' But as he hugged her close, his expression over her shoulder was one of such weary despair that I had not even been tempted to laugh, as I had been anticipating. I poured him a large whisky, and Kaye's gin and it, before retreating hastily upstairs. They were not long behind. I turned my record player up loud.

Christmas had no doubt been the last straw. Kaye had instigated a great deal of family visiting, to her parents and married sister, to Crystal Palace, introducing her relatives to Evelyn's. Evelyn had never been badly behaved, but had been demurely sarcastic, conveying almost incessantly an air of dangerous restraint, of scarcely contained outrageousness. I could not blame him in the least, but it had not helped. The socialising had been constrained, only the time at Crystal Palace remotely enjoyable or relaxing. In private, Evelyn had been exhausted and sulky, with the overtired petulance of a small child. I had avoided a great deal of the preparations and gatherings by working most of the holidays.

Now Kaye bravely blew her nose. 'The fact is, Lyn doesn't love me.'

'He . . . he's very fond of you.'

'Fond. That's about it.' She wiped her smudged eyes. 'You'll look after him, won't you?'

'Yes, of course.'

As soon as I politely could I said goodbye, took her new number, told her sincerely to take care of herself. I went out again, as I had arranged. Evelyn had still not come back. Kaye always made a particular fuss of him on Fridays. She would get him a large whisky, take off his tie, massage his shoulders and console, 'Never mind, Lyn. The weekend starts here.'

It was going to be a long weekend, I thought. But Evelyn seemed to cope surprisingly well. Although he drank a great deal, especially the first weekend, and began to go out in the evenings as he had used to, he did neither of these things as much as I had expected. Mainly he was preoccupied with the sale of the firm, endlessly going through everything with Richard over drinks, meals, cards, on the evenings they weren't working late.

The sale of the firm was finally completed not long before Easter. On Evelyn's last day, I arrived home from school to find Richard and Evelyn ensconced in the living-room. Richard, his head thrown back, his hands folded across his stomach, was snoring audibly. Evelyn drowsed on the sofa in shirtsleeves and socks. To complete the tableau, Berry lay stretched before the fire toasting her belly. I made tea and roused them.

'No, no, I shouldn't,' Richard declined the tinned fruit cake I'd opened.

'Nonsense. You've got to have something to soak up the alcohol.' I cut them both large wedges. 'Are you very drunk?'

'I'm sorry to have to say this, Evelyn, but you've reared a child who has no respect for her elders.'

I squeezed Evelyn's shoulder. 'Was it very awful?' I knew he'd been dreading it.

'Even Connie cried.'

'My God.' I could not imagine the redoubtable Mrs Crawford even surreptitiously wiping the corners of her eyes behind her glasses. 'Did you eat any lunch at all?'

'Don't fuss, Alex. I'm fine.' He hungrily attacked his cake. 'So's he.'

I inspected their cards and presents. There were many cards and telexes from customers, as well as from staff. They had both received presentation cuff-links with inscriptions, rather more tasteful than the late Robertson's bequest to Evelyn. They also had personal presents from the secretaries, Evelyn an italic fountain pen, Richard, boxed classical records. I knew that Evelyn and Richard had clubbed together with the Financial Director, Mr Norton, to get lavish presents for their three secretaries, as well as voting them a bonus for their help over Richard's illness and the sale. Evelyn also had a present from Dieter, some expensive German camera attachments.

I was puzzled over the whole business of Dieter Fuchs. I was well aware that he regarded Evelyn as his mentor, that Evelyn had given him his first big chance in business. And certainly they were good friends. The gift seemed a typically generous gesture from Dieter. But perhaps it was in expiation of guilt.

The night Kaye had left I was sure I had seen him get out of a taxi outside our flat as I glanced back. He had been expected, and I knew that Evelyn planned to treat us to an expensive evening out on the Saturday. I had returned home late, and found Evelyn alone. He had not, as I'd half expected, persuaded Kaye to change her mind about going.

'You might have bloody told me.'

'I didn't know until just now.'

'I know you didn't want her here. But to go conspiring behind my back!'

'I didn't. I didn't have any idea what she was up to.' It took me a while to convince him that I hadn't known about Kaye's flight. By then I was angry that he could suppose I'd do that to him.

'All right, love, all right. But how do you suppose I felt just to come back to a note? No one here, even the bloody cat out on the tiles.'

'Didn't you talk to her?'

'I didn't clap eyes on her.'

'But she was waiting for you, she intended to see you. I expect she couldn't wait any longer. She was in a terrible state, all wound up.'

Evelyn jumped up and poured himself another whisky. He didn't seem nearly as drunk and morose as I'd feared.

'Are you all right, Evelyn?'

His face softened. 'Yes, of course, love. I just wish she'd told me. For God's sake, what did she think I'd do?'

'I think she was worried that you'd talk her out of it.'

He smiled ruefully and flung himself into an armchair. 'I daresay it's for the best, really.'

'Poor Evelyn.' I perched on the arm of the chair, patted his shoulder.

'I'll be all right.' But he shuddered and leaned on me. I rubbed his back and he hid his face against my side, hugged me. After a time he got a new drink and gave me one. If he cried later, I didn't hear him. He was much quieter in all his emotions than Kaye had been.

When we were going upstairs I remembered. 'Did you see Dieter?'

'Oh God. I'd forgotten about that. I'll have to ring him tomorrow.'

I supposed that Dieter had tactfully gone away. But there was no trace of him at his usual hotel when Evelyn rang, and he did not contact Evelyn. On Monday, Evelyn had received a wire at work; Dieter had been detained and would not now be in England for another few weeks. Perhaps I'd been mistaken.

I rang Kaye to find out how she was getting on. She didn't like the bedsit, but hoped to move into a flat with one of the girls from work soon. She was worried about Evelyn. He had visited her to be sure she was all right, and had not, she thought, looked at all well.

'What happened that night? How long did you wait for Evelyn?'

She said that Dieter had arrived, it had been very embarrassing under the circumstances, but she'd asked him to wait. Evelyn couldn't make a fuss with someone else there, and Dieter could look after Evelyn when she'd gone. 'He was so kind, Alex. In the end he got me a taxi and helped me move. And then he took me for a drink, and let me talk, tried to cheer me up.'

'I can imagine.'

'Alex! That's *horrible*. It wasn't like that at all. He was very sweet, very understanding.'

I was inclined to believe Kaye. She was not that sort of girl, besides being a very bad liar. But why had Dieter pretended he hadn't been in England at all if nothing had happened? I wondered if they'd been having a clandestine affair. Regretfully I decided it wasn't possible. I was sure Kaye wasn't up to being that devious. She wouldn't have had much chance anyway, he wouldn't have time to get to London very often, even secretly. And I couldn't imagine anyone desiring him as a lover, although he was not unattractive in a fair, florid sort of way. I found it amusing that anyone quite so huge was called 'diet-er'.

The fact remained that Dieter had behaved very oddly. Perhaps he was merely apprehensive that Evelyn would jump to conclusions and be angry. If he supposed that Evelyn lost his temper in the way he did himself, then it was understandable that he avoided Evelyn until things had blown over. I didn't see any point in mentioning anything about Dieter to Evelyn. His visit a few weeks later passed without incident, except for an extravagantly mawkish drunken weeping fit over the imminent end to his business association with his dearest and oldest friend.

Evelyn collapsed into retirement. I had been worried about him after Kaye's departure, but the protracted drinking bout that I had half anticipated never occurred. Mainly he had slept a lot, lying in half the afternoon at weekends, lounging around in his dressing gown playing records, dozing over a book. After the firm was sold he was never up before noon.

I saw very little of him. Ostensibly I worked in the school library after school. Usually I would go to Christina's or sometimes to Philip's. Evelyn was seldom in when I arrived home, at the pictures, yet another obscure arty film with subtitles, or on one of his marathon walks around London. He did not even follow my suggestion that he should try his new camera gear. In the evenings one or other of us was often out. At first, when Kaye had gone, I was careful to be around a lot, in case he desired company. But he did not seem to need me.

Richard went to Italy as soon as the sale was complete. After being packed off for a few weeks in the autumn to enforce his convalescence, he now said that he wanted to see more of the country, keep up the Italian he'd worked on. It was vaguely planned that Evelyn and I would go at Easter. But Evelyn didn't suggest it again and I didn't push him. I had no wish to be restricted to his companionship when he was in such a remote mood. And I supposed that if it was left to the summer, our holiday could be much longer.

He did not pick up the threads with Ben and Molly. They had been invited once to meet Kaye. They had been very kind and evidently much taken aback, with little to talk about without excluding Kaye, and we had not seen them since. I did not think that Evelyn was angry, merely embarrassed. But without them or Richard he had little mental stimulus. The intermittent long screeds from George had petered out months since, and in any event, it was scarcely satisfactory to conduct political debates by air mail.

Aunt Louisa took care not to push him either. 'I expect he's tired, dear, what with one thing and another.' She patted my hand. 'He's been like this before. He'll bounce back, he always does.'

'But he's much older now.'

Her spectacles glinted balefully. 'And he's not nearly in such a state as I've seen before now.'

'When? What?'

'Oh, well.' She reflectively fondled the ginger tom. 'He's never made things easy for himself. He didn't have a very easy time when he was your age. And after the war, he wasn't well at all. And when Aubrey died, on top of that . . .'

'Is that when he went abroad?'

'What do you know about that?'

'He told me he went East, Saigon and Hong Kong.'

'Mmm. I don't think he had an easy time then. He wired for money a few times, and I'm sure he wouldn't have done such a thing if he hadn't been quite desperate.' Her hands tightened on Tobermory and he jumped down. 'We all thought his health was ruined then.' She smiled. 'The wretched boy is like a cat, always lands on his feet, no matter how you throw him.'

'Ruined? What was wrong with him?'

'Well, it was only glandular fever in the end. But he was carried off the plane to hospital. The first we knew he was back was the police coming round. I was next of kin in his passport, you see.'

'It took him months to get over that,' Aunt Hetty said. 'He was here all winter, shaking and shivering, huddling over the fire. So thin, poor darling. I don't think he'd ever properly got better after the war. It's not something he ever talks about, but I'm sure he had a very bad time in the war. He saw a lot of front line duty.'

'But he was all right in the end,' I jollied them.

'No thanks to himself.' Aunt Louisa snorted. 'That ridiculous job.'

'He got a job long distance lorry driving,' explained Aunt Hetty.

'Lorry driving!'

'He said it was the only thing he'd learned in the army that was wanted in civilian life.'

'Nonsense,' interjected Aunt Louisa. 'He fancied himself the proletariat or some such. Wouldn't even think of a black coat job. I thought he'd learned better after Spain.'

'I don't think that's fair, dear. I think he was just too unsettled for an office routine.'

'Anyway,' Aunt Louisa recalled herself. 'It all worked out in the end.'

'Did you make Richard give him a job?'

'Of course not, dear. It was nothing to do with me. Or anyone else. He had several sales jobs and did very well. It was Richard himself who suggested Evelyn apply when the sales manager left.' She made a philosophical gesture with her hands. 'I've given up worrying over him long since. He'll be fine in the end. Just bear with him a little.'

'I've been bearing with him for ages,' I said sulkily. 'I thought it would be better once we got rid of Kaye.'

'You seem to forget, dear, just how much he's borne with you all these years. All the upset when you first came. You worried him dreadfully. And I daresay he'll have a lot to bear yet,' she said drily.

2

My 'O' level exams were as unrelievedly awful as I had expected. The only high point was my French oral, when I succeeded in making the examiner lapse into English during the conversation. All the usual questions, my parents were *morts*, I resided *chez mon uncle, avec ma chatte et* (and stretching the point for effect) *la maitresse de mon uncle*.

'Now look.' He sternly waved his glasses at me, rather in the manner of Richard. 'If you're not going to take this seriously.'

My injured innocence seemed sufficiently plausible to convince him.

'*En Français, s'il te plait*,' he said irritably.

Christina had fared badly. 'Such an odious little man. So common.' She sniffed and threw her hair back. He had evidently been unimpressed by the glimpse of her black lace suspender belt afforded by her rolling her skirt up at the waistband, and the provocatively unbuttoned blouse. (She had taken her bra off in the 'Ladies' beforehand.)

Evelyn was unexpectedly helpful about the exams. Having showed no interest in what I was doing all year, he had salvaged the whole situation at the eleventh hour. I had done very little work, having the excuse of so much domestic upheaval. I had been put in for far too many exams, and could not possibly make up lost ground for nine subjects. Over Easter I abandoned any attempt to recoup my fortunes and sullenly lay on my bed playing records all day, reading Doris Lessing instead of studying, having previously informed Mr Wainwright that I would be too busy revising to work extra hours over the holiday. Evelyn didn't organise us into any sort of outing except a few meals out.

Eventually I threw a panicky tantrum, blaming Evelyn for the whole and saying a great many things about Kaye and the relationship and his character that I had managed to leave unsaid even in the moments of greatest provocation at the time. Astonishingly, he had meekly accepted the blame, apologised for imposing on me so appallingly. He had looked at everything I was supposed to be doing and at his suggestion I abandoned two of the nine subjects to the extent of not even sitting the papers.

Evelyn was extremely useful with revision. I made more progress with him with French in weeks than I had all year. He also arranged for Richard to help me with maths and Latin. He pulled himself together and organised our domestic arrangements. Someone came in and did for us again. He made sure always to have a meal for me in the evenings and to be available if I wanted help. When the exams started, he opened a bottle of good wine on the evenings before the papers to ensure that I would sleep. In the morning he would be up in time to make coffee for me before I left, and drive me if it was raining.

I couldn't help feeling smugly certain that I was going to do much better than Christina. She was not stupid, indeed she was enviably quick with mathematics. But she had learned even less than I had, and didn't have such a good memory for last minute cramming. She had no interest in or general knowledge of things like history or geography and could rely little on bluff. Her mother was no help at all; Christina was so disaffected that she spent a great deal of time at my house. I was finding her increasingly boring, but I didn't want to force the issue at such a critical time for us both. It did not make things easier with Evelyn. When she wasn't there he referred to her as 'Lady Docker' or 'her ladyship'.

She did most of her revision at my house. Typically, in the hot afternoons, Christina and Berry lolled on my bed, leaving me to devise essay plans at the desk. Idly she examined the wedding photo of my parents with a picture of Evelyn over the corner. 'Poor man.'

'What?'

'He's aged so dreadfully. So grey these days. And haggard. He really was quite good-looking. But now . . .' She sighed extravagantly. 'It must be so awful when one's looks go, if one's relied on them.'

'I'm not going to do all this for you.'

'It's the strain of keeping up with voracious younger women. It's taking its toll. So pathetic. I bet he needs all sorts of kinky stuff to get him going these days.'

'Look, if you don't do some of this, I won't show you what I've done.'

'Have you looked in his room? There might be whips and handcuffs, or – Ow!' She sulkily rubbed her arm. Berry, having jumped away from my aimed textbook, stretched herself through the open window and bounded down the fire escape. 'Your parents look . . . sweet,' she placated. 'What did they die of?' She luridly drooled over ocean liners sinking, planes plummeting in flames, cars tumbling end over end into gorges, lovingly described jostling for life boats, burning alive, severed limbs.

'My father died in a car crash,' I allowed.

'They didn't die together?' She was disappointed. 'Was it a bad crash?'

'How should I know? I was only two.'

'What did your mother die of?'

'I don't know.' I thought, tried to remember what I'd been told. 'I can't remember. Haemorrhage.'

'Haemorrhage? What do you mean?'

'What do you mean, what do I mean? Are you planning do to any work?'

'That doesn't mean anything. Brain haemorrhage? Stomach?' She pleasurably dwelt on the possibilities, the desperation of hospital staff as they struggled to save her, the last words. 'Or – I know! It must have been an abortion. She bled to death after a backstreet abortion. What was her lover like? Was he handsome?'

'Will you either get some work done or piss off!' I shouted.

'Really, Alexandria. I don't know what's got into you lately. You're so *touchy*.' She opened the book. 'Is your period due?' she asked solicitously. She made an incredible fuss of her own periods, whimpering and moaning, doing nothing for days, invariably missing at least one day from school each month.

Suddenly I was sympathetic to George and Matthew, understood their frantic application, their implacable demands on Evelyn. I remembered the very bad winter in the run-up to their finals. They had both practically camped here, huddling close to the fire, making more and more notes, filling index cards, accepting sustenance with perfunctory thanks, irritable at any interruption. I felt badly at how I'd behaved. I'd tried not to resent their presence, to be friendly and helpful, but I hadn't the remotest conception of what they were going through. Evelyn had been as kind and reassuring to them as he was now to me.

Once, in the middle of the exams, I took a Saturday evening off and went to a party. Returning home, I ran into Evelyn's old girlfriend, Jean, just outside the house. She didn't see me. I realised that she was very distressed, and crying.

I touched her arm. 'What's happened? What's he done?'

She blew her nose and shook her head. 'It's not his fault.'

'But why . . . He could have at least got you a taxi. I'll walk with you up to the station and you can get one there.' I felt protective. She had always been nice to me when I was little, and now she was much smaller than me and needed looking after.

After we had walked a bit she said, 'He just thinks he can turn up after a year as if nothing's changed. He's done it before. Good old Jean, she's always available if there's nothing younger and prettier. Well, he's not exactly a spring chicken himself,' she said savagely. 'I swore I wasn't going to get tangled up again, it's my own fault, I shouldn't have been so bloody soft.' The tears started again.

'But what did he do?'

'Oh God, nothing really. He's just so – takes everything for granted. Turning up out of the blue like that, expecting . . .' She snuffled determinedly. 'He's such an arrogant bastard. He always seems to think that everyone will want him.' She laughed weakly. 'Trouble is, they do. I'm old enough to know better, it's not his fault. There's no point expecting him to change after all these years. I know I'm being silly, really. It's not his fault,' she repeated.

She emphasised how kind Evelyn had always been, how concerned with her problems. She had frequently been disaffected with her accountancy job, complained of being treated as a menial, given all the most boring work to do. She had recently finally qualified as an accountant and immediately changed jobs. It was Evelyn who had persuaded her to stick out the training, insisted that she mustn't let her boss get the better of her, encouraged her to fight for the same concessions granted to her male colleagues. I remembered numerous occasions when Evelyn had let her have a moan, cossetted her, bolstered her determination. Never had he belittled her ambition or allowed her to give in to discouragement.

There were no taxis on the rank. Jean shivered in the cool night air. I bought us tea from a stall, stirred lots of sugar into Jean's.

'Thanks.' She sipped gratefully. 'Never be a good sport, Alex. I've always been a good sport. Shoulder to cry on, home comforts. I've lost track of the number of men who've cried to me about the women they really love, or why they can't leave their wife just yet. Look at me. I'll be thirty-five next birthday. I'll never have a husband and kids now.'

'You don't know that. I'm sure you will.'

'Can you see Evelyn as husband and father? Come on. I wouldn't have him now if he asked.'

'You might meet someone else.'

'I might. I've missed a lot of chances hanging about being a good sport.' She gulped tea. 'I'd have liked kids.'

When I got in Evelyn said, 'And what sort of time do you call this?'

'And what sort of a way is that to treat Jean? Sending her out in the night in tears. You might have got her a taxi.'

'I'll thank you to mind your own damned business.'

'Well, it is my business. She's my friend too. I walked her up to the station and got a taxi and then she dropped me off.'

He drew in his mouth. 'But you were late anyway.'

'That's just too fucking bad.'

'Don't you talk to me like that.'

'If you don't mind, Evelyn, I'm tired, and I'm going to bed.'

The row was horrible and I derived no satisfaction from reducing Evelyn to silence, hurrying away shocked at the spectacle of his bowed shoulders, his dark eyes gleaming wetly. Evelyn was carefully considerate for the next few days, and I responded magnanimously. But I was very frightened at what I had done, worried that things would never mend. The amount of revision I had to do provided sufficient reason for my lack of sociability.

On the eve of my last paper, Evelyn came home in an ebullient mood to announce, 'I've bought a house.'

3

'Really, my dear, no one lives in *Putney*,' chided Christina.

Evelyn and I had already argued this through. He had no intention of living in Putney. A business acquaintance of Richard's had needed cash in a hurry, and offered the house with sitting tenant absurdly cheap. Richard was away again, driving round the Derbyshire Peaks, before taking a job sorting out production difficulties for an electronics firm. So Evelyn had taken up the bargain. I made a number of rude comments about Rachman landlords and objected to his lack of consultation. I could not imagine Richard having the sort of friends who needed to raise quick cash in such a fashion.

This conversation with Christina degenerated into a serious row, and a great number of long-suppressed home truths were exchanged on both sides. A great lassitude set in. I lay in even later than Evelyn, read a great deal until very late and didn't bother to see anyone much.

I felt nostalgic for the companionship of Bobby. As we had outgrown espionage fantasies, he had developed numerous ways to make money. The simplest way was to pick up guileless tourists and regale them with outrageous historical 'fact'. I had been very good at this. I had much real knowledge, and the interweaving of truth and fabrication had often impressed even Bobby by its plausibility. Usually we would be tipped or taken for a real English tea for our pains. One of Bobby's favourites, if we weren't in need of cash, was to draw a small map of the area including a large triangle, and stop passers-by to ask if they could help us find the Great Pyramid.

I would go out in the afternoon, to change library books or listen to new releases in Imhof's basement, or just walk around. I was not so much bored as overwhelmed by *ennui*. I began to understand what Evelyn had gone through when he finished work, after the gruelling time he'd had when Richard was ill, Jamie Robertson dying, Kaye leaving.

Evelyn's purchase of a house had made him think. He could see no reason not to buy somewhere else for us to live. The lease on the flat was due to run out shortly and he had suddenly been faced with a massive rent increase. He had been increasingly dissatisfied with it, bemoaning the lack of space, not having a spare room. When Kaye had moved in, it was obvious that the flat was too small. In any event, everything needed redecorating.

We looked at various places. Evelyn's instinct was for something modern, with central heating. But such places were poky, and could not possibly accommodate the bulky furniture he had inherited from his father. I knew from Christina's flat that they were badly built and noisy; next door could be heard in the loo. Nothing was decided and the lease was running out.

Philip haunted the flat. His devotion during the exams had been almost touching. He had sat his own 'O' levels the previous year, and was very sympathetic, tolerating even more short-tempered scorn than he did normally without a murmur. Now he was forever organising picnics at Kew, or trips on the river. His mother's packed lunches were always thoroughly planned and beautifully executed, crusts trimmed, butter to the edges of the bread, twists of salt. Philip was deliciously scandalised when once I took a corkscrew and a bottle of wine from Evelyn's rack. He was giggling and pink-eared before he'd managed to consume his half.

If we stayed at home, we would climb out on the fire escape in the sun. I no longer had access to the garden, now Mrs Carey was gone. She had slipped on the ice in the bad winter and broken a hip. After that she could never really manage, and eventually her son had moved her to a home near him in Bexhill. It was probably as well, I thought, that she had not been faced with the Kaye situation. I kept meaning to go and see her but I never got around to it. Her beautiful garden was an overgrown mess now but Berry liked the wilderness.

If we sat in my room, Philip was always scrupulous about keeping the door ajar and sitting on a different surface from me, as he did in his bedroom at home, presumably under orders. Evelyn would sometimes irritably shut the door if the record player was on. Once Evelyn slammed the door on my music while Philip was brushing my hair. With increasing temerity he begged to be allowed to do so any time we were alone, spending ages raptly absorbed while I read something. His deferential manner and his antiseptic cleanliness, vaguely redolent of his father's surgery, made it feel more like a Harley Street consultation than an amatory encounter. The ritual was unvarying, medically methodical.

Later he flushed guiltily when Evelyn asked amiably if he was staying to eat. While I was laying the table, he said to Evelyn, 'I'd like to assure you, Mr Parrish, that my intentions are strictly honourable.'

'That's what worries me.' Evelyn turned the Spanish omelette on to a plate. 'Make yourself useful and open some beer. Yes, three, unless you don't want one.'

'You don't understand.' Philip sounded near tears.

'We're all sixteen sometime.'

'It's not like that. I'm seventeen now.' I had never heard him so irritated.

'Forgive me, dear fellow, but what has it got to do with me?'

'Don't you care about her at all?'

Evelyn clattered plates. 'I think we should allow that as unsaid, don't you?'

'I beg your pardon,' he stammered.

'I assure you, Philip, that I'm well able to look after Alex. If I supposed for a moment that . . . Will you carry that through?'

Dr Marigard came to pick up Philip after being called out and he and Evelyn chatted easily over large whiskies. Evelyn didn't offer us another beer.

'You shouldn't trifle with the poor thing,' Evelyn reproved later.

'I'm not trifling. He knows exactly what I think. He doesn't have to keep coming round. I wish he wouldn't.'

'Well then, send him on his way. I don't think you realise, Alex, what delicate plants young men of that age are. Much more so than girls.'

'I bet you weren't a delicate plant.'

'Cheek.'

In the end Evelyn suggested that we store everything and travel for the rest of the summer, before taking something temporary while we looked in the autumn.

'What about Berry?' Now that we had to decide quickly, I didn't want to move at all.

'Oh God.'

'You've never liked her,' I accused. I knew I was being ridiculous. Berry's favourite perch was lying full length on Evelyn when he was stretched on the sofa. I remembered when I had first got Berry, the fuss I made over her. Evelyn had been goaded often to remark, 'You care more for that bloody cat than you do for me.' I had never denied it. I relented. 'Do you think Aunt Louisa would have her back?'

'If you think she would be happy there . . .' conciliated Evelyn.

It was a melancholy task sorting through the accumulation of childish possessions and souvenirs. I was much more ruthless than I'd been when leaving Platea. Evelyn had even more belongings to sort through. He steeled himself to have a major purge of his books and got Mr Wainwright to take the boxes he'd weeded out. Mr Wainwright enjoyed himself immensely, discussing obscure editions, regaling Evelyn with scurrilous stories about me and consuming his beer for an entire afternoon, but made little concession when it came to business. Evelyn decided to have the storage firm box up everything except personal effects, but even so we had to work very hard to be out in time.

I was particularly reluctant to leave Tim's seascape. As a child I had loved it, stayed in the bath for ages, imagining myself part of the scene. But it was in sorry condition, blistered and peeling, colours faded. Although the artwork was as good as anything Tim had done, he had not been experienced in fresco techniques, and the steamy atmosphere had not helped. The scale of the undertaking had been immense; he and Evelyn must have been quite close for Tim to have invested so much effort. Or probably, I decided, Evelyn had magnanimously hired Tim when he was unemployed.

Evelyn would miss the bathroom. The tub was so long he could soak comfortably, topping up the hot for hours. In the worst time after Richard's heart attack he would sit in the water with a stiff whisky and no light except the orange glow of the electric bar. Not infrequently he fell asleep and had to be woken by Kaye.

The flat looked pitifully dingy stripped of pictures and decoration. In Evelyn's room the paper looked new where all his photographs had covered the alcove. He had not, I noticed, put up a picture of Kaye. No impression of her had been left. Everything was Evelyn's taste, Evelyn's choice, and, I suddenly realised, she had never more than camped out in the accumulated clutter of Evelyn's life. Although he had made space for her belongings, he had not encouraged her to make changes or adapt her surroundings to make herself feel more at home. She had not cared for Evelyn's decor, simultaneously unconventional and out of date. The first time her father had gone to the loo in the flat, he was in there for almost ten minutes. She was embarrassed by such deviation from the usual, at a loss to justify it to her family.

I recognised most of the people in the photos now. There were wedding pictures of Ben and Molly, Diana and Gordon, many family groups. There were portraits of Evelyn's father, Richard and Tim. But never had he told me anything about the army pictures.

'Why have you got a picture of Richard's wife?' I had never noticed before that an autographed studio picture of a glamorous young woman was in fact Richard's second wife, Megan.

'Well, I thought it was rather a good picture, don't you?'

'Did you take it?;' He had taken many of Kaye, some of them very fine.

'Mmm.' He began swaddling the frames in newspaper.

'Did you know her? I thought he was hardly married to her for ten minutes.'

'She . . . she was very kind to me when Daddy died, helped me to get organised. What do you know about it anyway?'

'Is it true that she ran off with another man?'

He snatched the picture away and wrapped it. 'If there's anything you want to know about Richard's private life I suggest you ask Richard.'

'All right, I will.'

'Alexandria, if you dare . . .'

'Stupid.' I said sulkily, 'I don't see why you can't tell me.' Evelyn continued wrapping. 'Why hasn't she got any clothes on in that picture?'

'Of course she bloody has clothes on. It was an evening dress.'

'Strapless?'

'It was very fashionable. It was green, like her eyes.'

'Were you in love with her?' I asked, awed.

To my surprise he burst out laughing. 'Trust you to be so melodramatic. No, I was not in love with her. Really, Alex.'

4

Evelyn was unexpectedly energetic about leaving the flat, in contrast to his desultory approach to searching for a new establishment. Plans quickly slipped beyond my control. First it had been agreed that we would go to Italy for a time, then that Aunt Louisa and Aunt Hetty would accompany us. I had imagined that Evelyn and myself would meander through Europe as the whim took us, just the two of us, as it had used to be. I did not really object to Italy, or to the old people, but it seemed disappointingly tame, and everything would be wholly predictable, all our usual walks and drives, museums and sights, constrained by the pace of the aunts, swallowed in the circle of Uncle Sebastian's in-laws.

I was getting on reasonably well with Evelyn, but there wasn't the same comfortable closeness that there had been before Kaye. Evelyn was always cordial, refrained from imposing too many restrictions on me. But he was fundamentally aloof. He didn't seem to mind at all the expansion of our arrangements, no longer was annoyed that I organised my weekends separately. I was very hurt that he showed no inclination to pick up where we had left off. I wondered whether he had been so wounded by

Kaye that he was still unable to make any effort. He had not seemed really upset, a bit down for a week or so, but not remotely devastated. It didn't occur to me that he was being careful not to crowd me too much. If he wasn't bothered that things were no longer the same, then I was not going to allow him to suppose that I was either.

The last straw was the further addition to the family gathering of his sister, Aunt Diana. I announced my refusal to go to Italy, my determination to remain in London.

'I see. And where do you suppose you could live?' said Evelyn sarcastically.

'I can find a bedsit. Like I was going to before. You said I could before.'

'I never said any such thing!' he exploded.

'You said we'd see,' I said sullenly.

During Kaye's residence it had been my oft repeated refrain that I would move out as soon as I was sixteen. I had not, of course, been allowed to do so, but I insisted frequently, provocatively, that I had merely deferred the move until my 'O' levels were taken. Evelyn had never risen to the bait, turning aside my melodrama with some bland prosaic remark in his usual fashion.

Now the row was prolonged, grumbling on for an entire day. Finally I said, 'I never wanted to go to Italy anyway. I never said I did.'

'Then where would you like to go?' he said wearily.

Taken by surprise by the sudden conciliation, I replied, 'I don't want to go anywhere with you. It will be horrible. You'll be scheming to get rid of me all the time so you can get off with people.'

'You mean that's what you'd be doing,' he retorted.

'I don't want go with you.'

'Well, it would have saved a great deal of trouble if you'd said so in the first place instead of stringing me along. If that's how you feel, we'll see what can be arranged,' he said stiffly. Before I could retract anything he had grabbed his jacket and ran out. I cried and cried, wished him back, but he did not come until the small hours, slipping quietly to his room before I could steel myself to intercept him.

'I've arranged for you to stay with Richard,' he told me the next evening, quite abruptly at the end of our strained meal.

'Richard?'

'Take it or leave it, Alex. I'm not having you running loose in London by yourself and that's absolutely final and non-negotiable. Is that understood?'

'Yes, but . . .'

'I said *no*, Alex.' He carried our used plates into the kitchen and appeared in the doorway in his raincoat. 'I'm going to the pictures. I should be back by half ten and you'd bloody well better be in when I get here, is that clear?'

'Yes, Evelyn.'

I was vehemently glad that he had given me no chance to pour out my carefully rehearsed apologies, my assurances that I hadn't meant it, that I wanted more than anything to remain with him.

Despite his grumbling about my capriciousness, Mr Wainwright was sufficiently pleased to have me full time after all to gave me a raise in wages. I found a full week in the shop rather less diverting than one day only, and it was very tiring not to have two days at the weekend. I was never given Monday as my day off in lieu, being last in the pecking order. Hillyard was going through a bad patch as well, his affairs even more tangled than ever. Mr Wainwright, by contrast, was in fine form, trilling 'Come into the garden, Maud' or 'Tit Willow' as he priced stock, which made Hillyard even more dismal.

Richard made things very easy for me domestically. He had

not after all taken up the troubleshooting job, deciding on closer inspection that his position would be far too invidious to little avail. He seemed to have nothing at all to do except look after me, waking me in the morning with a cup of tea, providing me with evening meals, Sunday drives, outings to theatres and restaurants.

What I had not imagined was how much I would miss Evelyn. The intensity of my longing for him was childish, idiotic. Not even to Hillyard would I admit my weakness. I resented Richard for not being Evelyn, indulged unforgivably in tantrums and sarcasm at the slightest provocation. Even more I resented Evelyn for not realising that I wanted him back. Evelyn wrote to me several times each week, describing with stilted blandness the sights and events, reiterating his affection in the tamest of terms.

My replies to Evelyn were less frequent, sulkily sketchy. I became convinced that he was enjoying himself much more without me, that he had not the slightest interest in us being together again. I knew the conventional expressions of endearment betrayed his utter indifference.

When he returned at the end of the month, we were given no chance to sort things out. Evelyn lodged at Crystal Palace while I continued with Richard. I had no intention of submitting meekly to the inevitable lectures from Aunt Diana, or the acerbic cosy chats with Aunt Louisa, and avoided contact as much as possible. Several times Evelyn took me out for the evening, but this was always constrained, like a first date, pleasant, anodyne, no one daring to broach the real issues.

Evelyn was soon irked by the suburban constraints of Crystal Palace; the difficulties and justifications of late nights out; the elderly fussing of Louisa and Hetty; the advice from Diana; the whining of his nephew Christopher, cramming for resits of his first year exams (he was reading Geography at Southampton). Within a couple of weeks he bolted.

Conspiratorially he confided his intentions to me, invited me to go with him. I wanted to, was eager to be coaxed, persuaded, coerced.

'I can't disappoint Mr Wainwright,' I demurred perfunctorily.

'No, of course not. But there's the small matter of Richard. I don't see why he should be lumbered with you.'

'He doesn't mind.'

'Not in the least,' agreed Evelyn. 'He thinks you ought to stay here. He doesn't think I'm fit to have charge of you.'

'Is that what he says?'

'They're all agreed I've made a botch of it. Just like they always knew I would.'

'Don't be silly. I'm not complaining.'

'It might be said that you've . . . voted with your feet.'

I couldn't begin to find words, remorse, apology, conciliation.

'Is there any point in me staying here? Do you want a new place like we planned?'

'Yes, of course. But I don't see why you should forgo your holiday on my account.'

'I see,' he said heavily. 'Your enthusiasm overwhelms me.'

He left for France two days later.

'What is it, Missy? You've been looking rotten all day.' Hillyard left the heaps of change on the counter and came over to me, awkwardly patting my shoulder. The unexpected sympathy was enough to cause me to give way to tears at last.

Nothing had gone as I calculated. Evelyn had not cajoled and wheedled, had not seemed markedly eager for my company. My rehearsed scenes of hesitant compliance had been wasted. And whatever Richard may have said to Evelyn, it was clear that he did not approve of how I had treated Evelyn. I was beginning to realise how horrible I'd been to Evelyn and now it was too late. I had ruined everything.

I had not allowed for how weary Evelyn was, for how upset he had been by the strictures of the family. I had utterly betrayed Evelyn, given him bound into the hands of Diana. All the assiduous complicity of seven years was disavowed. Time and again we had confounded prediction, been seen to manage very well, even if it was unsuitable. Evelyn had skated dangerously near the brink with Kaye. But however unpleasant I was to them at home, ranks were closed to outsiders.

I had been so shocked at his lack of ardour that I had not merely let him go without attempting to patch things up, to create an occasion for assuring him of my devotion. On his last evening I had provoked a horrible row, saying many things I had managed hitherto to leave unsaid, many more that he had already stood accused of. I could not even think of why I had done this now, when the worst was past. There was not the slightest justification. But I had repudiated Evelyn and it was irrevocable.

I could think of nothing except the watery glistening of his big eyes as he pecked my implacable cheek, the elderly sag of his shoulders as he had left me. I no longer had the excuse of being a child, being insecure, having had a difficult time. It would not seem a childish freak, but deliberate, calculated, malicious. And now there could be no allowance made; this time he would not forgive me.

I kept thinking of all the nice times we had had when I was a child. I had loved it when people remarked on the resemblance of his little girl to himself, basked in the attention when Evelyn commanded services by speaking of 'my little girl'. No longer would I be able to derive pleasure from having people refer to 'your Dad'. I had ruined everything.

'There, there, dear.' Hillyard let me sob for a time, and

finished cashing up while I pulled myself together. He locked up the shop and we walked to the night safe. In the pub he bought me a pint. I was touched; he could ill afford it. 'You take it from me, ducky, he's not worth it. There's not a man on earth who's worth crying over. You can't tell me anything about men. All the same, all bloody rotten. You forget all about him and go out and have some fun, that's my advice.'

5

'Evelyn tells me you've quarrelled about me.' This frontal attack was unexpected. Richard had refrained from saying anything about Evelyn for some days, and I was beginning to feel easier. I supposed he wasn't going to say anything. I had been completely off my guard during the excellent meal he had treated me to, accepted a liqueur at home, feeling as cosy as I had used to with him. 'I mean, about Meg.'

'Not really. It just got mentioned in passing.' I had accused Evelyn point blank of having run off with Richard's wife. When, much to my surprise, he had not denied it, I added that to the catalogue of his sins, castigating his complete lack of principle, his total callousness towards Richard, his uncontrolled lust.

'I really don't see that it's any business of yours.' Richard's eyes were icy. 'I strongly advise you not to meddle in what doesn't concern you.'

'It's very late. I think I'll go to bed now.'

'In due course. But since you have meddled, you'll hear what I have to say first.' He topped up his glass. 'I'd like you to understand that as far as I'm concerned, the whole thing is ancient history.' He smiled wryly. 'I'm not being magnanimous, I assure you. I daresay I emerge with even less credit than anyone else.'

I forgot my sulks. 'Do you mean you were having an affair with someone else?'

'How dare you!' He added petulantly, 'As if I had time for that sort of thing.' He explained that it had been obvious that his marriage had been a mistake as soon as he was back from the war, that he had been preoccupied with attempting to sort out the mess the firm was in. 'I know I'm very much to blame. I never really made an effort to make it work. I gave Meg very little time, I was hardly at home. And she was very young, very much at a loss over the whole business. She felt I was comparing her unfavourably with Angela all the time.'

'Were you?'

'I hope I never said so.' He sipped his drink and said with difficulty, 'I should have at least tried to make an end of it. But I just left her to go on best as she could until I had some time. She . . . she had no one to turn to, you see. All her ATS friends had gone home, married here and there. And neither her mother nor my own could have been the least help. Uncle Aubrey was very kind to her. And when Evelyn and Alec were back, she spent a lot of time there, it was much livelier, young people around all the time.' He smiled, almost impishly. 'It was your father everyone saw fit to warn me about. The poor fellow languished after her dreadfully.'

'Didn't you do anything?'

'Well, no. I thought it would solve everything.'

'Wait until she was unfaithful under everyone's nose and then divorce her?'

'She would have divorced me. Which she did in the end. Vastly creditable, wasn't it?'

I looked wistfully at the Cointreau and Richard nodded. 'And then?'

'Well, Evelyn wasn't at all well, and she spent a lot of time visiting, just talking, cheering him up. I think she found Alec a bit . . . young. And when Uncle Aubrey died, Evelyn took that very hard. I never really wanted to ask about all the ins and outs of it. Shall we just agree that he was much in need of consolation.'

'Consolation,' I said witheringly.

'Don't you take that tone over things you don't know anything about,' he said stiffly. 'Grief does strange things. How do you suppose I got myself into the whole mess to start with?'

'What happened in the end?'

'Evelyn decided to travel abroad, and I gave Meggie the money to book a passage to New York too.'

'New York? I thought he went out East.'

'He got that far eventually.'

'What happened to Megan?'

'I believe she got as far as California with Evelyn. She had a fancy to get herself into the pictures.'

'Did she?'

'Good God, no. She wasn't nearly ruthless enough to break into that sort of racket. And I don't suppose she had the right sort of looks.'

'She looked very pretty, I thought.'

'Oh yes, but not tall and elegant, like Diana. She tended to look fat in photographs.'

'Where is she now?'

'Still out there. She married some sort of film technician, and they have several children. I've lost track.'

'Didn't she . . . love Evelyn?'

'Who knows? I don't suppose so, any more than he did her.'

'He wasn't in love with her?'

'He was fond of her, I think. But he was most put out over the whole business. He wasn't best pleased to be saddled with her on his travels. Not part of his plans.'

'Why did he take her?'

'Well, he didn't really have much choice, did he?' Richard's smile seemed positively sinister.

'How do you mean?'

'If he was going to take my wife off my hands, I damned well wasn't going to let him get away with half measures.' He swirled his brandy.

'But . . . you mean you made them run away together?'

'It wasn't as bad as that. Evelyn was certainly in no state to look after himself, he had to have somebody. And Meggie was quite happy. She wanted to go with him, she was keen to see America.'

'But . . . how could you . . .'

'Anyway, it's all worked out in the end. Meggie certainly seems to be happy. And Evelyn admits that they had fun together, says she looked after him very well. It was very cold when they got to New York, apparently, and he wasn't up to much.'

'But . . . Aunt Louisa . . . Uncle Cecil . . . Uncle Theodore . . .'

'Well, yes. That was a bit awkward,' Richard admitted.

'You mean you just let them think . . .'

'It was perfectly true. He didn't have to make love to my wife.'

'I think that's really horrible, Richard.'

'I did explain to Louisa, and Cecil when Evelyn came back. Told them what had really happened.'

'I bet they thought you were just being nice. No wonder everyone always picks on Evelyn all the time. You ought to be ashamed.'

'I assure you, my dear, Aunt Louisa is under no illusions about me.'

'Is that why you gave Evelyn the job?'

'By no means.' He smiled. 'I did try to give him a job – not the one he had later – but he wasn't having it. I suppose it was understandable that he had a bit of a chip on his shoulder. I admit I would have felt better to make it up to him. In the end I suggested he apply for a vacancy in the usual way. He had relevant experience by then, and I thought he would be fun to work with. Really, my dear, you have no idea how dull most businessmen are. If you take my advice, you'll never marry a businessman. You'd hardly ever see them and when you did you'd be monumentally bored.'

'No doubt Megan was monumentally bored with you,' I snapped.

'Oh certainly,' he agreed. He swirled his brandy again, reflectively.

'Did my father go to America to try to find her?'

'Oh no. I believe he fell passionately in love several more times before he went away. He never seemed to settle. He didn't do badly, got into insurance sales, but he was very restless. I think he decided that what was good enough for Evelyn was good enough for him. He was always one for doing whatever Evelyn did. Fortunately, I don't think he had the slightest idea of half of what Evelyn did do.' He laughed.

'Like what?'

'Never you mind. If there's anything you want to know about Evelyn, you ask him.'

But I had him on the defensive now. 'Why haven't you ever married again?'

'It's a question of meeting the right person. I'd have quite liked to marry again, have children. Ah, well. It's a bit late now.'

'You never know.' My anger melted, and I felt sorry for him.

'I don't think so. I don't think it's a good thing for children to have an elderly father like I did.'

'Do you think your father was better with Aunt Isabel and your brother?'

He poured more brandy. 'I suppose not.' He looked amused. 'Anyway, I'm telling you all this in the hope that you might think better of jumping to conclusions and judging private matters you know nothing about in future.' He added perfunctorily, 'Is there anything else you'd like to know?'

'Yes. There is, actually.' I took more Cointreau without being offered it. 'How did my mother die, Richard?'

He gulped brandy. 'What have you been told?'

'Why can't you give me a straight answer?'

'I really think it's up to Evelyn, if he thinks . . .'

'That's right. Push everything on to Evelyn, as usual. Look, all I want is a simple "yes" or "no". Did she die of an abortion?'

'Really, Alexandria. You shouldn't know anything about such things. Of all the melodramatic . . .'

'Yes or no, Richard!'

After a long moment he said irritably, 'I'd like to know who told you, that's all.'

'Does that mean yes?'

Almost imperceptibly he nodded.

I had been thinking about my mother. Try as I might, I could remember feeling little except irritation and boredom, even contempt. I understood suddenly what had prompted Bobby to be so horrible to Mrs Best all the time; she asked for it. But now I was enraged. I could not imagine my mother succumbing to the dubious blandishments of Mr Jansen. It was not that I had been so young as to find him repulsive and elderly; he had been objectively appalling. The attrition of his overweening complacency must have finally won the day.

I was anguished now at what she must have felt. She was

devoutly religous. It would have been awful enough merely to have transgressed to the extent of allowing Jansen to have his way. But what threats, what pressures had been brought to bear to make her agree to an abortion did not bear thinking of. Certainly she would have felt unable to confide in anyone, not even Janet. I supposed that he must already have been married since he hadn't married her. I wondered if she had been conscious, had a priest, so as not to die in mortal sin. I thought of his slimy mouth, the presumptuous possessiveness in his eyes, and felt murderous. I was glad I hadn't ended up with Jansen for a stepfather. I remembered the cut on Evelyn's eye when we had left Platea, thought of a half-heard conversation between him and Richard. I wanted Evelyn to come back.

6

I continued to rely very much on Richard. Christina and Philip were both away. I avoided going to Sophie and Leo's, managed without Lennie and David's existentialist circle. I didn't want to hear whatever Sophie would have to say about either Evelyn or myself. Likewise, I didn't get in touch with Jean or Tim. I knew that they wouldn't approve in the least. Hillyard was very friendly to me at work and sometimes he would go for a drink with me after we locked up the shop, or even to the theatre. But he had a busy social life of his own, or as he referred to it, his love life.

'I'm sorry, lovey. I've shocked you,' he apologised once after a particularly graphic confidence. 'I keep forgetting you're only a kid.'

'Don't be silly. Some of my best friends are . . .'

He looked enquiring. 'You'll have to introduce me. Anyone dishy?'

But I did not feel up to discussing Tim. I wondered sometimes about him and Evelyn, tried to puzzle out the situation without becoming childishly melodramatic. Obviously Evelyn wasn't homosexual. I knew about the episode of Richard's wife; they had evidently lived together for many months. I was aware of, or presumed on circumstantial evidence, involvements with many women in the time that I had known Evelyn.

It had been Christina who had clarified everything. I had talked often of Tim, the attractive older man. To my surprise, she had not even bothered to simper at him. 'Really, Alexandria. I don't know what all the fuss is about. Complete waste of time. I think pansies are so pathetic, don't you?'

I had felt simultaneously sick and silly. I thought of all the years of making an idiot of myself, how kindly Tim had handled me. Evelyn's amused smile took on entirely new and unpleasant overtones. I didn't feel surprised, I must have known, really. But we were friends, I loved Tim, and he cared about me. What he did was irrelevant. I felt such a blinding venom for Christina that I trembled. Nothing I could possibly think of was vicious enough to say to her.

Kaye had disliked Tim; she had been cold to him from the outset. She was such a gentle soul she did not seem to dislike even her husband or father. Things between Evelyn and Tim seemed to have been sorted out. Tim had visited a few times after Kaye had gone and they had appeared friendly enough, although Tim never stayed very long. I had not talked to him about his private life. He had prematurely presumed on my sophistication, but there was nothing that needed discussion now.

I couldn't ask Tim about Evelyn. I didn't know how he would react. I didn't like to think of Evelyn being homosexual. I was sure I would not mind, really, but I decided he wasn't. I couldn't see how he possibly could be. I supposed he was close to Tim, took him under his wing in the way that he had with George and Matthew. And Tim and Evelyn had much more in common, always too much to talk about. It was typical of Evelyn to be broadminded about the activities of his friends. And if Tim had started out having a crush on a younger and more handsome Evelyn, it had been handled with sufficient delicacy not to impair the friendship.

Many times I was on the verge of sending a postcard to Tim, always I refrained when I thought of how angry he would be at my treatment of Evelyn.

I told Hillyard that Tim was not his type and he did not press further. Hillyard's fancy was monotonously predictable, large, wholesome, tiresomely masculine. Unfortunately, the normalcy of appearance was usually the outward manifestation of the strict orthodoxy of orientation. But even those whose appearance belied their tastes seldom seemed suited to Hillyard. 'They're all the bloody same, these butch types. Always dumping you for every woman in sight to reassure themselves they're not like that *really*,' he would moan. 'Never again. I'm not going to get caught like that again,' he always resolved.

The void of Richard's frequent bridge evenings was increasingly filled by Hillyard. His precarious juggling of his complicated involvements seemed at last to have undone him. Although he declared himself to have at last fallen *really* in love with predictable regularity, on no previous occasion had he been so far gone as to forswear flirtations, *divertissements* and bits on the side in general. Unfortunately, the object of his passion behaved as he normally did himself, breaking dates if something more interesting came up, calculatedly evoking fits of jealousy, quite incapable of monogamy, bored by truthfulness.

Richard didn't care for me to go drinking straight from work, but as it was only Hillyard, and as I was back at a reasonable hour, he didn't force the issue, merely becoming rather less punctilious about providing me with a hot meal and waiting on me if I returned late. Despite Hillyard's despondency, we had a great deal of fun. Sometimes we queued for cheap theatre seats or went to the pictures. Always we seemed to have something to talk about, usually with lots of silly jokes and giggling. He was much more satisfactory a best friend than Christina had ever been.

On one of our drinking evenings we encountered an old friend.

'Well, Justin.' The greeting was typically temperate, the voice the same hoarse, weary tones as always.

Hillyard murmured something, tried to divert my attention.

'Is your name really Justin?' I would not be distracted.

'Bloody hell! Alex?' The indifference, the voice cracked.

'William!' I hugged him, much to his chagrin, and then he sat at our table. He hadn't changed at all, emaciated, ragged and grubby even in his conductor's uniform.

'I might have known I'd find you in a place like this,' he said wryly.

'A pub, you mean?'

'That too.' He laughed, asked after Evelyn.

The conversation did not recover from that constraint. It emerged that William still painted, earned his crust on the buses, hoped Justin might know of someone who wanted a room in his house temporarily, had lost touch with Tim. Presently his friends arrived and he left us.

'It's no good looking at me like that,' Hillyard reproached.

'Not my type at all.' He sipped beer. 'Nor yours, I'd have thought.'

'Justin. He's a very distinguished older man.' We laughed. Many of Christina's phrases had become our jokes. 'How do you know him, then?'

It transpired that he had been the close friend of a friend. Hillyard was much amused to learn that William had been my chief babysitter. 'That explains a great deal,' he said. This made us giggle excessively.

The reunion with William had considerable repercussions. It occurred to me that I might myself rent the vacant room in his house until Evelyn came back. Justin, as I made a point of calling him now, was unwilling to give me the beer-mat scribbled with William's address. I put it down to his reluctance to have me learn anything about him that he didn't choose to divulge himself. It did not cross my mind that he felt I might be rebuffed by William, or that if not, I would sadly cramp his style. William too seemed hesitant, but when I counted out pound notes on the spot, the need for the cash overcame any scruples or reservations.

'I've taken a bedsit. I thought I might move in this evening,' I said casually over breakfast. Despite retirement, Richard was up by eight at the latest every morning, always woke me.

'You'll damned well do no such thing!' He was alarmingly puce, eyes bulging. Too late I remembered that it was only a year ago that he had had a heart attack. I refrained from further provocation. Detachedly I noticed his hands, square and sturdy, pink with fine gold hairs, so unlike Evelyn's elegant hands. The newspaper crumpled in his grip, slipped to the floor. He took off his reading glasses and slowly wiped them.

'I'll be late for work.' I jumped up and kissed his brow, conciliatorily smoothed his thin hair. Try as I might, I could think of nothing else as I stood on the tube except Richard's wounded expression, the two tears that had escaped down his cheeks.

'I wish you'd tell me what I've done. Isn't there anything I can do to make you change your mind?' By evening he was all soft persuasion, anger gone.

'Don't be silly.' I smiled warmly. 'You've been marvellous. I just think it's time I stopped imposing on you.'

'My dearest girl, if you don't know you're more than welcome . . . And besides, you're only sixteen.'

'I know. Silly. But I'm old enough to manage on my own now I'm earning.' Despite his sincerity, I felt also that he was humouring me as a child. 'Besides, it will be much cheaper for me,' I couldn't resist adding.

Richard was charging me board now. It had been part of the ploy to make working seem less attractive and convince me to start school again in September. But I had decided I had no intention of doing so. Now Evelyn had given up the flat I was in the wrong catchment area to go back to my old school. I didn't really want to go back anyway. I felt that was so far past as to be ancient history.

I insisted there was no point in starting school from Richard's, as I would probably have to change when Evelyn came back. Evelyn had written, indicating his willingness to return forthwith, but I had replied that it was much too late now, we would be lucky to be permanently established by Christmas. I said that there was no rush, he must do as he pleased. I added untruthfully that I would be quite willing to consider starting 'A' levels next autumn.

Richard helped me to move. Naturally, I was equipped with his sheets, his towels, his crockery and cutlery, as well as being ferried by his car. When everything was unloaded he lingered, made tea, talked of how he had left home when he came down from Oxford, how his mother had wept and entreated. 'Of course, I was a lot older. Twenty-two.' He had made me promise that I would ring every day to let him know I was all right.

'You never had any intention of living with Evelyn again at all,' he said abruptly.

'Of course I did. Do.'

'I don't think it's fair to string him along like this. I think you should be honest with him at least.' He set aside his cup. 'Really, Alex, I don't know what he's done, but I can't imagine he could do anything so awful that he deserves being treated like this. If you're still resenting things that are no concern of yours . . .'

'Of course not.'

'He's at the end of his tether. He doesn't understand what he's done. You must let him know where he stands.'

What Evelyn had done? It was what I had done. I could not imagine that he could really want me back after all that, that he could honestly forgive and forget, that there would not now forever be that shadow between us. It was like Evelyn to be so generous. I could see now how he'd got into the whole mess with Kaye; he'd been too soft and too kind, allowed her to cling. But I was quite sure that he had not really wanted to live with Kaye.

It was no better with Richard. He had not reproached me on his own account. But I knew I had hurt him. He had asked what he'd done too, offered to make amends for uncommitted wrongs. That was the crux of the matter. I felt suffocated by him. He arranged everything around me, did everything for me. I felt boxed in, in a way that Evelyn had never made me feel. It was almost as bad as being crowded by Philip.

I thought of all the nice times we'd had when I was a child, the excitement of staying overnight away from home, Gilbert and Sullivan operettas, outings in the country. I remembered how understanding he'd been about Kaye, providing refuge for me, diverting me, never pressing or nosing, never criticising Evelyn. We had been very close after his heart attack. We talked for hours, he reminisced about his boyhood and youth, told me many things I hadn't heard before. When my 'O' level results came through, he had opened champagne. (I hadn't done nearly as badly as I had supposed, even scraping through Latin.) We had never had our holiday together. And now it was too late for that too. I wished I was dead.

Aunt Louisa came to visit me. 'It's not very nice,' she said forthrightly.

'It's all right. I'm not here very much.' This was true. Several nights a week I went to Richard's for a meal, or went out with him. Most other evenings I queued for cheap theatre seats after work or went to the cinema. Sundays were the worst. I spent a lot of time in museums.

'Does Evelyn know? Have you written to him?'

'I will. I haven't had time yet. I'll do it at the weekend.'

'Make sure you do. He worries. He's longing to hear from you.'

'Is that what he says?'

'I suppose this was really necessary?'

I poured tea. 'I just thought it was time I stopped imposing on Richard. I'm old enough to manage myself.'

She accepted the tea with a noise of indignation.

'Just because you never left home.' Too late I remembered. Aunt Louisa had been married for several years before her husband had been killed in the First War. She had moved back when her parents were ailing and elderly. 'I'm sorry,' I whispered.

She regarded me unmoved. 'It's high time Evelyn came back. If I were ten years younger . . . I'll write to him.'

'I don't want him to come back if he doesn't want to.'

She snorted again and clattered her cup into her saucer. She took her leave, without attempting to persuade me to go back to Richard, or even to Crystal Palace.

7

My independence seemed the worst of all possible worlds, with neither the comforts of home life nor the excitement of Swinging London. The house was inconveniently located miles from the tube south of the river. Like all the previous houses William had lived in, there was little in the way of amenities. No one worried about cleaning or meals. My attempts to domesticate the menage were doomed to failure, tidying bitterly resented, catering scoffed without gratitude, without reciprocation. Soon I learned to keep my scanty supplies of bread and milk and butter in my room.

It was the smallest room, over the kitchen and loo downstairs and the roof leaked badly. The furniture was rickety, the bed sagged, mattress stained unspeakably. The bathroom geyser was covered in warnings from the gas board that it had been condemned. I bathed at Richard's or went dirty.

My fantasies of the conviviality of a shared house were illusory. William worked odd shifts, and conducted his private life away from home. He was only at home sometimes in the day to paint. No one else spent any more time in the house than was essential, leading frenetic social lives round the art college. Never did I end up going for a drink with anyone, and I could certainly not invite anyone round to such a distant and awful establishment.

Even the independence was a sham. I discovered that Richard had met with William before allowing me to move, and, I had no doubt, consulted with Aunt Louisa and probably Evelyn. William left me to my own devices, keeping much less of an eye on me than I supposed that he had assured Richard he would, but, I reflected bitterly, if I did get up to anything remotely interesting, like taking a lover, William would be sure to inform on me at once.

I wallowed in misery. My room was damp, and the electric bar gobbled shillings, so that I could never get warm. I spent much time in bed. The loo was disgusting. I took a bundle of sheets each week to be exchanged for clean ones at Richard's as well as most of my washing. Even Richard showed scant concern for me. I saw him one or two evenings each week. Although he was generous and accommodating, he never volunteered anything; I had always to ask. Never did he suggest I move back to him.

Work was little better. Everything reeked of paraffin from the elderly guttering heaters. I refused to service the heaters, was terrified of them. Despite the heaters it was freezing. I was not eating very well either. I gave up trying to cook in the filthy kitchen, and subsisted on bread and cheese and the meals at Richard's flat. I felt badly now about how much I had resented George.

It was not surprising that I became ill. Hillyard sent me home early one day, and the next William rang Richard. He took me, unprotesting, back to his flat. I was feverish for several days. I lay hating Evelyn for abandoning me, for not realising intuitively at once that I was on my deathbed. As I recovered, I revelled in lying around in Richard's warm clean guest room, idly reading whodunnits.

I constantly reread Evelyn's most recent letter. 'My dearest Chimp . . .' He described where he was, what it was like, renewed his offer to come back at once. Or, he suggested, I could come out to him. But no doubt he was living with some woman who snuggled up, smiled coyly at him in the taverna when their tune was played. He would find it very awkward to have me there too. And if he really wanted me, why didn't he come?

After a week I returned to work, but I did not return to my rented room. Richard had fetched all my things and paid William up until the end of the year when the usual occupant was due back. I was grateful for his high-handedness, made not even a token protest.

Everything seemed on the verge of collapse at work. All in turn had succumbed to the virus before I had. Mr Wainwright's usual mordant manner degenerated to the frankly morose, and he made not the slightest effort to check his spleen, several times reducing Hillyard to tears. Even Mr Kirkup was much more aggressively unbalanced than usual.

Hillyard, enfeebled by his illness, was loosing his grip at least as much as any of the others. He appeared quite unable to think or speak of anything except his blighted loved affair. It took several consecutive evenings in the pub to coax him into any semblance of his old self. But eventually he seemed to have talked himself out, was teased into our usual jokes, our scurrilous assessment of the talent in the shop or pub, our po-faced winding up of Mr Wainwright.

The abyss of Hillyard's despair frightened me. I did not suppose that he was prone to an excessive degree of emotional instability owing to his susceptibility. I imagined rather that anyone could be struck down with such paralysing passion without warning, rather like the flu we had all had. The prospect of such a thing happening to me was horrifying. Although I looked forward to the sophistication of having affairs, I did not wish to fall in love.

I wondered if Evelyn had suffered over Kaye as Hillyard now

pined. If he had, he had managed to disguise it remarkably well, I concluded. Yet I could not imagine why he had bothered over Kaye at all if his judgement hadn't been overborne by some degree of infatuation. Whatever that might mean. Perhaps Evelyn, like Hillyard, was quite incapable of falling for anyone remotely suitable.

I pictured Evelyn mooning after vacuous Slavic-faced young women, too ardent to care that I had practically been on my deathbed. But ardency was not his style, certainly not with Kaye. Nor was Kaye particularly a stereotype. It occurred to me that I had never known what was his type. Jean was completely different from Kaye, pretty rather than striking, small, fat, lively, formidably intelligent. I had a vague impression of a few others, but mostly just names from notes and phone calls. Evelyn had been assiduous in compartmentalising his life, I realised.

I tried, circumspectly, to talk to Hillyard about Evelyn, whether he thought Evelyn was too preoccupied to think of me. His advice was unexpectedly unpalatable. 'If I were you I'd hang on to your Uncle Richard. He's a poppet if ever there was one.'

'But I want Evelyn.'

'I've bloody told you, they're all the bloody same, these ambidextrous types. Unreliable. Charming and unreliable, couldn't care less for anything except what they want.' Hillyard was irritated by my childishness.

'But Evelyn's right-handed.'

'Oh God,' he said. 'I keep forgetting you're only a kid.' After a time he took my hand. 'Please. I'm sorry. I didn't mean it; you don't want to pay any attention to me moaning on.'

'I don't see why whatever else he does should make a difference to being my dad.'

'No, of course not, Missy. Of course not.' He squeezed my hand. His was small, cold, nails bitten and grubby. 'I don't see why you don't just write to him. How should he know that you miss him if you don't say so?'

'But he doesn't miss me.'

'How do you know that?'

It was many years since I had wondered whether Evelyn wanted me or not. I had actually dared to ask him once, the autumn after I had absconded from Hellisford, if he would not really rather I went away to school. We had been shopping for the start of the term, new shoes, uniform, a geometry set, and ended up having a lavish tea.

Surprisingly, Evelyn had not adjured me in bracing tones not to be silly, instead leaning across the tablecloth and taking my hands.

'Now please, love, that's enough. You know that perfectly well.' He drew back, knocking his cup, steadied it. 'For God's sake, what more do I have to do to prove that you're wanted?' He continued, in a calmer tone, 'It's all worked out for the best, you know. I've never really been very good at being on my own. I don't know how I'd manage without you now.' He smiled, squeezed my hands, and I believed him.

Now I worried, not merely about having made him not want me any longer, but about him being on his own. Richard needed to look after someone, but Evelyn needed to be looked after.

'You're right,' I told Hillyard. I covered his little boy hand with mine and then got us fresh pints of cider.

'So you'll write to him then?' He grinned tentatively.

'Mmm. Tonight.' I drank the pint down to the bulge in the glass. 'Justin? What you said about . . . How do you know?'

'Well, it stands to reason.'

'Does it?'

'I don't know, I just assumed . . . William said . . .' He gulped his drink. 'It's nothing to do with me. Don't pay any attention to me; you know what a dirty mind I've got. I've probably got it all wrong, don't give it a thought.'

'No, you're right,' I said again, finally.

'You don't know that. Maybe . . .'

'Just because you're so bloody intolerant. Do you think it matters to me what Evelyn does in private?'

He grinned relievedly. 'Missy, I'm sorry, I didn't think . . .'

'Idiot.'

The next day was gruelling. It was very busy, and we were even more short of staff than usual. The exiguous arrangements for intermittent, temporary and part-time help that kept the shop going had collapsed completely with the flu epidemic. In addition, Mr Wainwright himself was away on a buying trip. 'And books aren't the only thing,' Hillyard muttered darkly. Our hangovers, on many pints of cider, made even basic functioning difficult.

Hillyard's triumph over a runner hoping to take advantage of the gaffer's absence was short-lived. A fire was narrowly averted when I snatched someone's shopping from the top of a heater. I vented my fright by bawling the customer out. He did not take it well but Hillyard loyally backed me and routed the man.

The afternoon was punctuated by a shattering row between Mr Bassett and Mr Kirkup. The row dredged up every long-buried grudge, every imagined slight, every mistake.

'And what about that time you let the Virginia Woolf first go for half a dollar!' shrilled Mr Bassett.

'At least I didn't let him walk out with the Dulac plates under his mackintosh!' retorted Mr Kirkup.

Eventually Hillyard sent me up to quiet them. Mr Kirkup threw Mr Bassett's index drawers across the room and ran upstairs. I helped Mr Bassett gather up the cards, carefully keeping fanned bundles in order to lessen the sorting work. He wiped his nose frequently on his frayed cuff. By the time I finished I was snuffling too from the proximity of the mildewy, frayed carpet scraps that covered the crumbling lino. The astonishing thing was that none of the customers paid the least attention, continuing to browse in the middle of the battlefield. One had narrowly missed being brained by a drawer in flight without seeming to notice.

'I'm just nipping out to get something for tea,' I told Hillyard. I felt drastic measures were called for. I got a half bottle of whisky rather than biscuits or cakes. I had not lived with Evelyn for years for nothing. Mr Bassett, still sniffling intermittently, sipped his laced tea and then smiled, showing brown and chipped teeth.

'You're all right, Missy,' he allowed.

In trepidation I continued to the top. Mr Kirkup was on the stepladder, busily tearing pages from a book to wedge round the skylight. I left his cup and fled. I hadn't put any whisky in his, I thought it might overexcite him further. And there had been no need to spoil Mr Bassett's work like that.

Hillyard and I retreated behind the counter and did no further work. He slugged the whisky from the bottle in the stockroom in a professional manner, ruining the effect by choking. Presently he took another swig and spent the remainder of the afternoon leaning on the counter smiling seraphically. I felt better too for the medicinal fortification.

I was exhausted and wheezing from the dust. Richard had not wanted me to start back at work yet. But it was as well I had. Hillyard couldn't have managed without me. Richard had insisted on driving me the past few days, he wouldn't have me getting soaked to the skin. Soon he would come to fetch me; I was grateful. He had been very forbearing about my lateness, my inebriation the previous night, tucking me up with a hot drink, and in the morning refraining from remark on my fragility.

We spent the rest of the afternoon playing the Ruskin Game. Mr Wainwright did it all the time, but never consciously realised it was a game. The idea was to disparage whatever the customer requested. 'Ruskin? *Ruskin?* There are a few things upstairs, not that we get much call for that these days. Fancy, my dear Hillyard, this fellow wants that charlatan Ruskin.' And so on. Mr Wainwright did it best; he would have made a superb Lady Bracknell. But we would not have got away with playing the game when he was there.

'Don't you ever worry about getting stuck here?' I didn't like to think of Hillyard getting like Kirkup and Bassett eventually.

'All the time, Missy, all the time.'

'Sorry.'

'Oh well.' He grinned. 'Some day my prince will come.' He stood, wobbling, on the stool rungs and shouted, 'Closing in five minutes!' I began to tidy up in the stockroom. The bell clanged. Hillyard would be annoyed that I had forgotten the CLOSED sign. 'Are you looking for anything particular, sir?'

'I am as a matter of fact. Perhaps you can help me.'

'Chance would be a fine thing. Sir.' Hillyard had cracked under the accumulated stress of the day.

'Idiot! It's Evelyn!' I pushed past him and ducked under the counter, upsetting the remains of a cuppa. I flung myself at Evelyn as if I were ten again and he had just got back from a business trip and he held me tight as if I were a child once more.

'Well.' But Hillyard sounded only mildly aggrieved and delicately blotted the spilled tea with some handy customer correspondence. 'Some people have all the luck.'

Founded in 1986, Serpent's Tail publishes the innovative and the challenging.

If you would like to receive a catalogue of our current publications please write to:

FREEPOST
Serpent's Tail
4 Blackstock Mews
LONDON N4 2BR

(No stamp necessary if your letter is posted in the United Kingdom.)